The Landower Legacy

From the moment Caroline met the dashing
Captain Jock Carmichael she was aware of the
affinity between him and her beautiful mother.
When the Captain began to show an interest in
the young Caroline a dark secret was betrayed
to Robert Tressidor.

The discovery meant the banishment of
Caroline from her opulent London home to
remote Cornwall where she found herself
caught up in an entirely different environment.
There she made the acquaintance of the
Landower brothers, Jago and Paul. When she
was recalled to London the memory of those
weeks in Cornwall stayed with her.

Then once more Paul Landower came into
her life. Returning to Cornwall a shock awaited
her for the Landower estates had to be saved at
all costs and Paul had forced himself to save
them.

Caroline found herself at the centre of events
which shook the community. About her moved
an array of colourful characters: her beautiful,
selfish mother; the hypocritical Robert
Tressidor who, she discovered, was devoted to
pursuits other than good works; the worldly
Rosie; the mild peace-loving Olivia; and the
Landower brothers, merry Jago and tragic Paul
who found the price he had to pay for Landower
had shut him off from all that he most wanted in
life.

VICTORIA HOLT

The Landower Legacy

FONTANA/Collins

First published by William Collins Sons Co. Ltd 1984
A continental edition first issued by Fontana Paperbacks 1985
This edition first issued in Fontana Paperbacks 1986

Copyright © Victoria Holt 1984

Made and printed in Great Britain by
William Collins Sons & Co. Ltd, Glasgow

CONTENTS

Golden Jubilee

It was at the time of the Queen's Golden Jubilee when events took a dramatic turn and changed the entire course of my life. I was only fourteen years old at the time and although those momentous occurrences were taking place around me – and I myself played a part in them – I was not aware of their importance until much later. It was as though I looked through a misty glass; I saw them, but I did not understand their significance.

To the casual observer, ours would have seemed to be a very fortunate household. But how often are things what they seem? We were what is called 'well-to-do'. Our London residence was in one of the fashionable squares not far from Hyde Park; our comforts were presided over by Wilkinson, the butler, and Mrs Winch, the housekeeper, between whom there was a perpetual state of armed neutrality as each was very anxious to maintain superiority over the other. In the early hours of the morning, before members of the family left their beds, the lower echelons of the domestic staff scuttled about, removing the remains of the previous day's fires in all the grates, polishing, dusting, getting the hot water, so that when we arose, as if by magic, all we needed was waiting for us. They all knew that my father was most displeased if any of them made their presence known, and the sight of a cap and apron scuttling away could mean the dismissal of their possessor. Everyone in the household dreaded his displeasure – even my mother.

Papa was Robert Ellis Tressidor – one of the Tressidors of Tressidor Manor of Lancarron in Cornwall. The family had owned large estates since the sixteenth century and these had been greatly increased after the Restoration. The great West Country families – with very few exceptions – had been firmly for the King at that time – and none was more royalist than the Tressidors.

Unfortunately the family mansion had passed out of my father's hands and had been annexed (that was the word and I had had to look it up to see what it meant, for I was an inveterate listener and gleaned most of my information about the family from keeping my ears and eyes open) by Cousin Mary. Cousin Mary's name was always spoken by my father and his sister Imogen, who was his devoted admirer, in a tone of contempt and loathing – but with a flash of envy, I fancied.

I had discovered that my grandfather had had an elder brother who was Mary's father. She was his only child and as he was the elder, Tressidor Manor and all its land had gone to her instead of to my father who, apparently, had every right to it, because although he was the son of a younger son he belonged to that superior sex which no woman should attempt to rival.

My Aunt Imogen – Lady Carey – was as formidable in her way as my father was in his. I had heard them discussing the contemptible behaviour of Cousin Mary who had cheerfully taken possession of the family house and not paused to think for a moment that she was robbing the rightful heir. 'That harpy!' Aunt Imogen called her, and I imagined Cousin Mary with a woman's head and trunk, a bird's wings and long claws flapping at my father and Aunt Imogen as the harpies did over poor blind King Phineus.

It was difficult to imagine anyone's getting the better of Papa, and as Cousin Mary had done so I guessed she must be very formidable indeed and I could not help feeling a certain admiration for her, which, said my sister Olivia, when I told her of it, was decidedly disloyal. But however much Papa had been defeated over his inheritance, he was certainly the master in his own house. There he ruled supreme, and everything must be done as he ordained. There was a big staff of servants – necessary because of his

8

public life and the entertaining that entailed. He was the chairman of committees and organizations – many of them for the good of humanity, such as the Useful Employment of the Poor and the Rehabilitation of Fallen Women. He was the leader of good causes. His name was often in the papers; he had been called another Lord Shaftesbury and it was hinted that his peerage was long overdue.

He was obviously a great friend of many important people, including Lord Salisbury, the Prime Minister. He did have a seat in Parliament, but he did not take Cabinet rank – which it seemed could have been his for the asking – because he had so many interests outside Westminster. He thought that he could better serve his country by following them than giving his complete attention to politics.

He was a banker and on the board of several companies. Every morning the brougham would come round from the mews and draw up in front of the house. The carriage must be highly polished and the coachman's livery absolutely correct; and even the little 'tiger' who stood at the back as they drove along and whose duty it was to leap down when they reached their destination and open the door, must be equally immaculate.

He possessed the two most important qualities of a gentleman of our times: he was rich and he was virtuous.

Miss Bell, our governess, was very proud of him.

'You must remember that your father is the fountain from which all your comforts flow,' she told us.

I immediately pointed out that I had noticed people were not very comfortable in his presence, so perhaps it was not exactly comfort which flowed from that particular fountain.

Our governess often despaired of me. Dear Miss Bell – so earnest, so eager to do well in that task to which God – and the great Mr Tressidor – had called her. She was conventional in the extreme, overawed by the virtues of her employer, accepting without question his own valuation of himself – which in fact was the general one – constantly aware that however efficient she was, however well she performed her duties, she was merely a member of the inferior sex.

I must have been an irritating child, because I never accepted what I was told and lacked the sense to keep quiet about it.

'Why,' said my sister Olivia, 'do you always have to turn everything round to make it different from what we are told?'

It was probably, I replied, because people did not always tell the truth and said what they thought we ought to believe.

'It's easier to believe them,' said Olivia, which was typical of her. It was why they called her a good child. I was a rebel. I often thought it was strange that we should be sisters. We were so different.

Our mother did not rise until ten in the morning. Everton, her lady's maid, took her a cup of hot chocolate at that hour. She was a great beauty, and there were frequent pieces about her in the society columns of the newspapers. Miss Bell showed them to us from time to time: 'The beautiful Mrs Tressidor' at the races . . . dining out . . . at some charity ball. They always described her as 'the beautiful Mrs Tressidor'.

Olivia and I were overawed by her beauty just as we were by our father's towering goodness. I remarked that they both made ours rather an uneasy home. My mother was sometimes very affectionate towards us, at others she did not seem to be aware of us. She would embrace us and kiss us fervently at times – especially me. I noticed that and hoped Olivia didn't. She had sparkling brown eyes and masses of chestnut hair, the colour of which, Rosie Rundall, our very extraordinary parlourmaid, whispered to me, Everton took great pains to preserve with mysterious lotions. Keeping our mother beautiful was an absorbing task, apparently. Everton was good at it, and she kept the whole household at bay, demanding absolute quietness throughout when our mother was resting with ice pads on her lids or being gently massaged by Everton's expert

10

hands. There were continual discussions about the latest fashions.

'It is an exhausting business being a beauty,' I remarked to Olivia, and Rosie Rundall, who happened to be there at the time, agreed with a 'You can bet your life on that!'

Rosie Rundall was the most unusual parlourmaid I had ever known. She was tall and good-looking. In fact, parlourmaids were always chosen for their appearance. They were the servants seen by visitors, and ill-favoured ones could give a bad impression of a household. I often thought that in Rosie we had the supreme in parlourmaids.

Rosie could be extremely dignified with guests. People noticed her. They gave her a second glance. She was aware of it and received this silent homage with an equally silent dignity. But when she was with Olivia and me – which she contrived to be quite often – she was a different person altogether.

Both Olivia and I were very fond of Rosie. I suppose there were not many people to whom we could show affection. Our father was too good, our mother too beautiful; and although Miss Bell was very worthy, and good for us, I was sure, she was not exactly affectionate.

Rosie was warm-hearted and not averse to flying in the face of authority. When Olivia spilt gravy on her clean pinafore, with a wink Rosie had whisked it away, washed it and ironed it in such a short time that nobody knew anything about it; and when I broke a Sèvres vase which stood on a what-not in the drawing-room, Rosie took it away and stuck it together again, craftily placing it in an inconspicuous position.

'I'll be the one to dust it,' she said with a grin. 'Nobody will know. What the eye don't see, the heart don't grieve for.'

It occurred to me that Rosie went about the world saving a lot of hearts from grief.

On her nights out – one a week (she had insisted on those nights when she first came, and Mrs Winch, delighted to acquire such a good-looking girl, gave in), Rosie would dress up like a lady. She became quite a different person from the one we knew in white cap and apron. She would look very grand in a silk dress and a hat with a jaunty feather and gloves and a parasol.

When I asked where she went she gave me a little push and said: 'Ah, that's telling. I'll tell you when you're twenty-five.' That was a favourite expression of hers. 'One of these days, when you're twenty-five, you'll know.'

I was always interested to see the important people who came to the house. In the hall there was a beautiful staircase which wound round and round to the top of the house, with a well in the middle so that from the top floor – where the servants' sleeping quarters, the nurseries and the schoolroom were situated – one could look right down and see what was happening in the hall. Voices floated upwards and it was often possible to glean all manner of surprising pieces of information in this way. There was nothing so maddening – nor so intriguing – as to have a conversation cut short at some vital point. It was a game I thoroughly enjoyed, though Olivia thought it was somewhat shameful.

'Listeners,' she said, quoting adult philosophy, 'never hear any good of themselves.'

'Dear sister,' I retorted, 'when do we ever hear *anything* of ourselves – good or evil?'

'You never know what you might hear.'

'That's true and that's what makes it exciting.'

The plain fact was that I enjoyed eavesdropping. There was so much which was kept from us – unfit for our ears, I supposed. I just had an irresistible desire to know these things.

So peering down at the guests as they arrived was a source of great enjoyment. I liked to watch our beautiful mother standing at the top of the stairs at the first floor, on which were the drawing-room and salon where well-known artistes – pianists, violinists and singers – often came to perform for our guests.

Poor Olivia would squat beside me in torment lest we should be discovered. She was a very nervous girl. I was always the ringleader when it was a question of acting adventurously, although she was two years my senior.

Our governess, Miss Bell, used to say: 'Speak up, Olivia. Don't let Caroline call the tune every time.'

But Olivia was always retiring. She was really quite pretty, but the sort of person people simply did not notice. Everything about her was pleasant but ordinary. Her face was small and pale; I was already taller than she was; her features were small, except her eyes, which were large and brown. 'Like a gazelle's,' I told her, at which she did not know whether to be pleased or hurt. That was a characteristic of Olivia. She was never sure. Her eyes were beautiful but she was short-sighted and that gave her a helpless look. Her hair was straight and fine, and no matter how it was restricted, strands would escape, to the despair of Miss Bell. There were times when I felt I had to protect Olivia; but for the most part I was urging her to reckless adventure.

I was quite different in looks as well as in temperament. Miss Bell used to say that she would not have believed two sisters could be so unlike. My hair was darker, almost black; and my eyes were a definite shade of green which I liked to accentuate by wearing a green ribbon in my hair, for I was very vain and aware of my striking colouring. Not that I went so far as to think of myself as pretty. But I was noticeable. My rather snub nose, wide mouth and high forehead – in an age when low ones were fashionable – precluded me from a claim to beauty, but there was something about me – my vitality, I think – which meant that people did not dismiss me with a glance, and they invariably took a second look.

This was the case with Captain Carmichael. To think of him always gave me a thrill of pleasure. He was magnificent in his uniform – the scarlet and the gold – but he always looked very handsome in his riding clothes or dressed for the evening. He was the most elegant and fascinating gentleman I had ever seen and he had one quality which made him irresistible to me: he singled me out for his especial notice. He would smile at me and, if there was an

13

opportunity, would speak to me, treating me as though I were an important young lady instead of a child who had not yet emerged from the schoolroom.

So when I peeped through the stairs I was always looking for Captain Carmichael.

There was a secret I shared with him. My mother was in it, too. It concerned a gold locket, the most beautiful ornament I had ever possessed. We were not allowed to wear jewellery, of course, so it was really very daring of me to wear this locket. True, it was under my bodice, which was always tightly buttoned up so that no one could see the locket; but I could feel it against my skin and it always made me happy. It was exciting, too, because it was hidden.

It had been given to me when we were in the country.

Our country house was about twenty miles from London – a rather stately Queen Anne building standing in parklands of some twenty acres. It was very pleasant, but it was not Tressidor Manor, I had heard my father say with some bitterness.

However, most of our days were spent there, our needs provided for by a bevy of servants and Miss Lucy Bell, whom I called the matriarch of the nursery. She seemed old to us but then everyone over twenty seemed ancient. I think she was about thirty years old when she came to us and at this time she had been with us for four years. She was very eager to fulfil her duties adequately, not only because she needed to earn a living, but, I was sure, because she was in a way fond of us.

In the country we had our nurseries – large pleasant rooms full of light – at the top of the house, giving us delightful views over woodland and green fields. We had our own ponies and rode a good deal. In London we rode in the Row, which was exciting in a way because of the people who bowed to our mother on those occasions when she rode with us; but for the sheer joy of galloping over the springy turf, there was nothing like riding in the country.

It was about a month before we came up to London when

our mother arrived unexpectedly in the country. She was accompanied by Everton with hat-boxes and general luggage and everything my mother needed to make life agreeable. It was rarely that she came to the country and there was a great deal of bustle throughout the house.

She came to the schoolroom and embraced us both warmly. We were overawed by her beauty, her fragrance, and her elegance in the light grey skirt and the pink blouse with its tucks and frills.

'My dear girls,' she cried. 'How wonderful to see you! I wanted to be alone for a while with my girls.'

Olivia blushed with pleasure. I was delighted, too, but perhaps a little sceptical, wondering why she should suddenly be so anxious to be with us when there had been so many opportunities which she had allowed to slip by without any apparent concern.

It was then that the thought occurred to me that she was perhaps less easy to understand than Papa. Papa was omnipotent, omniscient, the most powerful being we knew – under God, and then only just under. Mama was a lady with secrets. At that time I had not been given my locket, so I had no great secret of my own – but I did sense something in Mama's eyes.

She laughed with us and looked at our drawings and essays.

'Olivia has quite a talent,' said Miss Bell.

'So you have, darling! Oh, I do believe you are going to be a great artist.'

'Hardly that,' said Miss Bell, who was always afraid that too much praise might be harmful.

Olivia was blissful. There was a lovely innocence about her. She always believed in good. I came to think that was a great talent in life.

'Caroline writes quite well.'

My mother was looking blankly at the untidy page presented to her and murmured: 'It's lovely.'

'I did not mean her handwriting,' said Miss Bell. 'I mean her construction of sentences and her use of words. She shows imagination and a certain facility in expressing herself.'

'How wonderful!'

The expression in the lovely eyes was vague as she regarded the sheet of paper; but they were alert for something else.

The next day the reason for Mama's visit to the country arrived. It was one of those important occurrences which I did not recognize as such at the time.

Captain Carmichael called.

We were in the rose-garden with Mama at the time. She made a pretty picture with the two girls seated at her feet while she held a book in her hand. She was not reading to us but looked as though she might be.

Captain Carmichael was brought out to us.

'Captain Carmichael!' cried my mother. 'What a surprise.'

'I was on my way to Salisbury and I thought: Now that's the Tressidors' place. Robert would never forgive me if I were in the neighbourhood and did not call. So . . . I thought I would just look in.'

'Alas, Robert is not with us. But it's a lovely surprise.' My mother rose and clapped her hands together, looking like the child who has just been awarded the fairy from the top of the Christmas tree.

'You can stay and have a cup of tea with us,' she went on. 'Olivia, go and tell them to bring tea. Caroline, you go with Olivia.'

So we went, leaving them together.

What a pleasant tea-time that was! It was early May, a lovely time of the year. Red and white blossom on the trees and the scent of newly cut grass in the air, the birds singing and the sun – a nice benign one, not too hot – shining on us. It was wonderful.

Captain Carmichael talked to us. He wanted to hear how we were getting on with our riding. Olivia said little but I talked a great deal and he seemed to want me to. He kept looking at my mother and their glances seemed to include

16

me, which made me very happy. One thing Olivia and I lacked was affection. Our bodily needs were well catered for, but when one is growing up and getting used to the world, affection, really caring, is what one needs most. That afternoon we seemed to have it.

I wished it were always like that. It occurred to me how different life would have been if we had had someone like Captain Carmichael for a father.

He was a most exciting man. He had travelled the world. He had been in the Sudan with General Gordon and was actually in Khartoum during the siege. He told us stories about it. He talked vividly; he made us see the hardships, the fear, the determination – though I suppose he skirted the real truth as too horrible for our youthful ears.

When tea was over he rose and my mother said: 'You mustn't run away now, Captain. Why don't you stay the night? You could go first thing in the morning.'

He hesitated for a while, his eyes bubbling over with what could have been mischief.

'Well . . . perhaps I might play truant.'

'Oh good. That's wonderful. Darlings, go and tell them to prepare a room for Captain Carmichael . . . or perhaps I'll go. Come along, Captain. I am so glad you came.'

We sat on – Olivia and I – bemused by the fascinating gentleman.

The next morning we all went riding together. My mother was with us and we were all very merry. The Captain rode beside me. He told me I sat a horse like a rider.

'Well, anyone is a rider who rides a horse,' I replied, argumentative even in my bliss.

'Some are sacks of potatoes – others are riders.'

That seemed to me incredibly funny and I laughed immoderately.

'You seem to be making a success with Caroline, Captain,' said my mother.

'She laughs at my jokes. The nearest way to a man's heart, they say.'

17

'I thought the quickest way was to feed him.'

'Appreciation of one's wit comes first. Come, Caroline, I'll race you to the woods.'

It was wonderful to ride beside him with the wind in my face. He kept glancing at me and smiling, as though he liked me very much.

We went into the paddock because he said he would like to see how we jumped. So we showed him what our riding master had taught us recently. I knew I did a great deal better than Olivia, who was always nervous and nearly came off at one of the jumps.

Captain Carmichael and my mother applauded and they were both looking at me.

'I hope you are going to stay for a long while,' I said to the Captain.

'Alas! Alas!' he said, and looking at my mother raised his shoulders.

'Another night, perhaps?' she suggested.

He stayed two nights and just before he left my mother sent for me. She was in her little sitting-room and with her was Captain Carmichael.

He said: 'I have to go soon, Caroline. I have to say goodbye.'

He put his hands on my shoulders and looked at me for a few seconds. Then he held me against him and kissed the top of my head.

He released me and went on: 'I want to give you something, Caroline, to remember me by.'

'Oh, I shan't forget you.'

'I know. But a little token, eh?'

Then he brought out the locket. It was on a gold chain. He said: 'Open it.'

I fumbled with it and he took it from me. The locket sprang open and there was a beautiful miniature of him. It was tiny but so exquisitely done that his features were clear and there was no doubt that it was Captain Carmichael.

'But it's lovely!' I cried, looking from him to my mother.

18

They both looked at me somewhat emotionally and then at each other.

My mother said practically: 'I shouldn't show it to anyone if I were you . . . not even Olivia.'

Oh, I thought. So Olivia is not getting a present. They thought she might be jealous.

'I should put it away until you're older,' said my mother.

I nodded.

'Thank you,' I murmured. 'Thank you very much.'

He put his arms about me and kissed me.

That afternoon we said goodbye to him.

'I shall be back for the Jubilee,' he told my mother.

So that was how I received the locket. I loved it. I looked at it often. I could not bear to hide it away, though, and it gave me added excitement because I had to keep it secret. I wore it every day under my bodice, and kept it under my pillow at night. I enjoyed it not only for its beauty, but because it was a secret thing, known only to myself, my mother and Captain Carmichael.

We came up to London on the fifteenth of June – that was a week before the great Jubilee day. Coming into London from the country was always exciting. We came in from the east side and the Tower of London always seemed to me like the bulwarks of the city. Grim, formidable, speaking of past tragedies, it always set me wondering about the people who had been imprisoned there long ago.

Then we would come into the city and on past Mr Barry's comparatively new Houses of Parliament, so magnificent beside the river, looking, deceptively, as though they had weathered the centuries almost as long as the great Tower itself.

I could never make up my mind which I loved more – London or the country. There was a cosiness about the country, where everything seemed orderly; there was a serenity, a peace, which was lacking in London. Of course Papa was rarely in the country and on those occasions when he came, I had to admit peace and serenity fled. There would be entertaining when he came, and Olivia and I had to keep well out of the way. So perhaps it was a matter of where Papa was that affected us so deeply.

But I was always excited to be returning to London, just as I was pleased to go back to the country.

This was a rather special return for no sooner did we reach the metropolis than we were aware of the excitement which Miss Bell called 'Jubilee Fever'.

The streets of the city were full of noisy people. I watched them with glee – all those people with their wares who rarely penetrated our part of London; they were there in full force in the city – the chair-mender, who sat on the pavement mending cane chairs, the cats'-meat man with his barrow full of revolting-looking horseflesh; the tinker, the umbrella-mender, and the girl in the big paper bonnet carrying a basket full of paper flowers to be put in fireplaces during the summer months when there were no fires . . . Then there were the German bands which were beginning to appear frequently in the streets, playing popular songs of the music halls. But what I chiefly noticed were the sellers of Jubilee fancies – mugs, hats, ornaments. 'God Bless the Queen,' these proclaimed. Or: 'Fifty Glorious Years'.

It was invigorating, and I was glad we had left the country to become part of it.

There was excitement in the house too. Miss Bell said how fortunate we were to be subjects of such a Queen and we should remember the great Jubilee for the rest of our lives.

Rosie Rundall showed us a new dress she had for the occasion. It was white muslin covered in little lavender flowers; and she had a lavender straw hat to go with it.

'There'll be high jinks,' she said, 'and there is going to be as much fun for Rosie Rundall as for Her Gracious Majesty – more, I shouldn't wonder.'

My mother seemed to have changed since that memorable time when Captain Carmichael had given me the locket. She was pleased to see us, she said. She hugged us and told us we were going to see the Jubilee procession with her. Wasn't that exciting?

We agreed that it was.

'Shall we see the Queen?' asked Olivia.

'Of course, my dear. What sort of Jubilee would it be without her?'

We were caught up in the excitement.

'Your father,' said Miss Bell, 'will have his duties on such a day. He will be at Court, of course?'

'Will he ride with the Queen?' asked Olivia.

I burst out laughing. 'Even he is not important enough for that,' I said scornfully.

In the morning when we were at lessons with Miss Bell, my parents came up to the schoolroom. This was so unexpected that we were all dumbfounded – even Miss Bell, who rose to her feet, flushing slightly, murmuring: 'Good morning, sir. Good morning, madam.'

Olivia and I had risen to our feet too and stood like statues wondering what this visit meant.

Our father looked as though *he* were asking himself how such a magnificent person as he was could possibly have sired such offspring. There was a blot on my bodice. I always got carried away when writing and made myself untidy in the process. I felt my head jerk up. I supposed I had put on my defiant look which I invariably did, so Miss Bell said, when I was expecting criticism. I glanced at Olivia. She was pale and clearly nervous.

I felt a little angry. One person had no right to have that effect on others. I promised myself I would not allow him to frighten me.

He said: 'Well, are you dumb?'

'Good morning, Papa,' we said in unison. 'Good morning, Mama.'

My mother laughed lightly. 'I shall take them to see the procession myself.'

He nodded. I think that meant approval.

My mother went on: 'Both Clare Ponsonby and Delia Sanson have invited us. The procession will pass their

21

doors and there will be an excellent view from their windows.'

'Indeed, yes.' He looked at Miss Bell. Like myself, she was determined not to show how nervous he made her. She was, after all, a vicar's daughter, and vicars' families were always so respectable that daughters of such households were readily preferred by employers; she was also a lady of some spirit and she was not going to be cowed before her pupils.

'And what do you think of your pupils, eh, Miss Bell?'

'They are progressing very well,' said Miss Bell.

My mother said, again with that little laugh: 'Miss Bell tells me that the girls are clever . . . in their different ways.'

'H'm.' He looked at Miss Bell quizzically, and it occurred to me that not to show fear was the way to behave in his presence. Most people showed it and then he became more and more godlike. I admired Miss Bell.

'I hope you have thanked God for the Queen's preservation,' he said, looking at Olivia.

'Oh yes, Papa,' I said fervently.

'We must all be grateful to God for giving us such a lady to rule over us.'

Ah, I thought. She is the Monarch, though a woman. Nobody took the crown from her because she was a woman, so Cousin Mary has every right to Tressidor Manor. Thoughts like that always came into my mind at odd moments.

'We are, Papa,' I said, 'to have such a great *lady* to rule over us.'

He glared at Olivia, who looked very frightened. 'And what of you? What do you say?'

'Why . . . yes . . . yes . . . Papa,' stammered Olivia.

'We are all very grateful,' said my mother, 'and we shall have a wonderful time together at the Ponsonbys' or Sansons' . . . We shall cheer Her Majesty until we are hoarse, shall we not, my dears?'

'I think it would be better if you watched in respectful silence,' said my father.

'But of course, Robert,' said my mother. She went to him and slipped her arm through his. I was amazed at such temerity but he did not seem to mind. In fact he seemed to find the contact rather pleasing.

'Come along,' she said, no doubt seeing how eager we were for the interview to end and growing a little tired of it herself. 'The girls will behave beautifully and be a credit to us, won't you, girls?'

'Oh yes, Mama.'

She smiled at him and his lips turned up at the corners, as though he could not help smiling back although he was trying hard not to.

When the door shut on them we all heaved a sigh of relief.

'Why did he come?' I asked, as usual speaking without thinking.

'Your father feels he should pay a visit to the schoolroom occasionally,' said Miss Bell. 'It is a parent's duty and your father would always do his duty.'

'I'm glad our mother came with him. That made him a little less stern, I think.'

Miss Bell was silent.

Then she opened a book. 'Let us see what William the Conqueror is doing now. We left him, remember, planning the conquest of these islands.'

And as we read our books I was thinking of my parents, wondering about them. Why did my mother, who loved to laugh, marry my father, who clearly did not? Why could she make him look different merely by slipping her arm through his? Why had she come to the schoolroom to tell us we were going to see the procession, either from the Ponsonbys' or the Sansons', when we knew already.

Secrets! Adults had many of them. It would be interesting to know what they really meant, for when they said one thing, they very often meant something else.

I felt the locket against my skin.

Well, I too had my secrets.

As the great day approached the excitement intensified. No one seemed to speak of anything but the Jubilee. The day before there was to be a dinner party and that meant in addition to Jubilee Fever there was the bustle such an occasion always demanded.

In the morning Miss Bell took us for our usual morning walk. The streets near the square, usually so sedate, were filling with traders selling Jubilee favours.

'Buy a mug for the little ladies,' they pleaded. 'Come on. Show respec' for 'er Gracious Majesty.'

Miss Bell hurried us past and said we would go into the Park.

We walked along by the Serpentine while she told us about the Great Exhibition which had been set up largely under the auspices of the Prince Consort, that much lamented husband of our dear Queen. We had heard it all before and I was much more interested in watching the ducks. We had brought nothing to feed them with. Mrs Terras, the cook, usually supplied us with stale bread, but on this morning, because of the coming dinner party, she was too busy to be bothered with us.

We sat down by the water and Miss Bell, always intent on improving our minds, turned the subject to the Queen's coming to the throne fifty glorious years before, and she went over the oft-repeated tale of our dear Queen's rising from her bed, wrapped in her dressing-gown, her long fair hair loose about her shoulders, to be told she was the Queen.

'We must remember what the dear Queen said – young as she was and wise . . . oh, so wise even then. She said: "I will be good." There! Who would have believed a young girl could have shown such wisdom? And not much older than you, Olivia. Imagine! Who else could have made such a vow?'

'Olivia would,' I said. 'She always wants to be good.'

It occurred to me then that good people were not always wise, and I couldn't help pointing out that the two qualities did not always go hand in hand.

Miss Bell looked faintly exasperated and said: 'You must learn to accept the conclusions of those older and wiser than yourself, Caroline.'

'But if one never questions anything, how can one find new answers?' I asked.

'Why seek a new answer, when you have one already?'

'Because there might be another,' I insisted.

'I think we should now be returning,' said Miss Bell.

How often, I ruminated, were conversations brought to such abrupt terminations.

I did not care. Like everyone else, I was thinking about tomorrow.

From our bedroom we could see the carriages arriving with all the guests and on such a night as this the square seemed full of them. I supposed we were not the only ones who were giving a dinner party.

It was about eight o'clock. We were supposed to be in bed, for we must be fresh for the morning when we would be leaving the house early so that we should be in our places before the streets were closed to traffic. The carriage was to take us to the Ponsonbys or the Sansons – we had not been told which invitation had been accepted. As we were going with our mother Miss Bell would have to take her chance in the streets and she was accompanying Everton to some vantage-point. The servants had made their arrangements. Rosie was going by herself.

'Alone?' I asked and she looked at me and gave me a little push.

'Ask no questions and you'll hear no lies,' she said.

I think Papa was at some function. All I cared about was that he should not be with us. He would have cast a decided gloom over the day.

Having seen the carriages arrive, I went with Olivia to our nook by the banisters and watched the guests received.

Our mother was sparkling in a dress trimmed with pink beads and pearls. She wore a little band of diamonds in her hair and looked exquisite. Papa stood beside her and in his black clothes and frilled shirt he looked magnificent.

We could hear their voices and catch the occasional comment.

'How good of you to come.'

'It is such a pleasure to see you.'

'What a wonderful prelude to the great day.'

And so it went on.

Then my heart leaped with pleasure, for approaching my parents was Captain Carmichael.

So he was back in London as he had said he would be. He looked very handsome, although he was not in uniform. He was as tall as my father and as impressive in his way as my father was in his – only whereas my father cast gloom, he brought merriment.

He had passed on and the next guest was received.

I felt bemused. I dared not wear my locket for I was in my night attire and it would be seen. It lay under my pillow. It was safe there, but I should have liked to be wearing it at that moment.

When the guests had all been received I just wanted to sit there.

'I'm going back to bed,' said Olivia.

I nodded and she crept away, but I still sat on, hoping that Captain Carmichael would come out and I should get another glimpse of him.

I listened to the sounds of conversation. Soon they would go down to the dining-room which was on the ground floor.

Then my mother came out with Captain Carmichael. They were talking very quietly and soon were joined by a man and woman. They stood for a while talking – about the Jubilee, of course.

I caught scraps of the conversation.

'They say she refused to wear a crown.'

'It's to be a bonnet.'

'A bonnet! Fancy!'

'Hush! Lese-majesty.'

'But it's true. Halifax has told her that the people want a

gilding for their money and Rosebery says an Empire should be ruled by a sceptre, not a bonnet.'

'Will it really be a bonnet? I don't believe it.'

'Oh yes, the order has gone out. Bonnets and long high dresses without mantle.'

'It will not be much like a royal occasion.'

'My dear, where she is there could be nothing but a royal occasion.'

Captain Carmichael said, and he had a very clear voice which was audible right to the top of the house, 'It's true, I hope, that she has insisted on modifying the Prince Consort's rules about divorcees.'

'Yes. Incredible, is it not? She wishes the poor ladies who are innocent parties to divorce to be admitted to the celebrations.'

My father had come out a few seconds before.

'Reasonable, of course,' said the Captain. 'Why should they be penalized for what is not their fault?'

'Immorality *should* be penalized,' said my father.

'My dear Tressidor,' retorted the Captain, 'innocent parties are not guilty. How otherwise could they be innocent?'

'The Prince Consort was right,' insisted my father. 'He excluded *all* who were involved in these sordid affairs, and I am glad to say that Salisbury has put his foot down about inviting foreign divorcees.'

'There has to be some human feeling, surely,' went on the Captain.

My father said in a very cold voice: 'There are principles involved.'

And my mother cut in: 'Let us go to dinner, shall we? Why do we stand about here?'

She was clearly changing the subject and as they started downstairs someone said to her, 'I hear you will be at the Ponsonbys'.'

'I was kindly asked by Marcia Sanson. My little girls are so looking forward to it.'

The voices faded away.

I sat there for some time thinking: I believe that Captain Carmichael and my father do not like each other very much.

Then I crept into bed, felt my locket safe beneath the pillow and went to sleep.

We were up early next morning and Miss Bell was very careful with our toilettes. She had long pondered, going through our moderate wardrobes deciding on what garments would best do justice to our mother; she picked bottle-green for me and crushed-strawberry for Olivia. Our dresses were both made on the same lines with flounced skirts, decorous bodices and sleeves to the elbow. We wore long white stockings and black boots, and carried white gloves, and each of us had a straw hat, mine bearing a green ribbon and Olivia's crushed-strawberry.

We felt very smart. But when we saw our mother we realized how insignificant we were beside her splendour. She looked every bit 'the beautiful Mrs Tressidor'. She wore pink, a favourite colour of hers and one which was most becoming. The skirt of her dress was full and flounced and so draped to call attention to a waist, which in that age of small waists, was remarkable. The tightly fitting bodice further accentuated the charm of her figure; she wore a pale cream fichu at the neck which matched the lace at the cuffs of her sleeves. Her hat was the same mingling shades of cream and pink and perched jauntily on the top of her magnificent hair, while its cream-coloured ostrich feather fell over the brim and reached almost to her eyes as though to call attention to their sparkle. She looked young and excited and we all set off in a fever of anticipation.

The carriage was waiting for us, and Olivia and I sat one on either side of her as we rode out of the square.

The horses trotted along for a while and my mother suddenly called to the driver: 'Blain, I want you to go to Waterloo Place.'

Blain turned in surprise as though he had not heard correctly. 'But, Madam . . .' he began.

She smiled sweetly. 'I've changed my mind. Waterloo Place.'

'Very good, Madam,' said Blain.

'Mama,' I cried, 'are we not going to Lady Ponsonby's?'

'No, dear. We are going somewhere else instead.'

'But everyone said . . .'

'Plans are changed. I think you will like this place better.'

Her eyes were brimming with mischief and an excitement gripped me. I had an inspiration. I had seen that look in her eyes before, and it recalled a certain person who, I believed, had put it there.

'Mama,' I said thoughtfully, 'are we going to see Captain Carmichael?'

Her cheeks turned pink which made her prettier than ever.

'Why? Whatever made you say that?'

'I just wondered . . . because . . .'

'Because what?'

'Does he live in Waterloo Place?'

'Close by.'

'So it is . . .'

'We shall get a better view there.'

I sat back in my seat. Something had been added to the day.

He was waiting to greet us, clearly expecting us. I thought it rather odd that we should have set out as for the Ponsonbys when this must have been arranged the evening before.

However, I was too excited to think much about it. We were here and that was all that mattered.

Captain Carmichael's rooms were small compared with ours but there was a lovable disorder about them which I immediately sensed.

'Welcome!' he cried. 'My lovely ladies, welcome all.'

I liked being referred to as a lovely lady, but it clearly embarrassed Olivia, who was perfectly sure that the description did not fit her.

'You are in good time,' he went on.

'Which is absolutely necessary if we were to get here,' said my mother. 'These streets will be closed to traffic soon.'

'The procession will pass this way on the outward journey to the Abbey,' he said, 'but you will not be able to leave until after it has returned, which pleases me very much since it will give me more of the most delightful company I know. Now let me show my beauteous ladies the seating accommodation, and I expect the girls would like to watch what is going on in the streets.'

He led us to chairs in the window from which we had a good view of Waterloo Place.

'The route will be from the Palace through Constitution Hill, Piccadilly, Waterloo Place and Parliament Street to the Abbey, so you are in a good position. Now I dare say you would like some refreshment. I have some very special lemonade for you young people and some little biscuits to go with it – a speciality made for me by my cook, Mr Fortnum.'

My mother giggled and said: 'I believe that to be incorrect. They were made by Mr Mason.'

'Fortnum or Mason, what matters it?'

I laughed immoderately because I knew that Fortnum and Mason was a shop in Piccadilly, and Captain Carmichael meant he had bought the biscuits from them.

'I will come and help you with the lemonade,' said my mother.

I was astonished. The idea of her getting anything was so surprising. At home she would ring if she wanted a cushion for her chair.

They went out together. Olivia looked a little dismayed.

'It's exciting,' I said.

'Why did we come here? I thought we were going to the Ponsonbys'. And what does he mean about his cooks? Fortnum and Mason is a shop.'

'Oh, Olivia,' I said, 'you are so solemn. This is going to be fun.'

They were quite a long time coming with the lemonade

and when they did, my mother had removed her hat. She looked flushed but very much at home, and she made a great show of pouring out the lemonade.

'Luncheon will be served later,' said Captain Carmichael.

I can still remember every moment of that day. There was a certain magic about it, a certain feeling of waiting, like the moment in the theatre when the curtain is about to go up and one is not quite sure what is going to be revealed. But I might have thought that afterwards in view of everything that happened, as one is inclined to do, looking back on important days in one's life, imagining they were pregnant with foreboding . . . no, hardly foreboding. I felt nothing of that, only a tremendous excitement, as though something really important was going to happen.

There came the great moment when we could hear the approaching procession. I loved the Handel march; it seemed most appropriate; and there she was – a rather disappointing little figure and yes, in a bonnet. True, it was a rather special bonnet, made of lace and sparkling with diamonds, but nevertheless a bonnet. The cheers were deafening, and she sat there acknowledging them now and then with a lift of her hand, not so appreciative as I thought she might have been of this show of excessive loyalty. But it was a wonderful sight. Her carriage was preceded by the Princes of her own House – her sons, sons-in-law and grandsons. I counted them. There were thirty-two in all; and the most grand among them was the Queen's son-in-law, Crown Prince Frederick of Prussia, clad in white and silver with the German Eagle on his helmet.

There was procession after procession. I was thrilled by the sight of the Indian Princes in their magnificent robes sparkling with jewels. There were among them envoys from Europe, four Kings – those of Saxony, Belgium, Denmark and the Hellenes; and Greece, Portugal, Sweden and Austria – like Prussia – had sent their Crown Princes.

The whole world, it seemed on that day, was determined

to pay homage to the little old lady in her lace and diamond bonnet, who had reigned for fifty years.

Even when the procession had passed, I still felt dazed by the spectacle; the music was still ringing in my ears, and I could still see the magnificently caparisoned horses and their brilliant riders, while my mother disappeared with the Captain, having mentioned something about luncheon.

The Captain wheeled in a trolley on which was cold chicken, some crusty bread and a dish of butter.

He brought a little table to the window. There was just room for the four of us to sit at it. Deftly he covered it with a lacy cloth.

What a luncheon that was! Later I thought it was like the end of an era, the end of innocence. That delicious cold chicken was like tasting the tree of knowledge.

The Captain opened a bottle which had been standing in a bucket of ice, and he produced four glasses.

'Do you think they should?' asked my mother.

'Just a thimbleful.'

The thimblefuls were half-glasses. I sipped the fizzy liquid in ecstasy, and felt intoxicated with a very special sort of happiness. The world seemed wonderful and I envisioned this as the beginning of a new existence when Olivia and I became our mother's dearest friends; we accompanied her on expeditions such as this one which she and the Captain between them conspired to arrange for our delight.

Crowds were beginning to gather in the streets below and now that the procession had passed the streets were no longer closed to traffic.

'On the return journey from the Abbey to the Palace she will go via Whitehall and the Mall,' said the Captain, 'so the rest of the day is ours.'

'We must not be back too late,' said my mother.

'My dear, the streets will be impassable just now and will be for some time. We're safe in our eyrie.'

We all laughed. Indeed, we were laughing a good deal

and at nothing in particular, which is perhaps the expression of real happiness.

The sound of voices below was muted and remote – outside our magic circle. Captain Carmichael talked all the time and we laughed; he made us talk too, and even Olivia did . . . a little. Our mother seemed like a different person; every now and then she would say 'Jock!' in a tone of mock reproof which even Olivia guessed was a form of endearment.

Jock Carmichael told us about the Army and what it was like to serve in it. He had been overseas many times and expected to go to India. He looked at our mother and a faint sadness touched them both – but that was for the future and seemed too far away to worry about.

He was an old friend of the family, he told us. 'Why, I knew your mother before you were born.' He looked at me when he said that. 'And then . . . I was sent to the Sudan, and I didn't see any of you for a long time.' He smiled at my mother. 'And when I came back it seemed as if I had never been away.'

Olivia was having difficulty in keeping her eyes open. I felt the same. A dreamy contentment was creeping over me, but I fought hard against sleep, as I did not want to lose a moment of that enchanted afternoon.

Then the street life burst forth. A hurdy-gurdy had appeared and was playing tunes from *The Mikado* and *The Pirates of Penzance*. People started singing and dancing; the hurdy-gurdy was rivalled by a one-man band, a versatile performer who carried pan-pipes fixed under his mouth, a drum on his back – to be beaten by a stick tied to his elbows; cymbals on his drum were clashed by a string attached to his knees; and he carried a triangle. The dexterity with which he performed won the great admiration of all, and the pennies rattled into the hat at his feet.

There was one man selling pamphlets. 'Fifty Glorious Years,' he called. 'Read about the Life of Her Majesty the Queen.' There were two gipsy women, dark-skinned, with big brass earrings and red bandana handkerchiefs tied about their heads. 'Read your fortune, ladies. Cross the palm with silver and a fine fortune will be yours.' Then came the clown on stilts – a comical figure who made the children scream with delight as he stumped through the crowds, so tall that he could bring his hat right up to the windows. We dropped coins into it; he grinned and bowed – no mean feat on stilts – and hobbled away.

It was a happy scene – everyone intent on enjoying the day.

'You see,' said Captain Carmichael, 'how impossible it would be to get through the streets just yet.'

Then the tragedy occurred.

Two or three horsemen had made a way for themselves through the crowds who, goodnaturedly, allowed them to pass through.

At that moment another rider came into the square. I knew enough about horses to see at once that he was not in control of the animal. The horse paused a fraction of a second, his ear cocked, and I was sure that the masses of people in the square and the noise they were creating alarmed him.

He lifted his front legs and swayed blindly; then he lowered his head and charged into the crowd. There was a shout; someone fell. I saw the rider desperately trying to maintain control before he was thrown into the air. There was a hushed silence and then the screams broke out; the horse had gone mad and was dashing blindly through the crowds.

We stared in horror. Captain Carmichael made for the door, but my mother clung to his arm.

'No! No!' she cried. 'No, Jock. It's unsafe down there.'

'The poor creature has gone wild with terror. He only needs proper handling.'

'No, Jock, no!'

My attention had turned from the square to those two – she was clinging to his arm, begging him not to go down.

When I looked again the horse had fallen. There was chaos. Several people had been hurt. Some were shouting,

34

some were crying; the happy scene had become one of tragedy.

'There is nothing, nothing you can do,' sobbed my mother. 'Oh, Jock, please stay with us. I couldn't bear . . .'

Olivia, who loved horses as much as I did, was weeping for the poor animal.

Some men had arrived on horseback and there were people with stretchers. I tried not to hear the shot as it rang out. I knew it was the best thing possible for the horse, who must have injured himself too badly to recover.

The police had arrived. The streets were cleared. A hush had fallen on us all. What an end to a day of rejoicing.

Captain Carmichael tried to be merry again.

'It's life,' he said ruefully.

It was late afternoon when the carriage took us home. In the carriage my mother sat between Olivia and me and put an arm around each of us.

'Let's remember only the nice things,' she said. 'It was wonderful, wasn't it . . . before . . .'

We agreed that it had been.

'And you saw the Queen and all the Kings and Princes. You'll always remember that part, won't you? Don't let's think about the accident, eh? Don't let's even talk about it . . . to anyone.'

We agreed that would be best.

The next day Miss Bell took us for a walk in the Park. Everywhere there were tents for the poor children who were gathered there – thirty thousand of them, and to the strains of military bands each child was presented with a currant bun and a mug of milk. The mugs were a gift to them – Jubilee mugs inscribed to the glory of the great Queen.

'They will remember it for ever,' said Miss Bell. 'As we all shall.' And she talked about the Kings and Princes and told us a little about the countries from which they came, exercising her talent for turning every event into a lesson.

It was all very interesting and neither Olivia nor I

35

mentioned the accident. I heard some of the servants discussing it.

' 'Ere, d'you know? There was a terrible accident . . . near Waterloo Place, they say. An 'orse run wild . . . 'undreds was 'urt, and had to be took to 'ospital.'

'Horses,' said her companion. 'In the streets. Ought not to be allowed.'

'Well, 'ow'd you get about without 'em, eh?'

'They shouldn't be allowed to run wild, that's what.'

I resisted the temptation to join in and tell them that I had been a spectator. Somewhere at the back of my mind was the knowledge that it would be dangerous to do so.

It was late afternoon. My mother, I think, was preparing for dinner. There were no guests that evening, but even so preparations were always lengthy – guests or no guests. She and my father would dine alone at the big dining table at which I had never sat. Olivia reminded me that when we 'came out', which would be when we were seventeen, we should dine there with our parents. I was rather fond of my food and I could not imagine anything more likely to rob me of my appetite than to be obliged to eat under the eyes of my father. But the prospect was so far in the future that it did not greatly disturb me.

It must have been about seven o'clock. I was on the way to the schoolroom where we had our meals with Miss Bell and where we always partook of bread and butter and a glass of milk before retiring, when to my horror I came face to face with my father. I almost ran into him and pulled up sharply as he loomed up before me.

'Oh,' he said. 'Caroline.' As though he had to give a little thought to the matter before he could remember my name.

'Good evening, Papa,' I said.

'You seem in a great hurry.'

'Oh no, Papa.'

'You saw the procession yesterday?'

'Oh yes, Papa.'

'What did you think of it?'

'It was wonderful.'

'It is something for you to remember as long as you live.'

'Oh yes, Papa.'

'Tell me,' he said, 'what most impressed you . . . of everything you saw?'

I was nervous as always in his presence and when I was nervous I said the first thing which came into my head. What had impressed me most? The Queen? The Crown Prince of Germany? The Kings of Europe? The bands? The truth was that it was the poor horse which had run amok, and before I had realized it I had blurted out: 'It was the mad horse.'

'What?'

'The – er – the accident.'

'What accident?'

I bit my lip and hesitated. I was remembering that my mother had implied that it would be better not to talk of it. But I had gone too far to retract.

'The mad horse?' he was repeating. 'What accident?'

There was nothing for it but to explain. 'It was that horse which ran wild. It hurt a lot of people.'

'But you were nowhere near it. That happened in Waterloo Place.'

I flushed and hung my head.

'So you were in Waterloo Place,' he said. 'That was not as I thought.' He went on murmuring: 'Waterloo Place. I see . . . I think I see.' He looked different somehow. His face had turned very pale and his eyes glittered oddly. I should have thought he looked bewildered and a little frightened, but I dismissed the thought; he could never be that.

He turned away and left me standing there.

I went to the schoolroom. I had done something terrible, I knew.

I was beginning to understand. The manner in which we had gone there in the first place when we thought we were going somewhere else . . . it was significant, the way Captain Carmichael had been expecting us, the looks he and my mother exchanged . . .

37

What did it mean? I knew the answer somewhere at the back of my mind. There are things the young know . . . instinctively.

And I had betrayed them.

I could not speak of it. I drank my milk and nibbled my bread and butter without noticing what I was doing.

'Caroline is absent-minded tonight,' said Miss Bell. 'I know. She is thinking of all she saw yesterday.'

How right she was!

I said I had a headache and escaped to my room. Miss Bell usually read with us, each taking turns for a page – for half an hour after supper. She thought it was not good for us to go to bed immediately after taking food, however light.

I thought I would get into bed and pretend to be asleep when Olivia came up, so that I should not have to talk to her. It was no use sharing suspicions with her. She would refuse to consider them – as she always did everything that was not pleasant.

I had taken off my dress and put on my dressing-gown. I was about to plait my hair when the door opened and to my dismay Papa came in.

He looked quite unlike himself. He was very angry and he still wore that rather bewildered look. He seemed sad too.

He said: 'I want a word with you, Caroline.'

I waited.

'You went to Waterloo Place, did you not?'

I hesitated and he went on: 'You need not fear to betray anything. I know. Your mother has told me.'

I was obviously relieved.

He continued: 'It was decided on the spur of the moment that you would get a better view from Waterloo Place. I don't agree with that. You would have been nearer at either of the others which had been offered. But you went to Waterloo Place and were entertained by Captain Carmichael. That's so, is it not?'

'Yes, Papa.'

'Did you not wonder why the plans had been changed so abruptly?'

'Well, yes . . . but Mama said it would be better at Waterloo Place.'

'And Captain Carmichael was prepared for you, he provided luncheon.'

'Yes, Papa.'

'I see.'

He was staring at me. 'What is that you are wearing round your neck?'

I touched it nervously. 'It's a locket, Papa.'

'A locket! And why are you wearing it?'

'Well, I always wear it, not so that it can be seen.'

'Oh? In secret? And why, pray? Tell me.'

'Well . . . because I like wearing it and . . . it shouldn't be seen.'

'Should not be seen? Why not?'

'Miss Bell says I am too young to wear jewellery.'

'So you have decided to defy Miss Bell?'

'Well, not really . . . but . . .'

'Please speak the truth, Caroline.'

'Well – er – yes.'

'How did you come by the locket?'

I was unprepared for the shock my answer gave him.

'It was a present from Captain Carmichael.'

'He gave it to you yesterday?'

'No. In the country.'

'In the country. When was that?'

'When he called.'

'So he called, did he, when you were in the country?'

He had snapped open the locket and was staring at the picture there. His face had turned very pale and his lips twitched; his eyes were like a snake's and they were fixed on me.

'So Captain Carmichael made a habit of calling on you when you were in the country.'

'Not on me . . . On . . .'

'On your mother?'

39

'Not a habit. He came once.'

'Oh, he came once, when your mother was there. And how long was his visit?'

'He stayed two nights.'

'I see.' He closed his eyes suddenly as though he could not bear to look at me nor at the locket which he still held in his hand. Then I heard him murmur: 'My God'. He looked at me with something like contempt and, still holding the locket, he strode out of the room.

I spent a sleepless night, and I did not want to get up in the morning because I knew there was going to be trouble and that I had, in a way, created it.

There was a quietness in the house – a brooding menace, a herald of disaster to come. I wondered if Olivia sensed it. She gave no sign of doing so. Perhaps it was due to my guilty conscience.

Aunt Imogen called with her husband, Sir Harold Carey, and they were closeted with Papa for a long time. I did not see Mama but I heard from one of the servants that Everton had said she was confined to her bed with a sick headache.

The day wore on. The brougham did not come to take Papa to the bank. Mama remained in her room; and Aunt Imogen and her husband stayed to luncheon and after.

I was more alert even than usual for I felt it was imperative for me to know what was going on, and my efforts were rewarded in some measure. I secreted myself in the small room next to the little parlour which led off from the hall and where Papa was with the Careys. It was a cubbyhole really, in which was a sink and a tap; flowers were put into pots and arranged by the servants there. I had taken a vase of roses and could pretend to be arranging them if I were caught. I could not hear all the conversation, but I did catch some of it.

It was all rather mysterious. I kept hearing words like scandalous, disgraceful and: 'There must be no scandal. Your career, Robert . . .' and then mumbles.

I heard my own name mentioned.

'She should go away,' said Aunt Imogen emphatically. 'A constant reminder . . . You owe yourself that, Robert. Too painful for you . . .'

'It must not seem . . .'

I could not hear what it must not seem.

'That would be too much . . . It would provoke Heaven knows what . . . There's Cousin Mary, of course . . . Why shouldn't she? It's time she did something for the family. It would give us a breathing space . . . time to make some plan . . . to work out what would be best . . .'

'Would she?' That was my father.

'She might. She is rather . . . odd. You know Mary. She feels no remorse . . . Probably has forgotten all the upset she's caused. It's an idea, Robert. And I do really think she should go away . . . I'm sure that's best. Shall I get in touch with her? . . . Perhaps better coming from me. I'll explain the need . . . the urgent need . . .'

What the urgent need was I could not discover; and I could not stay fiddling with a vase of roses any longer.

The days dragged on and the sombre atmosphere prevailed throughout the house. I did not see either my father or my mother. All the servants knew that something unusual was going on.

I caught Rosie Rundall alone in the dining-room and I asked her what was happening.

She shrugged her shoulders. 'Looks like your Mama has been too friendly with Captain Carmichael and your Papa don't like it much. Can't say I blame her.'

'Rosie, why are they blaming me?'

'Are they?'

'I was in the flower room and I heard them say I should go away.'

'No, not you, love. I expect that they meant your Mama. That's who they meant.' She shrugged her shoulders. 'This will blow over, I reckon. Such things happen in the highest circles, believe me. Nothing to do with you . . . so you stop worrying.'

At first I thought she must be right and then one morning Miss Bell came into the schoolroom, where we were waiting to begin our lessons and said: 'Your mother has gone away for a rest cure.'

'Gone where?' I asked.

'Abroad, I think.'

'She didn't say goodbye.'

'I expect she was very busy and she did have to leave in rather a hurry. Doctor's orders.' Miss Bell looked worried. Then she said: 'Your father has told me that he puts great trust in me.'

It was all very strange.

Miss Bell cleared her throat. 'You and I are going to make a journey, Caroline,' she said.

'A journey?'

'Yes, by train. I am going to take you to Cornwall to stay with your father's cousin.'

'Cousin Mary! The harpy!'

'What?'

'Oh nothing. Why, Miss Bell?'

'It has been decided.'

'And Olivia?'

'No. Olivia will not accompany you. I shall travel with you to Cornwall, stay a night at Tressidor Manor, and then return to London.'

'But . . . why?'

'It is just a visit. You will come back to us in due course.'

'But I don't understand.'

Miss Bell looked at me quizzically, as though she might not understand either – and yet on the other hand she might.

There was a reason for this. Possibilities flitted into my mind like will-o'-the-wisps on misty swamps. None of them was quite tangible enough to offer me an explanation which I could accept.

The Ghosts
in the Gallery

❧

Sitting in the first class carriage opposite Miss Bell, I felt
that what was happening to me was quite unreal and that I
should soon wake up and find I had been dreaming.

Everytning had come about so quickly. It had been on
a Monday when Miss Bell had told me that I was going
away, and this was only Friday and here I was on my
journey.

I was excited, naturally. My temperament made it impossible for me not to be. I was a little scared. All I knew
was that I was going to stay with Cousin Mary, who was
kindly allowing me to visit her. The duration of the visit had
not been mentioned and I felt that was ominous. In spite of
my craving to experience new ways of life I felt a sudden
longing for the old familiar things. I was surprised to
discover that I did not want to leave Olivia, and that had
she been coming with me my spirits would have been
considerably lightened.

She was going to miss me even as I missed her. She had
looked quite desolate when I had said goodbye.

She could not understand why I should be going – and to
Cousin Mary of all people. Cousin Mary was an ogre, a
wicked woman who had done something dreadful to Papa.
Why should I be going to her?

Pervading all my emotions was a terrible sense of guilt. I
knew in my heart that I had brought about this terrible
calamity. I had betrayed my mother; I had told that which
should have been kept secret. Papa should never have
known that we had been to Waterloo Place on Jubilee Day;

and in addition to telling him that, I had carelessly allowed him to see the locket.

He was annoyed about my mother's friendship with Captain Carmichael and I had betrayed it; and it seemed that, as a punishment, I was being sent to Cousin Mary.

I wanted so much to talk of it but Miss Bell was uncommunicative. She sat opposite me, her hands folded in her lap. She had seen the luggage deposited in the guard's van. One of the men servants had come with us to the station and looked after it, under the supervision of Miss Bell, of course, and all we had with us in the carriage was our hand luggage safely deposited in the rack above. I felt a rush of affection for Miss Bell, for I should be losing her soon because her duty was merely to take me to Cousin Mary and then return. I should miss her well-meaning authoritative manner at which I had often laughed with Olivia and which had, I knew, because of an absence from any other quarter, brought serenity and security into my life.

Occasionally I caught a glimpse of compassion in her eyes when they rested on me. She was sorry for me and that made me sorry for myself. I was angry. I knew that married ladies should not have romantic friendships with dashing cavalry officers; they should not meet them secretly. Yet knowing this, I had betrayed my mother. If only I had not talked to my father! But what else could I have done? Could I have lied? Surely that would not have been right. And he had come upon me so suddenly when I was in my dressing-gown and had not had the time to hide my locket.

It was no use going over it. It had happened and because of it my life had been disrupted. Now I was snatched from my home, from my sister, from my parents . . . well, perhaps that did not matter so much as I saw so little of Mama and far too much – for my comfort – of Papa. But everything was going to be new now, and there is always something alarming about the unknown.

If only I *knew* everything. I was too old to be kept in the dark; at the same time they considered me not old enough to know the whole truth.

Miss Bell was talking brightly about the countryside through which we were passing.

'This,' I said with a touch of irony, 'will be a geography lesson with a touch of botany thrown in.'

'It is all very interesting,' said Miss Bell severely.

We had pulled up at a station and two women came into the compartment – a mother and a daughter, I guessed. They were pleasant travelling companions and when we lapsed into easy conversation they told us that they were going as far as Plymouth and that they made the journey once a year when they visited relatives.

We chatted comfortably and Miss Bell brought out the luncheon basket which Mrs Terras, the cook, had packed for us.

'You will excuse us,' she said to the ladies. 'We left early and we have a long journey ahead.'

The elder of the ladies said how wise it was to come so prepared. She and her daughter had eaten before they left and there would be a good meal awaiting them on their arrival.

There were two legs of cold chicken and some crusty bread. I remembered Waterloo Place with a sudden pang of misery. It seemed far away – in another life.

'It looks delicious,' said Miss Bell. 'I'm afraid we shall have to use our fingers, though. Dear me!' She smiled at our companions. 'You will have to forgive us.'

'It is difficult travelling,' said the elder woman.

'I have a damp flannel which I brought with me, suspecting something like this,' went on Miss Bell.

We ate the chicken and the little cakes which had been provided by a thoughtful Mrs Terras for our dessert. Miss Bell produced a bottle of lemonade and two small cups. Yet another reminder of Waterloo Place.

I felt rather drowsy and, rocked by the rhythm of the train, dozed. When I awoke I was startled, for a moment wondering where I was.

Miss Bell said: 'You've had a long sleep. I must have nodded off myself.'

'We've come into Devonshire now,' said the younger of the two ladies. 'Not much farther for us to go.'

I looked out of the window at the woodlands, lush meadows and the rich red soil. We went through a tunnel and when we emerged, there was the sea. I was enchanted by the sight of the white frilled waves breaking about black rocks. I saw a ship on the horizon and thought of my mother going abroad. Where? When would she come back? When should I see her again? When I did I would ask her why *I* had been sent away. I know I told my father that we had been to Captain Carmichael's but it was only the truth, and I know that he saw my locket. But why send me away because of that?

Melancholy descended on me as I wondered what Olivia was doing at that moment.

Our travelling companions were collecting their things together. 'We shall soon be in Plymouth,' they said.

'Then,' added Miss Bell, 'we shall cross the Tamar and be in Cornwall.'

She was trying to inspire me with enthusiasm. I was interested but I could not stop thinking of Cousin Mary – the harpy – who had to be faced at the end of the journey, and the dreadful knowledge that Miss Bell would go away and leave me there. She had suddenly become very dear to me.

We were coming into the station.

The ladies shook hands and said it had been pleasant travelling with us. We waved goodbye and they went hurrying away to meet someone who was waiting for them.

People were scurrying along the platform. Many were getting off the train and some were getting on. Two men passed and looked in at the window.

Miss Bell sat back in her seat, relieved when they passed on.

'For a moment I thought they were coming in,' she said.

'They scrutinized us and decided against us,' I said with a laugh.

'They probably thought we would prefer to travel with ladies.'

'Very considerate of them,' I commented.

But apparently I was wrong, for just as the guard was blowing the whistle, the door was thrust open and the two very same men came into the compartment.

Miss Bell drew herself back in her seat, not at all pleased by the intrusion.

The two men settled themselves in the vacant corner seats, and as the train puffed out of the station I took covert looks at them. One was little more than a boy – I imagined he was two or three years older than I. The other I imagined to be in his early twenties. They were elegantly dressed in frock coats and bowler hats, and these last they took off and laid on the empty seats beside them.

There was something about them which claimed my attention.

They both had thick dark hair and dark, heavy-lidded eyes – very bright as though they missed little. I knew what it was that attracted me. It was a certain vitality; they both seemed as though it were something of an ordeal for them to sit still. I guessed they were related. Not father and son – the difference in age was not great enough. Cousins? Brothers? They had similar strong features – somewhat prominent noses which gave them an arrogant look.

I must have been studying them very intently, for I caught the elder one's eyes on me and there was a certain glint in them which I did not understand. He might have been laughing at my curiosity – or annoyed by it, I was not sure. In any case I was ashamed of my bad manners, and I flushed slightly.

Miss Bell was gazing out of the window rather studiedly, I thought, as though to indicate that she was unaware of the men. I was sure she believed it rather inconsiderate of them to have come into a compartment where two females were alone.

It was only when we were crossing the Tamar that her instinct for instruction prevailed over her displeasure.

47

'Just look, Caroline. How small those ships look down there! Now this is the famous bridge built by Mr Brunel. It was opened in er . . .'

'Eighteen-fifty-nine,' said the elder of the men, 'and if you would like the gentleman's name in full it was Isambard Kingdom Brunel.'

Miss Bell looked aggrieved and said: 'Thank you.'

The man's lips lifted at the corners. 'It has a central pier in the rock eighty feet below high water mark . . . if you are thirsting for more knowledge,' he went on.

'You are very kind,' said Miss Bell coolly.

'Proud, rather,' said the man. 'It is an extraordinary engineering feat, and the climax of that amazing gentleman's work.'

'Indeed, yes,' remarked Miss Bell.

'An impressive approach to Cornwall,' he went on.

'I am sure you are right.'

'Well, Madam, that you can witness for yourself.'

Miss Bell bowed her head. 'We are coming into Saltash,' she said to me. 'Now . . . we are in Cornwall.'

'I say Welcome to the Duchy,' said the man.

'Thank you.'

Miss Bell closed her eyes to indicate that the conversation was at an end and I turned my attention to the window.

We travelled in silence for some time while I was very much aware of the men – particularly the elder one – and I knew Miss Bell was too. I felt faintly annoyed with her. Why did she suspect them of indecorous behaviour towards two unprotected females? The thought made me want to laugh.

He had noticed my lips twitch and he smiled at me. Then his eyes went to my travelling bag on the rack.

'I believe,' he said to his companion, 'that this is rather a pleasant coincidence.'

Miss Bell continued to look out of the window, implying that their conversation was of no interest to her and indeed that she could not hear it. I could not attain the same nonchalance – nor could I see why I should pretend to.

'Coincidence?' said the other. 'What do you mean?'

The elder one caught my eye and smiled. 'Am I right in assuming that you are Miss Tressidor?'

'Why, yes,' I replied in some amazement; then I realized that he must have seen my name on the label attached to my travelling bag.

'And you are on your way to Miss Mary Tressidor of Tressidor Manor in Lancarron?'

'But yes.'

Miss Bell was all attention now.

'Then I must introduce myself. My name is Paul Landower. I am one of Miss Tressidor's close neighbours. This is my brother, Jago.'

'How did you know my charge is Miss Tressidor?' demanded Miss Bell.

'The label on her luggage is clearly visible. I trust you have no objection to my making myself known?'

'But of course not,' I said.

The younger one – Jago – spoke then: 'We did hear you were coming to the Manor,' he said.

'How did you know that?' I demanded.

'Servants . . . ours and Miss Tressidor's. They always know everything. I hope we shall be seeing you during your stay.'

'Yes, perhaps so.'

'You gentlemen . . . er . . . you have been visiting Plymouth?' asked Miss Bell, stating the obvious; but I guessed she wanted to take charge of the conversation.

'On business,' said the younger.

'You must allow us to help you with your luggage when we reach Liskeard,' the elder one said.

'It's kind of you,' Miss Bell told him, 'but everything has been arranged.'

'Well, if you need us . . . I suppose Miss Tressidor will send her trap to meet you.'

'I understand we are being met.'

Miss Bell's manner was really icy. She had a notion that perfect gentlemen did not speak to ladies without an introduction. I think the elder one – Paul – was aware of this and amused by it.

Silence prevailed until we came into Liskeard. Paul Landower took my travelling bag and signed to Jago to take Miss Bell's, and in spite of her protests they came with us to make sure that our luggage was put off the train. The porter touched his cap with the utmost respect and I could see that the Landowers were very important people in the neighbourhood.

My trunk was carried out to the waiting trap.

'Here are your ladies, Joe,' said Paul Landower to the driver.

'Thank 'ee, sir,' said Joe.

We were helped into the conveyance and we started off. I looked back and saw the Landower brothers standing there looking after us, their hats in their hands, bowing – somewhat ironically, I thought. But I was laughing inwardly and my spirits were considerably lifted by the encounter.

Miss Bell and I sat face to face in the trap, my trunk on the floor between us, and as we left the town behind and came into the country lanes, Miss Bell seemed very relieved. I guessed she had regarded the task of conveying me to Cornwall a great responsibility.

' 'Tis a tidy way,' our driver, Joe, told us, 'and it be a bony road. So you ladies 'ud better hold tight.'

He was right. Miss Bell clutched her hat as we went along through lanes where overhanging branches threatened to whisk it off her head.

'Miss Tressidor be expecting you,' said Joe conversationally.

'I hope she is,' I could not help replying.

'Oh yes, 'er be proper tickled, like.' He laughed to himself. 'And you be going back again, soon as you'm come, Missus.'

Miss Bell did not relish being called Missus, but her aloof manner had no effect on Joe.

He started humming to himself as he went on through the lanes.

'We'm coming close now,' he said, after we had been going for some time. He pointed with his whip. 'Yon's Landower Hall. That be the biggest place hereabouts. There's been Landowers here since the beginning of time, my missus always says. But you'm already met Mr Paul and Mr Jago. On the train, no less. My dear life, there be coming and going at Landower these last months. It means something. Depend on it. And there's been Landowers here since . . .'

'Since the beginning of time,' I put in.

'Well, that's what my missus always says. Now, there you can see it. Landower Hall . . . squire's place.'

I gasped in admiration. It was a magnificent sight with its gatehouse and machicolated towers. It was like a fortress standing there on a slight incline.

Miss Bell assessed it in her usual manner. 'Fourteenth-century, I should guess,' she said. 'Built at the time when people were growing away from the need to build for fortification, and concentrated more on homes.'

'Biggest house hereabouts . . . and that's counting the Manor too . . . though it runs it pretty close.'

'Living in such a house could be quite an experience,' said Miss Bell.

'Rather like the Tower of London,' I said.

'Oh, there's been Landowers living there for . . .' Joe paused and I said: 'We know. You told us. Since the beginning of time. The first man to emerge from primeval slime must have been a Landower. Or do you think one of them was the original Adam?'

Miss Bell looked at me reprovingly, but I think she understood that I was a little overwrought and more than ever indulging in my habit of speaking without wondering what effect my words might have. During the journey I had still been part of the old life; now the time was coming for a change – a complete change. It is only a visit, I kept telling myself. But the sight of that impressive dwelling and the

51

memory of the two men on the train whose home it was, made me feel that I had moved away from all that was familiar into a new world – and I was not sure what I was going to find in it.

I was overcome by a longing for the familiar schoolroom and Olivia there looking at me with her short-sighted eyes, reproving me for some outspokenness, or with that faintly puzzled look which she wore when she was trying to follow the devious wanderings of my comments.

'Not far now,' Joe was saying. 'Landowers be our nearest neighbours. Odd, they always says, to have the two big houses so close. But 'tas always been so and I reckon always will.'

We had come to wrought-iron gates and a man came out from a lodge to open them. I judged him to be middle-aged, very tall and lean with longish untidy sandy hair. He wore a plaid cap and plaid breeches. He opened the gate and took off his cap.

'Thank 'ee, Jamie,' said Joe.

Jamie bowed in a rather formal manner and said in an accent which was not of the neighbourhood: 'Welcome to you, Miss Tressidor . . . and Madam . . .'

'Thank you,' we said.

I smiled at him. He had an unlined face and I wondered fleetingly if he were younger than I had at first thought. There was almost a childishness about him; his opaque eyes looked so innocent. I took a liking to him on the spot. As we passed through the gates I had a good look at the lodge with its picturesque thatched roof; and then I saw the garden. Two things struck me; the number of beehives and the colourful array of flowers. It was breathtaking. I wanted to pause and look but we were past in a few moments.

'What a lovely garden!' I said. 'And the beehives, too.'

'Oh, Jamie be the beekeeper hereabouts. His honey . . . 'tis said to be second to none. He be proud of it and that fond of the bees. I do declare he knows 'em all. They be like little children to him. I've seen the tears in his eyes when any one of 'em comes to grief. He be the beekeeper all right.'

The drive was about half a mile long and as we rounded the bend we came face to face with Tressidor Manor – that beautiful Elizabethan house which had caused such bitterness in the family.

It was grand – but less so than the one we had just passed. It was red brick and immediately recognizable as Tudor – and Elizabethan at that, because from where we were it was possible to define the E-shape. There was a gatehouse, but it looked more ornamental than that of Landower, and it formed the middle strut of the E, two wings protruding at either side. The chimneys were in pairs and resembled classic columns, and the mullioned windows were topped with ornamental mouldings.

We went through the gatehouse into a courtyard.

'Here we be,' said Joe, leaping down. 'Oh, here be Betty Bolsover. Reckon she have heard us drive in.'

A rosy-cheeked maid appeared and bobbed a curtsey.

'You be Miss Tressidor and Miss Bell. Miss Tressidor 'er be waiting for 'ee. Please to follow me.'

'I'll see to the baggage, ladies,' said Joe. 'Here, Betty, go and get one of 'em from the stables to come and give me a hand.'

'When I've took the ladies in, Joe,' said Betty; and we followed her.

We passed through the door and were in a panelled hall. Pictures hung on the walls. Ancestors? I wondered. Betty was leading us towards a staircase, and there standing at the top of it was Cousin Mary.

I knew who she was at once. She was such an authoritative figure; moreover, there was a certain resemblance to my father. She was tall and angular, very plainly dressed in black, with a white cap on her pepper-and-salt hair which was dragged right back from a face which was considerably weatherbeaten.

'Ah,' she said. She had a deep voice, almost masculine, and it seemed to boom through the hall. 'Come along,

53

Caroline. And Miss Bell. You must be very hungry. Are you not? But of course you are. And you have had an exhausting journey. You can go now, Betty. Come along up. They'll see to the baggage. There'll be food right away. Something hot. In my sitting-room. I thought that best.'

She stood there while we mounted the stairs.

As we came close she took me by the shoulders and looked at me and although I thought she was going to embrace me, she did not. I soon learned that Cousin Mary was not prone to demonstrations of affection. She just peered into my face and laughed.

'You're not much like your father,' she said. 'More like your mother, perhaps. All to the good. We can't be called a good-looking lot.' She chuckled and released me, and as I had been about to respond to her embrace I felt a little deflated. She turned to Miss Bell and shook her by the hand. 'Glad to meet you, Miss Bell. You have delivered her safely into my hands, eh? Come along. Come along. Hot soup, I thought. Food . . . and then I thought bed. You have to be off again in the morning. You should have had a few days' rest here.'

'Thank you so much, Miss Tressidor,' said Miss Bell, 'but I am expected back.'

'Robert Tressidor's arrangements, I understand. Just like him. Drop the child and turn at once. He should know you need a little rest after that journey.'

Miss Bell looked uncomfortable. Her code would never allow her to listen to criticism of her employers. I did not feel the same compunction to hear my father spoken of in this way, and I was rather intrigued by Cousin Mary, who was quite different from what I had been imagining.

We were taken into a sitting-room and almost immediately hot soup was brought in.

I think Miss Bell would have preferred to wash first but she knew that one in her position did not go against the wishes of people in authority and there was no doubt that Cousin Mary was accustomed to command.

The room was cosy and panelled but I was too uncertain

54

and tired to notice very much and in any case I should have plenty of time to discover my surroundings. The soup was served immediately and we did need it. There was cold ham to follow and apple pie with clotted cream – and cider to drink.

Cousin Mary had left us while we were eating.

I whispered to Miss Bell: 'I do wish you could have stayed for a day or so.'

'Never mind. Perhaps it is better thus.'

'Just think. You'll have that long journey again tomorrow.'

'Well, I shall have the satisfaction of knowing that you are here.'

'I am not sure that I am going to like it. Cousin Mary is rather . . . rather . . .'

'Hush. You don't know what she is like yet. She seems to me very . . . worthy. I am sure she is a lady of great integrity.'

'She is like my father.'

'Well, they are first cousins. There is often a family resemblance. It is better than being among complete strangers.'

'I wonder what Olivia is doing.'

'Wondering what you are doing, I imagine.'

'I wish she were here.'

'I dare say she wishes she were.'

'Oh, Miss Bell, why did I have to go away so suddenly?'

'Family decisions, my dear.'

Her lips were clamped together. She knew something which she was not going to tell me.

I was surprised that I could eat so heartily, and as we were finishing the meal Cousin Mary came back.

'Ah,' she said. 'That's better, eh? Now, if you're ready I'll take you to your rooms. You'll have to be up early in the morning, Miss Bell. Joe will take you to the station. You should get a good night's sleep. We'll give you a packed lunch and return you to my cousin in the good order you left. Come with me, now.'

We mounted the staircase. The long gallery was on the first floor. As we passed through it, long dead and gone Tressidors looked down on me. The fast-fading light gave it an eerie look.

There was a staircase at the end of the gallery and this we mounted. We were in a corridor in which there were many doors. Cousin Mary opened one of them.

'This is yours, Caroline, and Miss Bell's is next to it.'

She patted the bed. 'Yes, they've aired it. Oh, there's your trunk. I shouldn't unpack it until tomorrow. One of the maids can help you then. There's hot water. You can wash off the train smell. Always think you carry that with you for a while. And then I should think a good night's sleep – and in the morning you can start to explore . . . get to know the house and our ways. Miss Bell, if you'd step along with me . . .'

At last I was alone. My bedroom was high-ceilinged, the walls panelled; a little light filtered through the thick glass of the windows. I noticed the candles in their carved wooden sticks over the fireplace. My trunk had been placed in one corner; my hand-case was on a chair. I had a nightgown and slippers in it so I could well leave unpacking until the morning. The floor sloped a little and mats covered the boards; the curtains were heavy grey velvet; and there was a court cupboard which looked solid and ancient, and an oak chest on which stood a Chinese bowl. On a dressing-table with numerous drawers was a swing-back mirror. I took a look at myself. I was paler than usual and my eyes looked enormous. There was no mistaking the apprehension in them. Who would not be apprehensive in such circumstances?

The door opened and Cousin Mary came in.

'Good night,' she said brusquely. 'Go to bed. We'll talk tomorrow.'

'Good night, Cousin Mary.'

She gave just a nod of the head. She was not unwelcoming, but she was not warm either. I was not sure yet of Cousin Mary. I sat down on the bed and resisted the impulse to cry weakly. I was longing for my familiar room, with Olivia seated at the dressing-table plaiting her hair.

There was a knock on the door and Miss Bell came in.

'Well,' she said. 'Here we are.'

'Is it how you thought it would be, Miss Bell?'

'Life is rarely what one thinks it will be – so therefore I make no pre-judgements.'

I felt myself smiling in spite of everything.

Oh, how I was going to miss my precise Miss Bell!

She sensed my emotion and went on: 'We are both exhausted, you know. Much more tired than we realize. What we need to do is rest. Good night, my dear.' She came to me and kissed me. She had never done that before and it aroused a sudden emotion in me. I put my arms round her and hugged her.

'You'll be all right,' she said, patting me brusquely, ashamed now of her own emotion. 'You'll always be all right, Caroline!'

Comforting words!

'Good night, my child.'

Then she was gone.

I lay in bed. Sleep eluded me at first. Pictures crowded into my mind, shutting out my tiredness. The men on the train, the great fortress which was their home, Joe driving the trap, the man with the bees . . . and finally Cousin Mary who was like my father and yet . . . quite different.

In time I should know more of them. But now . . . I was very tired and even my apprehension could not keep sleep at bay.

I was awakened by Miss Bell sitting on my bed, ready for her journey.

'Are you going . . . already?'

'It's time,' she said. 'You were in a deep sleep. I wondered whether to wake you, but I thought you would not want me to go without saying goodbye.'

'Oh, Miss Bell, you're going. When shall I see you again?'

'Very soon. It's just a holiday, you know. I shall be there when you come back.'

'I don't think it is going to be quite like that.'

'You'll see. I'll have to go. The trap is down there. I must not miss that train. Good luck, Caroline. You're going to have an interesting time here and you won't want to come back to us.'

'Oh, I shall. I shall.'

'Goodbye, my dear.'

For the second time she kissed me, and then she hurried from the room.

I lay wondering as I had so many times before what life was going to be like.

There was a knock on my door and Betty, the maid I had seen on the previous evening, came in with hot water.

'Miss Tressidor said not to disturb you if you be sleeping, but the lady what brought you be gone and I reckoned her'd come and say goodbye, wouldn't her?'

'She did, and I am awake and glad to have the hot water.'

'I'll take away last night's,' she said. 'And Miss Tressidor says that if you're up you can have breakfast with her at half past eight.'

'What's the time now?'

'Eight o'clock, miss.'

'I'll be ready, then. Where will she be?'

'I'm to be here to take you down to her. You can get lost in this house till you know it.'

'I'm sure you can.'

'Anything you want, Miss, just ring the bell.'

'Thank you.'

She went out. My homesickness was being replaced by a desire for discovery.

Precisely at eight-thirty Betty reappeared.

'This be the bedrooms up here, Miss,' she told me, 'and there's another floor above, too. We've got plenty of bedrooms. Then above them is the attics . . . servants' quarters, as they say. Then there's the long gallery and the solarium . . . then there's the rooms on the ground floor.'

'I can see I have a lot to learn if I am to find my way about.'

We came down the staircase.

'This be the dining-room.' She paused, then she knocked.

'Miss Caroline, Miss Tressidor.'

Cousin Mary was seated at the table. Before her was a plate of bacon, eggs and devilled kidneys. 'Oh, there you are,' she said. 'The governess left half an hour or more ago. Did you have a good night? Yes, I see you did, and now you're ready to take stock of your surroundings, eh? Of course you are. You'll want to eat a good breakfast. Best meal of the day, I always say. Stock yourself up. Help yourself.'

She showed a certain amount of concern for my well-being, which was comforting, but her habit of asking a question and answering it herself made for a certain one-sided conversation.

I went to the sideboard and helped myself from the chafing-dishes.

Cousin Mary took her eyes from the plate and I felt them on me.

'Feel a bit strange at first,' she said. 'Bound to. You should have come before. I should have liked to have visits from you and your sister . . . and your father and mother . . . if he'd been different. Families ought to keep together, but sometimes they're better apart. It was my inheriting this place they didn't like. There was no doubt about that. I was the rightful heir, but a woman, they said. There's a prejudice against our sex, Caroline. I don't suppose you've noticed it much yet.'

'Oh yes, I have.'

'Your father thought he should step over me and take this place because I was a woman. Only over my dead body, I said; and that's what it amounts to. If I died, I suppose he'd be the next. That's a consummation devoutly

59

to be wished – for him, I don't doubt. But I feel very differently about the matter, as you can imagine.' She gave a little laugh which was rather like a dog's bark.

I laughed with her and she looked at me with some approval.

'Cousin Robert is a very able man but he still lacks the power to get rid of his Cousin Mary.' Again that bark. 'Well, we've done without each other all these years. You can imagine how taken aback I was when I got the letter from Cousin Imogen telling me that they'd be glad if I invited you for a month or so.'

'They clearly wanted to be rid of me. I wonder why.'

She looked at me with her head on one side and, as I already realized was unusual with her, hesitated. 'Let's not bother about the whys and wherefores. You're here. You're going to be the means of healing the rift in the family . . . perhaps. I'm pleased you came. I've a notion that you and I are going to get on.'

'Oh, have you? I'm so glad.'

She nodded. 'Well, you'll settle in. You'll be left to yourself quite a bit. It's a big estate and I keep myself rather busy on it. I've managers but I hold the reins. Always have done. Even when my father was alive and I was younger than you . . . or as young . . . I'd work with my father. He used to say, "You'll make a good squire, Mary, my girl." And when there was all that raising of eyebrows and tittering about my being a woman, I was determined to show them I could do as well – and better – than any man.'

'I am sure you did show them, Cousin Mary.'

'Yes I did, but even now, if anything goes wrong they're ready to say "Oh well, she's a woman." I won't have it, Caroline. That's why I'm determined to make Tressidor's the most prosperous estate hereabouts.' She looked at me almost slyly and went on: 'You must have come past Landower Hall.'

I told her we had done so.

'What did you think of it?'

'I thought it was magnificent.'

She snorted. 'Outside, yes. Bit of a ruin inside . . . so we hear.'

When I told her we had met Mr Paul and Mr Jago Landower, she was very interested.

'They made themselves known,' I said, 'when they noticed the name on my luggage. They seemed to know I was coming here.'

'Servants,' she said.

'Yes, that's what the younger one said. Their servants . . . your servants . . .'

'It's like having detectives in the house. Well, it's natural, and as long as there are some things we can keep back, we have to put up with it. The Landowers keep a sharp lookout on what's going on here . . . just as we do on them.' She laughed again. 'There's rivalry. We're both squires, as it were. What possessed our ancestors to build so close, I can't imagine. And the Tressidors are the culprits. Landowers were here first. They're proud of that. Look on us as upstarts. We've only been here three hundred years. Newcomers, you see! We're on speaking terms, but only just. We're the rival houses – Montagu and Capulet. We don't go about biting our thumbs or thrusting rapiers into each other's gullets in the streets of the town, but we're rivals all the same. Friendly enemies, perhaps you could call us. We haven't had our Romeo and Juliet . . . not yet. I'm hardly made for Juliet and Jonas Landower is no Romeo. Certainly not now. Couldn't really have fitted the part in his young days any more than I could Juliet's. However, that's how it is with us and the Landowers. You say you met them on the train. Coming from Plymouth, I don't doubt. Been to see the lawyers . . . or the bank, more likely. Things are not going well at Landower, that much I know. Cost of keeping up the place is astronomical. It's creaking. It's about two hundred years older than Tressidor . . . and one thing I've always made sure of is to keep the place in order. The first little sign of decay . . . and it's dealt with. Costs less that way. You understand? Of course you do. Over the years the Landowers have thrown up some feckless characters like old Jonas. Drink, women, gambling . . . the Landower pattern. Tressidors have had their old reprobates, but on the whole we're a sober lot . . . compared with the Landowers, that is.'

'They helped us with our luggage,' I told her. 'Miss Bell was grateful.'

'Oh yes, very mannerly. Interested, too, in what goes on here. Opportunists, that's what they are. Always have been. Old Jonas thought he could retrieve the family fortunes at the gaming tables. Fools' game, that. Did you ever know anyone who was successful that way? Of course not. Always ready to take the main chance. Turncoats. Even in the Civil War they were for the King in the beginning, as most of us were in these parts, and when the King lost, the Landowers were for the Parliament. We suffered a bit at Tressidor then and they prospered.' She gave the bark which punctuated her speech and which I was beginning to wait for. 'Then the new King came back and they discovered that they were royalist after all. But that put us forward. However, they secured their pardon and managed to hang on to their estates. Opportunists. Now, of course, there are rumours. Well, we shall see.'

'It all sounds most exciting, Cousin Mary.'

'Life usually is when you take an interest in it. You've discovered that, haven't you? Of course you have. Well, my dear, you're going to have a little holiday here. You're going to learn something of what it is like to live in the heart of the country . . . that is, right away from the Capital. This is Cornwall.'

'The countryside seemed very beautiful. I'm longing to explore.'

'I always think this is the most beautiful part of the Duchy. We've got a touch of lush Devonshire and the beginnings of the rugged coast of Cornwall. When you get farther west it gets wilder, more stark, less cosy. You ride, don't you? Of course you do. There are horses in the stables.'

I said: 'We rode a good deal in the country and even in London.'

'Well, that's the best way of getting around. You'll amuse yourself all right. Don't stray too far at first and take a note of your bearings. I'll go round with you until you get to know your way a little. You have to be careful of the mists. They spring up suddenly and you can easily get lost and go round in circles. The moors are not far off. I should stay away from them at first. Keep to the roads. But as I say, someone will always go with you.'

'I thought the lodge cottage was very attractive.'

'Oh, the garden, you mean. Jamie McGill is a good fellow. Very quiet, very withdrawn. I think there's some tragedy there. He's a good lodgekeeper. I'm lucky to have found him.'

'I hear he's the neighbourhood's beekeeper.'

'Our honey comes from him. He does supply the neighbourhood, and very good it is. Pure Cornish honey. Here . . . try some. You can taste the flowers in it. Doesn't it smell fragrant?'

'Oh yes. And it's delicious.'

'Well, that's Jamie's honey. He came to me . . . it must be six years ago . . . no more than that, seven or eight. I was wanting an extra gardener. I gave him the chance and it wasn't long before we discovered he had a special way with plants. Then the old lodgekeeper died and I thought it was just the place for Jamie. So he went there and in a short time the garden was a picture – and he got his hives. He seems to be very happy there. He's doing what he likes best. People are very lucky when they have work they enjoy. Are you ready? I'll show you the house first, shall I? Yes, that's best. Then you can wander round the grounds for a bit and explore. This afternoon I'll take you for a ride. How's that?'

'I like the idea very much.'

'All right. We'll get along.'

It was an interesting morning. She showed me the attics where many of the servants had their quarters, though some lived in several of the cottages on the edge of the estate, and the grooms and stablemen lived over the stables. Then there were the bedrooms, many of them exact replicas of my own, and the long gallery with pictures of the family. She took me round explaining who they were. There were portraits of my father and Aunt Imogen when they were young, of my grandfather and his elder brother, Cousin Mary's father. Tressidors in ruffs, in wigs, in elegant eighteenth-century costumes. 'Here they are,' said Cousin Mary, 'the entire Rogues Gallery.'

I laughed protestingly and she said: 'Well, not all rogues. We had some good men among us and all of them were determined to keep Tressidor Manor as the family home.'

'That's understandable,' I said. 'You must be proud of it.'

'I confess to a fondness for the old place,' she admitted. 'It's been my life's work. My father used to say to me, "It'll be yours one day, Mary. You've got to love it and treasure it and show that the Tressidor women are as good as the men." And that's what I've been doing.'

There was the bedroom where the King had slept when he was on the run from the Roundheads. The fourposter bed was still there though the coverlet was threadbare.

'We kept that intact,' explained Cousin Mary. 'No one sleeps in this room. Imagine that poor man . . . with his own subjects against him. How must he have felt when he slept in that bed!'

'I doubt he had much sleep,' I said.

She took me to the window and I looked out over the rich green of the lawns, beyond to the woods in the distance. It was a beautiful view.

She pointed out the tapestry on the walls which depicted the triumphant return of the fugitive's son to London.

'That was put up in this room some fifty years after the King slept here. If I were fanciful, which I'm not, I would say that what part of him is left in this room would take some satisfaction from that.'

64

'You must be a little fanciful, Cousin Mary, to have such a thought,' I pointed out.

She burst out laughing and gave me a little push. She was not displeased.

She took me downstairs and showed me the small chapel, and the drawing-room and kitchens. We passed several servants during our perambulations and these she introduced to me. They bobbed respectful curtsies.

'Our hall is quite small,' she said. 'The Landowers have a magnificent hall. This house was built when halls were no longer the centre of the house, and more attention was given to the rooms. Much more civilized, don't you think? But of course you do. Building naturally should improve with the generations. I dare say at first it will be a little difficult to find your way around. Naturally. But in a day or so it will all become familiar. I hope you are going to like the house.'

'I am sure I shall. I do already.'

She laid a hand on my arm. 'After luncheon we'll go for that ride.'

I had had such a full morning that I ceased to wonder what Olivia was doing and how Miss Bell was faring on her homeward journey.

When I went to my room Betty came in and said that Miss Tressidor had suggested she help me unpack. This we did together and Betty hung up my clothes in the cupboard. She said that Joe would take my trunk and put it into one of the storage attics where it could remain until it was needed again.

After luncheon I changed into my riding habit and went down to the hall where Cousin Mary was waiting for me.

She looked very neat in her well-cut riding clothes, black riding hat and highly polished boots. She studied me with approval and we went to the stables where a horse was chosen for me.

We went down the drive, to the lodge. Jamie came out to open the gates for us.

'Good afternoon, Jamie,' said Cousin Mary. 'This is my

second cousin, Miss Caroline Tressidor. She is staying with us for a while.'

'Yes, Miss Tressidor,' said Jamie.

I said: 'Good afternoon, Jamie.'

'Good afternoon, Miss Caroline.'

'I noticed the bees when I came through last night,' I told him.

He looked very pleased. 'They knew you were coming,' he said. 'I told them.'

'Jamie always tells the bees,' said Cousin Mary. 'It's a custom. You must have heard of that. But of course you have.'

We rode on.

'He has an unusual accent,' I said. 'It's rather pleasant.'

'Scottish,' she said. 'Jamie's a Scotsman. He came to England . . . after some trouble up there. I don't know what. I've never asked. People's privacy should be respected. I suspect he came down here to make a new life. He's doing that very successfully. He's happy with his bees, and he does provide us with the finest honey.'

We rode on. She showed me the estate, and beyond it.

'This is Landower country,' she explained. 'They'd like to extend it. They'd like to take us in. We'd like to take them in, too.'

'Surely there's room enough for the two of you.'

'Of course there is. It's just that feeling there's been through the centuries. Some people thrive on rivalry, don't they? Of course they do. It's something of a joke really. I've no time for active feuding in my life and I doubt the Landowers have either. They've got other things to think about just now, I imagine.'

By the time we had returned to the house I felt I knew a great deal about Cousin Mary, the Tressidors, the Landowers, and the countryside. I was very interested and felt a great deal better than I had for some time.

The more I saw of Cousin Mary, the more I liked her. She was a great talker and I was playing a little game with myself to try to curb her flow and get a word or two in myself. I imagined I should be more successful at it later; but just now I wanted to learn all I could.

When I went to bed that night a great deal of my melancholy had lifted. I had been thrust into a new world which I was already finding absorbing.

I slept soundly and when I awoke and realized where I was my first feeling was one of expectancy.

A week had passed. I was settling into the household. I was left a great deal to myself now, Cousin Mary having introduced me to the countryside, as it were. This pleased me. It was a freedom I had not enjoyed before. To be allowed to ride out alone was in itself an adventure. Cousin Mary believed in freedom. I was of a responsible age, no longer a child, and by the time a week was up I was revelling in the new life.

I was given the run of the library. No books were forbidden, unlike at home where Miss Bell supervised all our books. I read a great deal – much of Dickens, all Jane Austen and the Brontës, which particularly intrigued me. I rode every day and I was beginning to know the country-side well. I had put on a little weight. Cousin Mary kept a good table, and I liked to do justice to what was served. I felt myself changing, growing up, developing a certain self-reliance. I realized that I had been somewhat restricted under Miss Bell's watchful eye.

Freedom from lessons was a relief. Cousin Mary said that as I found such pleasure in the library, the perusal of great writers was the best education I could get and would be more important for me in the future than the multiplication table.

It was certainly a pleasurable way of educating oneself.

Whenever I went out walking or riding I liked to go past the lodge gates where I often saw Jamie – almost always in his garden. He would call a respectful good morning. I wanted to stop and talk to him and ask about the bees, but there was something in his attitude which deterred me from doing this. But I promised myself that one day I would.

One day I came face to face with a rider in one of the narrow lanes.

'Why,' he cried, 'if it isn't Miss Tressidor!'

I recognized him as the younger of the travellers in the train.

He saw that and grinned. 'That's right. Jago Landower. That's a frisky little mare you're riding.'

'A little frisky perhaps. That doesn't bother me. I've ridden a great deal.'

'In spite of coming from London?'

'We ride there, you know. And we have a place in the country. When I'm there I'm always in the saddle.'

'I can see that. Are you going back to the Manor?'

'Yes.'

'I'll show you a new way.'

'Perhaps I already know it.'

'Well, you're not going the right way if you do. Come on.'

I turned the mare and walked her beside him.

'I've looked for you,' he said. 'I wonder I haven't seen you before.'

'I haven't been here very long, you know.'

'What do you think of Cornwall?'

'Very . . . fascinating.'

'And how long will you stay?'

'I don't know.'

'I hope you won't go away too soon . . . not until you have got to know us really well.'

'That's very welcoming, I must say.'

'What about the dragon?'

'The dragon?'

'The lady jailer.'

'Do you mean my governess, Miss Bell? She went back to London the next day.'

'So you are free.'

'She was not really a lady jailer.'

'Wrong words. A watch-dog. How's that?'

'She was sent to look after me and she did that.'

'I see you are a very precious young lady. I'm surprised that they let you out on your own. Oh, but that is My Lady Mary, teaching you self-reliance.'

'Miss Mary Tressidor has shown me the countryside, and I am quite capable of looking after myself.'

'I can see that. And how do you like the ancestral home? And how do you like Lady Mary? We always call her Lady Mary at Landower. She really is a very important lady.'

'I'm glad you appreciate that. This seems a long way round.'

'It is what is called a long cut as opposed to a short one.'

'So you are taking me out of my way?'

'Only a little. If we had gone the way you were going, our encounter would have been too brief.'

I was flattered and rather pleased, and I liked him.

I said: 'Your brother was very quick to notice the name on my luggage and realize who I was.'

'He's very bright, but on that occasion it did not require a great deal of perception. We had been informed that there was to be a visitor at Tressidor and we were well aware who. Your father was well known here. My father knew him and his sister Imogen. Some people thought he would inherit. But it went of course to Lady Mary.'

'Who was the rightful heiress.'

'But a woman!'

'Do you share the general prejudice?'

'Not at all. I adore your sex. And Lady Mary has shown she is as capable – far more, some say – as any man. I am just telling you why it was we knew you were coming and were to arrive on that particular day. Very few people travel down from London. We saw you when we passed the carriage and my brother said, "Did you see the girl with the lady who is obviously her governess? I wonder if that could be the much-heralded Miss Caroline Tressidor. Let's go back and find out." So we did.'

'I'm surprised that you went to so much trouble.'

'We go to a great deal of trouble to find out what's going

on at Tressidor. Look! There's Landower. Don't you think it's splendid?'

'I do. You must be very proud of such a home.'

He was momentarily downcast. 'Yes, we are. But . . . for how long . . .?'

I remembered what Cousin Mary had said about there being trouble at Landower and I said: 'What do you mean?'

'Oh, nothing. Yes, it is magnificent, isn't it? The family has been there since . . .'

'Since the beginning of time, according to Joe, the coachman.'

'Well, perhaps that rather overstates the case. Since the fifteenth century actually.'

'Yes. I heard you stole a march on the Tressidors.'

'How well versed you are in local history!'

'Not as well as I should like to be.'

'Well, there's time.'

I knew where I was now and I broke into a canter. He was beside me. Very soon I saw the lodge gates.

'Not such a long cut, was it?' he said. 'It's been delightful talking to you. I hope I'll see you again soon. Do you ride every day?'

'Almost every day.'

'I'll look out for you.'

I rode into the stables, well pleased with the encounter.

After that I saw him frequently. Whenever I rode out he seemed to be there. He became my guide and showed me the countryside and he talked a great deal about the old legends and the customs and superstitions which abounded in this part of the world. He took me on to the moors and pointed out the weird formation of some of the stones, which had been put there, some believed, by prehistoric man. There was an air of mystery about the moors. I could really believe some of the fanciful stories he told me of piskies and witches.

'What a pity you didn't come earlier,' he said. 'You could have taken part in the ceremony of Midsummer Eve when

70

we gather here at midnight and light our bonfires to welcome the summer. We dance round them; we become merry and a little wild and perhaps like our prehistoric forefathers. To dance round the bonfire is a precaution against witchcraft, and if you scorch your clothes that means you will be well protected. Ah, you should have been here for Midsummer Eve. I can see you dancing, with your hair wild – a real Tressidor.'

He showed me a disused tin mine and told me of the days when tin mining had made the Duchy prosperous.

'That's what we call an old scat bal,' he said, 'a disused mine. It's said to be unlucky. The miners of Cornwall were the most superstitious people in the world – apart perhaps from the Cornish fishermen. Their lives were full of hazards, so they looked for signs of good and evil. I suppose we should all be the same. Do you know, they used to leave food at the mine head for the knackers who could wreak evil on those who offended them. The knackers were supposed to be the spirits of Jews who had crucified Christ and could not rest. Why they should have travelled to Cornwall was never explained – nor how there could be so many of them. But do you know, there were miners who swore they'd seen a knacker – a little wizened thing, the size of a sixpenny doll, but dressed like one of the old tinners – that means an old miner. What do the knackers do now that so many mines are closed, I wonder? Perhaps they go back to where they belong. Now this particular shaft is said to be specially unlucky. You must not go near the edge. Who knows, some knacker might take a fancy to you and decide to take you with him to wherever he belongs.'

I loved to listen to him and urged him to tell me more, so I heard of the wassailing at Christmas when the great families provided spiced ale from which everyone drank. 'Waes Hael,' said Jago. 'That's Saxon and means "to your health". Lots of our customs go back before Christianity came here, which explains why we are such a pagan lot.'

He told me how they danced up at the big houses at Christmas, how the carol singers – called Curl Singers by the local people – came and joined in the merriment; how the guise dancers appeared on Twelfth Night, masked and disguised, dressed as historical characters, and frolicked out of doors and in and out of houses. Then there was Shrove Tuesday when it was permissible to rob the gardens of the rich, and how May Day was as important as Christmas and Midsummer Eve, when all ages assembled in the streets of the towns with fiddles and drums. They danced and feasted and set out to gather in the May, cutting branches of the sycamore trees and making them into whistles which sent out shrill sounds as they danced into the country and brought home the May. There was the Furry Dance, which was performed ceremoniously in Helston every year, and as fervently, if less orderly, all over Cornwall.

I had a notion that he was trying to show me how exciting life was here, and that he was pleased that I had come, and this made him very happy.

He loved to talk and I was a willing listener. He succeeded in making me feel that I wanted to witness for myself some of the customs about which he talked so enthusiastically.

But it began to dawn on me that often his gaiety was forced and I guessed that something was worrying him. When I asked him he shrugged it aside; but there came a time when he told me what was on his mind.

We had ridden past an empty farmhouse on the edge of the Landower estate. He said: 'The Malloy family lived here for generations. There was only one son and daughter left and they had no feeling for farming. The man went to Plymouth and became some sort of builder. He took his sister with him. So the farmhouse is vacant.'

'It's a very pleasant house,' I said.

'H'm.'

'I'd like to look at it. Could we go in?'

'Not now,' he said firmly, and turned his horse away as though he could not bear to look at the place.

Later I discovered why. We had taken our horses on to

the moor. It was invigorating there. I sat stretched out on the grass propped up by a boulder. Jago sat beside me.

I said: 'What's wrong? Why don't you tell me?'

He was silent for a few moments. Then he said: 'You know that farmhouse I showed you?'

'Yes.'

'That may be our home soon.'

'What do you mean?'

'We may have to sell Landower.'

'Sell Landower! What do you mean? Your family has been there since the beginning of time.'

'I'm serious, Caroline. We can't afford to live there. The place is almost falling about our heads and a fortune needs to be spent on it and soon . . . if it is going to survive.'

'Oh, I am sorry, Jago. I know how you feel.'

'Paul is frantic, but he can't get any help. He's staying in Plymouth now . . . seeing lawyers and bankers . . . trying to raise money. He won't give up, though they say it is hopeless and nothing can be done but let the house go. Paul thinks he'll do something . . . somehow. He's like that. If he makes up his mind he won't let go. He keeps saying he'll find a way. But you see, we need a fortune to spend on the structure and to save the roof. Everything has been neglected too long, they say. You think that because a house has stood for four hundred years it is going to stand forever. It would . . . if we could save it. But we can't, Caroline, and that's all there is to it.'

'What will you do?'

'They've come to the conclusion that we shall have to sell.'

'Oh no!'

'Yes. The lawyers say it's the only thing. My father is deeply in debt. Creditors are pressing. He has to find money somehow. We're lucky, the lawyers say, to have the farmhouse to go to.'

'How awful for you. And all those ancestors . . .'

'There's only one hope.'

'What's that?'

He burst out laughing. 'That nobody will buy it.'

I laughed with him. I was sure he was joking. He liked to tease me. Which was why I was never sure how much he was making up when he told me of the customs of the people.

Now I felt sure that he did not mean what he said. There was no danger of Landower's passing into other hands. How could it?

I raced him home. He waved a merry goodbye saying: 'Same time tomorrow.'

I was sure all was well at Landower, or at least it wasn't half as bad as he had said it was.

A few days later I was going for a walk and as I came to the lodge Jamie McGill appeared.

'Good afternoon, Miss Caroline,' he said.

'Good afternoon. It's rather sultry today. Do the bees know that?'

His expression changed. 'They do indeed, Miss Caroline. They know about the weather all right. They know fast enough when a storm's coming.'

'Do they really? They are fascinating, I know. I've always been interested in bees.'

'Have ye now?'

'Oh yes. I'd love to know more about them.'

'They're worth knowing.' A bee flew over his head and he laughed. 'He knows I'm talking about him.'

'Does he really?'

'Lazy old thing.'

'Oh, is he a drone?'

'Yes, he is. He does nothing but enjoy himself while the workers go about collecting the nectar and the queen's in the hive laying the eggs. His day will come, though. When the queen's off on her hymenal flight.'

'Have you always been interested in bees?'

'Interested in creatures, Miss Caroline. I've had hives before I came here. Never so many, though. They're miraculous little creatures. Clever, hardworking. You know what to expect from them.'

'That's a great asset . . . to know what to expect. Your flowers are lovely too. You have a way with those, I gather, as well as with the bees.'

'Yes, I love the flowers . . . all growing things. I've got a little bird in here.' He jerked his head towards the lodge. 'Broken wing. Don't think it will ever be quite right, but maybe it will mend a bit.'

A cat came out and mewing rubbed itself against his legs.

'Have you any other animals?' I asked.

'There's old Lionheart. He's the Jack Russell. He can give a good account of himself. He and Tiger the cat are permanent residents, so to speak.'

'And the bees, of course.'

'Oh yes, and the bees. The others come and go. This bird . . . he'll be here for a little while yet, but living in a cottage is no natural life for a bird.'

'How sad for it to be crippled. Particularly if it remembers the days when it was free. Do you think birds do remember?'

'I think God has given all creatures powers, Miss Caroline, just as He has given us.' He hesitated for a while, then he went on: 'Would you like to step inside for a while? You could see the little bird.'

I said I should indeed like to.

The dog came out rather fiercely to inspect me.

'All right, Lion. It's a friend.'

The dog paused, eyeing me suspiciously. Jamie stooped to pat him and the dog's slavish devotion was apparent.

It struck me then that this was a happy man.

He showed me the bird with the broken wing. He handled it lovingly and I saw that the bird, in his gentle hands, ceased to be afraid.

He had a pleasant little parlour, scrupulously clean, and in this we sat and talked about the bees. He said that if I cared to, one day, when it was a good time, he would take me out and introduce me to them.

'I'll have to protect you first. They don't always understand. They might think you had come to attack the hive.'

His conversation interested me in rather the same way that Jago Landower's did. I asked questions and he answered, obviously delighted in my interest. He told me how he had started with one swarm and now he had ten good stocks of bees in his garden.

'You see, Miss Caroline, you must understand them. Respect their feelings. They've got to know you for a friend. They know I'll shelter them against extremes of heat and cold. It's practical really to give them the best conditions for constructing the combs and rearing the young. Oh, I've learned a lot. Trial and error, you might say. I reckon now I must have the most contented apiary in Cornwall.'

'I'm sure you're right.'

'My bees have nothing to fear. They rely on me and I rely on them. They know they'll be looked after when the weather's too bad for them to forage for themselves. One day I'll show you how I feed them through wide-mouthed bottles full of syrup. That's when it gets cold, though. They mustn't have too much moisture. When I boil the sugar I put a little vinegar in it. That prevents it crystallizing. Oh, I'm being tiresome, Miss Caroline. Once get me on to the subject of bees and I don't know when to stop.'

'I find it very interesting. When can I actually look at the hives?'

'I'll speak to them tonight. I'll tell them all about you. I'll say there's a sympathetic soul . . . They'll understand. Mind you, they'd soon find out for themselves.'

I thought he was a little too fanciful but he interested me and I took to calling on him when I passed. Sometimes I went into the lodge, at others I had a little chat at the door.

Cousin Mary was rather pleased. 'It isn't everybody who'll take the trouble to show interest in him. He's a good man. I call him our Scottish Saint Francis. He was the one who was always looking after the animals, wasn't he? You know that. Of course you do.'

I felt now that I had three good friends – Cousin Mary, Jago Landower and Jamie McGill, and I was beginning to enjoy life in Cornwall. I could scarcely believe that it was such a short time ago when I had been dreading coming here.

Cousin Mary talked to me about the past when my father and Aunt Imogen used to stay at Tressidor for their summer holidays.

'The two brothers didn't get on very well, my father and your grandfather, that is. My father used to laugh and say, "He thinks he's going to get Tressidor Manor for his son. He's going to have a bit of a surprise." '

'I know how my father felt about that,' I said.

'Yes. I'd never give up Tressidor. It's mine . . . till the day I die.'

I asked her what she thought about the Landowers. Could it really be true that they might have to sell?

'There are rumours,' she replied. 'Have been for a long time. It will break the old man because it's his fault, you see. They've had gamblers in the family before but he's the one who's brought it all to a head. If Paul had been born a little earlier it might have stopped the rot. I've heard he really cares for the place and has a flair for management and might have had a chance of pulling the place round. The trouble is not only the old man's debts but the fact that the house needs instant repairs. Oh, it's folly not to take these things in time.'

'I believe Jago is very upset.'

'I dare say. But that's nothing to what his elder brother will be. Jago is young enough to recover.'

'Is Paul so much older?'

'Paul is a man.'

'Jago is nearly seventeen.'

'A boy really. They've brought it on themselves, though. If it had been an act of God, as they call it, one could have felt more sorry for them.'

'But I think people suffer more through misfortunes which have come about through their own fault, Cousin Mary.'

She looked at me rather approvingly, I thought, and patted my hand.

Later she said: 'Glad you came. Enjoyed having you.'

'That sounds like a goodbye speech to me.'

'I hope I shan't have to make one of those to you for a long time to come.'

Cousin Mary and I were certainly getting fond of each other.

In due course Jamie McGill took me out to introduce me to the bees. He covered my head with an extraordinary bonnet which tucked into my bodice and had a veil over my face for me to see through. I wore thick gloves. Then he took me out. I must say it was rather terrifying to have the bees buzzing round me. They buzzed round him too and some of them alighted on him. They did not sting, though.

He said: 'This is Miss Caroline Tressidor. I told you about her. She wants to learn about you. She's staying with her cousin for a while and she's a friend.'

I watched him take the combs out of the hive and I was amazed that they allowed him to do this. He was talking to them all the time.

Afterwards we went into the house and I was divested of the strange garments.

'They've accepted you,' he said. 'I know by their buzzing. *I* told them, you see, and they trust me.'

The bees' acceptance of me made a change in our relationship. Perhaps because the bees trusted me, he did. He became more open about himself. He told me that he was sometimes homesick for his native Scotland. He longed to see the lochs and the Scottish mists. 'Different from these down here, Miss Caroline, just as the hills are. Ours are grand and craggy – awesome at times. I long for them, aye, that I do.'

'Do you ever think of going back?'

He looked at me with horror. 'Oh no . . . no. I could

never do that. You see . . . there's Donald. It's because of Donald . . . and what he is . . . well, that's why I had to leave . . . get away . . . as far as I could. I was always afraid of Donald. We grew up side by side.'

'Your brother?'

'We were so alike. People didn't know us apart. Which was Donald . . . which was Jamie? No one knew . . . not even our mother.'

'You were identical twins.'

'Donald's not a good man, Miss Caroline. He's really bad. I had to get away from Donald. There. I'm boring you with things you don't want to know about.'

'I'm always interested in people. I like to hear their stories. I find them most interesting.'

'I can't talk of Donald . . . not what he did. I have to shut it right out of my mind.'

'Was he very bad?'

He nodded. 'There now, Miss Caroline, you've got to know my bees this afternoon.'

'I'm glad they accepted me as a friend. I hope you do, too.'

'I knew you were a friend right from the first.' He leaned towards me and said: 'Forget what I told you about Donald. I spoke out of turn.'

'I think it helps to talk, you know.'

He shook his head. 'No, I have to forget Donald. It has to be as though he never was.'

And I had to resist the urge to ask questions about Donald but I could see that speaking of him had already shaken Jamie McGill and that he was beginning to reproach himself for having talked of his brother.

After that one occasion he never mentioned him, although I did make several attempts to steer the conversation in that direction, but each time I was skilfully diverted, and I came to the conclusion that if I tried to get him to talk of his brother, I should no longer be welcome in the lodge.

I was writing quite frequently to Olivia. Writing to her

was like talking to her and I greatly looked forward to receiving her letters.

I gathered that life went on much as usual. She was mostly in the country. After the Jubilee celebrations there would be nothing for her to come to London for.

Miss Bell wrote once. Her letters were full of information which told me nothing. She had had a safe journey home; Olivia and she had started on Gibbon's *Decline and Fall of the Roman Empire.* The weather had been exceptionally warm. Such matters did not interest me.

There was one letter from Olivia which was different from the others.

Dear Caroline [she wrote],

I do miss you so much. They are talking now about my coming out. I shall soon be seventeen and Papa has told Miss Bell that he thinks I should be making my debut into society. I dread it. I hate the thought of those parties and meeting people. I'm no good at it. You would do very well. There's nobody here to talk to really . . . Miss Bell says it is to be expected and she is sure that if only I will make up my mind all will be well, it will.

Mama has never come back. She never will. I thought she had just gone away for a little while, but nobody speaks of her and when I mention her to Miss Bell she changes the subject as though it is something shameful.

I wish Mama would come back. Papa is more stern than ever. He is mostly in London and I am in the country, but if I "come out" I shall have to be there, shan't I? Oh, I do wish you would come back.

When *are* you coming back? I asked Miss Bell. She said it would depend on Papa. I said, "But surely Papa wants to see his own daughter?" And she turned away and said, "Caroline will come back when it is right and proper in your father's eyes for her to do so."

I thought that so odd. It is all so mysterious, Caroline, and I'm scared of going into society.

Do write often. I love hearing about the bees and that quaint man at the lodge, and about the Landowers and Cousin Mary. I think you are liking them all rather a lot. Don't like them more than you like me, will you? Don't like Cornwall more than you like home.

See if you can get Cousin Mary to send you home. Perhaps she could write to Aunt Imogen or something.

Remember, I do miss you. It wouldn't be half as bad if you were home.

Your affectionate sister,
Olivia Tressidor.

I thought a great deal about Olivia and wished that she could join me in Cornwall and share in this carefree absorbing life into which I had stepped.

Sometimes I used to feel that it was going on forever. I should have known better than that.

There were times when Jago Landower would lapse into a melancholy mood. I guessed he was really troubled as this was quite alien to his nature.

He admitted to me that there seemed to be no solution for his family but to sell the house.

I tried to comfort him: 'You'll have that lovely old farmhouse and you won't be far away.'

'Don't you see that makes it worse? Imagine being close to Landower and knowing that it belonged to someone else.'

'It's only a house.'

'Only a house! It's Landower! It's been our home for centuries . . . and we are the ones to lose it. You can speak lightly of it, Caroline, because you don't understand.' He paused. Then he went on: 'You've never seen it. Only from the outside. I'm going to show you Landower. Then perhaps you will understand.'

That was how I came to enter Landower and from then on I fell under its spell and I fully understood the anguish which the family was suffering.

I had grown to love Tressidor Manor. In spite of its antiquity, it was cosy. Landower was scarcely that. It was magnificent, splendid, crumbling perhaps, but as soon as I stepped inside, I felt that it was important that this house should not be allowed to fall into decay. As I approached I felt the full impact of the embattled walls and a shiver of delight went through me as I passed under the gateway and into the courtyard. I felt as though the centuries had been captured and were held fast within those walls. I was stepping right back into the fourteenth century when the place had been built.

There was a heavy nail-studded door through which we passed and we were in the banqueting hall. I was aware of Jago's immense pride and I now fully understood.

He said: 'Although Landower was built in the fourteenth century, it has been restored and built on since. Landower has grown with the centuries, but the banqueting hall is one of the oldest parts of the house. One thing they have changed. Originally the fire was in the centre of the room. I'll show you just where. The great fireplace was put in during Tudor times. That's the minstrels' gallery up there. Look at the panelling. That tells the age.'

I was speechless with wonder.

'Here is the family crest and look at the family tree; and entwined in the decorations over the fireplace, the initials of the Landowers who were living here at the time it was put in. Can you see anyone else living here . . . with everything that belongs to *us*?'

'Oh, Jago, it mustn't be. I hope it never happens.'

'That is the screens passage over there and the way to the kitchens. I won't take you there. I dare say the kitchen servants are nodding away, having an afternoon nap. They wouldn't be very pleased to see us. Come on.' He led me up a flight of stairs to the dining-room. Through the windows I could see the lawns and the gardens. Tapestry hung on the walls depicting scenes from the Bible; at either end of the table stood candelabra, and the table was set as though the family were about to sit down for a meal. On the great sideboard were chafing-dishes in gleaming silver. This did not seem like a doomed house.

There was a hushed atmosphere in the chapel into which he next led me. It was larger than ours at Tressidor and I felt overawed as our footsteps rang out on the stone flags. Scenes from the Crucifixion were etched on the stone walls; and the stained glass windows were beautiful, the carvings on the altar so intricate that I felt I should have to spend hours examining them to discover what they implied.

After that he took me to the solarium – a happy room with many windows, and as bright and sunny as its name implied. Between the windows and walls were portraits – Landowers through the ages and some notable people as well.

All about me was antiquity, the evidence of a family who had built a house and had made it a home.

Having seen something of my father's bitterness over the loss of Tressidor Manor, and Cousin Mary's pride in it, and determination to keep her hold on it, I understood the tragedy the Landowers were facing.

As I examined the tapestry I was aware that someone had come into the gallery. I turned sharply and saw that it was Paul Landower. I had not seen him since my arrival but I recognized him at once.

'Miss Tressidor,' he said with a bow.

'Oh, good afternoon, Mr Landower. Your brother is showing me the house.'

'So I perceive.'

'It's wonderful.' My lips trembled with emotion. 'I understand . . . I couldn't bear it . . .'

He said, rather coldly I thought: 'My brother has been talking of our troubles.'

'Well, why keep it a secret?' said Jago. 'You can bet your life everyone knows.'

Paul Landower nodded. 'As you say, no point in keeping

dark what will be common knowledge soon . . . very soon.'

'Is there no hope, then?' asked Jago.

Paul shook his head. 'Not so far. Perhaps we can find a way.'

'I'm so sorry,' I said.

Paul Landower looked at me for a few seconds, then he laughed. 'What a way to treat our guest! I'm ashamed of you, Jago. Have you offered her refreshment?'

'I just came in to see the house,' I said.

'Well, I'm sure you would like . . . tea. Is that so?'

'I'm quite happy just looking at the house.'

'We're honoured. We don't often have Tressidors calling.'

'It's a pity. I am sure anyone would consider it an honour to be invited here.'

'We don't do a great deal of entertaining now, do we, Jago? It is all we can do to keep the roof over our head and that, my dear Miss Tressidor, let me tell you, is in danger of falling in.'

I looked up in alarm.

'Oh, not immediately. We shall probably get a further warning. We have had little warnings already. What have you shown Miss Tressidor so far?'

Jago explained.

'There's more to see yet. I'll tell you what. Bring Miss Tressidor to my anteroom in half an hour. We'll give her some tea to mark the occasion when a Tressidor comes to Landower.'

Jago said he would do that and Paul left us.

'Things must have gone very badly for him to talk like that,' said Jago. 'He's usually so restrained about our troubles.' He shrugged his shoulders. 'Well, no use going over and over something that can't be helped. Come on.'

There was so much to see. The long gallery with more portraits, the state bedroom which had been occupied by royalty from time to time; the maze of bedrooms, ante-rooms and passages. I looked through the windows across the beautiful park and sometimes into courtyards where I could see the carvings on the opposite walls – often grotesque, gargoyles, threatening intruders, I fancied.

In due course we arrived at the anteroom which I believed to lead to Paul's bedroom. It was a small room with a window into a courtyard. There was a small table on which stood a tray containing everything that was necessary for tea.

Paul rose as I entered. 'Oh, here you are, Miss Tressidor. Have you still a high opinion of Landower?'

I said fervently: 'I have never before had the privilege of being in such a wonderful place.'

'You win our approval, Miss Tressidor. Especially as you come from the Manor.'

'The Manor is delightful, but it lacks this splendour . . . this grandeur.'

'How good you are! How gracious! I wonder if Miss Mary Tressidor would agree with you.'

'I am sure she would. She always says what she means and no one could fail to recognize the . . . the . . .'

'Superiority?'

I hesitated. 'They are so different.'

'Ah, loyal to Cousin Mary. Well, comparisons are odorous, we are told. Suffice it that you admire our house. What a mercy it is you came . . . just in time.'

I thought: He is obsessed by this tragedy, and I felt very sorry for him, far more than I ever had done for Jago.

He smiled at me and his expression, which before I had thought a little hard, softened. 'Now tea will be served. Miss Tressidor, will you do us the honour? It is supposed to be a lady's task.'

'I'd like to,' I said, and I seated myself at the tea-table. I lifted the heavy silver teapot and poured the tea into the very beautiful Sèvres cups. 'Milk? Sugar?' I asked, feeling very much at ease and grown up.

Paul did most of the talking. I noticed that Jago was quieter in his brother's company. Paul asked me about my impressions of Cornwall, about my home in London and the country. I talked vivaciously as I invariably did; but it was different when he spoke of my father. He had always seemed a stranger to me and never more than now. I was surprised how quickly Paul Landower sensed this. He quickly changed the subject.

I was deeply moved by this encounter. I was excited, of course, to be in this ancient house, and at the same time I was sad because of the agony the family was suffering at the prospect of losing it. I felt uplifted in the company of Paul Landower and so pleased that he had come across Jago and me in the house and that he was treating me like a guest.

He was so different from Jago. Jago I looked upon as a mere boy. Paul was a man and a man whose very presence excited me. I liked his virile masculine looks, but perhaps it was that touch of melancholy which stirred me so deeply. I longed to help him. I wanted to earn his gratitude.

I had the impression that he was thinking of me as a rather amusing little girl, and he was interested in me merely because I was a Tressidor, from the rival house. I longed to impress him, to make him remember me after I had gone – as I should remember him.

He talked about the feud between our families in the same way as Cousin Mary had.

'It does not seem much of a feud,' I said. 'Here am I a member of one side chatting amicably with members of the other.'

'We could not possibly be an enemy of yours, could we, Jago?' said Paul.

Jago said it was all a lot of nonsense. Nobody thought anything about that sort of thing nowadays. People had too much sense.

'I don't think it's a matter of sense,' said Paul. 'These things just peter out. It must have been rather fierce in the old days, though. Tressidor and Landower fighting for supremacy. We said the Tressidors were upstarts. They said we did not do our duty in the neighbourhood. Probably both of us were right. But now we have the redoubtable Lady Mary who is far too sensible for feuding with enthusiasm. And here are we in a sorry state.'

'I feel you will find a way out of your difficulties,' I said.

'Do you really think so, Miss Tressidor?'

'I'm sure of it.'

He lifted his cup. 'I'll drink to that.'

'I have a feeling,' said Jago, 'that no one will buy.'

'Oh . . . but it's so wonderful,' I cried.

'It needs a fortune spent on it,' replied Jago. 'That's how I console myself. It has to be someone fabulously rich so that life can be breathed into the tottering old ruin.'

'I still feel that it will come out all right,' I insisted.

When I rose to go I was reluctant to leave them. It had been such an exciting afternoon.

'You must come again,' Paul told me.

'I should love to,' I said eagerly.

Paul took my hand and held it for a long time. Then he looked into my face. 'I'm afraid,' he said, 'that we have rather overburdened you with our gloomy problems.'

'No, no . . . Indeed not. I was flattered . . . to be taken into your confidence.'

'It was really unforgivable. We're very poor hosts. Next time, we'll be different.'

'No, no,' I said fervently. 'I understand, I do.'

He pressed my hand warmly and I experienced a thrill of pleasure.

He was unlike any person I had ever known and it was his presence, as well as the splendours of the house, which had made this one of the most exciting afternoons I had ever spent.

His looks were outstanding; that strength, tempered with melancholy, appealed to my deep sense of all that was romantic. I wished that I had a great deal of money so that I could buy Landower and hand it back to him.

I was young; I was impressionable; Paul Landower was the most interesting person I had ever met and I was tremendously excited at the prospect of seeing more of him.

Jago said as we rode home: 'Paul was unlike himself. He's usually so restrained. I was surprised he talked so much . . . in front of you . . . about the house and all that. Very odd. You must have made some sort of impression, said the right things or something.'

'I only said what I thought.'

'He's not usually so friendly.'

'Well, I seem to have made a *good* impression.'

'I believe you and the whole of Cornwall have made a good impression on each other.'

When I reached home I wanted to tell Cousin Mary where I had been. I found her in the sitting-room. She looked rather subdued, I thought.

I burst out: 'You'll never guess where I've been. Jago took me to Landower to see the house and I met Paul again. He was very friendly and gave me tea.'

I had expected her to be astonished. Instead she just sat staring at me.

Then she said: 'I'm afraid I've had news from London, Caroline. It's a letter from your father. You are to go back. Miss Bell is coming next week to take you.'

I was distressed. It was over. I had had such freedom. I had grown to appreciate Cousin Mary. I wanted to go on calling on Jamie McGill, learning more and more about him and his bees and his wicked brother, Donald. Most of all I wanted to become friends with the Landowers.

I was fond of Jago but something had happened since that afternoon with Paul. I had thought about him after the meeting on the train, but that encounter in that most fascinating of houses had been a landmark in some way. How could a person one hardly knew loom so important in one's life?

I wasn't sure. There was a certain magnetism about him which I had never discovered in any other person. He was not handsome by conventional standards; he looked as though he might be prone to dark moods – but perhaps that was because of the desperate position in which he found himself now. I felt his tragedy deeply; I understood what he must be suffering at the prospect of losing his heritage; and

I longed to help. He felt it more than Jago ever could. Jago was by nature light-hearted, perhaps more resilient. I wondered about their father and what he must be suffering at this moment.

Why should I allow their misfortunes to colour my life? I hardly knew them, and yet . . . I felt so strongly that it must not happen, that some solution must be found.

I had felt great sympathy for Jago, but how much more strongly did I feel for Paul. I was growing up fast. I had begun to do so since that day when I had watched the Jubilee procession from Captain Carmichael's windows.

I knew now that my mother and he were lovers, that my father had discovered this and that I had, in a sense, betrayed them. He must have suspected them; I had just added the final proof. It was all becoming more clear. That was why he could not bear to see me. I had been the harbinger of disaster. I had forced him to see the truth, and for that reason he had wanted me out of his sight until he could bear to look at me again.

Yes, I was growing up and that made me more suscept-ible to emotions – certain rather special emotions which might be roused by a member of the opposite sex.

I wanted to be alone to think.

Cousin Mary had been upset too. She had been pleased to have me with her. I had an idea that she would have liked me to make Tressidor Manor my home. I could have done that quite easily, for I was beginning to realize that what I had thought of as 'Home' for so long was no real home at all if home meant love and security, as it should to a child. I had never had that. But I had found something like it with Cousin Mary.

She said: 'Well, you must come and stay again, Caro-line.'

She was not demonstrative but I could see that she was deeply moved.

I did not want to talk to anybody. I saddled my mare and rode out. I wanted to be alone. I went on to the moors. I rode over the grass, past huge boulders and trickling streams. Then I tethered my horse and stretched out on the grass and thought: This time next week I shall not be here.

Jago found me there. He had heard that I had ridden off in that direction from a woman in one of the cottages on the edge of the moor who had been pegging out her clothes and seen me ride by. He had been riding round for the last half-hour looking for me.

He sat down beside me.

I said: 'I'm leaving. I have to go back to London next week. My governess is coming to take me. My father says I must go.'

He picked up a blade of grass and started to chew it.

'I wish you'd stay,' he said.

'How do you think I feel?'

'You like it here.'

'I want to stay. There's so much . . .'

'I thought nothing much happened in the country and all the excitement was in London.'

'Not for me.'

'I ought to take you to the house,' said Jago. 'Paul took quite a fancy to you. He said you couldn't take it all in in one visit.'

'I should love to come. I should love to see more of the house, but . . .'

'Well, it won't be ours much longer. That seems to be the general opinion.'

'I am sure your brother will think of a way of keeping it.'

'That's what I used to say, but I can't think how. Paul's used to getting his own way, but this is different. They're determined on a sale. The trouble is to find someone who can afford to buy it.'

'If you sold it you'd be rich.'

'Rich . . . without Landower.'

'But your family's debts will be settled and you can start again.'

'With a farm . . . on the estate which was once ours!'

'It's tragic and I'm sorry.'

'And now you're talking of going. You're not going to let them send for you . . . just like that, are you?'

'What can I do?'

'Run away. Hide . . . until the old governess returns to London in despair without you.'

'How?'

'I'll hide you.'

'Where? In one of the dungeons at Landower, perhaps?'

'It sounds inviting. I'd bring you food every day, twice a day, three times a day. There aren't many rats there.'

'Only a few?'

'I'd see that you were all right. You might go to the farmhouse, the one that is going to be our home. No one would think of looking there for you. You could disguise yourself as a boy.'

'And go away to sea?' I said ironically.

'No. What would be the good of that? You might as well go to London. The plan is to keep you here.'

Jago went on making wild and absurd plans for my escape. I was comforted listening to him, even though I could not take anything he said seriously.

At last, reluctantly, I rose to go. I had wanted to be alone to think but I was glad he had found me for he had made me laugh with his ridiculous schemes, and in planning to escape from my unhappiness I had temporarily forgotten it. The fact that there were people who wanted me to stay did a little to alleviate my grief at the prospect of my departure. I was pleased to have so many friends. There was Jago, Cousin Mary and even Jamie McGill. He had hastened to tell me that the bees had buzzed mournfully and were sad that I should not be visiting the lodge much longer. Jago was really sorry and I wondered whether Paul would be.

It was fortunate that Jago had found me for on the way home I realized that something was wrong. Jago looked down at my horse and said: 'She's cast a shoe. That must be put right immediately. Come on. We're not far from Avonleigh and there's a smithy there.'

I dismounted and together we led our horses the quarter of a mile to the village of Avonleigh. We went at once to the blacksmith, who was at work. He looked up with interest when he saw us.

The not unpleasant smell of burning hoof was in the air.

'Good day, Jem,' said Jago.

'Why, if it b'aint Mr Jago. What can I do for 'ee, then?' He caught sight of me. 'Good day to 'ee, Miss.'

'The lady's horse has lost a shoe,' said Jago.

'Oh, be that so? Where's 'er to?'

'Here,' said Jago. 'How soon can you do it, Jem?'

'Well, soon as I've done with this 'un. Why don't you and the lady go along and take a glass of cider at the Trelawny Arms. 'Tis particular good . . . their own brew. I can tell 'ee so from experience. Go and do that and then come back. Like as not I'll have the little lady all ready for 'ee then.'

'It's the best thing to do,' said Jago. 'We'll leave both horses, Jem.'

'Just so, Mr Jago.'

'Come along,' said Jago to me. 'It's the Trelawny Arms for us. Jem's right. The cider is good there.'

It was a small inn, a hundred yards or so along the road from the blacksmith's. The signboard creaked in the faint breeze. It depicted that Bishop Trelawny of 'And Shall Trelawny Die' fame.

A woman who, I presumed, was the landlord's wife, came to talk to us. She knew Jago and called him by his name.

He explained that I was Miss Caroline Tressidor.

She opened her eyes wide and said: 'Oh, this be the young lady from the Manor, then. Come to stay with us for a little while. And what do 'ee think of Cornwall, Miss Tressidor?'

'I like it very well,' I assured her.

'Her horse cast a shoe,' Jago explained, 'and we've a little while to wait while Jem gets to work on it. So we thought we'd come along and try your cider. It was Jem who recommended it.

'Best in the Duchy, he always says. And although it be my own, I'm ready to agree with him.'

'I know. But Miss Tressidor will put it to the test, Maisie.'

'She shall do that, Mr Jago.'

We sat down at one of the tables in a corner. I studied the room with its small leaded windows and heavy oak beams. There was an array of horse brasses round the big open fireplace. It was a typical inn parlour and some two hundred years old, I guessed.

Maisie brought in the cider.

'Are you busy?' asked Jago.

'We've two people staying – a father and daughter. They're here for a day or two. It keeps us busy.' She smiled at me. 'We don't reckon so much on staying-guests. Most people stay in the town and we'm too near Liskeard. 'Tain't like the old days! 'Tis more an in-and-out trade, if you do know what I mean.'

I said I did and she left us to sample the cider.

'No need to hurry,' said Jago. 'Old Jem will be a little while yet. Just think . . . We'll probably never come here again. Let's make the most of it.'

'I don't want to think like that. I was beginning to forget that I had to go home soon.'

'We'll think of something,' promised Jago.

Just at that moment the guests came into the inn parlour – a man and a young woman who were clearly father and daughter. They both had the same sandy hair, alert light eyes and scanty brows. She might have been a year older than Jago. They gazed round the parlour and as the girl's eyes immediately fell on us they kindled with interest.

'Good day to you,' said the man. He had an accent which I did not recognize, except that I knew it did not come from near these parts.

We acknowledged his greeting and he went on: 'Cider good?'

93

'Excellent,' replied Jago.

'We'll have some, then. Gwennie, go and order it.'

The girl rose obediently and the man said: 'You don't mind if we join you?'

'Indeed not,' said Jago. 'This is a public room.'

'We're staying here,' said the man.

'For long?' asked Jago.

'Just a matter of days. So much depends on if what we've come to see turns out to be what we want.'

The girl returned and said: 'It's coming, Pa.'

'Ah,' he said. 'That's good. I'm as dry as a bone.'

Maisie brought in the cider.

'Are you all right, sir?' she asked of Jago; and he told her that we both found the cider excellent.

'You just let me know if you want more.'

'We will,' said Jago.

Maisie went out and Jago grinned at the man. 'It might be a little potent,' he said.

'That's so, but it's good stuff. Do you live round hereabouts?'

'Yes.'

'Do you know a place called Landower Hall?'

I opened my mouth but Jago flashed me a warning look.

'Indeed I do,' he said. 'It's the big house of the neighbourhood.' He threw me a mischievous glance. 'Though some might claim that the more important house is Tressidor Manor.'

'Oh, that's not for sale,' said the girl. 'It's the other one.'

Jago looked stricken for a moment. Then he said brightly: 'So you are interested in Landower Hall?'

'Well,' said the man with a laugh, 'it happens to be the reason why I'm here.'

'You mean that you are considering buying the place?'

'Well, a good deal will depend . . . It has to be suitable.'

'I think they're asking a high price.'

'It's not so much a matter of the brass. It's finding something that suits us.'

'You come from the North, don't you?'

'Aye, and thinking of settling in the South. I've still got interests up there, but there are those who can look after them for me. I fancy a different life. I plan to be a squire of some sleepy estate right down in the country . . . away from everything I've ever known.'

'Do you think you would like to be right away from the home you have known?' I asked.

'Can't wait to get away from it. My lawyer thinks this might be just the thing for us. What I've always wanted. Stately old home . . . somewhere with roots. Gracious, you know. Now that Mrs Arkwright's passed away – that's my wife – we've wanted to get away, haven't we, Gwennie?' The girl nodded. 'We've talked about it. Gwennie will be the lady of the manor; I'll be the squire. The climate's softer down here than where we come from. I've got chest trouble. The doctor's advice, you know. This seems just the place.'

'Have you seen this mansion yet?' I asked.

'No, we're going tomorrow.'

'We're so excited,' said Gwennie. 'I shan't sleep a wink tonight, thinking of it.'

'You like old houses, do you, Miss – er – Arkwright?' asked Jago.

'Oh, I do that. I think they're wonderful . . . standing there all those years . . . just facing the weather and getting the better of it. Think of all the people who've lived there. The things they must have done. I'd like to know about them . . . I'd like to find out.'

'You've always wanted to know what people were up to, Gwennie,' said Mr Arkwright indulgently. 'You remember what Mother used to say. She said you had your nose into everything. "Curiosity killed the cat," she used to say.'

They both smiled and then were a little sad, no doubt remembering Mother.

'I have heard that that house has not stood up so well to the weather,' said Jago.

I added my comment to his. '*I* heard that a great many

repairs had to be done . . . a complete restoration, some say.'

'Oh, I've gone into all that,' said Mr Arkwright. 'Nobody's going to pull the wool over John Arkwright's eyes. My lawyers are smart. They'll assess what's to be done and that will be taken into consideration.'

'So you have already considered that,' said Jago somewhat forlornly.

'I heard the place was falling down,' I said.

'Oh . . . it's not as bad as all that,' put in Mr Arkwright. 'It'll need a bit of brass spent on it . . . no doubt of that.'

'And you don't mind that?' asked Jago incredulously.

'Not for a place like this one. Roots in the past. I've always wanted to be part of such a place.'

'But it won't be *your* roots,' I pointed out.

'Oh well, we'll have to do a grafting job.' He laughed at his own joke and Gwennie joined in.

'You are a one, Pa,' she said.

'Well, I'm right. I'll be the squire. That's what we want. And don't you like the idea, eh, Gwennie?'

Gwennie said that what she had heard of the place made her feel it was just what they were looking for. 'There's a hall with a minstrels' gallery,' she added.

'We'll have dances there, Gwen. That we will.'

'Oh,' she said, raising her eyes ecstatically. 'That'll be . . .' She sought for a word. 'It'll be famous . . . really famous.'

'You won't be afraid of the ghosts, of course,' said Jago.

'Ghosts!' cried Gwennie in a tone which clearly implied that she was.

'Well, there are always ghosts in these old houses,' went on Jago. 'And they get very active when new people take over. All the Landower ancestors . . .'

Mr Arkwright looked in some concern at Gwennie. 'Oh, come on, Gwen. You don't believe in that nonsense, do you? There's no such thing, and if there are one or two . . . well, that's what we're paying good money for. They won't hurt us. They'll be jolly glad we've come to keep their home still standing.'

'Well, that's one way of looking at it,' said Gwennie, with a faint smile. 'Trust you, Pa.'

' 'Course it's the sensible way. Besides, ghosts give a bit of tone to an old place.'

Gwennie smiled but she still looked uncertain.

'Happen it is the place for us,' said Mr Arkwright comfortingly. 'Reckon our search is well nigh over.'

Jago rose. 'We've got to get back to the smithy. One of our horses lost a shoe. We came in to taste the cider while we were waiting.'

'It's been nice talking to you,' said Mr Arkwright. 'Come from these parts, do you?'

'Not far away.'

'Do you know the place well?'

'I know it.'

'Lot of rot about ghosts and things.'

Jago put his head on one side and shrugged his shoulders. 'Best of luck,' he said. 'Good day to you.'

We came out into the open and made our way to the smithy.

'Can you imagine them at Landower?' I asked.

'I refuse to think of it.'

'I believe you frightened Miss Gwennie.'

'I hope so.'

'Do you think it will do any good?'

'I don't know. He's only got to see the place to want it. He's got what he calls the "brass", and he's got his lawyer and he'll drive a hard bargain, I don't doubt.'

'I pin my hopes on Gwennie. You really scared her with the ghosts.'

'I rather thought I did.'

We started to laugh and ran the rest of the way to the smithy.

I had agreed to meet Jago that afternoon. He looked excited and I guessed that he had one of his wild plans in his mind and that he wanted to talk to me about it. I was right.

'Come to the house,' he said. 'I've got an idea.'

'What?' I asked.

'I'll explain. First come along.'

We put our horses in the Landower stables and went into the house. He took me in by way of a side door and we were in a labyrinth of corridors. We mounted a stone spiral staircase with a rope handrail.

'Where are we?' I asked.

'This part of the house isn't used much. It leads directly to the attics.'

'You mean the servants' quarters?'

'No. The attics which are used for storage. I had an idea that there might be something of value tucked away there . . . something which would save the family fortunes. Some Old Master. Some priceless piece of jewellery . . . something hidden away at some time, perhaps during the Civil War.'

'You were on the side of the Parliament,' I reminded him, 'and saved everything by changing sides.'

'Not till they were victorious.'

'There is no virtue in that, so don't sound so smug.'

'No virtue . . . only wisdom.'

'I believe you're a cynic.'

'One has to be in this hard world. However, we saved Landower, whatever we did. I'd do a lot to save Landower, and that's been the general feeling in the family throughout the ages. Never mind that now. I'll show you what I'm driving at.'

'Do you mean you've really found something?'

'I haven't found that masterpiece . . . that priceless gem or work of art or anything like that. But God moves in a mysterious way and I think He has provided the answer to my prayers.'

'How exciting! But you are as mysterious as God. You are the most maddening creature I know.'

'God,' he went on piously, 'helps those who help themselves. So come on.'

The attic was long, with a roof almost touching the floor at one end. There was a small window at the other which let in a little light.

'It's eerie up here,' I said.

'I know. Makes you think of ghosts. Dear ghosts, I think they are coming to our aid. The ancestors of the past are rising up in their wrath at the thought of Landower passing out of the family's hands.'

'Well, I'm waiting to see this discovery.'

'Come over here.' He opened a trunk. I gasped. It was full of clothes.

'There!' He thrust his hands in and brought out a pelisse of green velvet edged with fur.

I seized it. 'It's lovely,' I said.

'Wait,' he went on. 'You've seen nothing yet. What about this?' He brought out a dress with large slashed sleeves. It was made of green velvet and very faded in some places, but I was sure the lace on the collar had once been very fine. There was an overskirt which opened in the front to reveal a petticoat-type skirt beneath. This was of brocade with delicately etched embroidery. Some of the stitching had worn away and there was a faintly musty smell about the garment. It was not unlike a dress one of the Tressidor ancestresses was wearing in her portrait in the long gallery at the Manor so I judged it to be the mid-seventeenth century. It was amazing to contemplate that the dress had been in the trunk all that time.

'Look at this!' cried Jago. He had slipped off his coat and put on a doublet. It was rather tightly fitting, laced and braided, of mulberry velvet and must have been very splendid in its day. Some of the braid was hanging off and it was badly faded in several places. He took out a cloak which he slung over one shoulder. It was of red plush.

'What do you think?' he asked.

I burst out laughing. 'You would never be mistaken for Sir Walter Raleigh, I fear. I do believe that if we were out of doors in the mud you would spread your cloak for me to walk on.'

He took my hand and kissed it. 'My cloak would be at your service, dear lady.' I laughed and he went on: 'Look at these hose and shoes to go with it. I should be a real Elizabethan dandy in these. There's even a little hat with a feather.'

'Magnificent!' I cried.

'Well, you in that dress and me in my doublet and hose . . what impression do you think we'd make?'

'They're different periods for one thing.'

'What does that matter? They'd never know. I thought that in the shadows . . . in the minstrels' gallery, we'd make a good pair of ghosts.'

I stared at him, understanding dawning. Of course, the Arkwrights were coming to view the house this afternoon.

'Jago,' I said, 'what wild scheme have you in mind just now?'

'I'm going to stop those people buying our house.'

'You mean you're going to frighten them?'

'The ghosts are,' he said. 'You and I will make a jolly good pair of ghosts. I've got it all planned. They're in the hall. You and I stand in the shadows in the minstrels' gallery. We'll appear and then . . . disappear. But not before Gwennie Arkwright has seen us. She'll be so scared that Mr A. for all his brass will have to give way to entreaties.'

I laughed. It was typical of him.

'Full marks for imagination,' I said.

'I'll have them for strategy as well. How could it fail? I want your help.'

'I don't like it. I think that girl would be really scared.'

'Of course she will be. That's the object of the exercise. She'll insist that Pa does not buy the place and they'll go off somewhere else.'

'It only postpones the evil day. Or do you propose that when the next prospective buyer comes along we perform our little ghostly charade again. You forget. I shan't be here to help you.'

'By that time I'm going to find something of real value in

100

the attics. All I want is time. I'm also working on some way of keeping you here.'

'I'm afraid you'd never frighten Miss Bell away with ghosts.'

'My dear Caroline, I have so many ideas going round and round in my head. I shall think of something. There is still time. What we have to concentrate on now is the Arkwrights. You are going to help me, aren't you?'

'Wouldn't one ghost do?'

'Two's better. Male and female. Come on. Don't be a spoilsport, Caroline. Put on the dress. Just see how you look.'

I couldn't help falling in with the plan. The dress was too big for me but it did look effective. There was an old mirror in the attic. It was mottled and gave back a shadowy vision. Reflected in it we certainly did look like two ghosts from the past.

We rolled about laughing at each other. I was sober suddenly, wondering how we could give way to such merriment with disaster hanging over both our heads. He was about to lose his beloved home and I was soon to leave a life which had become interesting and exciting to go back to one of dreary confined routine. Yet there could be these moments of sheer enjoyment. I was grateful to him for making me forget even for such a short while.

I said: 'I'll help.'

'All we have to do is stand there. We want to catch Gwennie on her own if we can. Perhaps while Pa is examining the panelling and calculating how much brass will be required to put it in order. There is a movement from the gallery. Gwennie looks up and sees standing there, glaring down at her, two figures from the past. Perhaps we shake our heads at her dismally . . . warningly . . . menacingly . . . but clearly indicating that she should not bring her father to Landower.'

'You make the wildest schemes.'

'What's wild about this? It's sheer logic.'

'Like keeping me in the dungeons with rats for company?'

'That was a figure of speech. I hadn't worked that out properly. This is all carefully thought out.'

'When do they arrive?'

'Any time now. Paul will show them round . . . or my father will. We'll choose our moment. We must be prepared.'

'What about my hair?'

'How did they wear it in those days?'

'Frizzy fringes as far as I know.'

'Just tie it right back. But perhaps if you have it piled up . . .'

'I've no pins. I wonder if there is anything in the trunk? A comb or something.'

We looked. There were no combs but there were some ribbons. I tied my hair with a bow of ribbon, so that it stuck out like a tail at the top of my head. The ribbon didn't match the dress but it was quite effective.

'Splendid!' cried Jago. 'Now we'll take up our places in the gallery so that we are all ready for the great moment.'

I giggled at myself wearing the elaborate dress with my riding boots protruding incongruously from the skirt.

'They won't see your feet,' said Jago consolingly. 'Now we reach the gallery by way of a side door. It's the door through which the musicians enter. It's concealed by a curtain. When we leave we can cut through a corridor to the stone staircase and up to the attics. Couldn't be better.'

I knew afterwards that I should never have agreed to this mad adventure. But who cannot be wise after the event?

Trying to suppress our laughter we came down the stone staircase. I had to tread cautiously for such medieval staircases were dangerous at the best of times, but with a long skirt which was far too big for me trailing at my feet, I had to watch every step.

Jago, ahead of me, impatiently urged me on, through the corridor to the side door. He drew aside the curtain and we walked in. For a fraction of a second, which seemed at least like ten, we stood there. Jago had miscalculated. Our intended victim was not in the hall as he had planned; she

102

was actually in the gallery. I saw her face freeze into an expression of absolute fear and horror. She screamed. She stepped backwards and caught the rail of the balustrade. It came away in her hands and she fell forward, and down into the hall below.

We stood there for a few seconds staring at her. There was a shout. Mr Arkwright ran to her. I saw him bending over her. Paul was running towards them.

Jago had turned pale. He drew me back hastily behind the curtain. I could hear Paul shouting orders.

'Come . . . quickly,' said Jago; and grasping my hand he pulled me out of the gallery.

We stood in the attic, the open trunk before us.

'Do you think she was badly hurt?' I whispered.

Jago shook his head. 'No . . . no . . . Just a fall . . . nothing more.'

'It was a long way to fall,' I said.

'They were all there to look after her.'

'Oh, Jago . . . what if she dies?'

'Of course she won't die.'

'If she dies . . . we've killed her.'

'No . . . no. She killed herself. She shouldn't have been so scared . . . just at two people dressed up.'

'But she didn't know we were dressed up. She thought we were ghosts. That's what we intended.'

'She'll be all right,' he said. But I was not sure that I thought so.

'We ought to go and see what's happened.'

'What good would that do? They're doing all that can be done.'

'But it was our fault.'

He took me by the arm and shook me. 'Look! What good can it do? Let's get out of these clothes. No one will ever know that we wore them. What we've got to do now is slip out. We'll go the way we came. Get that dress off quickly.' He had already stripped off his doublet and was getting into his riding coat.

With trembling fingers I took off the gown. In a few

moments we were completely dressed and the trunk was shut. He took my hand and pulled me out of the attic.

We went out the way we had come in and reached the stables without being seen.

We mounted our horses and rode away.

I had said not a word. I was deeply shocked and filled with a terrible remorse.

He said goodbye to me and I rode home to Tressidor. I stayed in my room until dinner-time.

I wanted to be alone to think.

The next day I heard the news. Cousin Mary told me.

She said: 'There was an accident at Landower. Some people came to see the place and a young woman fell from the gallery into the hall. I told you the place was falling apart. The balustrade in the minstrels' gallery gave way. Apparently they had been warned about it, but the young woman fell all the same.'

'Is she badly hurt?'

'I don't know. She's staying there, apparently. The father is there, too. I think they couldn't move her.'

'She must be badly hurt, then.'

'I should think that would put them off buying the place.'

'Did they say why she fell?'

'I didn't hear. I take it she leaned against the woodwork and it gave way.'

I went about in a dream that day. I had forgotten even that my departure was imminent. I did not see Jago. I wondered whether he avoided me as I did him.

Once more I had the news from Cousin Mary.

'I don't think she's all that badly hurt but they're not sure yet. Poor girl. She says she saw ghosts in the gallery. The father pooh-poohs the idea. They're very practical, these Yorkshire types. The Landowers are making a great fuss of them . . . looking after them, showing them a bit of that gracious hospitality which they've come to find. At least that's what I've heard.'

'I don't suppose they'll want the place now.'

'I've heard to the contrary. They're growing more and more fond of it . . . so one of the servants told our Mabel. I gather that the man has convinced his daughter that it was the shadows which made her fancy she saw the ghosts.'

The time was passing. One more day and Miss Bell was due.

I went round to say goodbye to the people I had known. I lingered at the lodge and had tea with Jamie McGill. He shook his head very sadly and said the bees had told him that I would be back one day.

I did see Jago before I left. He looked sad and was a different person to me now. We were not young and carefree any more.

Neither of us could forget what we had done.

I said: 'We ought not to have run away afterwards. We ought to have gone down to see what we could do.'

'There wasn't anything we could have done. We would only have made it worse.'

'At least she would have known that she had not seen any ghosts.'

'She's half convinced that she imagined she did. Her father keeps telling her so.'

'But she saw us.'

'He says it was a trick of the light.'

'And she believes him?'

'She half does. She seems to have a high opinion of Pa. He's always been right. You want to confess, don't you, Caroline? I believe you've got a very active conscience. That's a terrible thing to go through life with. Get rid of it, Caroline.'

'Is she very bad?'

'She can't walk yet, but she's by no means dying.'

'Oh, I wish we hadn't done it.'

'So do I. Moreover, it's had the opposite effect from what I planned. They're staying in the house. Paul's treating them like honoured guests . . . and so is my father. They're liking the place more. They've decided to buy it, Caroline.'

'It's a judgement,' I said.

He nodded mournfully.

'Oh, I do hope she is not going to be an invalid for life.'

'Not Gwennie. Pa wouldn't allow it. They're tough, these Arkwrights, I can tell you. They didn't get all that brass by being soft.'

'And I shall be leaving tomorrow.'

He looked at me mournfully.

So all our schemes had come to nothing. Landower was to be sold to the Arkwrights and I was going home.

The next day Miss Bell arrived, and the day after that we left for London.

The Masked Ball

Three years had passed since my return from Cornwall and my seventeenth birthday was approaching.

For the first six months I thought often of Cousin Mary at Tressidor Manor, James McGill at the lodge and Paul and Jago at Landower Hall. I particularly thought of Paul. I experienced a feeling of nostalgic longing every morning when I awoke. I told and retold my adventures to Olivia who was avid to hear of them and listened entranced. Maybe I embellished them a little. Perhaps Landower Hall sounded like the Tower of London and Tressidor Manor a little like Hampton Court. I talked of Paul Landower more than anyone else. He had become a handsome hero endowed with every noble quality. He was something between Alexander the Great and Lancelot; he was Hercules and Apollo; he was noble and invincible. Olivia's lovely short-sighted eyes glowed with sentiment when I talked of him. I invented conversations with him. Olivia envied me my adventures; she was horrified at the outcome of the ghostly episode, and it never occurred to her to wonder why the omnipotent Paul had failed to save his own home.

Cousin Mary had written only once. She was not a letter-writer, I soon discovered, though I was sure that if I went back to the Manor we should take up our relationship where it had left off. In that one letter she did tell me that Landower Hall had been sold to the Arkwrights and that Miss Arkwright could not have been really badly hurt because she was now walking about. The Arkwrights were established in the Hall and the Landowers had moved to a farm on the edge of their estate. Apart from that, everything was much the same as usual.

I wrote back and that letter remained unanswered. I did not write to Jago but I was sure that the old farmhouse, which was now the home of the Landowers, would be a very melancholy household indeed.

My father expressed no pleasure at my return. In fact I did not see him until I had been back three days; and then he scarcely looked at me.

Resentment flamed into my heart and I felt wretchedly hurt and longed for the casual affection of Cousin Mary.

Miss Bell was her old self. She behaved as though I had never been away; but my great consolation was Olivia, who implied a hundred times a day how pleased she was to have me back.

She had her own problems and the greatest of these was her 'coming out'. She was extremely nervous and was being groomed by Aunt Imogen – an ordeal if ever there was one – and there were so many do's and don'ts that she was becoming quite bewildered.

I had not been home more than three weeks when I heard I was to go away to school at the beginning of the September term. This was a blow no less to Olivia and Miss Bell than it was to me.

Olivia had not gone away to school. I could only believe that my father still remembered that if it had not been for me he might have gone on in blissful ignorance of my mother's love-affair with Captain Carmichael, and for this reason could not bear the sight of me.

Olivia was going to miss me. Miss Bell was anxious about the post of governess; but she was reassured almost immediately. She was to stay on and look after Olivia and presumably me during holidays from school when – I imagined most reluctantly – my father would have to allow me to return to the family home.

We discussed school and coming out – both with their hazards – and our mother.

Olivia had heard that she was abroad with Captain Carmichael and that he had had to resign his commission in the Army because of the scandal. It seemed strange to me

108

that our mother could leave without wanting to see us – or at least to hear from us. And our father certainly did not want to see me. How different it had been with Cousin Mary!

There was an ache in my heart every time I thought of her.

Then life began to change – not suddenly, but gradually. I went away to school and after the first few weeks enjoyed it. I was extremely good at English literature and had a flair for languages. Miss Bell had taught us a little French and German and I rapidly progressed in those tongues. I played lacrosse with some success; I learned ballroom dancing and to play the piano; and in none of these activities was I a dunce, though I did not exactly excel in any of them.

I began to like school, my new friends, rivalries and all the drama and comedy which seemed to arise out of trivialities. I was not too different from the normal to arouse enmity, yet I had something which was unusual. I think it was a vitality, a tremendous interest in everything that was going on, and a willingness to try everything once. It brought me friends and it made my school life very acceptable.

But I always enjoyed coming home for holidays and in the beginning deluded myself into believing that it would all be changed. My mother would return; my father would be pleased to see me, and everything would be happy. Why I should have thought this, I could not imagine. It had never been so before.

Olivia was in the throes of 'coming out' and after the first few months finding it not so bad as she had thought it might be. She was not an outstanding success in society but she had never expected to be; all she hoped for was to get by, which was just what she was doing. She went to balls and even on occasions to Court – the Court of the Prince and Princess of Wales, that was. The Queen was not given to frivolity and was at Windsor most of the time or hiding herself away in the Isle of Wight. The Prince and Princess of Wales were those who held court and were courted.

But those occasions were rare. The Prince of Wales was what was called a little 'fast' and so the society which surrounded him was considered not ideal for young girls on the threshold of their entrance into society.

Between Miss Bell and Aunt Imogen, Olivia was very closely guarded; and she had overcome the dread she had felt at first and was beginning to find life not unpleasant. She still suffered from shyness; and wished that I could accompany her on her engagements. So did I. When there was a ball at the house I was not allowed to go and was resigned to my usual post at the top of the staircase – rather undignified for a girl who was fast becoming an adult.

My father then decided that I should go to a finishing school in France. Once again I was appalled and once again I was soon enjoying it. We lived in a château in the mountains and parties of us would walk into the town once a week and have a cup of coffee and the most delicious pastries, sitting outside a café under a brightly coloured sunshade while we talked of what would happen to us when it was our turn to 'come out'.

Time was passing. I had forgotten what Captain Carmichael looked like, though when we drank lemonade I remembered vividly sitting at the window on the day of the Jubilee, and how happy we had been then. But I never forgot Paul Landower. I used to sketch his face in one of the sketch-books which we took with us on rambles in the mountains. He grew more and more handsome, more and more noble with the passing of time. Girls would peer over my shoulder and say: 'There he is again. I do believe, Caroline Tressidor, that he is your lover.'

They were always talking about lovers. I used to listen and smile and pretend a little . . . well, perhaps more than a little. It gave one enormous prestige to have had an admirer. I began to hint at a romantic attachment. I invented episodes which had taken place during my stay in Cornwall. Paul Landower had been in love with me but nothing could be done about that because he considered me too young. He was waiting for me to grow up. I almost

110

had now. It became my favourite relaxation – making up little scenes between us, and I told them with such conviction that I began to believe them myself.

I mentioned that he was troubled and this made him even more attractive in their eyes. He was melancholy; he was like Lord Byron, said someone; and I did not deny it. It was no fault of his that his great house had had to be given up. If he had had time, he would have retrieved his family's fortunes.

I told the story of how I had played ghosts with his younger brother. Later, I romanced, I had confessed to Paul. He had taken me into his arms to comfort me. 'There!' he said. 'It is no fault of yours. You are not to blame.' 'And you don't love me any less for what I did?' I asked. 'I love you more than ever . . . because of it. You did it for me. I love you infinitely.'

Sometimes I came out of my fantasies and laughed at myself. We laughed a lot. Finishing school was fun. Discipline was not the same and as long as we spoke French all the time that was all that was required of us.

Then it was over. I was seventeen. I would now go home and I supposed my 'coming out' would begin. I imagined that I should be drilled by Aunt Imogen as Olivia had been. I thought the dressmakers would be coming to measure me and sew for me as they had for Olivia. But it did not turn out that way.

Once Olivia asked Aunt Imogen when I was going to come out and she reported that Aunt Imogen put her lips together in that way she had and which was like a trap shutting. She had turned away and not answered.

It seemed very strange.

Olivia would have been delighted if we could have gone to the parties together. She had a wardrobe full of beautiful dresses and I longed to have some like them.

'One can only wear them once or twice,' said Olivia. 'It's the same people everywhere and it wouldn't do for them to think you were so poor you had to go on wearing the same things over and over again.'

'Would it matter?'

'Of course. It's a sort of parade, isn't it? Everyone is supposed to be beautiful and rich. It's all part of one's assets.'

'Like a cattle market.'

'Yes,' she said thoughtfully, 'it is really. Papa is quite well off and nobody seems very eager to take me. I suppose I am not attractive enough even though Papa has enough money to make me worthwhile in the other respect.'

'Oh, Olivia, you sound cynical. I never thought you would be that.'

'I suppose it's the way life goes. You'll see when your turn comes.'

But my turn did not come.

Then I noticed a change in Olivia. She seemed to have grown prettier; she was absent-minded; I would find her staring into space, and when I spoke to her she did not always hear me.

'I'll tell you what,' said Rosie Rundall, with whom, now that we were growing up, we seemed to be on even more friendly terms than before. 'Miss Olivia is in love.'

'In love! Olivia! Oh, Olivia, are you?'

'What nonsense,' she said, but she was flushed and confused so we knew it was true.

'Who is it?' I demanded.

'It's nothing. It's no one.'

'But you can't be in love with no one.'

'Stop teasing,' she pleaded. 'What would be the good of my being in love with someone. He wouldn't be in love with me, would he?'

'Why not?' demanded Rosie.

'Because I'm too quiet and not pretty or clever enough.'

'Believe me,' said Rosie – 'and I know what I'm talking about – there's plenty who like their women that way.'

But however much we tried to probe, Olivia would tell us nothing. I presumed she nurtured a secret passion for someone who was scarcely aware of her existence. But she did not seem to dread going to parties so much – and even on some occasions looked forward to them. I confided to Rosie that it was because she hoped to see this young man, and Rosie thought that very likely.

Rosie herself seemed more lovely, more soignée than ever. She often used to come and show herself to us before going on those nightly jaunts of hers. We used to marvel at her clothes. Olivia, who had learned a great deal since coming out, said that the silk of her dress was of very good quality, and she wondered how Rosie could afford such garments.

Meanwhile I was more or less confined to the schoolroom. I did not have routine lessons but I used to read French with Miss Bell every day. Since my sojourn in France, I spoke that language better than Miss Bell did; candidly she admitted this, but decided it was good for me to 'keep it up' – so we conversed and read daily in French.

Olivia came in one day excited because there was to be a ball at Lady Massingham's. Everyone would be in fancy dress and masked. She liked the idea. 'When my face is covered up I don't feel so shy,' she said. 'I think I rather like masked balls.'

'Very exciting not to know to whom you are talking,' I agreed.

'Yes, and they unmask at midnight and you sometimes get a shock.'

'I wish I were going.'

'I can't think why . . . Moira Massingham was saying it was very odd that you don't come out. She says you're old enough and her mother was saying it was rather strange.'

'I expect it will happen soon,' I said.

'In the meantime you can't go to the masked ball.'

'Oh, how I wish I could.'

'What as?'

'Cleopatra, I think. I rather fancy myself in the role with an asp curled round my neck.'

Olivia began to laugh.

The next day she said: 'I was talking to Moira Massingham at the Dentons' place and she said you ought to go.

Why not? she said. No one would know and you could be like Cinderella and slip away before the stroke of midnight and the unmasking.'

The idea appealed to me.

'But I would be an uninvited guest,' I said.

'Not if Moira knew. After all, it's for her. Surely she can ask her friends?'

The prospect of going to the masked ball added zest to the days. Moira Massingham was thrilled by the idea. It had to be secret. She visited us for tea which we were allowed to have together and alone – a tribute to Olivia's maturity – and I was not sure whether I was expected to be present, but I managed to be.

'It's a shame you're not "out",' said Moira to me when Olivia had gone out of the room to get something she wanted to show to Moira. 'Perhaps they want to get Olivia married off first and think you might spoil her chances.'

'Why ever should I?'

'Because you're more attractive.'

'That hadn't occurred to me.'

'Never mind. You're coming to the ball.'

Olivia returned and I could not stop thinking of what Moira had said. I wondered if Olivia believed the same. Poor Olivia, she already had a notion that nobody found her attractive.

Getting me to the ball would need a certain amount of manœuvring. If it were discovered, the project would immediately be stopped. The fact that Moira wanted me to go eased my conscience about gatecrashing. But how was I to get out of the house in my finery without being noticed?

When Rosie Rundall heard of it – and we could not resist telling her – she immediately took command. 'It'll be tricky,' she admitted, 'but we'll manage. Leave it to me.'

She decided that Thomas, the coachman, would have to be a collaborator.

'He'll do it for me,' she said with a laugh. 'He's the only one who would be ready to risk his job because he knows he couldn't easily be replaced. They wouldn't find the mews in such good order if Thomas wasn't there. He'll help us.'

So it was arranged that I should go to the back door through a corridor which was not used very much, and out across the garden to the mews where Thomas would be waiting with the carriage. Rosie would see that the coast was clear. I should get into the carriage, cower back so that I could not be seen while Thomas brought the carriage round to the front door to pick up Olivia.

'Do you think Aunt Imogen will be going with Olivia?' I asked.

There was a problem. If she did go the whole plot would fail.

'I'll make them see that the whole idea of a masked ball is that nobody knows who is who,' said the forceful Moira. 'I'll impress on my mother that chaperones must be excluded on this occasion. I'll say we'll only ask the girls who can take care of themselves. None of the starters, the just-out brigade.'

We were all giggling at the prospect and gave ourselves up to the fun of planning.

'What will you go as, Caroline?' asked Moira, who was going as Lady Jane Grey.

'Oh, we've discussed that,' said Olivia. 'Caroline thinks of the maddest things.'

'I rather fancy Boadicea.'

'You'd have to have a chariot.'

'I should love to ride in scattering all before me.'

'Talk sense,' said Moira.

'Diana the Huntress. That would be fun. Helen of Troy. Mary Queen of Scots.'

'Think of the costume.'

'None of those is impossible.'

We went through Olivia's wardrobe. She had a beaded jacket with beads which reminded me of hieroglyphics. I tried it on and shook out my dark hair. I had come back to my original idea. I would be Cleopatra.

Moira clapped her hands. 'It's perfect,' she said. 'With a long black skirt. Here it is. Try it on.'

She looked at me critically, her head on one side, and said she had a necklace which looked like a snake. It had belonged to her great-grandmother. 'There is your asp.'

Excitedly we planned.

I was sure Olivia was more interested in my costume than her own, which Aunt Imogen had helped to create. She was to be Nell Gwynn with a basket of oranges as her badge of identity.

Thomas was eager to help – perhaps mainly to please Rosie. I think quite a number of servants thought I was badly treated and were eager to perform little services for me.

We were all waiting with the utmost eagerness for the night of the ball. Moira brought our masks. It was imperative that they should all be the same, she said. They were large and black and covered our faces so well that it would be difficult for anyone to recognize us.

Rosie tried on our dresses and would not have needed much persuasion, I felt, to come herself; but when I mentioned this she said: 'Oh no, ducks. It's one of my nights off. I've got my own fish to fry.'

The arrangement was that when we returned she should let me in by way of the back door. Olivia would be dropped at the front door, which would be opened by Rosie in her capacity of parlourmaid – for she must return from her own night out by eleven o'clock – and she was in fact to sit up to perform this duty. Then Thomas would drive me round to the mews. I would then cross the garden to the back door where Rosie would be waiting to let me in, making sure that I was not seen.

The evening came. We were on the alert all the time while Olivia helped me to dress. She had taken the precaution of locking the door. Finally I was ready in my beaded hieroglyphics and my snake necklace. My hair, which had been dressed by Olivia, fell over my shoulders. I wore a headdress which we had contrived from stiff cardboard, painted red, blue and gold. It looked most effective, and I

116

believe I did bear a resemblance – if a faint one – to the celebrated Queen of Egypt.

The dangerous moment had come, which was to get me out of the house undetected. We had eluded Aunt Imogen and Miss Bell; but the most perilous moments lay ahead, and I do not know what we should have done without Rosie. She it was who made sure that all was safe, and I crept out of the house to the mews where Thomas was waiting with the air of a conspirator. He bundled me into the carriage.

'Crouch down, Miss Caroline,' he said. 'My, you'll be the belle of the ball. What you supposed to be?'

'Cleopatra.'

'Who's she when she's out?' Thomas prided himself on his modernity and had all the catch-phrases of the day on his tongue.

'She was a Queen of Egypt.'

'Well, you'll be queen of the ball, Miss Caroline, and that's nearer than Egypt, eh?'

He laughed immoderately. Another of Thomas's characteristics was to laugh heartily at what he considered his jokes. The trouble was that no one else saw them in that light.

'Now keep out of sight,' he warned. 'Otherwise we'll be in trouble, and Miss Rundall wouldn't like that at all, would she? I'd be in the dog-house, I can tell you.'

We came round to the front of the house and Thomas leaped down to make sure that no one helped Olivia into the carriage but himself. Rosie stood at the door watching, all dressed in her night-out finery, and ready to set off for the frying of that fish she had mentioned. Olivia hurried into the carriage, nearly dropping her oranges, overcome as she was with excitement and nervousness.

Then we were trotting along to the Massinghams'.

Theirs was a large, imposing residence backing on to the Park and carriages were already lining up at the door while their masked occupants alighted. Passers-by watched with amusement as we went into the house.

117

There was no formal greeting for the whole idea was that nobody knew who was anyone else.

'Ten minutes to midnight,' said Olivia warningly, as we left the carriage. 'No later, Thomas.'

Thomas touch 1 his cap. 'I know, Miss Olivia. Before they take off their masks, eh? Wouldn't do for anyone to see who's who.' He was overcome with amusement.

'That's the idea, Thomas,' I said.

'Well, ladies, I hope you enjoy it. You can rely on old Thomas to get you back.'

He went off chuckling and Olivia and I went to the ball.

The salon was on the first floor and it made a sizable ballroom. It looked very grand decorated with flowers, and the musicians were playing as we entered. From the windows I could see the garden below – looking very romantic in moonlight. White chairs and tables had been set up down there, and beyond, the Park looked like a mysterious forest. I caught a glimpse of silver through the trees and guessed that to be the Serpentine.

I kept close to Olivia. Two men came up. One was dressed as a Saxon in a tunic and cross-over laces about his legs, and the other was a very elaborate gentleman from a long-ago Court of France.

'Good evening, lovely ladies,' said one of them.

We returned their greeting. One had taken my arm, the other Olivia's.

'Let's dance,' said one.

I had the Saxon and Olivia went into a waltz with Richelieu or whoever he was supposed to be.

The Saxon's arm tightened about me. 'What a crowd!'

'What did you expect?' I asked.

'I shouldn't be surprised if there are some uninvited guests here tonight.'

I felt myself go cold with fear. He knows! I thought. But how? Then I calmed my fears. He was just making conversation.

'It would not be difficult to walk in,' I said.

'Easiest thing possible. I assure you *I* received my invitation from Lady Massingham.'

'I am sure you did,' I said.

It was difficult to dance, so crowded was the floor. He said: 'Let us sit down.'

So we did, at a table in a corner among some green palms.

'I thought it would be fairly easy to discover who people were,' he said. 'After all, we do meet often, don't we? The same crowd all the time. This ball . . . that occasion . . . and out come all the young ladies to meet the elected young gentlemen – all carefully vetted by cautious mammas.'

'I suppose that is inevitable in a small community.'

'You call this a small community?'

'The accepted social circle is not very large.'

'Are you surprised when you consider the qualifications one must have to enter it?'

'I didn't say I was surprised. I was merely offering an explanation.'

'Have you guessed who I am?'

'No.'

'Nor have I guessed you. I know the young lady you were with, though. I've met her before.'

'You mean . . .'

'Didn't you know? I thought you came together. But I suppose you just met on the way. She was Olivia Tressidor. I'm sure of it.'

'How can you be sure? She was heavily masked like the rest of us?'

He laughed. 'I'm still puzzling over you. I intend to discover before masks off.'

A man had come over to us.

'Cedric the Saxon,' he said, 'are you being tiresome to the noble Queen?'

We laughed.

'I was trying to probe her disguise.'

The other sat down with us and leaned his elbows on the

119

table looking at me intently. He was dressed as a Cavalier. There were several Cavaliers present.

'That's part of the game, is it not?' said the Cavalier. 'To guess who's who before the final revelation?'

'I wagered Tom Crosby that I would discover the identity of more of our young ladies than he does,' said the Saxon.

'At least,' I put in, 'we now know you are not Tom Crosby. You have betrayed that much.'

'Ah, my dear and most gracious Queen, how do you know that I did not say that to deceive you? What if I am Tom Crosby?'

'Anyone would know you were not Tom Crosby,' said the Cavalier. 'I wish you luck with your gamble. Why don't we dance?'

He had bowed to me and I stood up. I was rather glad to escape from Cedric the Saxon who had probed Olivia's disguise so quickly. I thought he was too inquisitive and I wondered whether he had an idea that I was not one of the circle.

The Cavalier was a good dancer. I was quite good too, for a great deal of time had been devoted to that social grace at the finishing school.

We danced in silence. In any case there was too much noise and much suppressed laughter. I glanced at a Japanese lady, far too large for a kimono; she was fluttering her fan in a very coquettish manner towards a portly Henry the Eighth. My companion followed my gaze and laughed. 'A rather incongruous combination,' he said. 'I wonder how the geisha girl strayed into the Tudor Court?'

We had stopped dancing and were close to a window.

'It looks inviting in the garden,' he said.

I agreed that it did.

'Let's go,' he said.

So we slipped away. It was certainly very pleasant out of doors. He led me to one of the white tables and we sat down.

'You puzzle me,' he said. 'I don't believe I have ever met you before.'

'You probably did not notice me.'

'That's what puzzles me. I am sure I should have noticed you.'

'I don't know why.'

'Come, that's scarcely worthy of the serpent of old Nile. You look the part to perfection, by the way.'

I sat back in my chair. I was beginning to feel a great excitement. It was the atmosphere; the people in their masks; the balmy evening; the moonlight on the Park; the soft music which was coming from the salon. And perhaps the fact that I was not supposed to be here. It made the evening such an adventure.

I felt bold. These young men must discuss the girls whom they all knew because they were invited to every social function. I could imagine that Cedric the Saxon was not the only one who made bets about the girls. I was amused. None would guess who I was for the simple reason that none of them had ever met me before.

I said: 'Your companions in arms are here in force tonight.'

'Rallying against those despicable Roundheads.'

'I saw only one of those among all the Cavaliers. Who are you? Rupert of the Rhine?'

'I didn't aspire so high,' he said. 'I'm just an ordinary servant of the King, ready to defend him against the Parliament. Is it not pleasant here, Your Highness? I am not quite sure whether that is the right way to address a Queen of Egypt.'

'Highness will do until you find out.'

'Had I known I was to meet you I should have come as Mark Antony. Or perhaps Julius Cæsar.'

'I dare say Cæsar will appear sometime tonight.'

'I shall have to be careful, then. What chance would a mere Cavalier have against him?'

'It would depend on the Cavalier,' I said pertly.

Some couples had already begun to dance in the garden.

'Shall we?' he said. 'Did you not find our steps fitted perfectly?'

'I thought we performed quite well together.'

'How glad I am that I discovered you and rescued you from that boring Saxon.'

'I was not finding him boring – probing, rather.'

'The Saxons were very crude. Didn't they paint their faces with woad?'

'No, that was the ancient Britons.'

'The Saxons were almost as bad. Not refined in their tastes as the Cavaliers were. I'm surprised at James Eliot coming as a Saxon. I thought he would have wanted to be something more grand – the Great Cham or Marco Polo or something, wouldn't you?'

'Oh . . . I don't know.'

'I recognized him at once, didn't you?'

'N . . . no.'

'You didn't! I'm surprised. I thought it was obvious. At an affair like this you can guess most people. Their voices . . . the way they stand, the way they walk. I suppose it is because we all meet so frequently. But you, my dear gracious Queen, are the enigma. I don't think we can have met before. I am wondering if you will be very kind and lift the edge of your mask.'

'I shall do no such thing. I shall cower behind it until the moment I take it off.'

'How cruel! I grow more and more intrigued with every passing moment.' He had drawn me towards the garden wall. We leaned out, looking across the Park.

'What a beautiful night!' I said.

'I am finding it more delightful every moment.'

This was flirtation, I recognized. I quite enjoyed it, and I had to confess that I was finding the Cavalier's company very stimulating.

He said suddenly: 'You are different . . . from the other girls.'

'Every human being is different from every other,' I replied. 'That is one of the wonders of nature.'

'Is that so? I find a rather boring similarity in many of the young ladies I am called upon to escort.'

'Perhaps that is due to your own lack of vision.'

'I wish it could serve me better tonight. I should like to look behind the mask. Still, I intend to possess my soul in patience. I shall discover on the stroke of midnight when I am determined to be at your side.'

A faint tremor of uneasiness swept over me, but I dismissed it. It was early and I had not yet had the fun I intended to have this evening. I wondered fleetingly how Olivia was faring.

'You are a very mysterious lady,' he went on.

'Well, is not mystery the theme of this gathering? It is intriguing to talk with people and not know who they are. It should make one very cautious.'

'It is supposed to have the opposite effect of making us all careless, throwing off our inhibitions. What does it matter what I do tonight? No one will know who I am . . . until midnight.'

'Unless, like Cedric the Saxon, we make discoveries.'

'Oh, some are obvious. Did you see Marie Antoinette? I'd be ready to swear she is Lady Massingham. I thought to myself: The lady has acquired a little avoirdupois – and after her stay in the Conciergerie! And the gentleman who is our host . . . who is he? It is harder to guess who he is supposed to be than who he really is. Is it Dr Johnson? Or Robespierre? Surely one should be able to tell the difference between these two gentlemen – but I'm dashed if I can. You dance divinely.'

'And you pay empty compliments. It is quite impossible to know how one dances in a crowd like this.'

'Please, dear enchanting Queen of Egypt, whisper your name.'

'It is against the rules.'

'Do you always obey rules?'

I hesitated. 'Ah,' he said quickly. 'You do not. You are a rebel. Just as I am. How far do you rebel against the laws of society?'

'You would not expect me to admit my indiscretions to you, would you?'

'Why not? I don't know who you are, and do you know me?'

'One should never admit to indiscretions, even to people one does not know.'

'Oh, you are very profound. Perhaps when you know me better . . .'

'Tonight I cannot be anyone but Cleopatra and you are Rupert of the Rhine.'

'I have a feeling that tonight is only a beginning.' He gripped my hand suddenly and brought his face close to mine. I was aware of light blue eyes glittering through the mask; they studied me intently.

'Dear Serpent of the Nile,' he said, 'I have a feeling that you and I are going to know each other very well.' For a moment I thought he was going to kiss me and I half wanted him to. I was reckless on this night. I certainly was enjoying the world of romantic glamour into which Olivia had the right to enter, while I was an intruder.

He touched the necklace at my throat. 'What a clever touch to bring your asp. I hope you don't decide to carry your interpretation too far. Oh . . . I believe I have seen that asp before. It's really rather unusual. I remember seeing it on the neck of a young lady. Ah . . . yes, I have it. It was Lady Jane Grey . . . in other words, Moira Massingham. And you are not Moira Massingham, are you? A clue! You are a great friend of that young lady and she has lent you her necklace. Collusion, dear Queen. Conspiracy. Who is Miss Massingham's friend of the moment? I fancied it was Miss Olivia Tressidor. I saw you come in together. I noticed you at once. In spite of your mask you looked excited, ready to enjoy every moment. None of that blasé indifference which so many young ladies affect. You came in with Miss Olivia Tressidor when you were accosted by the crude Saxon. I was watching you, you know.'

I was growing more and more uneasy. I turned away from the Park. I said: 'I believe they are serving supper in the dining-room.'

'They are. Let me escort you.'

It was glittering and so exciting. I was amused and happy. I did not want the evening to end. I found my companion exhilarating, and the fact that I was afraid he would discover I had no right to be here only increased my enjoyment. What if he did discover? He would laugh, I was sure. He would never betray me. Not tonight, perhaps. But later he would laugh over the incident with his friends.

We grew very merry. He told me I had chosen wisely for I was possessed of infinite variety. It was a pity all that beauty should be destroyed by a venomous snake.

'We are a tragic pair. Poor Rupert, you found disgrace . . . in Exeter, was it?'

'Your historical knowledge is greater than mine. You are gracious to have elevated me to the rank of Prince and commander when I entered this house as a humble Cavalier.'

So the badinage continued.

I drank champagne and felt myself light-headed. We danced; we talked; he was at times earnest. He wanted us to be friends. 'I await midnight with impatience,' he said, 'and yet I don't want the evening to end.'

I certainly was not looking forward to midnight when I should be in the carriage worrying about getting into the house unseen. Most surely I did not want the evening to be over; it had been one of the most exciting I had ever known, and I did not want to say goodbye to my companion.

Servants, presided over by a splendid gentleman in blue and gold livery, stood behind a table laden with dishes; duck and chicken sizzled over braziers. Cutlets of salmon were laid out on dishes garnished with watercress and cucumber; and there were patties containing all sorts of delicacies.

When we had been served we took our plates to one of the tables for two and there we ate and talked again.

He said: 'Your eyes are green. I don't remember ever seeing such green eyes before. You are a mystery woman.

But soon I shall know. Do you realize that within an hour that mask will no longer hide your face.'

'Within an hour!'

'Dear Queen, it struck eleven some time ago.'

He was looking at me intently.

'Why are you so scared?' he asked.

'Scared? Of course I'm not scared. Why should I be?'

'You may have your reasons. Do you know, I am beginning to wonder if you should not have come as Cinderella. She was the lady who had to leave the ball before midnight, wasn't she?'

I laughed, but I did not think my laughter was very convincing. Now I had to concern myself with planning my retreat, which was not going to be easy, for he was going to be very watchful.

'Let us dance,' he said. 'Shall we go down to the garden?'

'No,' I said firmly, deciding it would be easier to escape from the crowded salon than from the garden.

There was a big clock in the salon. It had been decorated with flowers and put there for the occasion. It struck the hours and I could imagine the scene when it came to twelve.

It was now half past eleven.

I looked about. I could see nothing of Olivia. Was she equally nervous? We danced. The hand was slowly creeping up. Twenty minutes to go. At ten minutes to twelve Thomas would be there waiting. I had to find Olivia if I could. She would certainly be there – perhaps she was crouching in the porch waiting for me already.

A quarter to.

I dared not wait any longer.

'I need a drink,' I said. 'Could you get me a glass of champagne?'

'Are you bracing yourself for the revelation?' he asked.

'Perhaps. But please do get it for me.'

'Wait here. I'll be back in a moment.'

The bar was in a corner of the salon. I had to be quick. I hurried through the crowd . . . down the staircase to the

126

hall. The door was open and Olivia was in the porch.

'I thought you were never coming,' she whispered.

'It was difficult to get away.'

'Thomas is already there. Here.'

We ran. Thomas was opening the door of the carriage and we got in.

'All present and correct?' he said laughing.

We started up. I lay back in the seat – relieved, yet deflated because it was now all over.

'What was it like?' asked Olivia.

'Wonderful. What did you think?'

'I'm glad it's over.'

'Did you dance much?'

'Quite a bit.'

I said: 'The salmon was delicious and the champagne . . .'

'You didn't drink too much, did you?' she asked anxiously.

'What is too much? I only know that I felt light-headed and very excited and that it was the most wonderful evening of my life.'

'Here we are, ladies,' said Thomas.

Olivia said: 'You'll be all right. Rosie will be waiting to let you in at the back door.'

'It's all arranged,' I replied. 'Perfect strategy. This is an example of expert organization. It went without a hitch, I think, though I was pursued by a very inquisitive gentleman.'

'It's not over yet,' warned Olivia. 'I shall be on tenterhooks until you are out of the costume.'

Thomas alighted and went up the stairs to ring the bell.

The door opened and Olivia went in.

'Now we're off,' he said.

In a few minutes we were at the mews and I was running across to the back door.

I stood in the shadows waiting for Rosie. I waited. Nothing happened. Surely she would have come straight away to let me in. That had been the plan. I began to feel cold, then a little anxious. What had gone wrong? Where was Rosie? What could I do, locked out of doors, dressed in this absurd costume?

Suddenly the door opened. But it was not Rosie who stood there. It was Olivia.

'I couldn't get away before,' she whispered.

'Why? Where's Rosie?'

'Come in quickly. I'll have to make sure no one sees you.'

We made our perilous way to our bedroom. Olivia would not speak until we were there. She was pale and trembling.

'Something's happened. Rosie isn't here.'

'Where is she, then?'

'I don't know. One of the servants let me in. She didn't know where Rosie was, so I had to come and open the door for you.'

'It's most unlike Rosie to let us down.'

'I can't understand it. She was so interested. Never mind. We'll hear in time. You'd better get out of those things quickly. I shan't feel safe until you do.'

It was an anticlimax to a wonderful evening. What had happened to Rosie? She had always seemed an unusual person. No one would have suspected she was a domestic servant when she went off on her evenings. There had always been a fear at the back of my mind that one day Rosie would leave us. I knew that several of the men servants eyed her with relish. She would marry, I was certain. Indeed, I wondered sometimes if she had not done so already. There was a brooding speculation about her. Secrets in her eyes, little spurts of laughter – most of all when she came back from her evenings off.

There was nothing to do now but undress quickly. How sadly deflated I felt, shorn of my royal garments. I was no longer an exciting woman, hiding behind a mask. I was myself – a girl, not yet 'out', insignificant, far removed from that fascinating woman I had believed myself to be a few hours before.

That man had fostered my belief. Rupert of the Rhine! I

laughed to myself. I wondered who he was. Surely I should soon be brought out into society. I was only just turned seventeen, but it was time, as everyone said.

I slept little that night.

In the morning there was a certain tension in the household. I learned from one of the maids that Rosie had gone.

'Gone!' I cried. 'Gone where?'

'That's what we don't know, Miss Caroline.'

'Didn't she come home last night?'

'Well, Mrs Terras said she did come in. She was the only one who saw her. She's gone now, though.'

'Gone without saying goodbye?'

'Looks like it. Her things has all gone . . . all her lovely clothes.'

It was incredible.

I was so taken aback that I tried to question Miss Bell. I doubt whether she would have told us had she known, but it was obvious that she was as much in the dark as the rest of us.

Our father had not gone to the bank that morning. The carriage had come round and been sent away. He was in his study – not to be disturbed.

There was a strange atmosphere throughout the house. But perhaps I imagined that as I was so sad because Rosie had gone.

I was in the schoolroom reading with Miss Bell – Olivia had come in and sat with us as she sometimes did – when there was a knock on the door and one of the servants entered holding a dozen red roses.

'They've just been delivered, Miss,' she said.

Miss Bell rose. She read: 'For Miss Tressidor.' Then: 'Oh, Olivia. For you.'

Olivia flushed and took the roses.

I said:'They're lovely.' Then I saw the card attached. Written on it was: 'Thank you. Rupert of the Rhine.'

I turned away. I thought: He knew who I was. And he has sent the flowers for me.

Olivia was looking puzzled.

Miss Bell smiled. 'Obviously one of the gentlemen at the ball,' she said.

'Rupert of the Rhine . . .' began Olivia.

She looked at me.

'Rupert of the Rhine,' went on Miss Bell. 'He would have been in some sort of armour, I suppose. Rather difficult to achieve.'

'There was no one in armour.'

'It was evidently someone who noticed you,' said Miss Bell.

The maid was hovering. 'Shall I put them in water, Miss Olivia?'

'Yes,' said Olivia. 'Please do.'

I could not concentrate after that.

Miss Bell said: 'You are reading very badly this morning, Caroline.'

Olivia did not mention the flowers to me. I suppose it did not occur to her that anyone would have known that I was at the ball. I tried to figure out how Rupert knew.

While Olivia and I were taking tea with Miss Bell in the small sitting-room which was used for such occasions one of the maids came in to announce that Mr Jeremy Brandon had called. Miss Bell looked at Olivia who flushed a little. It was quite in order for young men who were interested in young women to call discreetly at the house and see the object of their interest in the company of a chaperone.

'Perhaps Mr Brandon would care to join us for a cup of tea,' said Miss Bell graciously.

He came in and I immediately knew him. His blue eyes rested on me and there was mischief in them. He took Olivia's hand and bowed to her and Miss Bell.

'And this,' said Miss Bell, 'is Miss Caroline Tressidor, Miss Tressidor's younger sister.'

He bowed to me, smiling that conspiratorial smile.

He seated himself next to Olivia. I was opposite. I averted my eyes from him though my thoughts were in a whirl. How soon had he known? He must have realized that I had no right to be there. I knew that it was not Olivia whom he had come to see, just as the roses had not been meant for her.

'It was an interesting evening,' he said. 'And the gardens were so suited to the occasion. I thought some of the costumes were delightful.'

'I had great difficulty in keeping my oranges in my basket,' said Olivia. 'I realized quickly that it was not a good idea to be encumbered with them.'

'I thought Henry the Eighth and Marie Antoinette were very amusing,' he said, 'and there was an enchanting Cleopatra.'

'I dare say,' said Miss Bell, 'that there was more than one.'

'I only saw one,' he said.

They talked in a desultory way for a few minutes. I kept very quiet. I think Miss Bell was wondering whether I should be present, and was coming to the conclusion that no harm could come of it, even though I had not passed the magical 'coming out' barrier.

He was determined to bring me into the conversation.

'Miss Caroline,' he said, 'did you enjoy the ball?'

I hesitated and Miss Bell said: 'Caroline has not yet come out, Mr Brandon.'

'Oh, I see. So we shall have to wait another season before we are able to see more of you.'

Olivia was fidgeting a little.

He then began to talk to me, asking about the finishing school in France. He said that France was a country he liked to visit. In a way he was shutting Olivia and Miss Bell out of the conversation.

I was feeling more of that excitement which I had known at the ball. He was very good-looking. His features were regular; he had twinkling eyes and a mouth which turned up naturally at the corners indicating that he found life very amusing.

But I was becoming aware of Olivia's dismay and the disapproving glances of Miss Bell.

131

When he left he asked permission to call again and Miss Bell said she was sure that would be most agreeable.

Olivia did not mention him to me which I thought strange. But she did seem to be a little bemused. I fancied she had believed at first that he had come to see her, which was natural, of course; and she did not connect his visit with the red roses.

For the first time in my life I felt restrained with her, a little shy of saying what was in my mind, so I resisted the impulse to tell her that Mr Jeremy Brandon was Rupert of the Rhine and that I had spent almost the entire evening with him.

The next day when I was walking in the Park with Miss Bell, we met him as if by chance; but I was delighted because I knew he had contrived the meeting.

He swept off his hat and bowed to us.

'Why, it is Miss Bell and Miss Tressidor, I do believe.'

'Good day to you, Mr Brandon,' said Miss Bell.

'What a pleasant afternoon. The flowers are beautiful, are they not? Have you any objection to my walking with you?'

I think Miss Bell would have liked to refuse since she was not sure of the propriety of this, but she could hardly do so without appearing brusque, and what harm could a young man do to a girl not yet 'out', simply by walking beside her in the Park?

He talked of the flowers and pointed out the various trees; and I had a notion that he was trying to create a good impression with Miss Bell. She joined in the discussion with enthusiasm.

I said: 'It is really becoming like a botany lesson.'

'Knowledge is so interesting,' he said. He pressed my arm and I knew that he was finding the situation very amusing. 'Do you not agree with me, Miss Bell?'

'I do indeed,' she replied with fervour. 'One misses gardens in London. Do you have a garden, Mr Brandon?'

He replied that there was a very fine one at his parents'

132

country house. 'What a joy to escape from Town to be in the peace of the country,' he added, giving me a look which suggested he felt exactly the opposite.

Miss Bell was warming to him. One would have thought that she was the object of his pursuit. I knew differently from this. I knew that he was acting just as much now as he had done at the masked ball and that he was no more a country-lover with a passionate interest in horticulture than he was Rupert of the Rhine or a nameless Cavalier.

He was with us for the best part of an hour and took his departure with a bow and fervent expression of thanks for an interesting time.

Miss Bell said: 'What a charming young man! It is a pity there are not more like him. I rather hope something comes of his interest in Olivia. It would be so good for her.' She was more communicative than usual and I think she had fallen a little under the spell of the captivating Jeremy Brandon. 'I have spoken to Lady Carey about his call at the house and I have told her about the flowers. I wonder if he sent them? It could well be. He comes of a good but impoverished family. A younger son, but I think . . . for Olivia . . . he might be acceptable.'

I burst out laughing.

'Really, Caroline. I fail to see what is so amusing.'

I replied: 'You have to admit it is rather like a market.'

'I never heard such nonsense,' she said shortly. Then she was silent and her mood softened. I imagined she was thinking of Jeremy Brandon.

During the week he called again. I was not present and Olivia received him. The visit was rather brief, and the next day Miss Bell and I met him in the Park. It was not so easy to pretend this was a chance meeting. I don't know what Miss Bell thought. I wondered whether it occurred to her that I might be the one in whom he was interested. We walked along by the Serpentine and then we sat on a seat and watched the horses in the Row. He talked knowledgeably about horses, but this was a subject in which Miss Bell was not interested as she was in horticulture.

133

She would clearly become suspicious if there were any more 'chance' meetings in the Park.

It was a week after the ball. There was no more news of Rosie Rundall. I was constantly trying to learn something from the servants but although they were willing to talk – for the mystery of Rosie Rundall was one of the main topics of conversation in the servants' hall – I could glean nothing, only certain descriptions of the clothes she had.

'To my mind, Miss,' said one of the maids, 'she must have gone off with a gentleman friend. She must have had one. Look at the clothes she had. I reckon he gave her them lovely things.'

So Rosie had disappeared leaving no trace. Olivia and I talked of her, speculated about her and deeply regretted her departure.

Then one morning there was great consternation throughout the house. When his manservant had gone to the bedroom with my father's hot water, he had found him lying in his bed, unable to move.

Within a short time the doctor's brougham arrived and Dr Cray hurried in.

The verdict was that my father was gravely ill. He had suffered a stroke and his life was in danger.

Everyone was subdued. This could mean great changes in the household and they were all deeply aware of that.

There were doctors in and out of the house. Two nurses were installed. Miss Bell, who added a knowledge of nursing to her many accomplishments, became attached to the nursing contingent and I saw less of her.

For a few days we expected my father to die, but he rallied.

Miss Bell told us that his health had been much impaired and that he would never be the same again but, as sometimes happened in these cases, a recovery could be made.

And it was. In a month's time he could leave his bed and walk about with the aid of a stick, though he dragged one leg a little.

After the first shock had subsided I began to realize that Miss Bell's involvement with the nurses meant that I had more freedom. I made the most of it.

Olivia and I were allowed to go out together and we enjoyed escaping from continual supervision. Jeremy Brandon had been considered by my Aunt Imogen, and as his family connections, although not brilliant, were passable, and Olivia had been 'out' for some time and had so far failed to capture a rich prize, he was acceptable.

He was allowed to take us to tea at the Langham Hotel, which was a great occasion.

We rode with him in the Park, too. I was allowed to accompany them and was amused to think of myself as a chaperone.

But Olivia, of course, was not long deluded. She knew that she was not the one in whom he was interested. It was a fact which even he could not hide; and finally I confessed to her that I had met him at the masked ball and that he was that Rupert of the Rhine who had sent the roses, which in fact were meant for me.

Now the secret was out we could talk about the ball, and we did over tea.

'Your sister was such a plausible Cleopatra,' he said to Olivia. 'Really, to talk to her was like being transported back to ancient Egypt.'

'What exaggeration!' I cried.

'Oh, it was so indeed. I was looking over my shoulder all the time expecting Mark Antony or Julius Cæsar to put in an appearance. There was an air of mystery about Cleopatra. I could not place her at all. I knew most of the girls in the circle. I was so surprised. I got the truth out of Moira Massingham. That was after the unmasking, when Cleopatra, the Cinderella of the ball had disappeared. I recognized the snake necklace. I knew it was Moira's. She told me the whole story.'

'It gave us many a qualm, didn't it, Olivia?'

She agreed that it did.

'Olivia was wonderful.'

He smiled at Olivia. 'I can well believe that.'

She flushed and cast down her eyes. I felt sorry for Olivia who, I was sure, had first thought he came to see her.

Sometimes with Jeremy as our escort we left the dignified streets and went into the byways. I loved the bustle of the little streets where you could sometimes see children hopping over chalk marks on the pavements, chanting as they did so. I loved the hurdy-gurdies playing the popular tunes, and I liked the pavement artists whom we would stop to admire. Jeremy would sometimes talk to the artist and always dropped some coins into his upturned cap. The wider streets always seemed to be congested with landaus and broughams and hansom cabs.

We went shopping for ribbons and such articles, at Jay's in Regent Street mostly, and every day we saw Jeremy Brandon.

I was intoxicated by this newly found freedom which my father's illness had brought me.

One day – it was almost a month after my father's stroke – Jeremy drew me a little aside and whispered: 'Why can I never see you alone?'

'It is just not allowed,' I said.

'Surely we can arrange it.'

'I'm not sure.'

'Oh come, when you consider all the effort which went into fixing the Cleopatra episode, what insurmountable difficulties could a meeting on our own present?'

'I'll see if I can slip out alone tomorrow afternoon,' I said. 'Be at the end of the street at half past two.'

Olivia, who had been a few paces behind us, caught up then. He squeezed my hand surreptitiously.

I believed that he was in love with me. He gave me every indication that this was so. As for myself, I was only too ready to follow him in this exciting adventure. I was a romantic. I had lived so much in a fantasy world, which I suppose young people do, especially when there is not a great deal of affection in their lives. I had Olivia, it was true, and I knew that she was a staunch friend as well as a sister. But who else was there? My mother had gone off with her lover and had not even written to her daughters; it was hard to imagine my father fond of anything but virtue; Miss Bell was a good friend and I knew had some affection for Olivia and me, but her governess-like attitude made her aloof. I dreamed of a reconciliation between my parents, of my father's suddenly experiencing a complete change in his character like Ebenezer Scrooge in *A Christmas Carol*. My mother, on her return, in my dreams, became the mother I had always wanted – loving, protective, but at the same time a confidante to whom one could talk of one's adventures, who would help and advise. Up to this time the centre of my dreams had been Paul Landower. Why I should have made such a figure of him I was not entirely sure. But there was logic in my dreaming. I hardly knew him. It was his brother who had been my friend. But Jago was not of the stuff of which heroes were made. He was just a boy – rather like myself when it came to making wild plans. There was nothing remote or romantic about him. And it was romance I was looking for. Romance was mysterious, exciting, the dream in which a girl like myself could indulge, setting the stage for all sorts of happenings – all, alas, the figments of her over-worked and event-starved imagination.

Thus I had set up Paul Landower as the archetypal hero. He had the right appearance. He was not too good-looking; he was essentially masculine and strong I used the word rugged in my imagination. He was the scion of a noble family forced into a difficult situation by the profligacy of his forefathers. He had a touch of melancholy – so becoming in a hero. He had great problems and my favourite dream was that I helped him solve them; I was responsible for bringing back the mansion which was about to pass out of his hands. I did it in various ways and one was that I discovered some healing herb which cured Gwennie Arkwright – for in this version she had suffered greatly from her fall from the minstrels' gallery – and Mr Arkwright was so grateful that he presented me with

Landower Hall which he had bought. I promptly handed it back to Paul.

'I shall be grateful to you for the rest of our lives,' he said. 'And there is only one thing which will make this gift acceptable. You must share it with me.' So we married and lived happily ever after and had ten children, six of them sons, and Landower was saved forever.

That was my favourite and wildest dream; and there had been many more.

I was longing to be in love, for I was sure that was the happiest state in the world. I had seen what it meant when we had been in Captain Carmichael's chambers at the time of the Jubilee. That was what I thought of as Guilty Love. Mine would be noble and all would be wonderful.

Paul Landower's appearance had changed a little. He had become darker, more mysterious, more melancholy; and it was the right sort of melancholy which only I could disperse.

Sometimes I came out of my dream world and laughed at myself. Then I said: 'If you saw the real Paul now, you probably wouldn't recognize him as yours!'

However, that was over now – ever since Jeremy Brandon had danced with me at the masked ball. I had a real figure to put in place of my dream one.

So I proceeded to rush, with habitual impetuosity, into love.

When I met Jeremy at the end of the street he said he wanted to talk to me seriously, and he was rather silent as we made our way to Kensington Gardens. We sat on one of the seats which surrounded the court in which stands the Albert Memorial, that dedication to her sainted husband by our grieving Queen – the symbol of faithful and devoted conjugal bliss.

The sun was shining on Albert, and I could hear the shrill laughter of children's voices and the admonishing or encouraging ones of their nannies telling them to walk sedately along the flower walk, frolic on the grass, or go to feed the ducks on the Round Pond.

Jeremy came immediately to the point.

'I'm in love with you, Caroline. It started at the masked ball and it's gone on in leaps and bounds from there.'

I nodded blissfully.

'I've been thinking about you so much . . . in fact I have thought about nothing else since our first meeting. I can't go on like this . . . just meeting you with someone else there all the time. I want you all to myself. There's only one answer. Will you marry me, Caroline?'

'Of course,' I answered promptly.

Then we began to laugh.

'You should have said, "Oh dear, this is so sudden!" I believe that is the conventional reply, even after a courtship that's been going on for months.'

'You'll have to get used to an unconventional wife.'

'Believe me, I would ask no other.'

He put his arms about me and kissed me. I was so happy. This was the perfect day. Here was the perfect lover. The melancholy rugged hero of my dreams had vanished completely. He was replaced by this handsome, charming, regular-featured mystery-lacking flesh-and-blood husband-to-be.

I was ecstatically in love.

'I will love you forever,' I promised him.

'Dear Caroline, you are so delightfully . . . unencumbered.'

'Unencumbered by what?'

'By conventions, by tiresome etiquette and all that is most boring in society. Life will be wonderful for us. I tell you what I plan to do. I shall write to your father and ask him if he will see me. Then I shall beg for his permission to ask you to marry me.'

'He'll never give it.'

'Then we shall have to elope.'

'I shall climb from my window by means of a rope-ladder.'

'That won't be necessary.'

'Oh, don't spoil it. I love the thought of a rope-ladder.

You'll be waiting below in a carriage to whisk me off. We shall be married immediately and live happily ever after. Where?'

'Ah,' he said. 'So you have a practical streak after all. This is what we have to decide. We'll have a small house near the Park so that we can come here often, sit on this seat and say, "Do you remember?" '

I looked dreamily into the future.

'Do you remember the day Jeremy asked Caroline to marry him,' I said dreamily. 'And she said, "Yes" . . . immediately and immodestly.'

'And he loved her for it,' went on Jeremy.

Then we kissed each other solemnly.

He said: 'I can't wait. I'm going straight home to write that letter to your father.'

I shook my head gloomily. 'He never liked people to be happy even when he was well. I believe he's even worse now.'

'We'll start with him in any case. I hope we can get his consent. It will save a lot of trouble.'

'Never mind. I'll soothe away your troubles. Haven't I told you that we are going to live happily every after?'

To my amazement, my father agreed to see Jeremy and then gave his consent to our engagement.

Life had changed completely. From being an insignificant member of the household I had become an important one. My hour of glory had begun. Moira Massingham called to see me. I was not present on sufferance this time. She regarded me with a kind of wonder. She thought it was so romantic – and me not even 'out'. Who had ever heard of anyone's securing a husband before she was launched into society? It was unprecedented. 'And to think it all began at our masked ball!' she marvelled.

It was not only with Moira that my stock had risen.

I was invited to several houses. I took tea at the Massinghams' and Lady Massingham regarded me with approval. There were other mothers present. I was something of a phenomenon – the girl who had acquired a fiancé without the cost of an enormously expensive season.

How I revelled in my glory.

I was sorry for Olivia who after two years had failed to achieve what I had before starting.

Even Aunt Imogen deigned to notice me now.

'It is the best thing that could have happened,' she said. 'The money your maternal grandfather left you is to be released. It is not much. There is a lump sum of a few hundred pounds, which was to come to you when you were twenty-one or on your marriage; and then you will have an income of fifty pounds a year. It is not a great deal. Your mother's family were not rich.' She sniffed with a certain degree of elegance to indicate her contempt for my mother's family. 'The money will be useful and we can start to plan your trousseau. June is a good month for weddings.'

'Oh, but we don't want to wait as long as that.'

'I think you should. You are very young. You have never been launched into society. It is most fortunate that this young man has offered to marry you.'

'He thinks he is rather fortunate,' I said complacently.

She turned away.

I thought: We are not going to wait until June. But when I broached the matter with Jeremy he said: 'If that is what your family want we should go along with it.'

We looked at houses. What a happy day that was when we found the little house in a narrow street – one of the byways of Knightsbridge. The rooms were not large but it had an air of elegance. There were three storeys with three rooms on each floor and a small garden in which a pear tree grew. I knew I could be happy in such a house.

The servants regarded me with a new respect. Jeremy was allowed to call at the house and he and I could go out together on certain occasions. I lived in a whirl. I was in love; I had never been so happy in my life – and I believed it would go on like that for the rest of it.

Jeremy of course was not exactly the catch of the season. He had just scraped into the magic circle set up by what he called the Order of the Questing Mamas. It was through family connections rather than wealth, and to make the perfect catch a man must have both. But one, in certain circumstances, could be regarded as enough.

How we laughed together! The days seemed full of sunshine, though I did not notice the weather. The wind could blow; the rain could teem down; and life was still full of sunshine. We were constantly together and so delighted because my father had given his consent – not that we could not have surmounted that difficulty, said Jeremy; but it was better not to have to. I was mildly surprised how much store he set by that. He said that he did not want any impediments. He was passionate and irritated by the restraints which were put upon us. He told me how he longed for the time when we could be together all through the days and nights.

I lived in an enchanted dream until one morning when our household was thrown into confusion.

When my father's manservant had gone to his room he found him dead. He had had another stroke – a massive one this time – and it had killed him.

Death is sobering – even that of people one has never really known. I suppose I could say I had never known my father; certainly there had been no demonstrative love between us, but he had been there in the house, though a figure who represented virtue and godliness. I had always imagined God was rather like my father. And now he was not there.

The Careys came at once and took over control. All the servants were in a state of tension, speculating as to what changes would be made in the household. There would certainly be some and they might well be out of employment.

Gloom pervaded the house. To smile would have been considered showing a lack of respect to the dead. Outside the house a funeral hatchment – a diamond-shaped tablet with the Tressidor armorial bearings – was fixed to a wall; and there were notices in the papers, besides his obituary,

142

which extolled his virtues and set out in detail the good works he had accomplished during a lifetime 'devoted to the service of his fellow men'. He had been a selfless man, we were told. He was one of the greatest philanthropists of our age. Many societies working for the good of the community were grateful to him and there would be mourning all over England for the passing of a great, good man.

Miss Bell cut out all the notices to preserve them for us, she said; and there was a great deal of activity over what was called 'The Black'.

We all had to have new black garments and we should attend the funeral with veils over our faces. We should be in mourning for six months, which was the specified period for a parent; Aunt Imogen escaped with two months since she was a sister, merely; but if I knew anything about her she would extend that period.

So Olivia and I should be in our black for six months and then, said Miss Bell, we should emerge gradually into greys, perhaps. No bright colours for a whole year.

I said I couldn't see why one couldn't mourn just as sincerely in red as black.

Miss Bell said: 'Show some respect, Caroline.'

Many of the servants were given black dresses and the men wore crape armbands.

Everyone – not only in the house but in our circle – talked of the goodness of my father, of his selfless devotion to his philanthropic work which had never flagged even when he suffered ill health and domestic trials.

I was relieved when the day of the funeral arrived.

People gathered in the streets to watch the cortège, which was very impressive. I saw it through my veil which gave a hazy darkness to the scene. The horses magnificently caparisoned in their black velvet and plumes; the solemn black-clad men in their deep mourning clothes and shiny top hats; Olivia seated opposite me, looking whitefaced and bewildered, and Aunt Imogen upright, stern, now and then putting her black-edged handkerchief to her eyes to

143

wipe away a tear which was not there, while her husband, seated beside her, contorted his face into the right expressions of grief.

And then to the family vault – grim and menacing with its dark entrance and its gargoyle-like figures defacing – rather than decorating – the marble.

I was glad to ride back to the house – far more quickly than we came. There were sherry and biscuits provided for the mourners and all, I guessed, were waiting for what I was sure was for them the great event of the day – the reading of the will.

The family was present in the drawing-room and Mr Cheviot, the solicitor, was seated at a table with documents spread out before him.

I listened without paying a great deal of attention to the legacies for various people and the large sums of money which were to be put in trust for some of the societies in which my father was interested.

He expressed appreciation of his dear sister, Imogen Carey, and she was rewarded financially for her support. He was a very wealthy man and I gathered that Olivia would be a considerable heiress. I was surprised when Mr Cheviot finished reading the will that I had not been mentioned. I was not the only one who was surprised. I was very much aware of the looks which were, somewhat furtively, cast in my direction.

Aunt Imogen came to me and said that Mr Cheviot would like to see me alone as he had something very important to say to me.

When I sat facing him in that room which had been my father's study, he looked at me very solemnly and said: 'You must prepare yourself for a shock, Miss Tressidor. I have an unpleasant duty to perform and I greatly wish that it was not necessary for me to do so, but duty demands that I should.'

'Please tell me quickly what it is,' I begged.

'Although you have been known as the daughter of Mr Robert Ellis Tressidor, that is not the case. It is true that you were born after your mother's marriage to Mr Tressidor but your father is a Captain Carmichael.'

'Oh,' I said slowly. 'I ought to have guessed.'

He looked at me oddly. He went on: 'Your mother admitted that your father was this man, but not for some years after your birth.'

'It was at the time of the Jubilee.'

'June eighteen-eighty-seven,' said Mr Cheviot. 'It was at that time when your mother made a full confession.'

I nodded, remembering: the locket, my mother's sudden departure, the manner in which he had ignored me. I could understand it now. He must have hated the sight of me because I was the living evidence of my mother's infidelity.

'There was a separation at the time,' went on Mr Cheviot. 'Mr Tressidor could have divorced your mother but he refrained from doing so.'

I said rather defiantly: 'He would not have wanted the scandal . . . for himself.'

Mr Cheviot bowed his head.

'Understandably he has left you nothing. But you will have a small inheritance from your mother's father, who left this money in trust for you when you came of age, or on your marriage, or at any time the trustees should consider it should be passed to you. I am happy to tell you that in view of your sudden impoverishment, the money is to be released to you immediately.'

'Some of it has already been released.'

'Yes, that was at the request of Lady Carey.'

'It has been spent on my trousseau . . . or most of it has.'

'I understand you are shortly to be married. That is very satisfactory and will solve many difficulties, I do not doubt. Mr Tressidor did say before he died that it was a solution for you who could not after all be blamed for the sins of your parents.'

'But even if I was not to be married he would still have left me with – what is it? Fifty pounds a year. Of course, he is such a good man. He has taken such care of all those philanthropic societies. It is no wonder that he cannot concern himself with his wife's daughter.'

Mr Cheviot looked pained. 'I am afraid recriminations do not help the situation, Miss Tressidor. Well, I had my duty to perform and I have done that.'

'I understand that, Mr Cheviot. I . . . I never thought of money before.' He did not speak and I went on: 'Do you know where my mother is?'

He hesitated and then said: 'Yes. There have been occasions when it was necessary, when acting for your father, to be in touch with her. He had made her a small allowance which he considered his duty, for in spite of her misdemeanours she was his wife.'

'And you will give me her address?'

'I can see no reason why it should be denied to you now.'

'I should like to see her. I haven't done so since the time of the Jubilee. She has never written to me or my sister.'

'It was a condition of her receiving the allowance that she did not get into touch with you. Those were Mr Tressidor's terms.'

'I see.'

'I will have the address sent to you. She is in the South of France.'

'Thank you, Mr Cheviot.'

When I left him I went straight to my room. Olivia came to me. She was very distressed.

'It's terrible, Caroline,' she cried. 'He has left me so much . . . and you nothing.'

I told her what the solicitor had told me. She listened wide-eyed.

'It can't be true.'

'Don't you remember how we went to Waterloo Place? It was my fault, Olivia. I blurted out that we'd been there. He saw the locket. Oh, you didn't know about the locket. Captain Carmichael gave it to me. It had his picture in it. You see, it was his way of telling me he was my father.'

'It's not the same between us, is it? We're not the same sisters.'

'We're half-sisters, I suppose.'

'Oh, Caroline!' Her beautiful eyes were full of tears. 'I can't bear it. It's so unfair to you.'

I said defiantly: 'I don't mind. I'm glad he wasn't my father. I'd rather have Captain Carmichael than Robert Ellis Tressidor.'

'It was cruel of him,' said Olivia, and then stopped short, realizing she was speaking ill of the dead.

I said: 'I shall get married . . . soon.'

'You can't while we're in mourning.'

'I shall not stay in mourning. After all, he is not my father.'

'It's so . . . hateful.'

I laughed rather hysterically. 'We always shared everything . . . governess . . . lessons . . . everything. Now you're the heiress and I'm the penniless one . . . well, not exactly penniless. I have enough to stop myself starving, I suppose. And you Olivia, quite suddenly, have become a very rich woman.'

'Oh Caroline,' she cried, 'I'll share all I have with you. This is your home. I'll always be your sister.'

We clung together, half laughing, half crying.

I had arranged to take another look at the bijou house with Jeremy and I decided that I would not let what had happened stand in the way of that.

Jeremy was strangely subdued. I supposed he was thinking of the funeral. I did not want to talk of it, I told him I wanted to look at the house and think about the future.

As soon as we opened the door and stepped inside he seemed to throw off his gloom. Hand in hand we went through the rooms; we discussed what we would turn them into, what colour carpets, what sort of curtains.

Then we went to the garden and stood under the pear tree, looking back at the house.

'It really is a gem,' said Jeremy. 'I could have been so happy living here with you.'

'Well, we are going to,' I replied.

'How shall we pay for it, Caroline?'

'Pay for it. I hadn't thought of that.'

'It's customary when buying something to have to pay for it, you know.'

'But . . .' I looked at him in astonishment.

He said with some embarrassment. 'You've always known I haven't much. The allowance from my father is adequate . . . but this would require a lump sum.'

'Oh I see, you thought – like everyone else – that I should have some money.'

'I thought that your father would help us with the house. A sort of wedding present. My family would have come up with something but I know they could never afford to buy the house outright.'

'I see. We shall have to find something less expensive.'

He nodded solemnly.

'Oh well, never mind. Houses are not all that important. I'd be happy anywhere with you, Jeremy.'

He held me tightly in his arms and kissed me with growing passion.

I laughed. 'Why are we looking at this house if we can't afford it?'

'It's nice to look at what might have been. Just for this afternoon I want to pretend that we are going to live here.'

'*I* want to get out of this house right away. I want to forget all about it. It's rather old. It's probably damp. And look at this tiny garden. One small pear tree. But it doesn't have any pears on it and when it does they'll be sour, I know. We'll rent . . . chambers. Is that what they call them? Somewhere right on the rooftops . . . on the top of the world.'

'Oh,' he said, 'I do love you, Caroline.'

I did not notice the regret in his voice.

It was two days later when I received the letter from him. I guessed it had taken him a long time to find the right words.

My dearest Caroline,

You will always be that for me. This is very hard for me to say, but I do not think it would be wise for us to marry. Love on the rooftops sounds delightful and it would be . . . for a time. But you would hate poverty. You have always lived in luxury and I have had enough. We should be so poor. My allowance and yours together . . . two people couldn't live on it.

The fact is, Caroline, I'm not in a position to marry . . . in the circumstances.

This breaks my heart. I love you. I shall always love you. You will always be someone very special to me, but I know you will see that it is simply not practical to marry now.

> Your heartbroken
> Jeremy, who will love you till he dies.

It was the end. He had jilted me. He had believed that because I was supposed to be the daughter of a very rich man he would be marrying an heiress.

He had been mistaken.

I felt my happy world collapsing about me.

His love for me had all been the greatest fantasy I had ever imagined. I did not weep. I was numb with wretchedness.

It was Olivia who comforted me. She kept assuring me that we should always be together. I must forget all that stupid talk about money. I was her sister. She would make me an allowance and I should marry Jeremy.

I laughed at that. I said I would never marry him. I would never marry anyone. 'Oh, Olivia, I thought he loved me . . . and it was your father's money that he wanted.'

'It wasn't quite like that,' insisted Olivia.

'How was it, then? I was ready to marry him . . . to be poor. He was the one who could not endure it. I never want to see him again. I have been foolish. I feel I've grown up suddenly. I shan't believe anyone any more.'

'You mustn't say that. You'll grow away from it. You will. You will.'

Then I looked at her and I thought: I believe she was in love with him. She didn't say so. She let me go ahead . . . and discover what he was worth.

'Oh, Olivia,' I cried. 'My dear, sweet sister, what should I ever do without you?'

Then I found the tears came and I felt better for crying there with her.

But there was a terrible bitterness growing in my heart.

Revelations
of an Intimate Nature

I had changed. I even looked different. I had grown up
suddenly. There was a glitter in my eyes, which had become a more vivid green. I piled my hair on top of my head;
it gave me height. I began to think about money – something I had never considered before. I was going to have to
be very careful if I were to live on my income.

I noticed a change in the attitude of the servants towards
me. There was less deference than there had once been. I
remembered a time when Rosie Rundall had laughed over
the protocol in the servants' hall. The ranks of society there
were more clearly defined and far more numerous than
above stairs.

Now I was no longer in the position of daughter of the
house. I was present more or less on sufferance. Respect
for Olivia had increased a hundredfold. She would one day
be mistress of the house.

This was for me a transient period – a time of decision. I
would wake in the morning and say, 'What are you going to
do?' And then I would think of Jeremy Brandon and all I
had hoped and planned. I had been so guileless, a foolish
romantic girl who had never realized for one instance that
when he saw our little home where we were to be so
idyllically happy, he was seeing the fortune he expected me
to inherit.

I was wretched. Sometimes I yearned for him; but at
most times I hated him. I think my hatred was more fierce
than my love had ever been. I had made a complete *volte
face*. Previously I had seen the world peopled by gods and

goddesses. Now I saw it inhabited by deceitful scheming people whose entire concern was to get what they could at the expense of others.

Olivia was the exception. She only was good and it was to her I continually turned for comfort, and she gave herself up entirely to the task of comforting me.

It did not matter that the money had been left to her, she insisted. It was ours. And as soon as it was hers she would give me half.

Dear, unsophisticated, loving Olivia!

I said to her: 'I can't stay here.'

'Why ever not?' she demanded.

'I don't belong here any more.'

'It's your home.'

'No. Everything's changed. The servants make that clear; Aunt Imogen always has ever since she has known, and that was the time of the Jubilee. Even Miss Bell has changed.'

'They're not important. This house and all in it will be mine. I shall have plenty of money. Caroline, please share it with me.'

I turned away. It was strange, but the simple goodness of Olivia could reduce me to tears whereas the mercenary deceit of Jeremy Brandon only filled me with bitter resentment and anger.

'I was thinking of going to see our mother,' I said.

'I'll come with you, Caroline.'

'Oh, Olivia, would you?'

'I can now . . . can't I?'

I was not sure. Aunt Imogen had taken up temporary residence in the house – 'Until everything is settled,' she said. Olivia was an heiress but she was not yet in possession of her fortune. She would not come into it until she was twenty-one or married and it seemed that the former would be the case – she was now twenty.

But I had not lost my desire to make plans – even though I now recognized the possibility of their not coming to fruition.

Aunt Imogen soon put a stop to Olivia's aspirations.

'My dear Olivia, you could not leave London now. It's such nonsense. You could not possibly go wandering all over France. What would everyone *think*?'

'Caroline would be with me.'

'Caroline may go if she wishes. But your father is scarcely cold in his grave.'

Of course Aunt Imogen won the day. Poor Olivia, I feared she would always be frustrated. The consolation was that she meekly accepted her fate.

Mr Cheviot turned out to be quite a kindly old gentleman.

He asked me to go to his offices and there he told me that he had written to my mother and she was delighted that I was going to see her. She was living in a village near a small town in southern France. If I wished, he would make the arrangements for my travel.

I was very grateful to him. He knew, of course, about my broken engagement and that seemed to have made him a little sorry for me.

I used to wake up some mornings in a state of fear. I suppose that was natural as everything had changed so drastically for me. I had suffered two blows; first, the house where I had lived all my life was no longer my home and in spite of my sister's affection I had no place there; secondly, there could be few experiences more heartbreaking and humiliating for a young woman than to be jilted on the eve – more or less – of her wedding.

I was amazed at my anger against those two men – Robert Tressidor and Jeremy Brandon. At least Robert Tressidor had never pretended to care for me and he must have paid for my education and kept me in his house all those years and I supposed I should be grateful for that. As for Jeremy Brandon, he was despicable. He had pretended to care for me when it was the inheritance which he had thought would be mine which was so glitteringly attractive.

Aunt Imogen had not entirely washed her hands of me.

'The Rushtons are travelling to Paris,' she said. 'They will take you with them. It is gracious of them. It is not fitting for one of your age to travel alone. They will see you in the train for the first part of the journey. I have discussed this with Mr Cheviot, and he thinks it is most satisfactory.'

I was a little relieved, for the thought of travelling so far alone was a little daunting. The Rushtons were quite pleasant people. They had two sons – both married – so they were not involved in the London seasons.

I made feverish preparations to depart and in fact looked forward to getting out of the house. I would be sad to leave Olivia, but she promised that as soon as she was free to do so, she would come to me in France.

It was about three days before I was due to leave when I received two letters. One was from Cousin Mary.

I read it eagerly.

My dear Caroline [she had written],

I have, of course, heard what happened.

I have not written before to you as I should have done but I am no letter-writer, and although I have thought of you often I have not got around to putting pen to paper. I remember well your visit and have wanted you to come back to see me. But then you were away at school and time flies.

Well, what I want to say now is, that I shall be glad to see you at any time. You can look on this as a home if you wish it. I myself would be pleased if you did.

It is strange to think that we are no longer related. But I never did think much of blood ties. Relations are thrust on us. Friends are of our own making and I believe – and I hope – that you and I will always be good friends.

My dear Caroline, I am well aware that at the moment you must be somewhat bemused. I want you to know that I heartily disapprove of my self-righteous cousin's action and I was shocked when I heard – as a member of the family – what had happened.

Bless you, my dear, and I repeat, there is a home for you here if you want it. Don't imagine that I offer this out of charity. I assure you I am thinking of my own pleasure.

Affectionately,
Mary Tressidor

I smiled as I read that letter. It brought back memories of her so vividly. I felt a longing to be with her, to see the old house, to ride out again past Landower . . . to see Jago and Paul whose image had been with me so long before it was replaced by Jeremy Brandon, the traitor.

That letter did a great deal to cheer me. I supposed if I had not been preparing to go to my mother I should have made plans to set out for Cornwall immediately.

I would write to Cousin Mary and explain.

I turned to the other letter which I had momentarily forgotten. I did not know the handwriting. I slit the envelope and read:

Dear Miss Caroline,

I've heard what's happened and it's a shame.

I wanted to talk to you, to explain why I was not there that night when I was to be there to let you in.

It wasn't my fault.

If you could come and see me on Wednesday, I'd tell you all about it.

Rosie (Rundall that was, Russell now).

I was astonished and very excited at the prospect of seeing Rosie again. I was on the point of showing the letter to Olivia but on second thoughts I decided not to. I would tell her after I had seen Rosie.

I looked at the address at the top of the letter. I knew the street well. It was one not very far away from us, with a row of delightful, though small, Georgian houses. She must have been married and married 'well' as they say.

155

No one tried to stop my going. I was no longer Miss Bell's concern. At least, I thought, I have gained my freedom. Perhaps something good – however slight – comes out of every disaster.

I arrived on time and when I knocked on the door it was opened by a smart parlourmaid. I said I had come to see Mrs Russell, and the girl said: 'Come in, please. Mrs Russell is waiting for you.'

I was taken to an elegantly furnished drawing-room on the first floor.

'Miss Tressidor,' announced the girl.

To my amazement, Rosie – soignée in a teagown of pale lavender – rose and took my hand, very much the mistress of the house.

The door shut on us and the formal hostess was immediately replaced by the Rosie Rundall I knew.

She laughed and hugged me.

'Miss Caroline!' she cried. 'My word! You've changed, you have.'

'I could say the same for you, Rosie.'

'That you could. Well, this is nice, eh? Here you are come to see me in my own little house.'

'So you married, Rosie?'

She winked at me. 'Not me. When my fortunes changed I changed my name. Rosie Rundall died a sudden death and Rosie Russell appeared. I reckon we ought to have some tea first. I'll ring for it . . . They'll bring it almost at once. It's all ready. I've got them well trained. Well, you'd expect me to, wouldn't you, seeing as how I was once in the business myself . . .'

'Rosie,' I said, 'this is incredible . . . and wonderful too. What happened? I always knew you were no ordinary parlourmaid.'

She put her fingers to her lips. 'Later. It wouldn't do for my maids to know *too* much. So just at first we'll talk about the weather and the little things ladies discuss when they pay friendly calls.'

The tea was wheeled in on a trolley by a different maid

156

from the one who had opened the door for me. Rosie eyed the tray with expert eyes.

'Thank you, May,' she said kindly but dismissively.

I felt laughter bubbling up within me.

Rosie poured the tea and then said: 'Now . . . We'll keep our voices low. Servants have a way of listening at doors. Don't I know it!' She winked at me in the old manner. 'I'm not complaining. I like them to talk with servants at other houses. It's the best sort of information agency you can get. Friends don't know what goes on in families like servants do.'

'Do explain everything, Rosie.'

'I've wanted to tell you for a long time. I didn't like you to think I'd just walked out and you coming back in all your Cleopatra clobber.' She laughed. 'I'll never forget the sight of you with that snake thing round your neck. You looked a treat. I said to myself, "My word, Miss Caroline . . . she's got what it takes." They'll be after you like flies round the honeypot. You'll have to make sure you're the one that gets the honey . . . not them.'

'Rosie, what is all this about?'

She poured out more tea and looked at me with her head on one side.

'You've grown up now, Caroline,' she said, 'and I know what's happened. You're not the heiress everyone thought you'd be. You've got a bit, but not much.'

'How do you know all this?'

'Gossip, dear. It was the talk of the town, wasn't it? That great, good man dying . . . him who'd looked after all the Fallen Women.' She was consumed with laughter. 'That's the bit I like,' she went on. 'And so he ought . . . considering he might on one or two occasions have tripped them up.'

'What do you mean, Rosie?'

'Well, I'm coming to that. I couldn't have told you before . . . though I wanted to on account of you thinking I might have let you down that night. You're on your own now. You're not one of the protected ones. You've got to know about things . . . life and all that. I figured that now all the wool should be pulled away from your eyes. You've got to look at what they call stark reality.'

'I agree with that. I've been a fool . . . ignorant . . . dreaming away . . . making everything look so lovely and quite different from what it really is.'

'That's how most of us are, love, when we start out. But we've got to grow up and the sooner we start doing it, the better for us. You remember when I was working at the house . . . the parlourmaid with a difference, eh? Well, the difference was that I didn't want to be a parlourmaid all my life. I had plans and I had the face and the figure and the brains to make my ideas work. I had to be in London. I had to have somewhere to live. I had to be right in the centre of things. So those nights . . . once a week . . . I used to go to Madam Crawley's in Mayfair. It was a beautiful house, very pleasant . . . the most expensive in London . . . or one of them . . . and she wouldn't take anybody. Now this might shock you a bit, but as I said you've got to face up to life. I used to go to Madam Crawley's to – er – entertain gentlemen.'

She leaned back to look at me and I felt the colour slowly flow into my face.

'I see you understand,' she said. 'Well, these things go on, and there's all sorts in them . . . people you wouldn't expect. Do you know I earned more in a few hours at Madam Crawley's than I did in a whole year in service? I worked it out. I was once as innocent as you used to be. I'd been in service from the time I was fourteen. There was the master of the house who took a fancy to me. He seduced me. I was too frightened to say anything. And after that I met someone in a teashop and she told me how she went on and how she was saving to make a life for herself and perhaps get married and live decent ever after.'

'I understand, Rosie, I do.'

'I knew you would. There's always rights and wrongs of any situation. Nothing's all good . . . nothing's all bad. I learned a lot, and I saved money . . . quite a tidy bit. I had plans to retire by the time I was thirty, say. Then I'd be very comfortable . . . but I had a windfall, and it's that I want to tell you about.'

Coming in addition to everything else that had happened so recently, this left me quite bemused. I should have guessed something like it, of course . . . those evenings out, those fine clothes . . . everything pointed to it. But perhaps that was how it seemed now that I knew. I was sure no one else in the house had had any notion of how Rosie spent her nights out.

'I was doing very well,' she went on. 'I had my nice nest-egg. And then there was this night. Oh, I could almost die of laughing, thinking of it. Caroline, are you sure you understand . . . that you want me to go on?'

'Of course I do.'

'Well, you're a big girl now. Cast your mind back to that night. There were you . . . all got up as Cleopatra. I was to open the door for Olivia and then nip round to the back and let you in. It was one of my nights out, remember? Well, as soon as you'd left for the ball I went out. I had to be back by eleven. Old Winch and Wilkinson were very sharp on that. They would have liked to stop my jaunts but I wasn't having any of that. They didn't want to get rid of me. I was a good parlourmaid. The mistress and master liked me to be seen by the guests. The right sort of parlourmaids are a very important part of a well run household.'

'I know that, Rosie. Do get on.'

'Well, on that night when you were at the ball, I went to Crawley's. Madam said, "There's a rich gentleman coming tonight. One of our best clients. I'm glad your visit coincides with his." She shook her head at me and said, as she was always saying, "I could put such good business in your way, if you would live in." But I wasn't for that. I wanted my freedom to come and go and once a week is all a girl needs at this sort of game. I had a beautiful silk dressing-gown which I used to receive my gentlemen in. There I was with nothing on but that and I went into the room where I found my gentleman. And there he was stark naked . . .

lying on a bed waiting for me. I stared at him. Who do you think he was?'

'I can't guess. Tell me.'

'Mr Robert Ellis Tressidor, pioneer of good causes, saviour of fallen women, advocate for the poor unemployed.'

'Oh no! It couldn't be.'

'Sure as I'm sitting here. He just sat up in bed and stared at me. I said, "Good evening, Mr Tressidor." He couldn't speak, he was so dumbfounded. His confusion was terrible. I even felt sorry for him. He was trembling. I doubt anyone's ever been caught so red-handed, you might say. It was his face that was red. And I didn't wonder at that. I reckon he could see the headlines in the paper. He said, "What are you doing here? You're supposed to be a respectable parlourmaid." That sent me into hoots of laughter. "Me?" I said. "It's clear what I'm doing here, sir. The funny thing is, what are you doing here, Mr Protector of Fallen Women. Helping them to fall a bit farther?" I was scared really and when I'm scared I always fight hard. Not for a moment did I doubt that he was in a worse position than I was. I was there in my dressing-gown. All he had was the sheet to cover him up. It was the funniest thing I ever saw. Me . . . the parlourmaid standing there and him the high and mighty, one of God's good men, lying naked on a bed.

'He calmed down a bit. He said, "Rosie, we shall have to sort this out." All very cajoling, equals now, none of the master and parlourmaid. He was a very frightened man. He said, "You shouldn't be living this life, Rosie." "Should you, sir?" I asked. "I admit," he replied, "to a certain weakness." That made me laugh. Then I saw the possibilities and I said, "I could make things very difficult for you, Mr Tressidor." He didn't deny it. I could see he was thinking . . . hard. It was in his eyes. Money, he was thinking. Money straightens out most things and he was right about that. "Rosie," he said. "I'll make it worth your while." And I said, "Now you're talking."

'I can laugh now. Him in the bed there and me standing

there in my dressing-gown – and we made terms. He wanted me out of the house. I understood that. He couldn't have me there all the time reminding him. And he wanted me out at once. He would give me a large sum of money as the price of my silence. He became quite human in his fear, and, by God, Caroline, he was afraid. He could see what I could see. "Philanthropist Robert Tressidor discovered in a brothel . . ." Well, we made an amicable arrangement. He would pay me well and I should leave at once. I should go to an hotel for the night . . . at his expense, of course, and stay there until something could be arranged for me. He owned a great deal of property in London and he would see what could be done about accommodation for me. He gave me all the money he had on him and promised to pay me a large sum. That would be an end of it. He had no intention of giving way to further blackmail. I did not want that either. It's a dangerous game. All I wanted was a good start in life – just what some people get by being born into it and others have to fight for. He quite understood my desire to break away from a life of service – my ambition, he called it, and he had a great respect for ambition. After all, he had a good deal of it himself. He was frank in a way, and do you know, I liked him better lying there in bed naked and being a bit humble . . . and in a way understanding . . . than I ever had the virtuous philanthropist. I said, "Look here, Mr Tressidor, you play fair with me and I'll play fair with you. I could expose you to the papers. There's nothing they'd like better than that sort of scandal. You'd be ruined." He admitted this, and said that he would honour his promises to me. But I was clever enough to understand he would not endure perpetual blackmail. He would pay the initial amount but that must be the end of the matter. I agreed. I'm not a blackmailer by nature, but I'm a girl who has to fight, and when you've got all the odds against you, you can't be over-nice. There! What do you think of that?'

'I can't stop thinking of him . . . always pretending to be so good . . . the way he behaved to my mother. Is the world full of deceitful people?'

161

'Quite a large number of the population, I shouldn't wonder. There! Was I right to tell you?'

'It's always best to know everything.'

'You've got to fight through life as I have had to. It's better to know people. The world is not always a pretty place. Oh, I reckon some go through and never see the seamy side. But look at your father . . . I mean Robert Tressidor. He was a man who had desires like most men. I know the sort. There were a lot of them like that at Crawley's. They're what they call sensual, and they can't get what they want at home. They have to play the gentleman there and maybe are ashamed to do what they really want, so they go for girls like me. Then they can do what they like. They don't have to worry about showing themselves for what they are. That's what it's all about.'

'I'm glad you told me, Rosie. I want to know everything. I never want to imagine things are not what they seem again. I think I hate men.'

'Oh, there are some good ones among the bad. Hard to find, it's true, but they are there.'

I shook my head. I kept seeing my father – why did I have to go on calling him my father? – I kept seeing Robert Tressidor cowering in that bed.

'It upset him terribly,' went on Rosie. 'I reckon it killed him really. He had that first stroke soon after that. He must have been almost out of his mind . . . when he thought what it could mean. I wouldn't have gone that far, though. I reckon I've been paid fair and square. Didn't stop him changing that rotten will about you, though, did it?'

I shook my head. 'Why should it?'

'Oh, he was very pompous and sanctimonious about your mother. We heard quite a bit when that little thing was going on. Such a great good man with such a naughty wife! How could she? And all the time there was sir, going to Crawley's for a little bit of slap and tickle on the sly.'

'It's so horrible,' I said.

'Do you think I'm awful?'

'No.'

162

ere was a bowl of flowers on the table in the hall and
pungent scent hung in the air.
his is a very small establishment,' Everton explained.
only have one *domestique* – as they call them here –
a man for the garden twice a week. You'll find it very
erent from . . .'
Yes, I suppose so. May I see my mother now?'
'Yes, come up.'
I was taken up a staircase and into a room. The shutters
ere closed and it was dark.
'Miss Caroline is here,' said Everton. 'I'll open the
shutters, shall I, just a little?'
'Oh yes. And are you really there, my darling? Oh,
Caroline!'
'Mama!' I cried, and running to the bed threw myself
into her arms.
'My dear child, it is wonderful to see you. But you will
find everything here . . . so different.'
'You're here and I'm here,' I said. 'I like the difference.'
'It is so wonderful that you are here.'
Everton went quietly to the door. She looked at me for a
moment and said: 'You must not tire her.' Then she went
out.
'Mama,' I said, 'are you ill?'
'My dear, let us not talk of unpleasant things. Here you
are and you are going to stay with me for a while. You can't
imagine how I have longed to see you.'
I thought: Then why didn't you make an effort to do so?
But I said nothing.
'I used to say to Everton, if only I could see my girls . . .
aroline particularly. Of course, you see how I live now
. in penury.'
I thought it seems a very pleasant house. The flowers are
ely.'
'm so poor, Caroline. I could never really adjust myself
overty. Did you know we have only one *domestique*
ne gardener . . . and not full time at that.'
now, Everton told me. But you have her.'

'A woman who sells her body, who's not averse to a little
blackmail?'
'I'm glad you got something out of him, Rosie. It's the
hypocrisy, the deceit, I can't bear. You were never like
that.'
'Open as the day, that's me. Well, I had to leave that
night, you see. That's why I wasn't there to let you in. I had
to pack up and be right out of the house by the time he came
back. It was part of the bargain.'
'I understand, Rosie.'
'It took me a long time to decide whether to tell you or
not. Then I heard you were going to France. How did I
know? Servants! They talk. I mix a bit on the edge of
society, too. There's gossip. They were all talking about
you being cut out and not his daughter and all that. That's
common knowledge. And I thought: Poor Caroline. She's
got a hard row to hoe. And I thought I'd ask you to come
and I'd tell you this. If ever you wanted a friend, Rosie's
here to help you. I'd ask you to stay here, but that wouldn't
be right for you. I do have the occasional gentleman friend
. . . my own choice, though, this time. And I've got a bit of
a reputation. One of these days I might settle down. I saw a
little fellow the other day playing in the Park with his
nanny. I thought . . . I dunno, there's something about
kids. Who knows, your old friend Rosie might fall for that
lark one day. And when, and if, I do, I'll have the right sort
of place to bring it up. There! But remember this, if ever
you think I could be of any help to you, you know where I
am.'
'Thank you, Rosie,' I said.
She rang for the tea to be cleared away. I watched her
with faint amusement mingled with awe.
She was a very clever woman, and in spite of the fact that
she had been a part-time prostitute and was confessedly a
blackmailer, she seemed to me to be a better human being
than quite a number I could name.
I made my way thoughtfully back to the house.
Yes, indeed I was growing up fast.

Night in the Mountains

I had come to Paris with the Rushtons as we had arranged and they had very kindly seen me on to the train which was to make its journey to the South of France.

It was difficult to believe that so much was happening to me. The journey did not bother me. Going away to school had given me a certain self-reliance, and this was not my first visit to France, although I was scarcely a seasoned traveller.

As I looked out of the train window I kept telling myself that I must put behind me all that had happened. I must start a fresh life. I might well discover that my true place was with my parents. I was romancing again.

I think what had shocked me almost as much as the knowledge that it was not me but my inheritance that Jeremy had wanted, was what I had just heard of the man whom I had believed to be my father. I could not keep out of my mind the picture of him on that bed. I could understand his need for sexual satisfaction, but not his hypocrisy. How could he make those speeches about fallen women when he himself was indulging in the practices he pretended to deplore?

'There's lots like him,' Rosie had said, and Rosie knew men.

And Jeremy? I would never forget opening that letter and realizing that I had been living in a fantasy world.

But it was over. I had to start again.

And here I was speeding through the French countryside . . . past farms, buildings, fields, rivers, hills. At least I was going to my mother and she wanted to see me. I thought of Captain Carmichael. He would be with her, I supposed,

and the thought of that cheered me. I h
by him when I was young, and not at
discover that he was my father.

It seemed a long journey. Miss Bell w
'France is a big country, much bigger tha
smiled fleetingly. Miss Bell would have kno
proportions.

That was long ago – in the past. I had to turn
all that life – stop thinking of it, because when I
only see those two deceivers – Jeremy Brandon an
Tressidor.

When I arrived at the station and left the train a ti
waiting for me.

I was told that Madame Tressidor was expecting me,
that the journey was not very long.

My fluent French was a great help to me, and my dri
was delighted that I could speak the language. He pointe
out the line of mountains in the distance and told me that
beyond them was the sea.

We stopped before a house. It was white – neither big
nor very small. There were balconies at two of the windows
in the front and bougainvillea made a colourful purple
splash against the walls.

As I alighted a woman came out of the house.

'Everton!' I cried.

'Welcome, Miss Caroline,' she said.

I took her hand and in my excitement would have k
her, but Everton drew back reminding me of her pla

'Madame is glad that you were coming,' she sai
isn't one of her good days . . . but she wants to se
soon as you arrive.'

'Oh,' I said, feeling a little deflated. I had ex
mother or Captain Carmichael to be waiting t
though I was glad, of course, to see the famili

'Come on in, Miss Caroline. Oh, there's y
The driver helped carry it into a tiled hall

I thanked him, gave him some coins, an
cap. Everton was coolly aloof.

'How could I do without her?'

'Apparently you don't have to. She seems as devoted as ever.'

'She's a bit of a tyrant. Good servants often are. She treats me as though I'm a baby. Of course, I suffer quite a lot. There is so much I miss. This is not London, Caroline.'

'That is obvious.'

'When you think of what life was before . . .'

'Mama,' I said, 'what of Captain Carmichael?'

'Oh, Jock . . . poor Jock. He couldn't stand it. It was idyllic in the beginning. We didn't seem to mind the poverty at first. We neither of us had been used to it, you know.'

'But you were in love. You had each other.'

'Oh yes. We were in love. But there was nothing to do here. For me . . . nothing. For him, too. No racing. He loved the races. And then, of course, there was his career . . . the Army.'

'He gave all that up . . . for you.'

'Yes. It was sweet of him. And for a while it was wonderful . . . even here. Your father . . . I mean my husband . . . was so vindictive. You know all about that now, I gather, from Mr Cheviot. He's been a good friend. He's looked after everything. He sends the money regularly. I don't know what I should do without that. My income from my father is infinitesimal. Jock had very little apart from his soldier's pay, and you know, that's not much. He was always in debt. No one should attempt to hold a commission in the Queen's regiments unless he has a good income.'

'But what happened? Where is he now?'

She took a lace handkerchief from under her pillow and held it to her eyes. 'He's gone. He died. It was in India. It was some awful disease he caught there. He had to resign his commission, you see. Poor darling, it was all because of the scandal. He went out there. He was going into some sort of business with people he knew. He was going to make a lot of money and come back to me. But the Army was the only thing he really wanted to do. The Carmichaels were all soldiers. He'd been brought up to it. But he used to say it was all worth while . . . in the beginning.'

'And he died!' I couldn't believe that laughing, charming man, whose company had been so delightful, was dead. 'It is such a short while ago really. Only four years . . . the Jubilee, you remember. But so much has happened that it seems like an age.'

'Four years . . . is that all? Four years ago and I was in London. There was so much to do there. Do you know, I have had hardly any new clothes since I have been here. One would have to go to Paris. Such a journey. Of course, Everton is good . . . but what do we know of the fashions down here?'

'I suppose that is the last thing you have to worry about.'

'We came here. We had to get out of England. That was one of Robert's conditions. He wouldn't have us there. He made me a small allowance on condition that I did not see you girls. That broke my heart. Particularly because of you, Caroline. Olivia was *his* daughter. I hated him, Caroline. I didn't want to marry him. He was the catch of the season . . . or one of them. So rich, you see, already making a name for himself. Well, he decided he would marry me as soon as he saw me, and although I would have preferred someone else I had to take him. It was expected of me and everyone said how lucky I was. Oh Caroline, I can't tell you how I hated him. I could not bear all that goodness. Do you know, he used to kneel by the bed before getting into it, praying for God's blessing on our union, and then . . . and then . . . but you wouldn't understand, Caroline.'

I thought of the man visiting Mrs Crawley's, lying naked in the bed, waiting for Rosie and I said: 'Yes, Mama, I think I do.'

'Bless you, my darling. Well, now you are here. I don't know how I go on living here. It's been so dull . . . ever since Jock went . . . and even before. There is nothing to *do*. If only I could go back to London. If only I had the money. When I think of all Robert had, I realize what a fool I've been. I had endured it for years . . . and only another four to go. Then I should be there . . . where I long to be.'

I said: 'It is very beautiful here. The scenery, coming down in the train, was quite dramatic.'

'I'm bored with scenery, dear. What can you do with mountains and trees and flowers, except look at them?'

'What of your health, Mama?'

'Oh my dear, a dismal subject! I have to rest every day. I don't get up until ten. Then I will sit in the garden until luncheon and after that I rest.'

'And in the evening?'

'Dull! Dull!'

'Are there no people around? Are you quite isolated?'

'There are people. They are very dull, though. I can't grasp their tiresome language very well. Did you see the château as you came in from the station?'

'No. So there is a château, is there?'

'Yes. The Dubusson family. At first I thought that might be interesting. The Dubussons are very old. Madame looks about ninety; there is a son and his wife – rather dismal. It's very run down. They seem quite poor. Like farming people. Quite hospitable, though. I sometimes visit and they have come here. There are one or two families in other houses scattered about. Then there are people who grow flowers and make perfume. And the town is a mile and a half away. So you see how we are situated.'

'Olivia wanted to come and see you.'

'Poor Olivia! How is she?'

'Very much the same as ever.'

'She was never attractive, poor child. I used to wonder how I had given birth to her. Of course she takes after her father.'

'Oh no! Olivia is a wonderful person.'

'That was what was said of her father.'

I found it hard to remain silent. I was beginning to sum

169

up the situation. I was seeing my mother as I had never seen her before. In my childhood she had been one of the goddesses who populated my world. Now I had cast aside my illusions. I looked life straight in the face and I was feeling more and more depressed every moment.

Everton came up after a while because she thought my mother would be tired. She showed me to my room. It was rather lofty and the walls were white: windows opened on to a wrought-iron balcony. I went to this and gasped at the beauty of the scenery. In the early evening light the distant mountains looked as though they had been tinted blue. Flowers grew in abundance – rich purple, red and blue. Their scent filled the air.

I thought it was beautiful and I imagined my mother and Captain Carmichael coming here to live out an idyllic dream – and finding the reality not quite what they had hoped for.

Their love had not lasted. It was an old story. But at least he had given up all for her, even though he did regret it afterwards and went away.

As for her, there was no doubt of her regrets.

I unpacked my bags and hung up my clothes. I changed and went down to dinner.

My mother had risen for this and she wore a pink silk dressing-gown over her night attire. She looked very romantic with her chestnut hair loose. It hadn't quite the same highlights as it had had once and I wondered practically whether Everton had difficulty in obtaining the necessary lotions here.

There was a courtyard attached to the house. It was beautiful, with clumps of bougainvillea growing from the walls. There was a table here and I saw that generally meals were eaten out of doors.

It could have been enchanting, but my mother did not see it so. All she saw was the social gaiety of a life she had lost and to which she longed to return.

When I went to bed that night I felt lost and depressed.

I thought longingly of Tressidor Manor and how different it would have been if I had accepted Cousin Mary's invitation.

It is amazing how quickly one can settle into a new way of life. I found my surroundings so beautiful, so peaceful, that they gave a certain balm to my wounded spirit. I could sit in the garden and read; I could sew a little, for Everton was continually at work on my mother's clothes and glad of a helping hand. I could meditate on life and think at least nature was beautiful. I wished that Olivia had come with me. It would have been pleasant to talk to her. But I could not imagine myself telling her what Rosie had told me. After all, he had been her father. Nor could I talk to her of Jeremy Brandon. I never wanted to think of him again. All the same, we could have been together, and Olivia was one of the few people for whom I had much regard these days. I had become cynical.

My mother noticed it. 'You've grown up a lot, Caroline,' she said to me one evening as we dined in the courtyard. 'You're attractive in an unusual way. It's those green eyes. They never used to be so green. They look as if they see into the dark.'

'They see into people's dark secrets, perhaps.'

She shrugged her shoulders. *She* never wanted to probe into people's thoughts; she was completely absorbed in her own.

'Well,' she said, 'you should have emeralds . . . earrings, pendants . . . They would bring out the green. And you should wear a lot of green. Everton was saying that she would like to dress you. You do well to dress your hair high on your head like that. It's right for your high forehead. Everton said she wouldn't have guessed high foreheads could be so attractive. It makes you look older, but it gives you something. You're not pretty but you look . . . interesting.'

'Thanks,' I said. 'I'm glad I'm not quite insignificant.'

'You never were that. Unlike poor Olivia. So the child

171

has not yet had a proposal. I wonder if she ever will. And you . . . you were spoken for without coming out!'

'My expected inheritance was spoken for, Mama, not me.'

She nodded. 'Well, you can't blame these impecunious young men. We all have to live.'

'I would rather live on my own efforts if I were a young man,' I said.

'But you are not, and in some ways you are very unworldly. It is a mercy you have that small income, but it is a pittance really. Robert Tressidor was a very mean man.'

Oddly enough, I went in to defend him. 'He has made *you* an allowance.'

'Another pittance! It could have been so much more and would have made no difference to him whatsoever. He was so afraid that Jock would benefit from his money so he gave me just enough to keep me on survival level . . . and he only did that because he wanted to keep up his image as a good man.'

'It's all long ago. It's lovely here. Let's forget about it.'

'It's so dull,' she moaned and lapsed into melancholy, contemplating the lost social whirl.

Sometimes Jacques the gardener would take his trap into the little town and I would go with him. I would wander round while he did what business he had to, and I would meet him at a specified time where he had left the trap. I enjoyed going into the little shops and chatting with the people; there was the inevitable café with the tables outside and I could sit there among the pots of flowering shrubs and drink a cup of coffee or an apéritif.

I often thought how much I could have enjoyed this in the days before what I called my awakening.

I had become clear-sighted. I saw my mother as she really was – a selfish woman who took refuge in imaginary illness to relieve the boredom which came from a shallow mind.

I wondered how much she had cared for Jock Carmichael. I wished I could have known him better, for I felt we might have meant something to each other. I could well understand his regrets, his need to get away. He had at least given up his career for the sake of love – the reverse really of Jeremy Brandon.

I would take strolls through the beautiful countryside. Often I walked the one and a half miles into the town. The shopkeepers began to know me and I found the recognition pleasant. They would call to me; they found it interesting to chat to me. My knowledge of French being fairly good, I could still amuse them with my occasional misuse of their language. I grew to know many of them. There was the woman who sold her vegetables on a stall every Wednesday when she came in from a village four miles away; girls at the café; the *boulanger* who raked the long crusty loaves out of the oven in his shop and served them hot to his waiting customers; the *modiste* who aped her Paris counterpart by showing only one hat in her window; the *couturière* who crammed hers full of her creations; and even the man in the *quincaillerie* where I once went with the *domestique* to buy a saucepan.

Living in a small house brought us closer together and I became on more intimate terms with the servants there than I ever had been in London – with the exception of Rosie, of course. I could imagine the disapproval which would have been expressed by Mrs Winch or Wilkinson if I had sat in the kitchen having long chats with the servants as I did with Marie, the *domestique*, or in the garden with Jacques.

But I felt these people were my friends and I wanted to learn as much about them as I could.

Marie had been 'crossed in love' and I shared her chagrin. He had been a bold and dashing soldier who had stayed in the town for a few months with his regiment. He had promised to marry her and then he had gone away and left her. After she had talked to me about him she would be heard singing a melancholy dirge:

> *'Où t'en vas-tu, soldat de France,*
> *Tout équipé, prêt au combat?*
> *Plein de courage et d'espérance,*
> *Où t'en vas-tu, petit soldat?'*

She forgot him after a while and treated us to other melodies like *Au Claire de la Lune* and *Il Pleut, Bergère* for she was not melancholy by nature.

I was not sure when this romance had flourished, for she was at this time near the end of her thirties, I imagined, and she was far from prepossessing with a faint moustache and several missing teeth. But she was a conscientious worker, good-hearted and very sentimental. I grew fond of her.

I also had a certain friendship with Jacques. He was a widower of three years standing; he had had six children, several of whom contributed to his support. Most of them lived nearby. He was now courting a widow who was something of a catch because she had inherited ten hectares of very good arable land, left her by her late husband.

I asked every time I saw him how his courtship was progressing. He would always pause and consider, shaking his head. 'Widows, Mademoiselle,' he would say, 'are very funny creatures. You never know how to take a widow.'

'I am sure you are right, Jacques,' I said.

They were pleased that I was there. Neither my mother nor Everton had ever taken an interest in them – except to give orders. When I spoke to my mother of Marie's faithless lover and Jacques' widow she had no notion of what I was talking about, and when I explained she said: 'You are quaint, Caroline. Of what interest can all that possibly be to you?'

I said: 'They are people, Mama. They have their lives just as we have. In London the servants were so much apart. In a small household like this we are closer. It is good in a way. It makes us aware of them . . . as people.'

It was an unfortunate remark.

'Ah, London,' she sighed. 'How different.'

And then she was sunk in melancholy, remembering.

I soon became acquainted with some of our neighbours. I visited the flower growers and saw how they distilled their essences and heard how they sold them to the *parfumeurs* all over France. It was very interesting. They had acres and acres on which they grew their flowers and I was amazed to discover how many were needed to produce one small flagon of perfume.

The scent of the jasmine was exquisite. They told me they gathered it in July and August but there was a second flowering in October, which was when the flowers were really at their best.

The roses from which they made attar of roses were wonderful.

The Claremonts employed several people from the town who came riding in on their bicycles in the early morning. I often saw them going home after the day's work.

I soon made the acquaintance of the Dubussons. I found them charming. It was true that their château was somewhat dilapidated. There were chickens in one of the courtyards and it really was more like a farmhouse than a castle. True, it had the usual pepper-pot towers which gave it an air of dignity, and the Dubussons were as proud of their home as the Landowers and Tressidors were of theirs.

I would sit in the big salon drinking wine with Monsieur and Madame Dubusson, and they would tell me how times had changed since the days of their grandeur. Their son and his wife were with them and they were very hardworking. Sometimes the family visited us and we were invited to the château. Then my mother would wear one of her exquisite gowns; Everton would spend a long time doing her hair and they would try to pretend it was like one of the old engagements which my mother had had in such abundance in the old days.

The Dubussons kept an excellent table, and Monsieur Dubusson liked a game of cards. We played a sort of whist. Monsieur Dubusson enjoyed a game of piquet – and so did my mother – but as only two could play at that, it was not one of the games which took place in the evening. Often I went over to see them in the afternoon and he and I would play piquet together, or a little chess, which he liked better. I had learned the rudiments of the game when I was at school in France and he liked to instruct me.

But although I could find plenty to occupy me I was beginning to feel somewhat restless. I was thinking more and more of Cornwall and I wondered a great deal about the Landowers and how they liked living in their comparatively humble farmhouse. I wrote to Cousin Mary and told her that I should love to come and see her one day.

Her reply was enthusiastic. When was I coming?

I had been three months with my mother. Autumn had come, and I was thinking more and more longingly of Cornwall. I wrote to Cousin Mary and told her that I would come at the beginning of October.

I was quite surprised when I told my mother what I had done.

'Going away from me!' she cried. 'Caroline, I shall miss you.'

'Oh, Mama,' I protested. 'You'll get along very well without me.'

'You like it, do you, with Cousin Mary? I always heard she was something of an ogre.'

'She can be a little gruff, but when you get to know her, you understand the sort of person she is. I grew very fond of her.'

'Robert disliked her intensely.'

'That was because she had the house . . . her rightful property.'

'It has been so wonderful for me to have you here.'

I said nothing, and when I looked up I saw the tears were falling down her cheeks.

Everton said to me: 'Your mother will miss you. She has been so much better since you came.'

'Was she very bad before?'

'She has cheered up wonderfully.'

'She is not really ill, Everton.'

'There is a sickness of the mind, Miss Caroline. She pines

176

for the life she has left, and I am afraid she will always do so.'

'But was she really contented when she was there?'

'She loved that life . . . all the people . . . all the admiration. It was everything to her.'

'But she left it.'

'For the Captain. It was a great mistake. But she would never have gone if she had not been forced to do so.'

The old guilt I had felt came surging back. I was the one who had carelessly betrayed her. If I had not met Robert Tressidor on the stairs and blurted out that I had seen the runaway horse, she might still have been in London, a rich woman. Captain Carmichael might not have died, but could be pursuing his career in the Army.

But I said: 'But there is nothing I can do, Everton. I can only remind her of the past.'

'She has been better since you came,' persisted Everton.

She, like my mother, was trying to persuade me not to go.

My mother said: 'I tell Everton that young people must live their own lives. One cannot expect sacrifices from the young. That is what I tell her.'

But they expected me to stay and I began to ask myself whether it was not my duty to do so.

In the quiet of my bedroom I admonished myself. Be sensible. You can do nothing here. The only good that can be done must come from herself. If she will stop yearning for the glitter of society, if she will interest herself in the life around her, she could be as well as she ever was.

No, I would not be foolish. Cousin Mary was expecting me to go to Cornwall – and I was going.

I had written several times to Olivia. I wrote in detail of the people around me. Her letters were affectionate and she expressed an eagerness to know of my experiences.

She was amused by Marie and Jacques; and loved hearing of the Dubussons and the perfume-makers.

I told her that I was going to Cornwall to see Cousin

Mary and that on my return from France I should have to stay in London. Perhaps I could be with her for a few days then.

That brought back a delighted reply. She longed to see me.

As the day for my departure grew nearer the air of melancholy in the house increased. My mother spent more time in bed and I often came upon her shedding tears. I felt very uncomfortable.

My bags were packed. I had said goodbye to the Claremonts and the Dubussons. In two days' time I should be on my way.

I promised my mother that I would come back to see her before long.

It was the evening of that day. I had been for a walk into the town and taken a last farewell of all my friends and had walked back to the house. I was washing and changing for dinner when Marie came bursting into my room.

'It is Madame,' she cried. 'She is very ill. Mademoiselle Everton says will you go to her at once.'

I hurried to my mother's bedroom. She was lying back in bed, her eyes tightly closed, her face colourless. I had never seen her look like that before.

'Everton,' I said, 'what is it?'

She said to Marie: 'Ask Jacques to go at once for the doctor.'

We sat by her bed. My mother opened her eyes and was aware of me. 'Caroline,' she said weakly, 'so you are still here. Thank God.'

'Yes, I'm here, Mama. Of course I'm here.'

'Don't . . . leave me.'

Everton was watching me intently and my mother closed her eyes.

'How long has she been like this?' I whispered.

'I came up to help her dress for dinner. I found her lying there . . .'

'What can it be?'

'I wish the doctor would hurry,' said Everton.

It was not long before I heard the sound of his carriage wheels on the road.

He came in – a little man, very much the country doctor. I had met him once at the Dubussons'.

He took my mother's pulse, examined her and shook his head gravely.

'Perhaps she has had a shock?' he suggested. He looked so knowledgeable on such a brief examination that I began to suspect his efficiency.

Both Everton and I followed him out of the room.

He said: 'She needs rest . . . rest and peace. She must have no stress, you understand? You are sure she has not had a shock?'

'Well,' said Everton, 'she was upset because Miss Tressidor was leaving us.'

'Ah,' said the doctor wisely. 'That is so, eh?'

'I came on a visit,' I said, 'and that visit is coming to an end.'

He nodded gravely. 'She needs care,' he said. 'I shall come tomorrow.'

We escorted him to his carriage.

Everton looked at me expectantly.

'Could you not stay a little longer . . . until she recovers?'

I did not answer.

I went back to my mother's room. She lay there pale and wan, but she was aware of me.

'Caroline,' she said weakly.

'I'm here, Mama.'

'Stay . . . stay with me.'

That night I slept little. I could not help thinking of my mother lying there on her bed, looking quite unlike herself. At first I had thought that she had feigned illness, and I still had a feeling that this was so. And yet I was not sure. How could I be?

What if I went away? What if she were really ill and died. Did people die of nostalgia? It was not so much that she wanted me. She had done very well without me for the greater part of her life. She felt none of the passionate attachment some mothers have for their children. I could see that my coming had enlivened her days to a certain extent. We played piquet now and then in the evenings and that passed the time – that and the endless talk of the old days.

Yet how could I be sure? It was through my action that her husband had turned her out of his house. Could I be responsible for her death as well?

I did not sleep until dawn and when I awoke I had made up my mind.

I could not go . . . yet.

I wrote letters to Cousin Mary and Olivia, explaining that my mother had been taken suddenly ill and I must stay with her a little longer.

When I told Everton what I had done, her face was illuminated with pleasure. I felt relieved. My mind was made up.

I went to my mother's room. Everton was already there. She had told my mother.

'She will get well now,' said Everton.

'Caroline, my darling,' cried my mother. 'So . . . so you are not going to leave me?'

I sat by her bed holding her hand and I felt as though a trap were closing round me.

My mother recovered slowly but for a while she was more of an invalid than she had ever been. Dr Legrand visited her often and had an air of complacency which suggested he believed he had brought about a miraculous cure.

Cousin Mary wrote to say that she hoped my visit would not be postponed for too long and Olivia expressed her regrets that she was not going to see me and that her mother was ill. She would have liked to come out but Aunt Imogen was against it; she thought she might come later on.

I was now planning to leave at Christmas, but every time

I hinted at it such gloom pervaded the house that I decided to say nothing, but to make my plans and then announce my imminent departure.

I was not so gullible as not to believe that my mother's indisposition had been in a great measure produced by herself. On the other hand, she was a woman of fierce desires and there was no doubt that frustration could make people ill.

I wanted nothing more on my conscience; but I thought longingly of Cornwall.

I admonished myself that I was falling into my old habit of building up a fantasy world. What was there so different about Lancarron compared with this little French village?

The days began to pass quickly. The long evenings had come. We no longer ate in the courtyard. Marie lit the oil lamps and we spent evenings playing piquet or looking through the press cuttings which Everton had pasted into a book; but that, of course, could often end in melancholy so I always tried for piquet.

I began to wonder what I should do with my life. Could I take some sort of post? What could I do? What did impoverished gentlewomen do? They became governesses or companions; there was little else for them. I could see myself as a companion to someone like my mother . . . spending a lifetime playing piquet or listening to reminiscences of past glories.

I was restive. I wanted to get away.

Then the bombshell came in the form of a letter from Olivia.

My dear Caroline,

I don't know how to write this. I don't know what you will think. It has been going on for some time and I have often been on the point of telling you and have decided against it. But you will have to know sometime.

I am engaged to be married.

You know they never thought I would be, but it has

181

happened. I could be very happy, but for one thing. Oh, I don't know what you will think of me, but I have to do it, Caroline. You see, I love him. I always have . . . even when he was engaged to you.

Yes, it is Jeremy. He was very sad when your engagement had to be broken. He has told me all about it. He did realize, though, that he was completely fascinated by you but it was not really lasting love. He discovered that in time. He felt you were too young to know your own mind. Before, you know, he had noticed me, but when you came along he saw only you. He really loves me now, Caroline. I know he does. And I could never be happy without him. So we are going to be married.

Aunt Imogen is delighted. But she insists that we wait till a year after my father's death before the marriage can take place. And then it will be very quiet.

Caroline, I hope you will have got over all that by now. I hope you won't hate and despise me for this. But I do truly love him and did even when he was engaged to you.

He would be very happy if you could forgive him.

Dear Caroline, do try to understand.

Your ever loving sister, Olivia.

I was stunned when I read that letter.

The barefaced effrontery! The toad! The snake! I said: 'Jeremy Brandon, how can you be so despicable? You were determined to enjoy Robert Tressidor's fortune, weren't you? And if you could not get it through one sister, you would through the other.'

I began to laugh bitterly, wildly; and my laughter was near to tears.

I sat down and thought of how different it might have been. I saw myself in that little house in Knightsbridge. How happy I might have been if he had been different, if he had been the man I had believed him to be – not just another of my fantasies!

I could not face anyone yet. I wanted to shut myself away. I went out of the house and walked for miles. I could not bear to talk to anyone for fear I should betray my fury, my resentment, my bitter, bitter anger.

I felt no better when I returned home.

I sat down and wrote a letter to Olivia.

How can you be so gullible? Don't you see him for the fortune-hunter he is? He is not marrying you. He is marrying your father's money. Of course he transferred his affections to you. He thought I should have a share of the money, that was why he fell so passionately in love. He's in love all right . . . but not with you, dear sister, any more than he was with me. He is in love with money.

Olivia, for heaven's sake don't ruin your life by giving way to this schemer . . .

And so on in such a strain.

Fortunately I did not post that letter.

That evening I had to talk of it. I supposed my mother would be informed in due course of her daughter's proposed marriage.

She had not noticed that I was different, though it must have been obvious. Marie had asked if I felt quite well. But my mother never saw anything that did not relate directly to herself.

I said: 'Olivia is engaged.'

'Olivia! At last! I thought she never would be. Who is the man?'

'You'll never guess. It is Jeremy Brandon, who was engaged to me until he heard that your husband was not my father and consequently had left me nothing. Then his affections declined. However, they have now settled on Olivia, who can keep him in that state to which he aspires.'

'Well,' she said, 'at least it is a husband for Olivia.'

'Mama,' I cried reproachfully, 'how can you talk so?'

She replied: 'It's the way of the world.'

'Then I want no part of that world.'

'But you *are* part of it.'

'It is not the whole world. I do not want to live among the bargain-hunters.'

She sighed. 'What can an impecunious young man do? You wouldn't have been happy living in poverty. Look at me.'

'Do you not believe in love, Mama?'

She was quiet for a moment, looking into the past, seeing no doubt the handsome Captain. But even his love had not survived the lack of money. That was what had made love turn cold for her more surely than another woman could have done.

'I've no doubt Olivia is delighted,' she said. 'Poor child. She didn't have many chances, did she? She'll be happy enough and glad, no doubt, that it all turned out as it did.'

I hated her view of life and yet . . . I knew she was right when she said Olivia would be happy.

I could see my sister going through life seeing only good and being unaware of evil.

I could not destroy her illusions.

I went to my room that night and tore up the letter I had written to her.

But I felt the bitterness eating into my soul.

I hated Jeremy Brandon a hundred times more than I had done before.

The Dubussons were giving a dinner party to which we were invited and although my mother despised their 'little evenings', as she called them, they did relieve the monotony and she would prepare herself for them – or rather Everton prepared her – with as much care as she had bestowed upon her London engagements.

She and Everton would be in close conference for a day or so deciding what she would wear, and her toilette would engross them both for several hours before our departure.

'Just a friendly little party,' Madame Dubusson had said.

'A gathering of neighbours. The Claremonts have some important business client staying with them and I have asked them to bring him along.'

My mother certainly looked very beautiful when we were ready. She was wearing a gown of her favourite lavender colour and her delicately tinted skin and shining hair accentuated her beauty. She looked much as she had when we were in London and I thought: If a Dubusson dinner party can do this, she would soon be perfectly well if she could once again enter fashionable society.

Everton had insisted on doing my hair and I had to admit that she had done it very well. She had brushed it with a hairbrush covered with some special silk and then piled it high on my head. She had selected an emerald brooch, belonging to my mother, which she had put on my grey gown; and Everton certainly knew what she was about.

The Dubussons had sent one of their somewhat decrepit old carriages for us. I saw my mother's distaste as she seated herself and I had to remind her that it was good of the Dubussons to provide transport for us as we had none of our own; all the same, her expression did not change when we entered the courtyard of the château, and she caught sight of a hen perched on one of the walls.

Madame Dubusson greeted us warmly. The guests were ourselves, Dr Legrand and the Claremonts with their visitor.

'We all know each other,' announced Madame Dubusson, 'except Monsieur Foucard.'

Monsieur Foucard came forward and bowed gravely. He was, I should say, in his middle fifties; he had a little goatee beard and sparkling dark eyes. His luxuriant hair was almost black and he was dressed with such elegance that one was immediately reminded of the lack of that quality in the other men.

He was somewhat fulsome. He was clearly rather startled by my mother's good looks which seemed to imply that he did not expect to find such elegance in this country community. He was equally gracious to me.

Madame Dubusson said we should have an aperitif and then dinner would be served.

It was clear that Monsieur Foucard was the guest of honour. He had a presence. There was no doubt of that. He had a way, too, of monopolizing the conversation. He seated himself between my mother and me and addressed himself mainly to us.

His stay was, alas, to be brief, he told us, and he was already regretting that. His eyes lingered on my mother. She seemed to sparkle; this was the sort of attention she so desperately needed. I was glad that she was enjoying this so much.

'You are a man of affairs,' said my mother. 'Oh, I do not mean affairs of the heart. I mean business affairs.'

He laughed heartily, his eyes shining with admiration.

It was true, he admitted. He had business all over France. It meant travelling a good deal. Yes, he was in the perfume business. What a business! He had been brought up in it. 'It is the nose, Mesdames. This nose.' He indicated his own somewhat prominent feature. 'I was able to detect all the subtleties of good perfume almost as a baby. At an early age I learned of the wonderful perfumes which could be made to suit beautiful women. I knew that the best cedar wood came from the Atlas Mountains in Morocco, and the essential oil we get from cedar wood is invaluable to give that tang . . . shall I say to set a scent . . . It's a fixative.'

'It's fascinating!' cried my mother. 'Do tell me more.'

He was only too ready and although he turned to me now and then and addressed the occasional remark in my direction, I could see he was carried away by my mother's mature charms.

I knew why my mother always found an immediate masculine response. She was entirely feminine. She looked frail and helpless; her large brown eyes appealed for protection; she put on an air of innocence, of ignorance, in order to flatter masculine superiority, and they loved her for it. What man would not feel himself growing in stature to be appealed to by such an enchanting creature?

She was now looking at him as though all her life she had been longing to discover the facts about the manufacture of perfume.

Madame Dubusson and the Claremonts were delighted to see that their important guest was enjoying the company so intensely.

The food was always excellent at the Dubusson table. Even my mother had to admit that. Eating to the Dubussons was a religion. The manner in which they attacked their food, the obvious relish with which they consumed it, exuded a kind of reverence. But I imagined that was a trait of the French in general rather than in particular. I was sure Monsieur Foucard was a typical Frenchman in that respect, but on that night he seemed far more interested in the company than the food.

My mother said: 'You must tell us more about this fascinating subject, Monsieur Foucard.'

'If you insist, Madame,' he replied.

'I do!' she replied with an upward smile at him.

'At all costs Madame must be obeyed.'

And, of course, what he wanted more than anything else was to talk of his business and when it was at the request of such an elegant and attractive woman he was delighted.

He talked; and I admit it was interesting. I learned a great deal, not only about the manufacture of perfume but its history. He was certainly knowledgeable on his subject and he talked of what perfumes the ancient Egyptians had used and he bemoaned the fact that at the present day perfume was not used to the same extent.

'But, my dear lady, we shall work on that. The presentation has been neglected. Things must look good, must they not, to please the eyes, and who is more insistent on that than the ladies? We are presenting them in such a way that they are irresistible. What is more delightful than a fragrant perfume?'

My mother laughed and halted him in his flow. 'You speak too fast for me sometimes, Monsieur Foucard. You must remember that I am such a novice at your language.'

'Madame, I never heard my language more delightfully spoken.'

'You are as great a flatterer as a *parfumeur*.' She tapped his hand playfully, which made him laugh.

'I am going to ask a great favour,' he declared.

'I am not sure whether I shall be able to grant it,' she replied coquettishly.

'You must or I shall be desolate.'

She leaned towards him, putting her ear close to his lips.

He said: 'I am going to ask you to allow me to send you a flagon of my very special creation. It is Muguet . . .'

'Muguet!' I cried. 'We call that lily of the valley.'

'Lillee of the vallee,' he repeated and my mother laughed immoderately.

'Madame is like a lily. It is the perfume I would choose for her.'

I felt that the evening was being given over to this flirtation between him and my mother. But no one minded. The kindhearted Dubussons liked to see people enjoying themselves; and the doctor was so intent on his food that that was enough for him. As for the Claremonts, they were delighted. They were greatly in awe of the important Monsieur Foucard and I guessed they relied on him to buy quantities of their essences. The Dubussons were also delighted to see their guests taking over the burden of entertaining each other and making a very good job of it.

My mother and Monsieur Foucard were clearly getting more satisfaction from the situation than anyone.

We sat over dinner sampling the wines. Monsieur Foucard knew a great deal about them, but it was obvious that his real interest was in perfume.

There were signs of regret from Monsieur Foucard when the evening came to an end.

Effusively he thanked Madame and Monsieur Dubusson. The Claremonts exuded satisfaction and when Monsieur Foucard heard that my mother and I were travelling home in one of the Dubusson carriages he insisted on accompanying us.

This he did, to my mother's immense satisfaction.

The evening had been a triumph for her.

Monsieur Foucard kissed first my hand and then my mother's – lingering over hers and looking into her eyes, he told her that he deeply regretted he must leave the next day for Paris.

'Perhaps I shall be returning,' he said, still holding her hand.

'I hope that may be so,' replied my mother earnestly, 'but I have no doubt that you will find this little village somewhat dull after the exciting places and people you must be meeting all the time.'

He looked very solemn. 'Madame,' he said, placing his hand on his heart with an elaborate gesture to indicate his complete sincerity, 'I assure you I have never enjoyed an evening as I have this one.'

Everton was waiting for my mother and I heard their excited conversation going on into the early hours of the morning.

I lay in bed thinking of the evening and its significance.

I cannot stay here much longer, I thought. I must get away.

For days there was talk of that evening and that amusing, intelligent man of the world, Monsieur Foucard. The Claremonts offered the information that he was one of the wealthiest distributors in France. He owned a large exporting business and numerous shops all over the country.

It was evidently a great honour to them that he had decided to spend a night under their roof; and how fortunate it was that his stay had coincided with the Dubusson dinner party!

My mother's high spirits began to wilt after a day or so, and then a magnificent flagon of perfume arrived, 'For the most beautiful lily of them all.'

That kept her happy for several days.

Christmas would soon be with us.

The Dubussons had asked us to spend the day with them and we had accepted.

My mother recalled past Christmases, which reduced her to even greater melancholy, and I promised myself that after Christmas I should definitely go to Cornwall. There I would be able to talk sensibly to Cousin Mary and discuss with her the possibility of doing something to earn money. I thought momentarily of Jamie McGill. Perhaps I could keep bees. Was it possible to make a little money that way? Jamie would be glad to teach me. Although I had enough money to live frugally, it would be useful to earn money to augment my income. I did not want to go to London, for there I should have to see Olivia.

At the beginning of November I went into the town to buy a few Christmas presents. I would need something for the Dubussons who were going to be our hosts for the day, and there were my mother, Everton, Marie and Jacques.

There was not a great deal of choice in the shops and I quickly made my purchases and went into the *auberge* where I was well known by now. There were no longer tables outside, so I sat in a room with windows looking out on the square, and there I ordered a glass of wine.

As I was drinking this a man came in and sat down quite near me. There was something very familiar about him. I stared at him. I must be dreaming. I had imagined him so often that for a few moments I could not really believe my eyes.

He had risen and was coming towards me. He was dark-haired, dark-eyed, rather lean, with a somewhat slouching walk. I felt the colour rush into my face.

'Forgive me,' he said, 'but you are English.'

I nodded.

'I think you are . . . I think you must be . . .'

I was recovering myself. 'You are Mr Paul Landower. I recognized you at once.'

'And you are Miss Tressidor.'

'Yes, I am.'

'I am so pleased to see you. We met such a long time ago. You were a little girl then.'

'I was fourteen. I didn't regard myself as little. It's four years ago actually.'

'Is it really?'

'I remember it clearly.'

'May I sit down?' he asked.

'Please do. Going to Cornwall was a great event in my life.'How is your brother?'

'Jago is well, thank you.'

'He and I were quite good friends.'

'He is more your age. A little older, in fact. He is doing quite well.'

I wanted to ask about Landower, how they liked living at the farmhouse. But I felt it might be a melancholy subject.

'I'll call for some more wine,' he said. He leaned his elbows on the table and smiled at me. I felt rising excitement. Here was the man who had occupied my thoughts for so many months until Jeremy Brandon had replaced him. It was a strange coincidence that he should have arrived in France and at the very place where I was staying.

'Are you on holiday here?' I asked.

'No. I had business in Paris and again in Nice. I thought I'd have a look at the country while I was here. These small places are so attractive, are they not? And one gets to know people so much better than one does in the towns.'

'I am staying with my mother,' I said.

He nodded.

'She lives here now. She has been here some years.'

'You like life here?'

'Life is interesting wherever it is.'

'That's so. It's a pity everyone does not see it that way.'

'How is Miss Tressidor? She is not a great letter-writer so I don't hear as much as I should like to.'

'She is well, I believe.'

'I forgot your family and hers don't mingle.'

'They do more now. I believe Miss Tressidor was hoping that you were going to visit her.'

'Did she tell you?'

He nodded.

'I should have gone to see her but my mother was taken ill.'

'She was very disappointed.'

'I shall go to see her one day. How is everything at Landower?'

'Very well.'

'I suppose . . .' I did not know how to put what I was going to ask, and decided it would be wiser not to talk of it. I said instead: 'Where are you staying?'

'In this very *auberge*.'

'Oh! Have you been here long?'

'I came yesterday.'

'Is it to be a short stay?'

'Oh yes, quite short.'

'Jago must be quite grown up now. I hope everything really is well with him.'

'Jago will always see that life goes as he wants it.'

'When I was there, there were some people . . . What was their name? Oh . . . it was Arkwright.'

'Yes, that's right. They bought Landower Hall.'

'Oh, they did buy it!' I wanted to ask about Gwennie Arkwright and I wondered how much Paul knew and whether Jago had ever confessed to what had happened in the minstrels' gallery.

'Yes, but now the family is back.'

'Oh, I'm so glad.'

'Yes, it came back into the family.'

'That must be a great relief.'

He laughed. 'Well, you know, it was the family home for hundreds of years. One feels certain ties.'

'Indeed yes. Jago always said that *you* would never let it pass right out of the family.'

'Jago had too high an opinion of me.'

'Well, it seems he was right.'

'In that instance . . . perhaps. But tell me about yourself. What have you been doing?'

'I went away to school after I returned to London, and I came to France, in fact.'

'Then you have an impeccable accent, I am sure.'

'I get by.'

'That must be a great help. Do you come into town often?'

'Yes, quite often. We're about a mile and a half out.'

'How is your mother?'

'She is not well sometimes.'

'I wonder if you will allow me to call?'

'But of course. She would be delighted. She likes to see people.'

'Then while I'm staying here . . . if I may . . .'

'How long will you be here?'

'I am not sure. Perhaps a week. I should not think longer.'

'I dare say there will be a great deal to do at Christmas.'

'There always is on the estate. All the old traditions have to be observed, as you can imagine.'

'I can indeed.'

I glanced at the watch pinned to my bodice.

He said: 'You are anxious about the time. May I take you back?'

'Old Jacques, our gardener, is waiting for me with his trap.'

'Then I'll take you to him. And . . . tomorrow . . . may I call?'

'Yes,' I said. 'We should like that.' And I gave him details of our address and how to find us.

Jacques was waiting with some impatience. It was unlike me not to be on time.

Paul held my hand firmly in his as he said goodbye.

I returned his gaze and felt happier than I had since I had read that cruel letter of Jeremy's.

My mother was excited at the prospect of a visitor. He came in the morning and sat in the courtyard with me while an excited Marie prepared the *déjeuner*.

193

The midday meal was usually the biggest of the day, as it was in most French households. My mother thought it most uncivilized to eat large quantities at midday; dinner was the great social occasion with her.

However, Paul was asked to luncheon.

My mother received him very graciously. His manner towards her was courteous but a little aloof. He was no Monsieur Foucard to be bowled over by her charms. She adapted her style to suit him and I marvelled at her expertise. Handling man and adjusting herself to what she believed would attract them was one of her obvious social assets.

As she was quite interested in Cousin Mary, of whom she had heard so much when she was married to Robert Tressidor, Cornwall, the life there and the two great houses made a long topic of conversation.

'I hear you have been quite unwell,' he said solicitously.

'Oh, Mr Landower, don't let's talk of my boring ailments,' she said, and went on to talk of them at some length.

He listened sympathetically.

He turned to me. 'Miss Tressidor, I remember when you stayed in Cornwall, you did a great deal of riding with my brother. Do you ride here?'

'Alas, no. I haven't a horse.'

'I believe I could hire horses. Would you care to show me the countryside if I could do this?'

'I should like it very much.'

'Caroline dear,' put in my mother, 'do you think it's safe?'

'Safe, Mama? I'm perfectly safe on a horse.'

'But a foreign horse, dear.'

I laughed and saw that Paul was smiling.

'Horses don't consider nationality in the same way as we do, Mama. They are much the same the world over.'

'But in a foreign country!'

'I should take care that no harm came to your daughter, Mrs Tressidor,' said Paul.

194

'I am sure you would. But I should be so anxious . . .'

I understood the way her mind was working. Much as she liked the monotony of her days to be relieved by the advent of visitors, she was a little wary of Paul Landower. Every man she saw she assessed as a possible husband or lover; and it was quite clear that he was making no plans which involved her. Therefore, she reasoned, I must be the target of his aspirations; and she did not want me to go to him any more than to Cousin Mary. I could see the speculation in her eyes.

I had allowed her to prevent my going to Cornwall, but she should not stop my riding with Paul. The thought of riding with him filled me with ecstatic pleasure.

I said: 'Do you think you really would be able to hire horses?'

'I'm certain of it,' he said. 'As a matter of fact I have already asked at the *auberge*. I have one bespoke as it were. I am sure there will be no difficulty in getting another.'

'I shall look forward to it.'

After lunch I showed him a little of the countryside. I met Monsieur Dubusson, who insisted on our going into the château to sample the wine his son had produced in his vineyard in Burgundy. Madame Dubusson greeted us with delight. They were very kindly people and already scented a romance. It was embarrassing in a way and yet I knew it came from the kindliness of their hearts and that they believed it was no life for a young girl – even though it might be her duty – to look after a mother who from time to time lapsed into invalidism.

Afterwards I introduced Paul to the Claremonts for, having included the Dubussons, I dared not leave them out. There was a great deal of talk about the flowers they produced and the essences they distilled; and they were very gratified to explain to a newcomer. From time to time the language became too fast and furious for Paul and I had the pleasure of translating.

As we were leaving Madame Claremont said: 'By the way, Monsieur Foucard is coming for the Christmas holiday. Oh, he will not stay here. We are not equipped for such as he is . . . not for more than one night. He is used to so much comfort. He will stay at the *auberge* in the town.'

'Tell him I thoroughly recommend it,' said Paul.

After we left the Claremonts we walked through the lanes and talked of the countryside and the Dubussons and Claremonts, the difference between the French and the English; and that seemed to me an enchanted day.

When I said goodbye to him he held my hand firmly and said: 'Tomorrow morning. Say about ten o'clock. We'll go off somewhere and we'll find some little *auberge* where we'll stop for luncheon. How's that?'

I said it sounded perfect.

'Tomorrow, then.'

He stepped back, took off his hat and bowed; blissfully I went into the house, aware of Marie peering through the kitchen window.

When I came into the hall, Marie was there. She said: 'Oh, he is a very grand gentleman. So tall . . . He reminds me of *mon petit soldat*.'

I suppose that was about the greatest compliment she could pay. Later I heard her singing dolefully '*Où t'en vas-tu, petit soldat*.' It was clear that Paul had found favour with Marie and Jacques as well as the Dubussons and Claremonts.

It was not the case with my mother. I guessed she had discussed him with Everton.

'So you are going riding tomorrow,' she said as we ate that evening.

'Yes, Mama.'

'I shall be very worried.'

'I don't think so, Mama. You'll forget all about it as soon as we've gone.'

'Caroline, how can you say such a thing!'

She saw what she called my mulish look setting about my lips and she knew that I was determined to go.

She said: 'There's something mysterious about him.'

'How, mysterious?'

'Those dark looks.'

'Do you think all people with dark hair are mysterious?'

'I'm not referring to his hair, Caroline. I know men.'

'Yes, Mama, I'm sure you do.'

'I should hate to see you make a terrible mistake.'

'What sort of mistake?'

'To rush into marriage.'

'Oh Mama, please! A man appears. He is a stranger in a strange land. He meets a fellow compatriot whom he saw once some years ago, he is friends – and you talk of marriage!'

'He seemed persistent . . . hiring horses.'

'It's nothing but a friendly gesture.'

She looked pathetically down at her plate and I thought she was going to weep.

Poor Mama, I thought. She visualizes lonely evenings – no piquet, no one but Everton to talk to of past triumphs. And Everton is years older than she is. I am young. She is terrified of my going away. How strange that when I was a child she had no time to spend with me; now I am grown up she cannot bear me to leave her for a day.

Then suddenly I remembered. The excitement of the day had completely driven this important piece of news out of my mind.

'I saw Madame Claremont today. She told me Monsieur Foucard is coming here for Christmas.'

The change in her was miraculous.

'Is that so?'

'Yes, he is staying at the *auberge*.'

'I'm not surprised. One could hardly expect a man like that to stay at the Claremonts'.'

'I dare say,' I said archly, 'that we shall be seeing something of him.'

'It may well be,' she answered; and I knew she was already planning her wardrobe.

My words had had the desired effect. There was no further mention of my day's riding.

It was a day I was to remember for a long time.

The sun was bright although there was a sharp wind. It was good to be in a riding habit again.

I went to say goodbye to my mother before I left.

She was sitting up in bed sipping the hot chocolate which Everton had brought to her just as she had done each morning in England. Everton was seated on a chair making lists of clothes.

The Christmas wardrobe, I presumed!

What luck that Monsieur Foucard had saved the situation and made everything so much smoother! I had been determined to have my day but it was pleasant to achieve it with the minimum of friction.

I kissed her and she said, 'Have a good day,' almost absent-mindedly.

Paul was waiting with the horses.

'A little chestnut mare for you,' he said. 'She's a bit frisky but I told them you were an expert.'

'She's lovely,' I told him.

'Now you know the countryside, you'd better decide where we shall go.'

'I only know the immediate environs. I never before had a chance to get away. Shall we go into the mountains?'

'That would be very interesting.'

What joy it was for me to be on a horse, and I had to admit that my companion added considerably to my pleasure. It was almost like one of those dreams come true. He might not look exactly like the knight in shining armour whom I had visualized in my girlhood, but he was Paul Landower, the hero of my imaginings.

He talked about Cornwall just as Jago used to, about the estate and the house and Tressidor too. But for a great deal of the time we were silent, for the road was so narrow that sometimes we had to go in single file.

At length we came to the foothills of the mountains where we paused to admire the grandeur of the scenery. On the other side of these Maritime Alps was the beautiful Mediterranean Sea.

'The air is like wine,' he said, 'which reminds me we are going to find that little *auberge*. Are you hungry?'

'Getting that way,' I said.

'It'll be uphill for a while. Madame at my *auberge* told me that she can recommend *La Pomme d'Or* which we ought to find fairly easily. She says the damson pie is the best she ever tasted and has made me swear a solemn oath to try it. I dare not return and tell her I have not done so.'

'Then it is a matter of honour for us to find *La Pomme d'Or*. I wonder why it is so called. After the famous golden apple which Paris gave to Aphrodite, as the fairest of women, I suppose, but I wonder how it got here.'

'I fancy,' he said, 'that that is one of the mysteries we shall never solve.'

The scenery was becoming awesome – mountains stretching as far as we could see; we passed gorges and silver waterfalls and streams trickling down the slopes.

'I hope the horses are sure-footed,' said Paul.

'I dare say they've been in the mountains before.'

'It must be getting quite late now.'

'Time for luncheon. We should find the golden apple soon.'

We came upon it unexpectedly. There it stood, white and glittering in the sunshine, built against the side of the mountain and facing a gap through which there was a glimpse of the sea.

We left our horses in the stable to be cared for and went into the dining salon.

We were welcomed warmly, especially when Paul mentioned that Madame at the *auberge* where he was staying had recommended *La Pomme d'Or*.

'She told us about the damson pie,' he said. 'It is hoped that it is available.'

Madame was large and plump and I soon realized that she possessed in an even greater degree than usual that reverence for food which was characteristic of her nation. She put her hands on her hips, and shook with laughter.

'Believe it or not, Monsieur, Madame,' she said, 'I cook

the most wonderful dishes . . .' She put her fingers to her lips and threw a kiss to those revered objects. 'My langoustines are magnificent. Crevettes . . . gigot of lamb . . . and such tarts as you never have seen . . . but always it is my damson pie.'

'It must be gratifying, Madame,' I said, 'to be so famed for such an achievement.'

She lifted her shoulders and her eyes sparkled as she told us what she could give us.

Hot soup was brought in. I had no idea what it contained but it was delicious. But I was living in an exalted state and anything, I imagine, would have tasted like ambrosia.

It is the mountain air, I told myself. That . . . and Paul Landower.

I studied him intently. My mother had said he had dark looks . . . secret looks. Yes, there was an element of that. I did not know him. Not as I had known Jago . . . or Jeremy. But had I known Jeremy? I could not have been more surprised when I had received that letter jilting me.

No, I had not known Jeremy. I was gullible where people were concerned. But I was changing. Once I would have believed my mother wanted me to stay with her because she loved me. Now I saw clearly that she only wanted me to relieve the boredom a little. If someone else could do that, I might go out for the day and she would not mind in the least.

I would be more prepared now for people to act in an unexpected way; and there was something secret, mysterious about this man. I longed to know what it was and I was excited at the prospect of discovering.

After soup there was lamb served in a way I had never had it before; it was delicious; and the wine, which was proudly shown to Paul before it was poured out, was nectar.

I said: 'I shall have no room for the famous damson pie.'

At last it came. Madame told us that during the season she set one of her maids doing nothing else but preserving damsons for several weeks.

She served it with her special garnishing and we both agreed that it came up to expectation.

Paul was amused to see me counting the stones.

'Ah,' he said, 'that looks significant. Tell me, what is your fate?'

'There are eight stones. They indicate whom I shall marry. Rich man, poor man, beggarman, thief.'

'You have too many.'

'Oh no. I just start again. Rich man, poor man, beggarman, thief. Oh dear! I'm destined for the thief. I don't like that at all. I think I'll try something else.

I began to quote:

> 'He loves me,
> He don't.
> He'll have me,
> He won't.
> He would if he could
> But he can't
> So he won't.'

Paul was laughing. 'You've one left over.'

'So I start again. He loves me. Well, that's a little more satisfactory. But if he is a thief I'm not very happy about my future.'

'You should be,' he said seriously. 'I have an idea that you are the sort of person who will be happy and make others happy.'

'What a charming assessment of my character. I can't imagine how you can be so knowledgeable in such a short time.'

'There are things one knows . . . instinctively.'

I thought: I am falling in love with him. What a fool I am. I have just been bitterly deceived. I have vowed I would never fall in love again, and here I am ready to begin it all once more. Oh, but I was never really in love with Jeremy. It was infatuation. This is different. Besides, wasn't I always in love with Paul Landower?

He was watching me intently. 'Your eyes are a brilliant green.'

'I know.'

'They glitter like emeralds.'

'I like the comparison. We had a cook once who used to say "Blue eyes for beauty, brown eyes for cherry pie" (which I believe in her eyes was another way of saying beauty) "green eyes for greedy guts." That must have been because I had filched some titbit from the table which I believe, at an early age, I was inclined to do.'

'You are revealed as a green-eyed monster.'

'That means jealousy.'

'Are you jealous?'

'I think I might well be.'

'Well, it's natural.'

'I think I should be a veritable fiend.'

'I can imagine how those eyes would flash. It would be rather like facing the gorgon.'

'We are getting very classical this afternoon. It all began with the golden apple, I suppose.'

'How do you feel?'

'Replete.'

'So do I. I hope they haven't fed the horses as well as they have fed us or they'll be too lethargic to move.'

'Is that how you feel?'

He nodded. 'I should like to stay here for a long time.'

'It's delightful in the mountains.'

'Awe-inspiring. I am glad I found you. I shall report my findings to Miss Tressidor. When can I tell her you will come to see her?'

'Soon. After Christmas . . . if I can get away.'

'Your mother will try to stop your going to Cornwall?'

'She is very frustrated here. She misses the old life. I suppose I help a bit.'

He smiled and continued to study me.

Our hostess came in and we told her that her damson pie was beyond our expectations and they had been very high.

We would extoll its virtues to all those with whom we came into contact.

She looked well pleased and told us not to hurry but to take a look round. 'The view's well worth seeing half a mile on. That's a regular beauty spot. You have a good view of the gorge there.'

We came out to the stables. 'We must not forget,' said Paul, 'that it gets dark early. Alas, I think we should be wending our way homewards. This delightful day is coming to an end.'

We rode in silence for a while. The path was uneven; we went down, then up, and there were a great many stones underfoot, so we had to pick our way with care. Paul was riding on ahead of me as the path was so narrow.

I was not sure how it happened. My horse must have tripped over a stone; in any case she side-stepped and caught me unaware. At one moment I was following Paul quite serenely and the next I was being thrown out of the saddle.

I cried out just as I saw the ground coming up to meet me. Then I lost consciousness.

From a long way off I could hear my name being called.

'Caroline . . . Caroline . . . oh, my God, Caroline . . .'

He was kneeling beside me. I felt his lips on my forehead and I opened my eyes and saw his face close to mine.

'Caroline . . . Are you hurt? . . . Caroline . . .'

In that moment I felt nothing but happiness. It was the tender way in which he said my name; it was the deep concern in his voice; it was the fact that he had kissed me.

'What . . . happened?' I asked.

'You fell.'

'I – I don't understand . . .'

'You're here with me in the mountains. Something happened. I didn't see. I was going on ahead. How do you feel? You can't have done much harm, we were only ambling. See if you can stand.'

He helped me to my feet, holding me tightly.

'How's that?'

'All right . . . I think.'

'Good.' He spoke with great relief. 'I don't think you've broken anything.'

I clutched him, feeling dizzy. The mountains swayed ahead of me.

'You fell on your head but your hat would have saved you. I don't think you should attempt to ride back.'

I was beginning to grasp the situation and the first thing I felt was shame. I had prided myself on my horsemanship and here I was coming a cropper when I was only walking my horse.

Paul said: 'I'm going to get you back to the *auberge*.'

'Oh no. We must go home. It'll soon be dark.'

'No,' he said authoritatively. 'I should be afraid for you to attempt that long ride. I think not much harm has been done but one can't be sure. I am going to get you back to the *auberge* and send for a doctor to have a look at you. Don't worry, we can get a message sent to your mother.'

'I'm sure I'm all right.'

'I feel sure you are too, but I'm not taking risks.'

'Oh dear, you must think me very stupid. I'm a good rider really.'

'I know you are.' He picked me up in his arms and sat me on his horse. 'There! We'll go back. We'll be there shortly.'

And leading the two horses he took us back to *La Pomme d'Or*.

Madame was deeply concerned. Yes, they had two rooms which were kept ready for travellers. Yes, she could send for a doctor, and yes, one of the stable boys could take a message to my mother.

'There,' said Paul. 'Nothing to worry about.'

'I feel so foolish.'

'Look at it like this. It give us a little more time in this really rather attractive place.'

He had a certain effect on me. I was able to cast aside my anxieties about my mother's reaction to the situation. I was sore and a little light-headed, but when the doctor came he said that I had broken no bones; he had left a little liniment

204

for the bruises and a sedative which I was to take before settling down for the night if I found sleep difficult.

He was sure I should feel a little stiff in the morning and might experience a few twinges of discomfort, but apart from that I should soon be perfectly all right. But I should rest until the effect of the shock wore off.

I was given a very pleasant room with a view over the mountains. Paul had the next room. There was a balcony with French windows leading on to it, and his windows opened on to the same balcony.

Darkness came. Oil lamps were lighted and the scenery in the glow of a faint crescent moon was like something from another world.

The mountain air was crisp and cold and our hostess gave me extra blankets. She said I should need them, for the nights were very cold in the mountains.

I can remember very vividly every waking moment of that strange night.

Paul and I took supper together in my room. There was soup and cold chicken served with a delicious salad; and we asked if there was more of the far-famed damson pie.

Paul studied the stones on my plate and asked: 'What have you got this time?'

There were six stones.

'Poor man,' I said. 'An improvement on the last. But the other isn't so good. Last time he loved me. This time he can't.'

'Your fate has changed within a few hours. I shouldn't have thought that possible, would you?'

'I suppose in life everything is possible.'

He looked at me steadily and said nothing.

The stable boy had returned with the news that he had delivered the note to my mother and impressed on her that there was nothing to worry about. I should be home next day.

The doctor had been right about the twinges. Some of the bruises were painful. I still felt somewhat light-headed, but I did wonder if that was due to all that was happening.

I kept thinking of coming out of my stupor and seeing Paul's face. I could feel the touch of his lips on my forehead. I thought: The world is a happy place after all. And I was glad that Jeremy Brandon had jilted me. My experience with him was to be welcomed rather than deplored.

I felt gloriously free to be happy.

And I was happy that night. I marvelled that out of disaster could come such pleasure. If I had not tumbled from my horse I should now be playing piquet at home or listening to my mother's account of what she would wear for the Christmas festivities, for she would have forgotten her fears about a possible marriage for me in the prospect of further flirtation with Monsieur Foucard.

So we sat in the lamplight and we talked. I told him quite a lot about myself, about the Jubilee and our visit to Waterloo Place and its consequences. I think he already knew that I was not Robert Tressidor's daughter. I wondered if Cousin Mary had told him. If so, the animosity between the two families must have diminished considerably. I hesitated about telling him of Jeremy Brandon, but I found myself blurting that out too.

'So you see it was the money he thought would be mine that he wanted. When he knew I wasn't going to get that, he didn't want me.'

'I see,' he said. 'Perhaps it was as well that you found out in time.'

'That's what I tell myself. But it is hard to see these things when they happen. And now he is going to marry my sister. I often wonder what I should do about that.'

'Does she want to marry him?'

'Oh yes . . . very much. She was in love with him before I knew him. I didn't realize that at the time, but I guessed there was someone. It turned out to be him. I wish I could make her see she must not marry him.'

'That would not make her very happy.'

'No, but he is marrying her for her money.'

'She wants him, you say.'

'Oh yes. But he is deceiving her. I can well imagine him.

He will tell her how much he loves her. He will urge her to marry him, explaining that he really loved her all the time . . . even when he was engaged to me. I can't believe it is right for me to say nothing. My mother thinks it is all right. In her world that is normal conduct.'

'In a lot of people's worlds, it would be.'

'I despise it.'

There was silence in the room. I could hear the faint sound of water rushing down the mountainside.

I said suddenly, 'Do you think I should warn Olivia?'

He shook his head. 'Let her be happy. It is what she wants. It is what he wants. She knows he was engaged to you. There is nothing new you can tell her. It must have been very hurtful to you.'

'Oh, I've got over it now.'

'I'm glad.'

He reached for my hand and pressed it.

'I'm also glad that you are not badly hurt,' he went on. 'When I turned and saw you on the ground . . . well, I cannot describe my feelings.'

I laughed happily. 'I was thinking that out of mishaps sometimes the nicest things come about.'

'You mean this . . . here. Are you enjoying it?'

'So much . . . more than I have enjoyed anything . . . for a long time.'

'Do you know,' he said, 'I can say the same.'

We smiled at each other and some understanding seemed to pass between us, some fellow feeling.

I never want this to end, I thought.

We sat there in silence and that seemed as wonderful as when we talked. A clock striking eleven broke in on the silence.

'The doctor said you were to go to bed early,' said Paul.

'I'm afraid I've been forgetting the time.'

'I forgot it too,' I replied. 'Surely that clock can't be right?'

'It is, I'm afraid. You must sleep now. You'll feel absolutely right in the morning, I am sure.'

'How quiet it is here! It seems so strange to be in the mountains.'

'You're not afraid?'

I shook my head vigorously.

'There's no need to be. I'm next door . . . to offer protection should you need it. Good night.'

'Good night,' I answered.

He leaned forward suddenly and kissed me on the brow, just as he had when I was coming into consciousness as I lay on the road.

I smiled at him. I thought he was going to say something, but he appeared to change his mind and went out.

I knew that I should not find sleep easily. I was not sure that I wanted to. I wanted to lie in my bed and look out over the mountains and go over everything that had happened on this wonderful day.

If I had not fallen from my horse I should not be here now. If Jeremy had not jilted me, this day would never have happened. Perhaps something good always comes out of evil. It was a comforting thought.

Was I in love? Perhaps. But I must remember that my emotions were easily aroused. I had adored Captain Carmichael. Then Jeremy had come and I had been over-ready to fall in love with him. And even before that I had made a hero of Paul Landower, and he had figured in my dreams ever since . . . apart from the time when I had been obsessed by Jeremy.

Could I really trust my feelings? I suppose people would say I was too young – and immature with it.

One thing I was sure of. I was happy. I would go to Cornwall soon. There I should see Paul often. Our relationship would strengthen. I was going to be happy.

I dozed and awoke with a start. I was not alone. I lay still, my eyes only half open, my heart beating wildly. The room was full of moonlight, and there was a shadow at the french window.

I knew that it was Paul who was standing there. He was looking in at me.

I dared not let him see that I was awake. I did not know what would happen if he did. He had his hand on the door. I thought: He is coming to me.

I felt a great yearning for him to do so. I was almost willing him to come.

But I lay there, my eyes half closed, feigning sleep.

And still he stood there and made no move.

I repressed a desire to call him. How could I welcome him into my room at that hour of the night? If I did, it could surely be for one purpose.

I must not . . . and yet I wanted him to come in.

I could hear my heart hammering beneath the bedclothes. I had shut my eyes tightly . . . waiting.

I was aware that the shadow had disappeared. I opened my eyes. He had gone.

I slept little but my sleeplessness was not due to my fall.

He said nothing about the night, but just asked how I had slept. I replied: 'Intermittently.'

He nodded. 'After such a shock you would expect to.'

I wanted to ask him, 'Why did you stand outside my window last night?' But I said nothing and he seemed different by morning light. The intimacy of the previous evening had gone, he was aloof almost.

He said: 'We must have breakfast and set off right away. Your mother will be anxious. How do you feel about mounting the chestnut?'

'Perfectly all right. It was my carelessness really. I should have been more watchful. The poor creature was plagued by that stony path.'

'You're too good a horsewoman to be bothered by a little spill, I'm sure.'

We had the usual French breakfast of coffee and brioche with lots of creamy butter and honey; and apart from a certain stiffness I did feel normal.

He regarded me with some concern. 'All the dizziness has gone?'

I nodded.

'You'll have those bruises to remind you for some time, I should imagine.'

'I shall remember after they have gone.'

'We'll neither of us forget, will we?'

'Oh, will you remember too?'

'But of course.'

He went on ahead as the road was narrow and very soon we had left the mountains behind us.

Everton came to the door when we arrived.

'Your mother has been so anxious,' she said.

'You had a message, did you not? The stable boy from the *auberge* . . .'

'Yes, yes,' said Everton, 'but your mother has been most upset.'

'Miss Tressidor has been upset also,' said Paul.

He had dismounted and helped me down.

'Would you like me to wait and see your mother?' he asked.

I shook my head. 'No, I think I'd better go in alone.'

'Au revoir,' he said.

He took my hand and held it firmly while he looked into my face with a certain inscrutable expression.

Then he went off with the two horses.

My mother was sitting up in bed, the empty chocolate cup on the table beside her.

'Caroline! My child! I've been so worried.'

'I hoped the message would explain.'

'My dear child, staying out like that . . . with that man!'

'I had an accident, Mama.'

'That's what they said.'

'Are you suggesting that there was no accident? I'll show you my bruises.'

I wondered then what tales she had made up to tell her husband when she had gone to see my father. I was becoming very unsympathetic towards her. I told myself I was overwrought. I had had an accident but it was not of that I was thinking so much as the thought of Paul standing outside my window. I was sure he had wanted to come in and that he had been grappling with his conscience. I wondered what his feeling would have been had he known that I had wanted him to come. I was very innocent and ignorant in the ways of the world, and I should very quickly have betrayed my feelings to him.

My mother was saying: 'What will people think?'

'What people?'

'Everton, Marie, Jacques, the Dubussons . . . everybody.'

'Everton will think what you tell her to and Marie and Jacques what I tell them. The Dubussons and the Claremonts would have no uncharitable feelings about anyone. As for everyone else, *Honi soit qui mal y pense*.'

'You always try to be clever. Olivia was never like that.'

I said: 'Please, Mama. I am tired. I had a fall from a horse and I want to go to my room to rest. I just came to see you to let you know that I am back.'

'Where is Mr Landower?'

'He left. He has taken the horses with him.'

'Well, I hope no one saw him and that the servants don't gossip.'

'I don't mind if they do, Mama. I have told you what happened and if people choose to disbelieve that, then they must.'

'You are getting dictatorial, Caroline,' she said.

'Perhaps I have been here too long and you would like me to go,' I retorted.

Her face crumbled. 'How can you say that? You know I should hate you to go. The very thought of it makes me ill.'

'Then,' I said coldly, 'you must not make me want to go, Mama.'

She looked at me in a certain surprise and said: 'You're getting very hard, Caroline.'

I thought: Yes, I believe I am.

That afternoon Paul came over to see me.

I was glad that there was no one about. Marie had gone into the town with Jacques to buy some stores and my mother was resting – and I presumed Everton was too.

I heard him ride up and went out to find him dismounting from his horse.

His first words were: 'How are you?'

'Quite all right really.'

'Are you sure? No after-effects?'

'None – only the expected bruises.'

'I am so relieved. And now I have come to say goodbye. I am leaving tomorrow.'

'Oh.' My disappointment must have been obvious. 'Come through into the garden,' I went on. 'It's quite warm in the sun.'

We went through to the walled garden.

'I didn't expect I should leave so hurriedly,' he said. 'I was hoping we could have done more excursions into the mountains.'

'With happier results,' I added, trying to speak lightly.

'That was quite an experience, wasn't it?'

'Were they all right about the horses?'

'Oh yes. They said there are hazards in the mountains for people who are not used to them. May I tell Miss Tressidor that you will be coming to Cornwall soon?'

'Tell her that I want to come very much. I was all prepared to before, you know, but my mother became ill.'

'And you think she might become ill again if you made plans to leave?' He stopped short. 'I suppose I shouldn't have said that,' he went on. 'But you must not stay here too long, you know.'

'It is so difficult to know what to do. I shall discover, though.'

'I will tell Miss Tressidor that you want very much to visit her and will do so at the earliest possible moment. May I give that message to her?'

'Please do.'

'I should so much look forward to seeing you again.'

'Yes, it would be pleasant.'

'I wish I could stay longer.'

We were silent for a while as we walked to the seat set against the stone wall.

I sat down and he was beside me.

'What time do you leave?' I asked.

'At the crack of dawn. It's such a long journey and the train will only take me as far as Paris. I'll have to change there and then there is the crossing and the long journey to Cornwall.'

We sat in silence for a while but I had the impression that he was trying to say something to me.

I said: 'Would you like some tea? My mother is resting. She usually does at this hour in the afternoon. Everton will take her tea at four o'clock.'

'No . . . no, thanks. I just came to see you. I couldn't just go off without saying goodbye.'

'Of course not. It was good of you to think of me.'

'But you know I think of you! I have . . . over the last years. But then I thought of you as a child with flying dark hair and green eyes. You haven't really changed very much. Do you remember when we first met?'

'Yes. In the train. You detected my name on my bag in the luggage rack.'

He laughed. 'Yes, and there was a dragon guarding you.'

'She still guards my sister and I expect will until her marriage.'

'But you escaped from your guardians.'

'Yes. Life has its compensations.'

'You're a person who would value freedom.'

'Very much.'

'You are not in the least conventional.'

'Certain conventions have come about because they make life easier. I think I approve of them. It is just the useless ones which I find restricting.'

He looked at me earnestly. 'You are very wise.'

That made me laugh. 'If you really mean that you must be the only person who thinks so.'

He said: 'Yes, I do believe it.'

I felt he was on the point of saying something very

serious to me. I waited eagerly, but the moment passed.

A cold wind had blown up and I shivered.

'You're cold,' he said. 'I should not keep you out of doors.'

'Come into the house.'

'Thank you, but I won't. There are certain things I have to do. I just came over to tell you I was leaving.'

Desolation swept over me. When should I see him again, I wondered.

If he wanted to see me, perhaps he would come here.

He turned to face me. 'I should go now.'

I nodded.

'I shall never forget,' he went on. 'The mountains were beautiful, weren't they? There was a sense of being apart there . . . away from everything. Did you feel that?'

'Yes, I did.'

'I felt that . . . well, never mind. I shall remember it . . . the room, the balcony . . . and the damson pie. What was the rhyme?'

'Rich man, poor man . . .'

'No, not that one, the other one.'

'Oh . . .

> He loves me,
> He don't.
> He'll have me,
> He won't.
> He would if he could
> But he can't
> So he won't.'

'Yes, that's the one.'

'Fancy your remembering.'

'I shall go on remembering.'

'It was a pity I was so stupid as to fall off that nice little chestnut.'

'At least it made our outing longer. Compensations, remember? Caroline . . . Let's drop Miss Tressidor. It's ridiculous after . . . after . . .'

'Our adventure in the mountains.'

'You will come to Cornwall?'

'When I can.'

'You must, you know. It's a mistake to let oneself be used. There. Forget I said that. I just hope that you will come.'

'I will,' I promised.

'Before long?'

'Before long,' I repeated.

He was looking at me intently now. 'There is so much I want to say to you.'

'Then say it.'

He shook his head. 'Not now. There isn't time.'

'Are you in such a hurry?'

'I think I should go.'

I held out my hand to him. He took it and kissed it.

'Au revoir, Caroline.'

'Au revoir,' I replied.

He looked at me appealingly and then suddenly he put his arms round me and held me tightly against him. He kissed me – not gently on the brow this time but on the lips and I sensed a sudden passion that was under an iron control. I could not help responding.

He released me with apparent reluctance.

'I must go. You see . . . I must go.'

'Goodbye,' I said.

'Au revoir,' he insisted.

I walked with him out to his horse. He mounted slowly, and rode away.

I stood watching him but he did not turn to wave goodbye.

A deep depression set in after he had gone. I wondered when I should see him again. I certainly would if I went to Cornwall. I *would* go to Cornwall. He had said: 'Don't let yourself be used,' and I knew to what he was referring.

I would speak to Everton.

My mother was clearly delighted that he had left. She

dismissed him from her thoughts and gave herself up to the joys of contemplating the coming visit of Monsieur Foucard.

December had come. Christmas was imminent. Marie had decorated the house with holly and mistletoe and Jacques had brought in what he called the Noël log.

It seemed to me that we were celebrating the advent of Monsieur Foucard rather than the coming of Christmas.

He arrived a week before Christmas Day. He had his own carriage and his manservant and they had taken rooms in the *auberge* where Paul had stayed.

One of the first things he did was visit us. The household was in a flutter, but my mother was calm, knowing that others would have to take care of the arrangements and all she had to do was receive him, look beautiful and indulge in a mannered flirtation; and that she could do very well.

She was lying on a sofa in the small salon when he arrived. She was dressed in a morning gown of sprigged muslin and looked at least ten years younger than she actually was.

He came in with an armful of hothouse flowers. I was present but he had eyes only for her. He sat by the sofa and they chatted vivaciously; after a while I made an excuse and left them together.

That was the beginning. His carriage was at the house every day. He took her out for drives in the country, to luncheon, to dinner. He dined with us.

'You must put up with our simple ways, cher Alphonse . . .' (They were on Christian name terms by this time.) 'Once I could have entertained you in a manner worthy of you. It is different now . . .'

She looked so pathetic and helpless that Alphonse's ever-ready chivalry must certainly come rushing to the fore.

I liked him. In spite of his bombast and flaunting of his worldly goods, there was a simplicity about him. His enthusiasm for his work, his belief in himself, his dedication, his almost boyish susceptibility to my mother's beauty coupled with his obvious speculation as to how such a beautiful woman could play the gracious hostess to his clients and replace his dead wife . . . these things endeared him to me.

I think he quite liked me – when he could spare a thought from my mother.

At first my mother was a little anxious because she said I looked older than my years and that made her seem older than she was. 'And when you put on that air of knowing everything and talk in that clever-clever way, it makes you seem even older. Men don't like it, Caroline.'

'If men don't like me, I shall retaliate by not liking them,' I replied.

'That's no way to talk. But if you could wear your hair down . . . instead of piled up in that ridiculous way . . .'

'Mama, I am nineteen years old, and there is no way of making me less.'

'But it makes *me* seem old.'

'You'll never be old.'

She was somewhat mollified, and as Monsieur Foucard did not seem to be aware of my mature looks, she decided to forget them. She tripped about the house now. There was no talk of illness; she even gave up the afternoon rest. The new excitement in her life did her more good than all the ice-pads and lotions and creams for her skin. She glowed.

Christmas came. Most of the entertaining was done by the Dubussons. They had the space and were delighted to play hosts. They loved romance and it was clear that this was brewing between the affluent Monsieur Foucard and the very beautiful Madame Tressidor. The Claremonts were delighted because it was in their territory that the important Monsieur Foucard had found his contentment.

I don't think any of us were surprised when the announcement was made.

Monsieur Foucard delivered a long speech telling the company that he had been a lonely man since he had become a widower and now he had been given a new lease of life. He would be lonely no longer for Madame Tressidor had paid him the supreme honour of promising to become his wife.

There was great rejoicing throughout the village, and nowhere more than in our house.

My mother was in a state of perpetual excitement. She talked incessantly of Alphonse's establishment in Paris and his house in the country near Lyons. He travelled about the country a good deal on business, and she would go with him.

'Bless him, he says he will not let me out of his sight!'

Everton was already talking about the Paris shops.

'They are the leaders in fashion, Madame, say what you will. No others can compete. I shall study them and we shall choose the very best.'

'Oh, Caroline,' cried my mother, 'I am so happy. Dear Alphonse! He has rescued me. I declare I could not have gone on much longer. I was getting to the end of my tether. It won't be a grand wedding. Neither of us wants that. After all, it's not the first time for either of us. There will be a great deal of entertaining later. It's so fascinating . . . all that perfume.'

'Mama,' I said, 'I am delighted to see you so happy.'

'There is so much to do. I shall keep on this house until I go to Paris. Alphonse thinks we should be married there. What a joy to escape from all this . . . squalor.'

'It's hardly that. It's really a very charming house.'

'Squalor compared with what I had.'

'Everton will go with you?'

'Of course. How could I do without Everton?'

'And Marie . . . and Jacques . . . they more or less go with the house. I hope the Dubussons will find good tenants.'

'Of course they will.' She glanced sideways at me. 'I suppose you will go and stay with Cousin Mary?'

I couldn't resist teasing her a little. 'Cousin Mary is not really related to me, is she? She is Robert Tressidor's cousin and he has made it clear that I am no connection of his.'

She was dismayed. 'Oh! But you wanted to go!'

I laughed and could not stop myself saying: 'You want me to go to Cousin Mary, don't you, Mama . . . *now*.'

'It will do you good and you liked it there. You were so eager to go a little while ago.'

'Yes, as eager as you were to keep me here then and as eager as you are for me to go now.'

She looked stunned.

'I do believe you are jealous, Caroline. Oh, fancy that! My own daughter!'

'No, Mama,' I said, 'I am not jealous. I do not envy you one little bit. I am delighted that you have found Monsieur Foucard. And I shall go to Cousin Mary.'

She laughed a little slyly. 'You'll be able to renew your friendship with that man.'

'You mean Paul Landower?'

She nodded. 'Well, you liked him. I must say he went off very abruptly. He's not a bit like Alphonse.'

'Not a bit,' I agreed.

She smiled complacently. Life was working out well for her.

I could understand her gratitude to Alphonse. I had to admit I shared it. Alphonse was not only my mother's benefactor; he was mine also.

Although everything was working out so satisfactorily, it was not until Easter that the marriage took place. There was a great deal to arrange. Shopping to be done; a visit to Paris for my mother and Everton where they could shop to their hearts' contentment.

I did not accompany them to Paris but remained in the house. There was a certain amount of packing to be done and every day when I woke up it was with the hope that Paul would come. I was indulging in my usual daydreams. I had let myself imagine that he would ride to the house one day and would tell me that he had come back to see me

219

because he had been unable to stay away. I believed that he had been on the point of saying something important to me when he had left – but for some reason had refrained from doing so.

Perhaps he had thought our acquaintance was too brief. He could not think I was too young now. So I let myself dream.

Therefore I was glad to stay in the house while my mother went to Paris. If he should return I must be there.

The spring had come, and I must say a rather regretful farewell to all the friends I had made. The kind Dubussons, the Claremonts who were so grateful to us for providing their greatest and most important business associate with such joy, to Marie with her memories of *le petit soldat* and Jacques who had still not succeeded in persuading his widow.

I was sorry to leave them and yet I was longing for complete freedom. I was looking forward to arriving at the station and finding the trap waiting for me. It all came back so vividly – the winding lanes, the lodge with the thatched roof and garden full of flowers and beehives, and Cousin Mary with her cool but staunch affection and her common sense. I wanted to see Jago again – and more than anything, I wanted to renew my exciting friendship with Paul Landower.

I had written to Cousin Mary and told her that my mother was about to get married. She wrote back with enthusiasm. I must come as soon as I could.

I had also written to Olivia.

Her wedding would soon take place and she hinted that she would be very happy if I came. But that was something I could not do. Since Paul had come back into my life I felt less bitter about Jeremy – but I did not think I could face seeing him married to my sister.

Olivia understood. Her letters were cautious. She did not want to say too much about her happiness, but it shone through. I sincerely hoped that she would not be disillusioned, but I did not see how she could fail to be.

I went to Paris for my mother's wedding and I stayed in a hotel with her and Everton for a few days, as Alphonse thought that my mother should not be under his roof until after the ceremony.

Alphonse had not exaggerated; there was no doubt that he was a very wealthy man. As for my mother, she looked younger and more beautiful every day. She was now attired like a lady of fashion, and Alphonse was so proud of her that I hoped he would never discover her somewhat shallow and selfish nature.

I decided that I would leave France the day after the ceremony although Alphonse said the house was at my disposal for as long as I wished; and if at any time I wanted to make my home with them, I was welcome.

I thought that very generous of him and told him so.

'My dear, you are the daughter of my dearest wife. This is your home.'

I told him he was charming and I meant it. And I marvelled at my mother's good fortune.

They went to Italy for their honeymoon. I saw them off on the train, my mother attracting glances of admiration from passers-by and Everton struggling with all the band-boxes, feverishly counting the cases, as happy as my mother to say goodbye to what they called penury.

Affluence suited them both.

I would cross the Channel and take the night train to Cornwall.

At last I was on my way.

The Lost Illusion

Seated in the train, watching the countryside rushing past, it was inevitable that I should recall that other occasion. It all came back so vividly. I could almost see Miss Bell sitting opposite me, making sure that I should profit from everything which came my way. I even remembered the two ladies who had left us at Plymouth although I had forgotten what they looked like.

I could remember so clearly that apprehension, that bewilderment, the terrifying experience of being wrenched away from all that was familiar, and being thrust without much warning into a new life. I could laugh now at my fears, of Cousin Mary the ogress, the harpy, who had turned out to be so different from my imaginings.

Crossing the Brunel bridge, looking down at the ships below, I was seeing those two, Paul and Jago, and laughing to myself at the memory of Miss Bell who had disapproved of their addressing us. That was the beginning, I thought.

When I alighted there was Joe waiting for me in the trap just as he had five years before.

'My patience me,' was his greeting, 'I wouldn't have known 'ee, Miss Caroline. You'm grown a bit since I last did see 'ee.'

'It's the usual thing, you know,' I replied. '*You* haven't changed a bit.'

'A few more of the white hairs, Miss Caroline, a wrinkle or two, I shouldn't wonder. Travelling alone this time you be. Last time it was that governess woman. A bit of a tartar, she was.'

'As you say, Joe, I've grown up.'

Then we were rattling along. No need to warn me this

time of the 'bony' road. I knew it well. Everything was agreeably familiar.

I said: 'It looks exactly the same.'

'Nothing much changed down here, Miss Caroline.'

'People change.'

'Oh . . . ah! They do grow older.'

'More white hairs, more wrinkles,' I said.

'You get along with 'ee, Miss Caroline.' He began to laugh. 'My missus was saying Miss Tressidor be right glad you'm coming.'

'Oh did she? That's a nice welcome.'

'She took to you, Miss Tressidor did. My missus says t'aint right for women to be all alone in this world. They want a husband and children . . . that's what they do want. So my missus says.'

'She should know, having acquired both.'

'Well, yes, Miss Caroline, there be our Amy married to the wheelwright over Bolsover way and our Willy he's doing well at Squire Trevithick's place near Launceston. Then there's our Jimmy who went out to Australia . . . caused us a bit of trouble, our Jimmy did.'

'You can't expect everything to work out smoothly, can you?'

' 'Tis something a man looks for, and I sometimes says to my missus, "Well, there be Amy and Willy . . . and we don't see so much of them . . . and there be Jimmy in Australia." And there's my missus herself . . . She keeps a tight hand on me. Sometimes I says to her, "Maybe the old maids 'as the right idea." That's if they're placed comfortable like Miss Tressidor.'

'People make their own way in life,' I said. 'The art is to be content with what you have.'

I thought I sounded just like Miss Bell.

Then I laughed and went on: 'This is a very serious conversation, Joe. What's been happening here at Lancarron?'

'There's been tidy changes at Landower. The family be back there now.'

'Yes, I heard. What changes, Joe?'

'Well, smart as a new pin, that's what. My patience me, there was workmen there all over the place . . . on the roof . . . banging and scraping. Nothing much wrong with Landower Hall now, I can tell 'ee. The old gentleman died, you know. That must be well nigh a year ago. But he saw the place righted afore he went, which made his passing easy, they say. And Mr Paul, he be the master now. Oh, there's changes, I can tell 'ee.'

'For the better, obviously.'

'You could say that and all . . . There be unease, Miss Caroline, on an estate what's going downhill. Don't I know it? And it was like that . . . for years it was like that. Not now, though. Mind you, they'm on their toes. It were different with the old gentleman . . . that it were. It were the tables with him . . . gambling the night away. That and the wine and the women, they do say. There's been wildness at Landower. My gran'fer could tell some tales and he did and all. That Mr Jago now.'

'What of Mr Jago? I remember him well. He was only a boy when I was here before.'

'He be a man now all right.' Joe started to chuckle. 'Well, least said soonest mended.'

Before I could probe further we had come to the lodge house.

There it was, the same as ever, the thatched roof, the neat garden, the flowers and, of course, the bees.

And there was Jamie McGill – plaid cap, plaid breeches and a game-keeper type of coat edged with leather.

His face lit up with pleasure when he saw me.

'Miss Caroline!' he said.

'Oh, Jamie, it's good to see you. Is all going well?'

'Indeed it is, Miss Caroline. I heard you were coming and pleased I am.'

'Did you tell the bees?'

'They knew something was in the air. They're as pleased as I am.'

'I hadn't expected a welcome from them!'

'They know. They have their likes and dislikes and you're one of their likes.'

'Jamie, I shall come and call . . . soon.'

'I'll look forward to that with pleasure, Miss Caroline.'

The trap moved on down the drive.

'A strange fellow he be, Jamie McGill,' mused Joe. 'My missus says she reckons something happened to him. Crossed in love, she reckons.'

'Well, he seems happy enough, so I expect that happened a long time ago.'

'There with all them bees . . . and the animals too. He's always got some creature there . . . something that's got hurt and he's putting to rights.'

'I like Jamie.'

'They all like Jamie, but my missus says 'tain't natural for a man. He ought to have a wife and children.'

'Your wife is a firm believer in marriage and all it entails,' I said. 'Oh . . . and there's the house . . . just as I remember it.'

I felt overcome by emotion as we passed under the gatehouse and rattled into the courtyard.

The door was opened almost immediately by one of the maids. Betty, I remembered.

'Oh, Miss Caroline, there you be. We've been waiting for 'ee. Miss Tressidor do say you'm to be took right up to her room, soon as you come. Bring Miss Caroline's bag to her room, Joe, and I'll take you to Miss Tressidor, Miss Caroline.'

I went into the hall. Cousin Mary was at the top of the stairs.

'Caroline, my dear,' she cried, rushing down.

I ran to her and we met at the bottom of the staircase and hugged each other.

'Well, well,' she said, 'at last. I thought you'd never come to see me. How are you? Well, I see. My word, you've grown. Had a good journey? Are you hungry? Of course you must be. You're here, at last!'

'Oh, Cousin Mary, it's good to be here.'

'Come along. What's it to be first? Refreshment, eh? What do you feel like? There's a good hour to dinner. They could put it forward. Perhaps just a snack to be getting on with.'

'No, thanks very much, Cousin Mary. I'll wait till dinner. I'm too excited to think about eating, anyway.'

'Then come and sit down just for a minute. Then I'll take you up and you can wash before supper. I expect that's what you'd like, eh? My word, you have shot up. Still, I'd have known you anywhere.'

'It's five years, Cousin Mary.'

'Too long. Too long. Come and sit down. Your room's the same one. Thought you'd like that. How did you come . . . all the way from France, eh?'

'It was a long journey. Fortunately I was in Paris, which is not so bad as being right down in the south. The journey from the south to Paris took almost the whole of a day.'

'And your mother married again! A kind of fairy prince, I gather.'

'A rather elderly one, but very nice.'

'Lucky for us all! If she hadn't, I expect you'd still be there.'

'I had made up my mind that I was coming, but it wasn't going to be easy unless . . .'

'I know. The last time she was ill.'

'She really was.'

'H'm. Convenient sort of illness, perhaps. Never mind. She's happy with her prince.'

'Honeymooning in Italy, and then they will return to his mansion in Paris and his château in the country. It is exactly what she needed.'

'She has become a lady of the French nobility.'

'Not exactly the nobility. He is a prince of industry.'

'Which probably means that his fortune is more sound. Well, let's leave your mother to her good fortune and think about us.'

'I'm longing to hear everything.'

'All is well here. The estate is flourishing. I see to that.' She glanced at the watch pinned on her blouse. 'I think, my dear, that you should wash and change now and then we can talk to our hearts' content this evening. Betty will be there to help you unpack. How's that? I just wanted a brief word and a look at you. We've got lots of time ahead of us.'

I followed her up the stairs, through the gallery. No longer my ancestors, I thought, and felt a faint regret.

There was my familiar room. I went to the window and looked out across the parkland to the hills in the distance. I could not see Landower, but it was close and the thought of that sent my heart racing with excitement.

'Betty?' called Cousin Mary and Betty came in.

'Help Miss Caroline unpack,' she went on. 'She will tell you where everything has to go. Will you come down when you are ready, Caroline?'

I was very happy. This was a wonderful welcome. Cousin Mary was just as I remembered her and my affection for her was growing with every minute.

I was happy to be back.

Betty was hanging up my things. 'Where do 'ee want this, Miss Caroline? Shall I be filling these drawers with your linen? Here. Let me hang that up. Miss Tressidor says if you haven't enough space you could use the next room. There be a big court cupboard there.'

'I have heaps of room, thanks, Betty.'

'Everybody be very glad you'm back, Miss Caroline. They do all remember 'ee as a little 'un.'

'I was fourteen when I came here. I don't think I was all that little.'

'You be a grown-up young lady now.'

I thanked her when she had finished and she reminded me that dinner would be served in about half an hour. 'Do you remember the dining-room, Miss Caroline?'

'I do, Betty. As soon as I entered the house I felt as though I had not been away.'

Cousin Mary was waiting for me in the dining-room. The

table was elaborately laid. I glanced at the tapestries on the walls and through the window to the courtyard.

'Come and sit down, my dear,' said Cousin Mary. 'We'll have a long chat this evening. Though I expect you'll want to retire early tonight. You must say when you want to go to bed. We've lots of time in front of us.'

I told her how happy I was to be here and while we were eating we talked of France and the events which had led up to my going there. I found I could talk of Jeremy Brandon without too much emotion.

'I suppose I should have gone to Olivia's wedding,' I said. 'It was cowardly not to.'

'There are times when it is better to be a little cowardly. I don't suppose the bridegroom would have been too happy to see you there – nor, I imagine, would Olivia.'

'You don't know Olivia. She is guileless. It comes of being so sweet-natured herself that she thinks everyone else is the same. She really believes that Jeremy was not influenced by the money – simply because he tells her he wasn't.'

'Sometimes people who don't ask too many questions are happier than those who do.'

'In any case, she is married now.'

'He is no longer of importance to you?'

I hesitated. It was impossible to be anything but frank with Cousin Mary.

'I was so eager to escape from the bondage of Miss Bell and the strict rules of the household. I was hurt because I sensed the hostility of the man I thought was my father. Jeremy was romantic and handsome and charming . . . and it was easy to believe he loved me. So I felt the same about him. Why I felt the same I am not quite sure. I think I was ready and eager to fall in love.'

'What they call being "in love with love".'

'Something like that.'

'And now . . .' I could not say, 'When I met Paul Landower again I was glad I was not married to Jeremy.' Did I really feel so strongly about Paul, did I want to escape

228

from the humiliation Jeremy had imposed upon me, was I still 'in love with love'? I supposed all people's feelings should be subject to analysis. Mine more than most.

I told her about the meeting with Alphonse and how he had immediately fallen under my mother's spell. There would be no questioning in that case. As long as he could keep her in luxury she would admire him. Contrary to the rules of morality, my mother was going to be the one who lived happily ever after.

The meal was over. I said I did not want to go to bed just yet.

'Let's go into the winter parlour. We'll have a little port wine. Yes, Caroline, I insist. It will make you sleep.'

We left the dining-room and went into the little room nearby. It was cosy and I remembered sitting there with Cousin Mary in the past. She took the port wine from the cupboard there and poured some into two glasses.

'There,' she said. 'Now we can talk without servants hovering.'

I said that nothing much had changed here. Old Joe was still being commanded by his tyrant missus, and Jamie McGill was the same with his bees. 'It all feels as though I've never been away.'

'Oh, there have been vast changes. You'll discover.'

I didn't want to broach the subject of the Landowers. I thought I might betray too much eagerness for information which would not escape the discerning eyes of Cousin Mary.

'So the estate is flourishing?'

'Oh yes, that's one of the things I want to talk to you about . . . but perhaps not tonight.'

'But you've whetted my curiosity. What about the estate?'

'It's just that I thought you might learn a little about it. You might help me.'

'Do you need help, then?'

'Could do with it. I just thought you might find it interesting.'

'I'm sure I should.'

'It's too involved for tonight. We'll talk about a lot of things tomorrow.'

'When you said there were vast changes . . .'

'I wasn't thinking of Tressidor so much as Landower.'

'Yes, Joe said something. How is . . . er . . . Jago?'

'Oh, Jago. He was a special friend of yours, wasn't he? He's become the Lothario of the neighbourhood. There are tales about Jago.'

'He must be twenty-one . . . or two. Is he married?'

'Oh no. But some say he ought to be. They say he'll go the way of his father. I don't know about the gambling, but he's certainly fond of the ladies. One hears these things and I'm not averse to a bit of gossip, particularly when it's about my neighbours and old rivals.'

'Does the feud still exist, then?'

'Oh no, no. It's not a feud. It hasn't been for years. We're very good friends on the surface. But the rivalry exists. In the old days when Jonas Landower was gambling away the estate we were far in advance and the winners. It's different now. Jago would never have done it. The new affluence would soon have disappeared under him, I'm sure. They say he has a mistress in Plymouth to whom he is quite devoted, but he doesn't marry her and he's not averse to sporting with the village girls.'

'I remember him well. He was an amusing companion.'

'He's all of that still. He goes around with a song on his lips distributing that indestructible charm to all beholders, particularly if they are young and personable. You won't want to get caught up with him. You won't. You're far too sensible.'

'I've learned a lesson, Cousin Mary.'

'Lessons are a blessing, providing one profits from them.'

'I don't think that indestructible charm would touch me.'

'No . . . perhaps not. Jenny Granger, one of the farmer's daughters, is making him pay for her baby . . . and it is said that it is possible he is not the father. Apparently there was a choice and she settled on him because she thought that would be more rewarding.'

'A risk a gentleman of his kind must take.'

'Now Paul, he's of quite a different genre.'

'I suppose it would be too much of a drain on the family fortunes to have two like Jago in it,' I said, trying to speak lightly.

'Paul is a very serious man. I have become rather specially friendly with him. There are visits . . . occasional ones . . . but neighbourly visits nevertheless.'

'That's interesting,' I said, hoping my voice did not sound too unnatural.

'I have a confession to make,' she went on.

'Really?'

'Yes. He was going to the South of France . . . Paul Landower, I mean. And I asked him to look you up.'

'Oh!'

'I was worried about your mother and wondering what the position really was. I felt sure she wasn't really ill but was determined to keep you there looking after her. I wanted to know because a selfish woman can chain a daughter to her side so that she has no life of her own. I talked to Paul about you and he saw the point. I said to him, "Could you call there? Go as if by chance . . . and spy out the land and then come back and let me know what's going on."'

'Oh,' I said again. 'I thought it was a chance meeting.'

'I hoped you would. I didn't want you to think I was fussing or prying. But I did want to know.'

'And what did he report?'

'Just what I thought. So you can imagine how delighted I was to hear of this Alphonse carrying off your mother to romance among the perfume bottles. You understand my feelings. Of course you do. Monsieur Alphonse is the fairy godfather to us all.'

I felt deflated. He had come because she had asked him. He had stayed so briefly. Then I thought of him, standing

231

on the balcony outside my bedroom . . . hesitating.

'Paul Landower is very shrewd,' said Cousin Mary, 'but for him there would not now be Landowers at Landower Hall. He has set everything to rights, which I am sure was always his intention.'

'He must be very gratified.'

'I gathered that you spent a little time with him.'

'Yes. We went riding in the mountains. Unfortunately I fell off my horse and we had to spend a night at the *auberge* in the mountains.'

'He didn't tell me that! A night in the *auberge* . . . with him!'

'Well, you see I was a bit bruised and shocked and they called in a doctor. He said I shouldn't make the journey back that evening.'

'I see.'

'Tell me about Landower. How did he manage to get it back in such a short time?'

'Didn't he tell you?'

'He didn't speak much about Landower.'

'Oh well, the Arkwrights bought the place. You knew that.'

'Oh yes. You must have told me at the time. There was a question of it before I went away.'

'There was an accident and the daughter hurt her back.'

'Not seriously, I believe.'

'Well, it hasn't prevented her having a child. There's a dear little boy, Julian.'

'Oh, she married then?'

'But of course she married. That's how it all came about. It was the best solution. Old Arkwright would never have made a squire. There's more to it than brass, as he would put it. He had the money to restore the house, to repair the tenants' cottages . . . but he was no squire. They wouldn't accept him with his northern accent and his northern ways, and he was shrewd enough to realize that. They preferred gambling old Landower any day . . . or Paul, who can strike fear into them, or Jago, who goes round seducing their daughters. They're squiral qualities. They wouldn't stand for the stern, down-to-earth, common sense of the northerner.'

'I should have thought they would have been glad if he repaired their cottages.'

' "He bain't no squire" . . . that was the tale wherever you went. They were against me for being a woman. "Tain't natural," they used to say. But I soon showed them it was. Whether Arkwright would have managed to convince them in time, I don't know, but the opportunity came and he was too hard-headed a man to refuse it.'

'What of the daughter, Miss Arkwright? I'm glad she wasn't crippled.'

'Oh no, they thought the injuries would be worse than they were. She said she had seen a vision up there . . . ghosts. She was nervous and I don't know how she felt about living in the house. But her father managed to convince her that she'd imagined the whole thing. Trick of light and all that. She stuck out that she'd seen something and the place has an even greater reputation now for being haunted than it had before.'

'Still, the Arkwrights bought the house. And the Landowers went into the farmhouse, I suppose?'

'For a while, yes. I didn't think they'd stay there long. And they didn't. It seemed the best solution. It might have been Jago, but that wouldn't have done so well, and I doubt Mr Arkwright would have accepted that. He wanted the elder . . . the serious one, for his son-in-law.'

'His son-in-law!'

'Didn't Paul tell you he'd married Gwennie Arkwright and that brought the property back to the Landowers?'

I hoped she did not notice my reaction. I was sitting up straight in my chair and I knew the colour had drained out of my face.

'No – no.' My voice sounded as though it came from a long way off. 'He – didn't say anything about that.'

I could not believe it and I was fighting hard to hide my emotions.

'You're tired,' said Cousin Mary. 'I shouldn't be keeping you up.'

'Yes . . . I am tired. It comes over one suddenly. I didn't notice how tired I was . . .'

'Well, come up to bed.'

'Just a little longer, Cousin Mary. It's so interesting. There was a marriage, then . . .'

'Well, it's quite three years ago. Yes, it must be. I think little Julian is two.'

'And there is a child?'

'Everyone said how sensible it was. Even old Arkwright. He died not long ago. A contented man, they said. It was soon after Jonas went, and the two men got on quite well at the end. Mr Arkwright used to say he'd made his pile of brass and had used it to buy an estate and the standing he'd always wanted for his daughter. Brass wasn't good enough without breeding, but he always used to say, "What you don't have, you buy. You've got the brass, you've got what it needs." I liked the old man. I became quite friendly with him. He was a man of the people – though brass-coated, he said. He had a colourful style of language; he was out-spoken . . . and straight. I wouldn't be surprised if he was the one who put forward the proposition. I could imagine his saying, "Marry Gwennie and the house will be hers, which means yours, and it's for the children Gwennie will have." His triumph was supreme when Julian was born, and he told me once that the best thing he'd ever done – apart from going into the building trade at the right moment – was to buy Landower and marry his daughter to the man who would have owned it if his family had known as much about making brass as the Arkwrights did. "It's an unbeatable combination – brass and breeding, and that's what my grandchildren will have." '

'I can see it worked out very satisfactorily for the Landowers.'

'Yes. They're back in the old house with the money to settle Jonas's debts, to restore the house and keep it up. A good stroke of business, wouldn't you say? Everyone was happy. All the people around in the cottages. They're real snobs, Caroline . . . much more aware of class than we are. They didn't want the Arkwrights for their squires. They wanted the old reprobate Landowers . . . and they got it. Julian is a regular little Landower by all accounts. Like a fairy story, don't you think?'

'Yes,' I said, 'a fairy story.'

'Well, I filled you in with the picture. That's what's been happening at Lancarron. So now we have Landowers back at Landower and Paul will see that the Arkwright brass is not frittered away. The estate is now as healthy as mine, and the rivalry to excel each other is once more rampant. Come on, my dear. To bed.'

She kissed me goodnight at my bedroom door.

I was glad to be alone. I felt bruised and humiliated. It was like reading that letter from Jeremy all over again.

I shut the door and leaned against it.

What a fool I had been! Once more I had let my dreams take possession of my life. All men were the same. They looked to the main chance – and they took it.

I thought of Jeremy holding me in his arms, kissing me passionately, telling me how much he loved me. I thought of Paul Landower standing outside my window. Suppose he had come in! How dared he! He would dare much, I knew. Could it really have been that he was contemplating coming in, taking advantage of my gullibility? Had I betrayed myself so much?

And all the time he was married – married to someone who could give him Landower – just as Jeremy was married to Olivia who could give him her fortune!

The pattern was the same. That was how men were. At least the Jagos of the world were honest. I thought of Robert Tressidor, the good man, the philanthropist. How shocked he had been by my mother's liaison with Captain Carmichael. He had turned her out of his house and turned his back on me. And all the time he was sneaking off to indulge his sexual appetites with prostitutes! And Jeremy Brandon had loved me most passionately until he found I had no fortune, when he turned his affection to my sister who had. And now Paul Landower. He had not attempted to make love to me, it was true, but somehow he had conveyed something . . . Or was I so foolishly fascinated by him that I had imagined it? He had gone away and left me with my dreams and hopes. I had not cared that he had no fortune. I had none either. I would have been prepared to live in a farmhouse . . . anywhere with him.

I wanted to cover my face with my hands to hide the shame I felt. I wanted to weep, but I had no tears. I felt my heart was bruised far more than my body had been by my fall in the mountains – and the scars that resulted were deeper and would never be cured.

I went to the window and looked out. Somewhere out there lay that great mansion which was more important to him than anything on earth. And somewhere far away Olivia and Jeremy were together, making love possibly . . . and what he really loved was the fortune which would be his. Such men do not love women – they love possessions.

'I hate men,' I said aloud. 'They are all alike.'

And, as I had when Jeremy had wounded me so deeply, I found solace in hating.

During the night, when I lay sleepless in spite of my tiredness after the journey, I told myself that I would not stay here. I would go right away. But where? Where could I live? I had no home. Alphonse had said my home could be with him and my mother. No, that would not do. Olivia had said there would always be a home for me with her. What! Shared with Jeremy Brandon, my one-time false lover! Cousin Mary implied that she would like me to stay with her. I had wanted this until I had discovered that Paul had married in the same manner as Jeremy had.

I can't stay here, I told myself. Yet in a way I wanted to. I wanted to show him my contempt. I wanted him to know that even though I had not the slightest interest in him, which was quite false, I despised him, which was a contradiction. What I must show was my indifference to him, my unawareness of him.

That would be difficult. It would be better to go away. But where?

All my joy in my return was gone. I must not let Cousin Mary realize this. She was so very pleased to see me; she wanted me to stay. I came back to the perpetual question. How could I? Yet where else could I go?

I started to make plans. I would get some sort of post. What post? I had gone into all this before. A governess to unruly children? Companion to some demanding old woman? What could one do? Why were women never trained to be independent? Why was it presumed they were worthy only to serve the needs of men?

Men are all the same, I told myself. They may seem charming but their charm is superficial and they use it to get what they want. All they think of is what is best for themselves.

I hate them all. Never will I allow myself to be deceived again. If ever I have a chance of showing my contempt for them, I shall seize it.

In the morning, in spite of an uneasy night, I felt better. There is something therapeutic about the daylight. One sees clearly that during the hours of darkness one has been a prey to one's emotions, unreasoning, letting one's heart, as they say, rule one's head.

Why should I feel so angry with Paul Landower? What had he done to me? Nothing. Except fascinate me – yet he had made no attempt to do so. It had just happened. It was true he had stood outside my bedroom door. Might it have been that he was just looking in to see if I were all right? After all, I had taken a nasty toss and one could never be sure what effect that would have. Had I misconstrued his intentions? How many times had I been wrong in the past? I had been a fool to imagine that he wanted to be with me, to be my lover. Because I had been attracted by him, it did not mean that he had been by me. And yet . . .

I despised him, of course, for selling himself to the

highest bidder. But wasn't I jumping to conclusions? Gwennie Arkwright might be a fascinating siren. I did not think so. I had met her on two occasions – once in the inn with Jago and once in the gallery when I had helped to frighten her. I was pulled up sharply at the thought of that. She had more reason to dislike me than I had to feel contempt for her husband.

I was being foolish again. I had allowed my dreams to take possession of reality once more.

Cousin Mary came in while I was having breakfast.

'Is that all you're having – coffee and toast!' she cried.

I said I was not very hungry.

'You're still feeling the effects of that travelling. Have an easy day. What would you like to do? You tell me. Are you still keen on riding? Of course you must be.'

'Yes, very. But I didn't have much chance in France. I only rode once.'

'That was when you had your fall.'

'Yes. It was when . . .'

'When Paul Landower visited you.'

'He hired the horses and we went into the mountains.'

'We haven't any mountains here. Only Brown Willy, and he won't match up to the Alps Maritimes.'

I laughed. It was good to be with her. She was so matter of fact, so full of normality. She was no dreamer.

I said impulsively: 'It's good to be with you, Cousin Mary.'

'I was hoping you'd feel that. Caroline, I want to talk to you very seriously.'

'What, now?'

'No time like the present. Have you thought about doing anything –'

'You mean . . . earning a living?'

She nodded. 'I know how you're placed. I got it all from Imogen. My cousin left you nothing, but you have a little from your maternal grandfather.'

'Fifty pounds a year.'

'Not exactly affluence.'

'No. I have been thinking a great deal. But then I was with my mother and it seemed I might have to stay. Alphonse very kindly offered me a home with them, but . . . Olivia too.'

'If I know anything about you, you're a young woman who wants her independence, are you not? Of course you are. Therefore I expect you will want to *do* something.'

'I could be a governess, I suppose. A companion to someone.'

'Ugh!' said Cousin Mary.

'I quite agree.'

'Definitely unsuitable. Of course it is.'

'When I passed Jamie McGill's lodge I thought of having a little cottage and keeping bees. Can one make money by selling honey?'

'Very little, I imagine. Oh no, Caroline, that's not for you. You say you've been thinking. I've been thinking, too.'

'About me?'

'Yes, about you. Now, I'm beginning to feel my age a bit. Not so spry as I used to be. A touch of what they call "the screws", meaning the old rheumatics in the joints. It slows you down a bit. I've thought of asking you many times . . . but it seemed you'd marry, which I suppose would have been the best thing for you if it had been the right man.'

'Why, Cousin Mary, you follow the general trend of thinking. The best thing a woman can do is pander to the needs of some man. Why shouldn't she keep her independence? You have done so . . . very successfully.'

She looked at me sharply. She said: 'Don't brood on that defaulter. Congratulate yourself rather. There are men and men. I know very well that a woman wants to choose very carefully and it often happens that she makes the wrong choice. I agree with you that it's better never to marry than to marry the wrong one. But if you could find that paragon of a man and have children of your own . . . well, that's about the best thing, I reckon. But don't set too great a store on it. The world's full of good things, and independence and freedom to be yourself is one of them. And in marriage you have to give that up to a certain extent. Make the most of what you've got. That's what I've always done and it hasn't turned out too badly. Now listen to what I have to say. I want you to help me. I want you to learn about the estate. There's a great deal to do. There are all the tenants to look after. Jim Burrows is a good manager, but it's the landowners who set the pace. I've always taken a personal interest. That's what was wrong at Landower . . . until now. I'd like you to learn about things, get to know the tenants, to write letters for me . . . and generally learn all about it. I'll pay you a salary.'

'Oh no, Cousin Mary. Certainly not.'

'Oh yes. It has to be on a business footing. Just as if I were employing you. But I shouldn't let it be known just yet that I was doing so. People are so inquisitive . . . they talk too much. You'd find it interesting. You'd earn some money. It would be more profitable than keeping bees, I assure you. Believe me, you'd find it very interesting. Now what's it to be?'

'I – I'm overwhelmed, Cousin Mary. I think you're doing this to help me.'

'I'm doing it to help myself. I can tell you *I* want help . . . but not from an outsider. I think you're cut out for the job. So that's settled.'

'You are so good to me.'

'What nonsense! I'm good to myself. You and I are two sensible women, are we not? Of course we are. I can't stand any other sort.'

'I had thought that I shouldn't stay here . . . that I ought . . .'

'Give it a chance,' she said. 'I shall never forget your woebegone little face when we said goodbye last time. I said to myself, "There's one who's got a feel for this place." And that's what it takes. It will be a great relief for me to have you with me.'

'Well, I don't want to be paid.'

'Now I'm beginning to believe you're not so sensible as I

240

thought after all. Didn't someone say the labourer was worthy of his hire? You'll be paid, Caroline Tressidor, and no nonsense about that. Why is it people always get on their high horse when it's a question of money? What's wrong with money? It's necessary. We can't go back to bartering goods, can we? Of course we can't. You shall be paid. Not excessively, I promise you. Just what I would pay someone I called in to give me a hand. And with that, and what you've got, you'll be an independent young lady. And there are no contracts or anything like that. You come and go as you please.'

I felt the tears coming to my eyes. It was strange that I, who had hardly shed a tear over Jeremy's perfidy and when confronted with the avarice of Paul, now wanted to weep for the goodness of Cousin Mary.

I said rather tremulously: 'When do I start?'

'There's no time like the present,' said Cousin Mary. 'Get into your riding things and I'll take you round and show you something of the estate this morning.'

Jamie McGill was in his garden as we rode out and he came to greet us.

'Lovely morning, Jamie,' said Cousin Mary.

'Aye, Miss Tressidor, Miss Caroline. It's a fine morning.'

'Bees all happy?'

'That they are. They're glad Miss Caroline is back.'

'It's very nice of them to be so welcoming,' I said.

'Bees know,' he told me gravely.

'There you are!' said Cousin Mary. 'If the bees approve of you, you're the right sort. That's so, is it not, Jamie? Of course it is.'

He stood with his cap in his hand while the light breeze ruffled his sandy hair.

'Poor Jamie,' said Cousin Mary as we rode on. 'Though perhaps I should say, Lucky Jamie. I've never known anyone who has that complete contentment. It's due to coming to terms with life, I suppose. Jamie has what he wants. He doesn't look beyond that. A roof over his head,

241

enough to eat, and his friends about him . . . chief of which are the bees.'

'Perhaps the simple life is the best.'

'There's a lot to be said for simplicity. Well, here we are. These woods along here are the dividing line between Tressidor and Landower. There used to be conflict in the old days. Whose woods were they? Now they're a sort of no-man's-land. I would first like to call on the Jeffs. Their cottage is decidedly damp and Jim Burrows thinks something ought to be done about it . . . I shall introduce you as my cousin's daughter,' she went on. 'That's what we thought you were. No point in going into complicated relationships.'

I said: 'It's odd to think that we are not related. I continued to think of you as Cousin Mary even after . . .'

'I never did believe in all that nonsense about blood being thicker than water. Who was it said we choose our friends but our relations are thrust upon us? How true! I never thought much of my cousin Robert, nor his sister Imogen for that matter. However, my cousin's daughter you stay. How's that? All right, eh?'

'If it makes it easier.'

'Just at first, anyway.'

We were received with pleasure by the Jeffs.

'I remember Miss Caroline,' said Mrs Jeffs. 'It must be well nigh . . . well, bless me, if I can remember how many years since she were here.'

'It's five,' I told her.

'My word, you've shot up since then. I remember how you used to ride round with Mr Jago.'

'Fancy your remembering.'

'Oh yes. That were the time when there was trouble up at Landower. I do recall how Jane Bowers and her husband Jim were that worried as to what was going to happen to the estate. My patience me, there was rumours going round. There's been Landowers up at the house as far back as anyone could remember. Jim Bowers's grandfather and great-grandfather . . . they'd all been on Landower property. Praise God, 'tis all well now and Landowers be where they belong to be and Landower tenants be safe in their homes.'

Cousin Mary discussed the damp at some length with Mr and Mrs Jeffs and when we left them and were riding alone in silence I thought of Mrs Jeffs's words about people being safe in their homes. So the marriage had brought some good to others as well as to the Landowers. He wouldn't have been thinking of that, though. He would merely have been considering what he would gain.

I felt the bitterness rising and I did my best to suppress it. I did not want Cousin Mary to know that I had been so foolish as to look on Paul Landower as someone very important to me.

We were soon calling at one of the other cottages to talk of further matters, and from there we set out for the farms.

As we were riding home Cousin Mary said: 'That's one of the most important parts of the job – to get to know the tenants. They're hardworking people for the most part and many of them work on the farms. I like to feel that they are comfortable and happy. That is how to make a contented estate and you can't have a prosperous one without that contentment.'

As we were riding through the gateway we met a woman coming out.

She seemed vaguely familiar.

'Oh, Miss Tressidor,' she cried. 'I was just calling on you. I see that your visitor has arrived.'

'You must come back to the house,' said Cousin Mary. 'This is Caroline Tressidor, my cousin's daughter. This is Mrs Landower, Caroline.'

I felt my heart begin to beat very fast. I could not stop myself studying her intently. She sat her horse well and her riding habit was immaculate. Her light sandy hair was visible under her riding hat; her eyes were light blue and very piercing. They were what I noticed first, for they were very lively and seemed to dart everywhere – almost avidly, as though their owner was intent on taking in every detail.

243

'Well, just for a moment,' she said. 'I just wanted to say welcome to Miss Caroline. As a matter of fact, I was calling to ask you if you would dine with us tomorrow evening.'

'That's good of you,' said Cousin Mary. 'We'd love to come, wouldn't we, Caroline? Of course we should. Ho, James,' she called to one of the grooms who was crossing the courtyard. 'Take our horses. Mrs Landower is coming in for a while.'

We dismounted and I saw that she was considerably shorter than I and I noticed – a little maliciously I admit – that she had rather a plump figure, which made her look dumpy.

'I've been showing Caroline something of the estate,' said Cousin Mary.

'Do you like the country, Miss Caroline?' she asked. I could detect the faint touch of the north in her speech and it brought back to me vividly that meeting at the inn with Jago when we had been waiting for my horse to be shod.

'Oh yes, yes, indeed I do,' I replied.

'You'll have something to drink,' put in Cousin Mary, making it a statement rather than a question.

'Thank you,' she replied.

'In the winter parlour, I think,' went on Cousin Mary. 'More cosy.'

One of the maids had heard us come in and was beginning to say, 'Mrs Landower called . . .'

'It's all right, Betsy. We were in time to catch her. Bring some wine, will you, to the winter parlour . . . and some of cook's wine biscuits.'

In the winter parlour we awaited the arrival of the wine.

'Your face seems familiar to me,' said Mrs Landower.

'Well, we did meet before. Do you remember the inn . . . before you saw the house.'

'Oh, of course. You were there with Jago. I do remember that. But you've changed so. You were only a child then.'

'I was fourteen.'

'But you've grown up a lot since.'

'Everyone here keeps telling me that.'

'It's something that happens to us all,' said Cousin Mary. The wine was brought and she poured it into glasses and I passed round the biscuits.

'Dinner, you say,' said Cousin Mary. 'That sounds delightful. I want Caroline to get to know everything that goes on here . . . quickly.'

'I was most anxious to meet her. After all, we are neighbours, aren't we? Did I see you only once? I can't believe it. You are so familiar to me . . . although you've grown so much. You'll have to meet my little boy.'

'Oh yes. Cousin Mary was telling me about him.'

'He's beautiful. They say he takes after the Landowers.' She grimaced.

'Oh,' said Cousin Mary, 'I expect he's got a bit of you in him. Perhaps he'll be like your father. Now, there's a man I respected deeply.'

'Dear old Pa,' said Gwennie Landower. 'A pity he had to go and die just when he'd got what he wanted.'

'At least he got it in time,' said Cousin Mary philosophically. 'Is your husband well?'

'Quite well, thank you.'

'And Jago?'

'Jago is always well. He's back from Plymouth. He's very anxious to see you, Miss Caroline. He was telling us how well you two got on together all those years ago. He said he wondered if you'd changed and hoped you hadn't . . . too much.'

'I shall look forward to renewing our acquaintance.'

She drained her glass.

'I should go. I only looked in to invite you. So it's all right, then? Can you come over about seven-thirty? Not a big dinner party . . . just the family. Getting neighbourly, you know. Jago said we must be the first to ask you.'

'That's appreciated, tell Jago,' said Cousin Mary.

We went out with Gwennie Landower to the courtyard and watched the groom help her into the saddle.

She lifted a gloved hand and waved as she went under the gatehouse.

As we returned to the house Cousin Mary said: 'Well, she is determined to be friendly.'

'She certainly seemed so.'

'She would want to see how you looked.'

'Why should she be so eager?'

'She likes to know everything that goes on. She's so inquisitive. It's been said that she can't keep her nose out of anything that's going on. They say that she knows which servant is courting and she can spot a baby on the way before its mother knows it's there. Our servants say she gossips with her servants. They don't like that. They expect a strict code of behaviour from employers, I can tell you. Gwennie – we always call her Gwennie – doesn't quite come up to what they think the squire's lady ought to be – any more than her father did as squire.'

'So you think she just wants to have a good look at me?'

'Oh, she likes to have people around, but I noticed she was giving special attention to you – and I think you were quite interested in her.'

'I wanted to see what Landower's benefactress was like, naturally.'

'Well, now you have. She's very pleased with herself. She got what she wanted.'

'So she is satisfied with her part of the bargain.'

'Doesn't seem any doubt of it.'

'I wonder whether he is.'

'Ah! I wonder. Well, do you want to change? You'd better have a rest after luncheon. I can see you are still rather tired. We'll talk some more tonight. You'll be completely restored tomorrow.'

'Yes,' I said. 'I must be fresh for the Landowers in the evening.'

'It will be interesting. You didn't go there before, did you?'

'Not as a guest. Jago gave me a sneak view of the place.'

'Well now you'll go in style. You'll enjoy that, I promise you.'

As I went to my room I wondered whether I should.

I was dressing for the Landower dinner party. I had slept soundly during the previous night. I must have been tired out. The day had passed quickly. I had ridden with Cousin Mary in the morning and seen a little more of the estate, and as Cousin Mary rested in the afternoon, I had sat in the garden reading a little but mostly brooding on how I should feel that evening.

I dressed with great care. I wished that Everton had been there to do my hair. I could never quite achieve the results that she had, she had said I should dress it high because of my high forehead, and it gave me added height, which I liked. I wore a cream dress with a tight bodice and very flounced skirt which had been bought in Paris for my mother's wedding. I had never before had such a dress and as it had had Everton's approval before the purchase, I felt it was the pinnacle of elegance. Moreover, I had the emerald brooch which my mother had given me as a parting gift. 'It does something for Miss Caroline' had been the comment – Everton's, of course. 'And really, Madam, it is not so much for you. The aquamarine is your stone . . . as we always said.'

And as my mother was going to be showered with jewels, she could part with the brooch without missing it, so it came to me; and Everton was right; it certainly brought out the green in my eyes.

When I looked at myself ready for departure I was struck by the brilliance of my eyes; they positively glittered. But I did look rather like a general going into battle. I intended to show Paul Landower that although I was not in the least interested in him, I despised his mercenary behaviour.

Cousin Mary had not take the same care with her appearance. I doubted she ever had.

'Goodness me,' she said when she saw me, 'you do look splendid.'

'It is a simple dinner dress really. My mother bought it for me . . . or I suppose Alphonse did . . . when we were in Paris. I had to be presentable for the wedding celebrations.'

'It's very *haute couture*. Is that what they call it? Very French too. But I doubt they'll know that in Cornwall. They'll just think you're a very elegant lady. What a lovely brooch! Our old trap seems hardly good enough.'

'It will suit me.'

'Let's get going, then. It was nice of her to ask us like this. *En famille*, as they say in France.'

I could not help being overawed as we approached the house. It looked magnificent and I remembered the first time I had seen it. The great stone walls, the battlemented tower, that fortress-like appearance – they were impressive. I could understand why a family who had owned it for generations, whose ancestors had built it, would be prepared to make great sacrifices for such a place. Perhaps it was natural that Paul had acted as he did.

We passed under an archway into the courtyard where a groom hurried forward to help us alight. A nail-studded door opened and a maid appeared.

'Will you please to come in, Miss Tressidor,' she said. 'Mrs Landower be waiting for you.'

'Thank you,' said Cousin Mary.

'I'll take the trap into the stables,' said the groom.

'Thank you, Jim.'

We went into the hall. Memories came back. I couldn't help looking up at the minstrels' gallery as our footsteps rang out on the stone-flagged floor. The rail must have been replaced. I glanced at the fireplace and the family tree which spread out over it and beyond. In the house it was even easier to understand how such a place made demands, how it would entwine itself about one's life, how it could well become of major importance.

I was making excuses for him.

The maid led us up the staircase.

'Mrs Landower is in the drawing-room,' she said.

She knocked and without waiting for a reply opened the door. I had not been in this room before. It was large and lofty; the windows were latticed and did not let in a great deal of light. I had time to notice the tapestry on the walls and the painting of some long-dead Landower over the fireplace.

Gwennie Landower came towards us.

'It's good to see you,' she said as though she meant it.

She took my hand and gazed at me. 'You look grand,' she said.

I felt embarrassed. Cousin Mary explained afterwards that in Gwennie's vocabulary 'grand' did not necessarily imply grandeur. It merely meant, 'You look very nice.'

'And you know my husband.'

He had come forward, he took my hand and held it firmly.

'How nice to see you,' he said. 'I hope you have recovered from your fall in the mountains.'

'Paul told us all about it,' said Gwennie. 'I scolded him. He was supposed to be looking after you, wasn't he? Miss Tressidor had asked him to go and see you because she was worried about you.'

'It was entirely my own fault,' I explained. 'Your husband was well ahead and we were going at a snail's pace. I was just not attending. You can't afford to do that on horseback.'

'Don't I know it! I had to learn to ride, didn't I, Paul?'

He nodded.

'I managed it, though, didn't I? Took me some time. But I thought: Well, if I'm going to be in the country I've got to be able to get about without fuss. But I was ill for a while . . . that was before I was married. I had a bad fall.'

'Oh yes,' I said quietly. 'I heard.'

'Ugh!' she shivered. 'Do you know, I can't go into that hall without looking up and wondering . . .'

'It must have been a shock.'

'Oh, here's someone you know.'

He was coming towards me. He had grown a great deal

since we had last met. He was the handsomest man I had ever seen. Tall, rather lean, with a somewhat swaggering walk. It was not that his features were perfect. His mouth was full and rather sensual; it looked as though it only knew how to smile; his heavy dark-lidded eyes, so like his brother's in shape and colour, shone with amusement as they surveyed the world; his thick dark hair grew in much the same way as Paul's; in fact they were very much alike but they seemed so different because of expression. Paul appeared to be over-serious whereas his brother looked as though he hadn't a care in the world, or if he had, refused to recognize it. He gave an impression of complete *joie de vivre*.

'It's Jago,' I said.

'It's Caroline,' he answered.

Throwing aside decorum, he put his arms round me and hugged me.

'What a delightful . . . I was going to say surprise . . . but the news of your impending arrival had already reached us . . . so I'll say occasion. You can imagine how thrilled I've been awaiting the reunion. Welcome back to Cornwall. You've grown up.' He looked at my hair and raised his eyebrows. 'Still the same green-eyed siren, though. I couldn't have borne it if you had changed.'

Gwennie said: 'Well, everybody's met before, haven't they? Even I met Miss Caroline once. Do you remember? It was at the inn where Pa and I stayed. You two came in and tried to put us off. You told us what a terrible place this was . . . on the point of collapse.'

'We didn't want to hide the truth from you, dear Gwennie,' said Jago.

'You were up to something . . . as usual.'

'What a day that was,' said Jago. 'The moors . . . Caroline's horse was in trouble and we had to go to the blacksmith. I can see that "do you remember" is going to be the theme of our conversation for some time to come.'

'And I can see that you are obviously well pleased with life, Jago,' I said.

'It's a mistake to be otherwise than pleased with life.'

'It is not always easy to be pleased with something which is not pleasing,' said Paul.

'It's what is called an approach to living,' explained Jago.

'Very glib,' commented Paul; and Gwennie said, 'Shall we go in to dinner?'

She came to me and slipped her arm through mine. 'I did explain,' she said in a conspiratorial whisper. 'It's quite informal tonight. Just the family. Mind you, we do entertain in style now and then. I like to get back to the old days of Landower glory . . . so does Paul . . . so does Jago.'

'I'm all for the glory,' said Jago, 'as you say, dear sister-in-law of mine.'

'We're not eating in the dining-room this evening,' went on Gwennie. 'We should all be at great distances from each other. We use it when we have guests but when we're just family we eat in the little anteroom next to the dining-room.'

'Tonight we have our most important guests,' protested Jago.

'They're neighbours, that's what I mean,' said Gwennie.

'Which is very pleasant,' put in Cousin Mary.

'Of course we do have big dinner parties now and then,' explained Gwennie. 'Sometimes so big that we use the old hall. Well, we have a position to keep up, don't we? It wouldn't do for us to forget our position in the Duchy . . . if you see what I mean.'

I glanced at Paul. He was biting his lips in annoyance. Jago was looking amused.

She led us through the dining-room to the smaller room. I could see what she meant. We should have been lost at that vast table and conversation would have been difficult. The dining-room was quite splendid with its lofty ceiling and tapestried walls; the other room was delightful, cosy, intimate with a small window looking out on a courtyard. The table was laid for five and there was a candelabrum in the centre, though the candles had not yet been lighted.

The ceiling was painted in delicate pastel shades, representing Neptune holding court.

'What a delightful room!' I said.

'You've restored it beautifully,' added Cousin Mary.

'It cost me something to have that ceiling done,' said Gwennie. 'You couldn't even see what it was meant to be. Like everything else, it had been neglected. I got an artist down here. He had to clean it and then restore it. I can tell you, a pretty penny had to be spent on this place.'

'Dear Gwennie!' murmured Jago. 'She has been so generous with her pretty pennies. Personally I have never cared whether they were pretty or plain. Any penny is good enough for me.'

'He likes to take a rise out of me,' Gwennie explained confidentially to me.

'Dear Gwennie,' went on Jago. 'No one could be more proud of this old house than she is. She's more of a Landower than any of us, are you not, dear sister-in-law!'

'A woman's family is the one she marries into,' said Gwennie sententiously.

'Which sounds as if it came out of the prayer book,' said Jago, 'but knowing our wise little Gwennie, I'll swear she made it up herself.'

Gwennie's lips were pressed tightly together. I thought there was tension between them all. Both Jago and Paul hated to have her money saving them. They should have thought of that before they took it, I thought severely.

She turned to Cousin Mary and me with a smile and indicated where we were to sit. Paul was at one end of the table, she at the other. I was on Paul's right and Jago was next to me. Cousin Mary faced us.

As the meal was served Cousin Mary talked a great deal about estate matters with Paul. I listened with attention and was able to offer a remark now and then. I had already learned a little and was finding it interesting. I was desperately seeking to divert my thoughts from all the unpleasantness I had discovered.

Jago leaned towards me and said *sotto voce*: 'There's a

lot for us to catch up on. I was wildly excited when I heard that you were coming and desolate when you were whisked away. It was rather sudden, wasn't it?'

'Yes, it was. I hated going.'

'We were such friends in that little while, were we not? What good times we had. I hope we are going on from there.'

'Oh, I dare say you have a lot to occupy you and I'm learning something about the Tressidor estate. It's very interesting.'

'I never allow business to interfere with pleasure.'

Paul overheard that remark and said: 'I assure you that this at least is one occasion when Jago speaks with sincerity.'

'You see how they treat me,' said Jago, raising his eyes to the ceiling.

'You're treated better than you deserve,' commented Gwennie.

'Hush! Caroline will think I'm a wastrel.'

'I dare say she knows that already,' said Gwennie. 'If she doesn't, she soon will.'

'You mustn't believe half they say of me,' said Jago to me.

'I always make my own judgements,' I assured him.

'Remember rumour is a lying jade.'

'But it is true,' said Paul, 'that the most convincing rumours are founded on truth.'

'The Oracle has spoken,' said Jago. 'But Caroline is going to consider me from the wisdom of her own experience.'

'I always believe in saying what I mean . . . right out,' Gwennie put in. 'No beating about the bush. Some people would tell any tale to get out of saying something that might not be polite. It's what my father used to call the perfidy of the southerner.'

'Compared with the sterling honesty of the northerners,' added Paul.

'There's a lot to be said for honesty,' persisted Gwennie.

'Sometimes it can be very uncomfortable,' I reminded her.

'It often happens,' said Paul, 'that people who are determined to say what they mean – however displeasing it may be to others – are not quite so happy when others are equally frank with them.'

'I'm all for the comfortable life,' said Jago. 'I am sure that is the best way of getting along.'

There was a certain asperity creeping into the conversation. Cousin Mary threw me a glance and started to talk about the pictures in the house.

'There was such a fine collection.'

But this was just another outlet for Gwennie's favourite theme.

'All going to rack and ruin,' she said sharply. 'There wouldn't have been anything left of them if Pa and I hadn't got that artist in to do them all up. My goodness, the change in this place!'

'Miraculous,' said Jago. 'We have learned the meaning of miracles since Gwennie took us in hand.'

I quickly asked a question about the Landower estate and how it compared with that of Tressidor. Paul talked at length about the different problems and Cousin Mary joined in enthusiastically. Jago was also involved in the management of Landower and added a remark or two, rather desultorily, while he made several attempts to engage me in asides. I did not encourage him. I wanted to hear what Paul and Cousin Mary were saying; and I believe Gwennie did too. She was clearly something of a business woman.

My feelings wavered between a deep perturbation and an exhilaration. I wanted to get away one moment and the next I was eager to remain. I was trying to assess my feelings for Paul. I had thought there was no doubt of them since I had discovered his mercenary act in marrying a woman for her money – an act similar to that which had made me so bitter against Jeremy Brandon; but for some reason I could not help feeling sorry for Paul. I had already seen that his life with Gwennie was not an easy one, and that he must be paying dearly for regaining his house. Perhaps he had hoped for a simple transaction. It was far from that.

When the meal was over Gwennie, determined to observe the conventions, said she would take us ladies into the drawing-room and leave the men over their port. How absurd that was, I thought, and wondered wryly what Paul and Jago would have to say to each other alone at the dining table.

In the drawing-room Cousin Mary exclaimed at the wonderful restoration of the ceiling which was beautifully moulded into delicate patterns, and Gwennie was off on what I had quickly learned was her favourite subject.

'The work we had to do on this house! You've no idea. But I was determined to do it absolutely right. So was Pa. The cost was more than he'd bargained for. I often wondered whether Pa would have taken it on in the first place if he'd known. When you start on a house like this you make a lot of discoveries.'

'You must have completed all the restoration by now,' I said.

'There's always something. I'm going to start on the attics one day. I haven't touched them yet. There's one room I'm very interested in. It's off the long gallery. I think there's something behind the walls.'

'A priest's hole or something like that?' I asked. 'Were the Landowers Catholics at one time?'

'The Landowers would be anything that was best for them,' said Gwennie, with a tinge of both contempt and admiration.

'I know they crossed from Cavalier to Roundhead and back during the Civil War,' said Cousin Mary. 'But they saved the house, I believe.'

'Oh, the Landowers would do a great deal to save the house,' said Gwennie with an expression which hovered between triumph and bitterness.

255

We seemed to come back and back again to that unfortunate subject.

'I'll tell you what,' she went on. 'I'll show you this room. See what you think of it. You've lived in Tressidor all your life, Miss Tressidor. You must know a great deal about old houses.'

'I know a great deal about Tressidor. All houses are different.'

'Well, come and look.'

'Won't the men wonder where we have gone?'

'They'll guess, I reckon. That room's my favourite project just now. It's off the long gallery. Come on.'

She took a lighted candle and led the way.

She turned to me. 'May I call you Caroline? We're much of an age. And two Miss Tressidors makes it a little awkward.'

'Please do.'

'And I'm Gwen . . . but everyone calls me Gwennie. Pa started it. He said even Gwen was not the name for a little scrap. Certainly not Gwendoline which is what I am really. It's friendly, in a way.'

'All right, Gwennie,' I said. 'I shall be very excited to see this room. Won't you be too, Cousin Mary?'

Cousin Mary said she would indeed, and we left the drawing-room.

'The nurseries are at the top of the house. Not right at the top . . . that's the attics . . . just below the attics. Julian is fast asleep now. Otherwise I'd show him to you. He's a lovely boy.'

'Two years old, I believe,' I said.

'Coming up to it. He was born within the year after we married. I'll tell you what. If you like, we'll have a quick peep at him.'

She led us up several staircases and opened a door. The room was in darkness apart from a faint glow from a night-light. A woman rose from a chair.

'It's all right, Nanny. I've just brought the Misses Tressidor. To show them Julian.'

256

The woman stepped back and nodded as we advanced into the room. Gwennie held the candle high so that the light fell on the sleeping child.

He was a beautiful boy with thick dark hair. I looked at him and felt envy because he was not mine.

'He's beautiful,' I whispered.

Gwennie nodded, as proud as she was over the restored ceilings and all the work she had done at Landower.

He doesn't love her, I thought. It's obvious. She's a source of irritation to him. But she had that beautiful child and I had not envied her until I saw him.

She led us to the door.

'Couldn't resist showing him to you,' she said. 'He's a pet, don't you think?'

Cousin Mary said: 'A lovely boy.' And I nodded in agreement.

'Well, come on, and I'll show you my room.' She led us down a flight of stairs and eventually we stopped before a door. 'Here it is.' She opened the door. 'We need more light. Here's another candle . . . I always keep plenty here. I don't like to be caught in the dark. Funny thing. Nothing else frightens me. It's just things that are not natural. I was always like that since I was a little one. In a place like this you'd expect to find ghosts, wouldn't you? I don't know why I'm so fond of it.' She turned to me, her eyes luminous in the candlelight. 'You wouldn't think I was the sort to have fancies, would you?'

I shook my head.

'Well, sometimes I get this zany idea that there are ghosts in that gallery and that they were making me come here . . . making me bring new life to the house.'

'An odd way of doing it,' said Cousin Mary practically, 'to frighten you so much that you fell over the rail and hurt yourself.'

'Yes . . . but up to then I thought Pa was against it. He was saying what a lot of work there was to be done. He liked the idea of living here but there would be other places in the country which wouldn't be in such a bad state. But when I fell I hurt myself so badly I stayed here and Pa stayed with me . . . and that was when the house started to . . . I don't know how to say it . . .'

I said: 'Put its tentacles about you.'

'That's right. And they held Pa fast. And then he had this idea about Paul and me . . . to make it right with everyone. He always cared more for my future than his own. He was, after all, right where he planned to be . . . except that he wasn't the squire. But father of the squire's lady was good enough for him.'

'So we come to the fairy tale ending,' I said ironically; but she did not notice the touch of asperity in my voice.

'Well . . . things have to be worked out,' she said rather sadly, 'and life is never what you think it's going to be. Look here.' She threw the light of the candle over the walls. There was a desk in the room and a cupboard – very little else. 'I don't think they ever used this room,' she went on. 'I had that cupboard moved. You see, it was over there. You can see the slightly different colour of the wall . . . even in this light.' She tapped the wall. 'There! Can you hear the hollow sound?'

'Yes,' said Cousin Mary. 'There could be something behind that.'

'I'm going to get them working on it,' said Gwennie.

I heard a sound behind us. We all started and a voice said: 'Boo!'

Jago was grinning at us and Paul was just behind him.

Jago said: 'I told Paul you'd be inspecting Gwennie's latest discovery.'

Jago stepped forward and tapped the wall.

'Is anyone there?' he enquired.

He turned to smile at Gwennie. 'Dear sister-in-law,' he said, 'I'm only teasing. There is only one thing in the world before which that stalwart northern spirit quails – and that is ghosts. As if any of them would want to hurt the one who has saved their habitation from crumbling into decay!'

Behind his banter there was a certain malice. I thought: Both of these brothers resent her, and she is determined to remind them at every moment of what she has done. There is more than resentment in this house. There is hatred.

'We shall soon see what is behind that wall,' said Paul.

'Did no one ever wonder about it before?' I asked.

'No one.'

'Until Gwennie came,' added Jago.

'Well, there is nothing to be seen here tonight,' went on Paul.

We came out into the gallery. Paul and Cousin Mary walked on ahead. Cousin Mary was talking about a similar experience at Tressidor. 'We took down a wall . . . oh, that was long ago . . . in my grandfather's day, and all that was behind it was a cupboard.'

Gwennie joined them and began asking eager questions.

'I can't say much about it,' said Cousin Mary. 'I only heard of it. I know the spot where it was done, of course.'

I paused to look at a picture which I thought was Paul.

'Our father as a young man,' said Jago.

'He is like your brother.'

'Oh yes. That was before his dissolute days. Let us hope that Paul doesn't go the same way. Not much hope . . . or fear . . . of that.'

'I should think it is hardly likely.'

The others had passed out of the gallery.

'He could be driven to it.'

'Oh?'

'Haven't you noticed the way it is? Never mind. I want to show you something. It's the view from one of the towers. It's just through here.'

'The others will wonder . . .'

'It will do them good to exercise their minds.'

'You haven't changed much, Jago.'

'The boy is father to the man. Aren't they the wise words of someone? You should know. You're the wise one. All that education in France . . .!'

'How did you hear about that?'

'Miss Tressidor is mighty proud of her young relative. She's talked a great deal about you.'

'It is nice to know that the two families have become friends.'

I had allowed him to lead the way out of the gallery. We had come to a winding staircase which we mounted. He cautioned me to hold the rope banister. Then we were on a tower, out in the open air. I stood still breathing in the fresh coolness. A faint moonlight showed the parapet and the battlements and park and woodlands stretched out before my eyes.

'It's magnificent,' I said.

'Can you imagine Gwennie's bringing my brother up here and saying: "Sell your soul to me and all this shall be thine"?'

'No, I can't.'

'Of course not. It would be a matter-of-fact transaction. Just imagine Pa, banging the table. "You've got the house, the background and the family. I've got the brass. Take my daughter and I'll save the house for you."'

'You resent it, don't you?'

'Mildly. *I* wasn't the one who had to take Gwennie.'

'Why do you dislike her so much?'

'I dislike her because I don't dislike her as much as I want to! Or rather I do dislike her and I know I shouldn't. She's not a bad sort, our Gwennie. If only she was less brass-conscious, if you know what I mean, and my brother was less proud . . . it might work.'

'Marriages of convenience should at least be convenient.'

'That's exactly what it is. Convenient. And there it ends.'

'You should have stayed at the farmhouse. That seems to me to have been the best bargain.'

'Younger sons never get the best of the bargain. The house will go to Paul's offspring. Young Julian is half Arkwright. That's part of the bargain.'

'You can always congratulate yourselves on saving the house.'

'I suppose we do. It's something we don't forget. But

what is past can't be altered. It is the future which concerns us. I'm glad you've come back, Caroline.'

I was silent, looking out over the moonlit grass. Was I glad? I was immensely excited. Life was certainly not monotonous as it had been in France. How different it would have been if Paul had decided to save his dignity and his honour rather than the house, and was living humbly in the farmhouse looking after the few acres which went with it – a poor man, but at least a proud one. I should have liked that better.

'You look sad,' said Jago. 'Has life been difficult?'

'Not exactly. Unexpected, perhaps.'

'That's how one wants it to be, surely. As soon as the expected happens it becomes dull.'

'Sometimes one's expectations are very important to one.'

'Don't let's get philosophical. Do you still ride as well?'

'Well, I did have a spill in the French mountains, of which you have heard.'

'I wish I'd known you were there. I would have come out to spy out the land. We would have had some fun and I should not have allowed you to fall off your horse.'

'It was I who allowed myself to do that. Jago . . . does Gwennie suspect?'

'Suspect what?'

'That a trick was played on her . . . in the gallery that time.'

'You mean the ghosts?'

I nodded. 'Sometimes she seems . . .'

'Gwennie is the most inquisitive person I have ever known. She wants to know everything about everyone, and she doesn't rest until she finds out. She doesn't suspect it was a trick. She insists she saw ghosts. They are the only things that can scare Gwennie, and it is comforting to know that such a formidable lady has one weak spot.'

'What do you think she would do . . . if she were to find out that we were the ghosts?'

'I don't know. It's so long ago, and if she hadn't fallen

and we hadn't played the good hosts everything might have been different. There might have been other people at Landower. There might have been no buyer at all, in which case this revered old place would be a crumbled ruin and we would be struggling in penury in our farmhouse. Who can say?'

'It is interesting to see how it brought about the opposite result to what we intended. Remember we played the ghosts to drive the Arkwrights away and we succeeded in bringing them in.'

'It was in our stars, as they say.'

'Ordained. The saving of Landower and the union of Gwennie with your brother.'

'I believe the old house arranged it. Naturally it didn't want to tumble down. You're very beautiful, Caroline.'

'Thank you,' I said.

'I've never seen such green eyes.'

'Which my mother's lady's maid would tell you came from my wearing this brooch.'

He bent his head to look at it and his fingers lingered on it; and just at that moment a voice said: 'Oh, you're here. I guessed you'd come up by way of the gallery staircase.' It was Paul.

'We wanted a little fresh air and I was showing Caroline the view.'

'It's very beautiful,' I said. 'And so is the house. You are very proud of it, I know.'

There was a coldness in my voice which he must have been aware of.

'Shall we join the others?' he said.

Jago gave his brother an exasperated look as we followed him down the staircase.

In the drawing-room Cousin Mary was saying that it was time we left.

'I was showing Caroline the view from the tower,' said Jago.

Gwennie laughed significantly.

Cousin Mary said: 'It's been such a pleasant evening and so kind and neighbourly of you to ask us.'

Eventually we took our leave and were soon bowling along the short distance to Tressidor.

Cousin Mary came up to my room with me. There she sat down thoughtfully.

'What an atmosphere,' she said. 'You could cut it with a knife.'

'They resent her,' I replied, 'both of them.'

'Jago was interested in you. You'll have to watch him, Caroline. You've already heard something of his reputation.'

'Yes, I know. They are not very admirable, are they? One the rake of the countryside and the other blatantly marrying for money.'

'Human frailties both, I suppose.'

'Perhaps. But having made the bargain, it should not be resented.'

'Oh, you're talking about the elder one. I know what you mean. Some men are like that . . . proud . . . holding firmly to the position into which they were born. One can understand it. They've been brought up to expectations and they're about to be robbed of them. Opportunity presents itself and they fall into temptation.'

'That woman . . .'

'Gwennie. The name doesn't suit her. She's as hard as nails.'

'She needs to be, with such a husband.'

'You despise him, don't you? I had the impression that when you were in France you rather liked him.'

'I didn't know then that he had sold himself.'

'What a melodramatic way of describing a marriage of convenience . . .'

'Well, that's what it amounts to.'

'It's hard for him. They are quite unsuited. I can see that her mannerisms, her blunt way of expressing her thoughts . . . the fact that she doesn't fit in . . . irritates him. If she had been a simple little girl – an heiress with Pa's money to

263

buy her a mansion and a handsome husband – it might have worked better. But there he is a proud scion of an old family married to a woman who has been brought up to an entirely different culture, you might say. Good manners, social subterfuge, an elegant and somewhat indolent way of living, against that of a girl brought up by a hardworking, shrewd father of not much education but possessed of great gifts . . . which to some extent she has inherited. It's like trying to mix oil and water. They never do. One won't absorb the other. And there you have it. Discord! I never noticed it so much until tonight.'

'Have you seen much of them together?'

'Occasionally. It was different tonight – more or less the family. You and I were the only outsiders. Generally when I have been entertained by them there have been a lot of people.'

'It was certainly an experience.'

Cousin Mary yawned.

'Well, you're settling in. I liked to hear you talking to Paul Landower about the estate. You're learning already.'

'I want to, Cousin Mary.'

'I knew it would absorb you, once you started. Good night, my dear. You look pensive. Still thinking of those people?' She shook her head. 'It wouldn't surprise me,' she went on, 'if there were trouble there one day. I got the impression of rumbling thunder in the distance. You know what I mean? Of course you do. Two strong natures there. I wish Gwennie had been a dear simple soul. I wish Paul was ready to accept what is. Well, it's their problem. Nothing to do with us, is it? Of course it's not. But a lot of people depend on the prosperity of Landower. All the people on the estate. It's the best way really. Keep the estate going . . . make up for the dissolute ways of those who have gone before and brought about the situation in the first place. I believe Gwennie will do her best. She's got her father's head for business. It's just the domestic side she can't manage. Well, as I said, no concern of ours. Good night again.'

I kissed her and she went out.

Then I sat down at my mirror and took off my emerald brooch. I studied my reflection. My eyes did look brilliant, even without the brooch to call attention to them. Whatever I said, whatever I tried to think, I could not banish the memory of Paul from my mind. I could not stop myself being sorry for him.

'It's his own fault,' I said aloud. 'He made his bed. He must lie on it.'

How apt! I could sense his dislike of Gwennie. There were moments when he could not hide it. I now knew the reason for the melancholy, for those secrets in his eyes.

I wanted to hate him. I wanted to despise him. But I could not. I could only feel sorry for him and I had an overwhelming desire to comfort him.

'It's no concern of ours.' Cousin Mary's words were in my ears. Of course it is no concern of ours, I said to my reflection.

But I still went on thinking of him sadly, yet with a vague hope . . . I could not say of what.

The next morning Cousin Mary stayed late in bed. I went to see her in some alarm.

'Oh, I'm feeling my age,' she said. 'I always lie in after a night out. I shall be up shortly.'

'Are you sure that's all?'

'Completely sure. I don't believe in driving myself. Particularly now that I have an assistant.'

'Not much use so far, I'm afraid.'

'I'll tell you what you can do this morning. Ride over to Brackett's farm and tell them Jim Burrows is looking into the matter of Three Acre Meadow, will you? There's some question about the soil there. Jim won't have time to go because he's got to go into Plymouth today. I said I'd see to it.'

I was pleased to be able to do something useful and practical and after breakfast I set out.

I sat in the Bracketts' kitchen and had a cup of tea and a hot scone which Mrs Brackett had just brought out of the oven. I passed on the message and Mrs Brackett said how pleased she was I had come to the Manor.

'I often thought it was lonely up there for Miss Tressidor, so it is nice for her to have you along with her, like. And she thinks the world of you. I said to my Tom, "It's nice for Miss Tressidor to have Miss Caroline with her." '

'Yes,' I said, 'and nice for me.'

'We're lucky to be on the Tressidor estate, I always say to Tom. Landower's now . . . well, there was a time not so long ago. I said to Tom, "It's not the same . . . Landower's changing hands . . . It makes you think." '

'But it is back to normal now.'

'Yes, but they say she keeps her hands on the purse strings . . . Of course she's not quite what you'd expect. There! I'm talking out of turn.'

I wanted her to go on. I was eager to learn all I could about what was happening at Landower. But naturally I must not gossip.

I came out of the farmhouse and turned my horse towards the moor. I wanted to gallop over the fresh turf. I wanted to feel the wind in my face. I wanted to think clearly about last night and what the future was going to be like. Cousin Mary was expecting me to stay and I wanted to, but having seen Paul last night and being aware of the strained relationship between him and his wife, made me feel very uneasy.

It was no use saying it was no concern of mine. I was well aware of the feelings he aroused in me and I was not sure whether I was right in thinking I had a certain effect on him. If this was so, then it could easily become a concern of mine. Unless, of course, I went away.

I believed I had to think very seriously about my future.

It was a warm day with a fairly brisk breeze which came from the south-west – the prevailing wind in these parts, and which I always felt carried with it a breath of the spices of Morocco. I inhaled with pleasure as I galloped along. In the distance I could see the old scat bal which Jago had once pointed out to me.

I went towards it.

It certainly looked eerie. I remembered the stories Jago had told me about the departed spirits who were said to inhabit old mines. Here, alone on the moors with the wind whistling through the grass, I could understand the reason why people were affected by old superstitions.

I approached near to the edge of the shaft. The wind sounded like hollow laughter. I drew back and looked about me. I could see right to the horizon on one side; on the other the view was blocked by several tall boulders.

I turned my horse away and as I did so I heard the sound of horse's hoofs and then someone was calling my name.

At first I thought I had imagined it or that it was one of those departed spirits Jago had said were called knackers. But the voice was familiar and among the boulders I saw the rider picking his way through the stones.

It was Paul.

'Good morning, Caroline,' he said.

'Good morning. I thought I was quite alone.'

'I was going to call on you and I saw you taking the path to the moor. You shouldn't go too near the old mine shaft.'

'It seems safe enough.'

'You can never be sure. It's supposed to be haunted.'

'That makes me all the more eager to have a look at it.'

'There's nothing much to see. About fifty years ago someone fell down the shaft and was killed. It was on a misty night. People said he had fallen out with a witch.'

'I know no witches and it is clear sunshine today, so I was perfectly safe.'

He had come up to me and was carrying his hat in his hand. The wind caught at his dark hair and his heavy-lidded eyes regarded me solemnly.

'It's a great pleasure to see you,' he said and his voice vibrated with feeling.

It moved me, piercing my indifference. It made me more and more certain of my feelings for him and I was angry

267

with myself for allowing my emotions to take control over my common sense; and I turned my anger on him.

'Congratulations,' I said.

He raised his strongly marked brows questioningly.

'For acquiring Landower,' I said. 'You must be proud of all the restoration.'

He looked at me reproachfully and said: 'The house will now stand safely for another two hundred years and be kept in the family.'

'A great achievement. Surely worthy of congratulation.'

'I was going to tell you about my marriage when we were in France.'

'Oh? What made you decide not to?'

'I found it very difficult to speak of it.'

'Why should you? It was all so natural, wasn't it?'

I turned my horse and started to walk away from the mine shaft. He was beside me. 'I wanted to talk to you.'

'You are talking to me.'

'Seriously.'

'Why don't you, then?'

'You're not as you were when we were in France. That was a very happy time for me, Caroline.'

'Yes,' I said. 'It was pleasant. Of course there was that unfortunate accident.'

'You suffered no ill effects?'

'None.'

'It helped us to get to know each other better.'

'I don't think it helped me to know you.'

'You mean . . .'

'Not as well as I do now,' I said coolly.

'I think you must know that I have a very special feeling for you, Caroline.'

'Is that so?'

'Oh come, let's be honest. Let's be frank. Here we are alone on the moors. There is none to overhear us.'

'Only the knackers, the spirits and the ghosts.'

'When we were in France, that little time we spent together . . . it's something I shall never forget. I've thought about you ever since. It was after that that everything seemed to become intolerable.'

I interrupted: 'I don't think you should talk to me like this. You should remember that you are married very satisfactorily . . . very *conveniently*.'

'I should never have done it.'

'What! When you saved Landower for the Landowers!'

'I hesitated for a long time. So much depended on it. My father . . . Jago . . . the tenants . . .'

'And yourself.'

'And myself.'

'I understand perfectly. I believe I told you when we were in France that I had been engaged to be married and when my fiancé discovered that I had no fortune he decided that he could not marry me. You see, I know the ways of the world.'

'You are cynical, Caroline, and somehow it doesn't suit you.'

'I am realistic and that is how I want to be.'

'I wish it could have been different.'

'You mean . . . you wish that you could go back to the days before your marriage. Then you would also go on living in your farmhouse. I'm sure you don't wish that.'

'Can I explain to you what Landower means to my family?'

'It's not necessary. I know. I understand.'

'I had to do it, Caroline.'

'I know. You bought Landower from the Arkwrights just as they bought it from you – only the currency used was different. The transaction was just the same. It is all perfectly clear. No explanations are needed. I could see last night that you were a little dissatisfied. Perhaps I am talking too frankly. It's being here on the moors, I suppose. I feel quite apart from the world of polite society. Do you?'

'Yes,' he replied. 'That's why I'm talking as I am.'

'We have to go back to the real world,' I said, 'where we study the conventions of polite society. You should not reveal so much and I should be speaking in a guarded fashion. We should be discussing the weather prospects and those of the harvests instead of which . . . I must go back.'

'Caroline . . .'

I turned to look at him. I said: 'You made your bargain. You got what you wanted. You have to go on paying for it. After all, it was a very costly purchase.'

I felt so bitter and unhappy that I wanted to hurt him. I knew that I could have loved him more deeply than I ever had Jeremy. I was mature now. When Jeremy had jilted me my feelings for him had quickly turned to hatred. Yet here was Paul as mercenary as Jeremy and I had to fight my impulses to take his hand, to caress him, to comfort him.

I could see danger ahead and I was filled with apprehension. I must not let him know how deeply he affected me.

I galloped across the moor. I could hear his horse's hoofs thundering along behind me. The wind pulled at my hair and I thought how different it could have been. And I almost wept with frustration. I could have loved him and I believe he could have cared for me; and between us there was Landower, which had had to be saved, and Gwennie, who had bought him so that he was bound to her for the rest of their lives.

The moorland scenery was changing, growing less wild. Now we were in the country lanes.

He said: 'I hope that nothing will interfere with our friendship, Caroline.'

I said shortly: 'We are neighbours . . . as long as I am here.'

'You don't mean that you are going away?'

I shrugged my shoulders. 'I am not certain.'

'But Miss Tressidor spoke as though you were going to make your home with her.'

'I really don't know what will happen.'

'You must stay,' he said.

'It won't make any difference to you whether I go or stay.'

'It will make all the difference to me.'

I wanted to make some bitter retort but I could not. I wondered if he noticed that my lips trembled. He might have. We were walking our horses side by side.

I did not want him to know how deeply he affected me.

I could see it all so clearly: the passion between us growing, becoming irresistible; secret meetings; secret guilt; Gwennie probing; servants prying. Oh no. I must not allow that to happen.

I rode ahead of him. There must be no more of this conversation.

I said goodbye to him when we came in sight of Tressidor. I went in and straight up to my room. I could not face anyone for a while. I was in too much of an emotional turmoil.

There was a certain joy in my heart because he was not indifferent to me; there was a feeling of deep desperation because he was not free; and any relationship between us other than the most casual friendship was out of the question.

But was it? Why had he spoken to me as he had? Was he in love with me? Was I in love with him? Was he suggesting that something should be done about it?

Perhaps they were questions it was better not to ask.

Perhaps I should go away . . . in time.

That afternoon I paid a visit to Jamie McGill.

There was an atmosphere of peace in the lodge and I felt I wanted to escape into it for a while. He was delighted to see me. He had increased his hives, he told me, since I had last been there.

'We've had our ups and downs,' he said. 'There was that cold winter. We don't get winters here like we did in Scotland, but that was a cold snap – just for a few weeks – and the bees didn't like it. Of course I protected them from the worst of it. They know that. They're grateful. More grateful than folks, bees are.'

271

He made the tea and said it would be a good idea if I went out and had a word with the bees.

'Wouldn't want them to think you were stand-offish.'

I smiled. 'Do you really think they would?'

'They know. But they'd take it as a good gesture if I took you out there. They know you're here. They knew before I told them. Sometimes I think bees knows these things . . . quicker than we do. Lionheart, he'll sometimes know what's going to happen before it does.'

The Jack Russell, hearing his name, wagged his tail. He was lying on the rug looking at his master with adoring eyes. The cat came and leaped upon his lap.

'Oh,' he said, 'mustn't forget Tiger. Tiger's a wise one, aren't you, Tiger?'

Tiger was black and sleek with slanting green eyes.

'What an unusual cat!' I said.

'Tiger's more than a cat, aren't you, Tiger? Tiger came to me one night. Outside the door he was . . . not exactly begging to come in. Tiger never begs. But demanding in a way. So he came and he's stayed ever since. Where did you come from, Tiger? You're not telling, are you?'

'You get great satisfaction from animals and bees,' I commented.

'They're different from people,' he said, 'and I always got along with them better. I know them and they know me . . . and we trust each other. There's Lionheart. Now in his eyes I can do no wrong. That's a good friend to have. Tiger . . . well, he's not so predictable. It's my privilege to have him, if you understand. That's how Tiger sees it.'

'And the bees?'

'They're a cross between these two. We live side by side. I do what I can for them and they do what they can for me.'

'It's a good life you've made for yourself here, Jamie.'

He did not answer. His eyes had a faraway expression as though he were looking beyond the cottage and me and even the animals.

'It would be a good life,' he mused, 'but for Donald. I never know when he might find out where I am.'

'Your twin brother,' I said, remembering what he had told me in the past.

'If he were to come here, all this peace . . . it would be gone.'

'Do you expect him to come, Jamie?'

He shook his head. 'There's whole days . . . weeks . . . when I don't think of him. I forget him sometimes for months at a stretch.'

'Well, you've been here a long time, Jamie. It's hardly likely that he'll come now.'

'You're right, Miss Caroline. It's foolish of me to worry. He won't come.'

'Apart from that, you have made everything as you want it.'

'I reckon that's so. Miss Tressidor has been good to me . . to give me this lovely house and garden to live in.'

'She's good to all the people on the estate.'

'I'll never forget what she's done for me.'

'I'll tell her. But I think she knows. Did you really mean that you wanted me to see the bees?'

'Oh yes. We must do that.'

He dressed me up in the veil and gloves which I had worn on a previous occasion and I went out to the hives. I felt a momentary panic when the bees buzzed round me, even though I knew I was well protected.

'Here she is,' said Jamie. 'Come to see you. Miss Caroline. She takes a great interest in you.'

I saw some alight on his hands and some on his head. He was not in the least perturbed and nor were they. He must be right. They did know him.

Back in the lodge he divested me of the veil and gloves.

'It's wonderful,' I said, 'how they know you.'

'No,' he answered, 'it's natural.'

'They seem to have a thriving community. They don't seem to be bothered by the troubles which beset us humans.'

'There can be trouble. Sometimes there are two queens in one hive.'

'Couldn't the two of them live side by side?'

Jamie laughed. 'They're like people after all. You couldn't have two wives in one home, could you? You couldn't have two queens ruling a country.'

'What happened?'

'They fought. One killed the other.'

'Murder!' I said. 'In your ideal colony!'

'Jealousy is a terrible thing. There's only room for one . . . so the other gets rid of the one in the way.'

'You've spoilt my illusion.'

'It's better to have the truth than illusions, Miss Caroline.'

'So bees are not perfect after all.'

The black cat sprang on to my lap.

'Tiger likes you,' he said.

I was not sure. The cat was staring at me with its green satanic eyes. Then suddenly it settled down and started to purr.

There was a brief silence in the room broken only by the sound of the ticking clock.

There is peace here, I thought. Perfect peace. No, not quite perfect. I kept thinking about the queen bees who had fought to the death of one; and the niggling fear in Jamie's mind that one day his wicked brother would find him.

I received a letter from Olivia. It moved me deeply.

My dear Caroline,

I have great news for you. I am going to have a baby. That will make my happiness complete. Everything has been so wonderful for me since I married. Jeremy is so delighted. It was what we both wanted to crown our happiness. Jeremy wants a boy, of course. I suppose men always do. As for myself I really don't mind – except for Jeremy, of course. It will be quite soon. I put off telling people for as long as I could. I had a funny feeling as I always did about wonderful

274

things – afraid that something might go wrong if I talked too much about them. So I kept it to myself. It will be at the end of July.

I know you will share my joy in this. How do you fancy being an aunt? It's hard to imagine you as one. I do wish you would come up some time. I long to see you. I want you to promise that you will be the baby's godmother. Please write to me soon and tell me that you will.

I love your letters. I can imagine it all. Perhaps one day I'll come to Cornwall. It will be difficult for a while because of the baby, but you must come here, Caroline. It is a long journey but I should so love to see you.

Miss Bell is still here, of course. She is so excited about the baby. It will be a new one for her to 'governess'. I am afraid she felt her post here was something of a sinecure since I can hardly be said to be in the schoolroom now. She 'directs' me, as she calls it. Jeremy is amused by her.

You will think about coming, won't you? You will have to for the christening. It is usual for godmothers to attend.

Do go on writing to me. I do so look forward to your letters. I love to hear about the Landowers and the people on the estate and of course Cousin Mary and the quaint man with the bees. I should have loved to see you in that veil and everything.

> With much love,
> Your affectionate sister,
> Olivia.

Olivia a mother! It was hard to believe. I felt a twinge of envy. She had avoided telling me because she had been unsure of what my feelings would be. I had not been at her wedding. She knew why. Sensitive to a degree herself, she always thought of others. She put herself in their places. It was one of her most endearing qualities.

And Jeremy was a good, devoted husband. Of course he is, I thought cynically. He is living comfortably.

Dear Olivia! She had been used by him . . . as I should have been . . . as any woman would have been who had the means to keep him in the style to which he aspired.

I would be free and independent.

I thought of Jeremy – excited by the prospect of a child. I thought of Paul and a terrible desolation came over me.

A Visit to London

I was finding the company of Cousin Mary more and more comforting. She was discerning enough to realize that I was far from serene and happy, and I believe she attributed this to Jeremy's treatment of me, and yet at the same time she was aware of an uneasiness in the relationship between myself and Paul Landower. She was too wise to attempt to probe obviously, and I knew she was trying to make life easy for me. To have been rejected as I had been was understandably a great shock to one's *amour propre* and naturally would colour one's relationships with every other man who crossed one's path for some time to come.

She believed in healing me by turning my thoughts in another direction and that was the management of the estate. She was right up to a point, for I found myself becoming absorbed in these affairs. I would sit with her and the manager, Jim Burrows, over the accounts; schemes would be discussed in my presence. I said little but I listened avidly; and I really did find myself forgetting everything but the matter in hand for long periods at a time.

There was a certain amount of entertaining.

Cousin Mary said: 'I never gave myself up to it entirely. In fact I avoided it whenever I could, but since the Landowers have plunged into such activity with the coming of the new mistress of the house, entertainment in the neighbourhood has become more frequent.'

It was not a large community, although now and then squires from some way off visited Landower and there were house parties. We were never house guests, being so close, but we were invited to these gatherings. Gwennie revelled in them; she was, as she said, bringing Landower back to what it had missed for so long. I believed Paul disliked these occasions but Jago was amused by them.

Cousin Mary said: 'She tries too hard to be a Landower, that's Gwennie's trouble. She doesn't realize that the very essence of what she is trying to achieve is a certain nonchalance. She quite misses the point. She tries to call attention to the fact that she is of noble birth, when the true aristocrat automatically assumes that there is no doubt of it. Poor Gwennie, I wonder if she will ever learn.'

Cousin Mary gave small dinner parties – repaying hospitality, she called it. 'We didn't have to bother until Gwennie's day,' she complained.

Dr Ingleton and his wife with their middle-aged unmarried daughter were visitors; so were the vicar, his wife and sister-in-law; the solicitor who lived in Liskeard and one of the directors of the bank were others – with their families, of course.

I was being caught up in the community.

'It is as well you get to know all these people as well as those on the estate,' said Cousin Mary.

Each day she implied that Cornwall was to be my permanent home; and each day I wondered what I should do.

I avoided Paul and I believe he avoided me. I think we were both aware that there was a great attraction between us, and it must never be allowed to flourish. It was like a banked up fire at the moment – smouldering. Instinctively I knew – and I fancied he did too – that it could flare up suddenly.

Relations with Jago were easier to handle. I met him often. He had a way of appearing when I rode out alone – and then of course he was always present at the gatherings.

I couldn't help enjoying his company. He was amusing, light-hearted, and all the time he kept up a bantering kind of flirtation which we both enjoyed.

I had the impression that he was not all that intent on seduction but would welcome it if it came. Jago had too

278

many strings to his bow. He was the kind of man to whom sexual adventure was as natural as breathing. He was successful in his amorous adventures because of those striking good looks which together with his laughter-loving nature were irresistible to many.

He did not exactly pursue anyone, I was sure. Conquest came too easily, so there was no challenge. I reckoned I was one of the few who resisted him; in some cases that might have aroused a determination to succeed with me. Not so with Jago. He was all for ease and comfort. There was no need for him to attempt difficult tasks. All around him was easy success.

I was glad of this and amused by it. I had to admit that being in Jago's company did cheer me quite a bit. His attitude to life, I told him, was that of a butterfly, flitting from blossom to blossom, dancing in the sunlight, with no thought of the future. He retorted that he would never have believed butterflies had an attitude to life if I hadn't told him.

I used to remonstrate with him in a light-hearted way. 'Remember what happened to the grasshopper?' I asked him once.

'I never was attracted by grasshoppers in general and am quite unaware of the fate of this particular one, which I presume by the tone of your voice was tragic, and a lesson to us all.'

'Jago, you must know the La Fontaine fable.'

'I don't even know La Fontaine.'

'Of course you know it. Everyone does. The grasshopper sang and danced all through the summer and had nothing stored for the winter. She then tried to borrow from the ant. "What did you do in summer?" asked the ant. "Danced and sang very happily," she replied. "Well, dance now," said the ant.'

'I fail to see the analogy. Who is this ant? I realize you have cast me in the role of grasshopper.'

'When you get old and grey . . .'

'Perish the day! I shall never be old. It is not in my

nature. I shall tint my locks if necessary. But I shall never be old or grey.'

'You'll have to settle down one day.'

'What do you mean by settle?'

'Live seriously.'

'I am very serious. I am determined to enjoy living. I am completely serious about that.'

It was impossible to talk gravely to him about anything. It suited my mood, and being with him always raised my spirits.

The weeks began to speed past.

I thought a great deal about Olivia. I had long conversations with Cousin Mary about her.

'It's always an anxious time having a baby,' I said. 'And I feel there is a kind of plea in her letters. I feel I ought to be there with her.'

'Well, if you feel like that you should go.'

'I can't make up my mind. I should hate it in a way. I don't want to see Jeremy Brandon again.'

'That's understandable. Perhaps it is better for you not to go. You don't know what Olivia will be feeling.'

'She would understand, I think.'

'You'll go for the christening?'

'Yes, I'll have to go for that. Then I shall know that she is all right.'

The days passed and anxiously I waited for news.

It came at the end of July, a letter from Olivia herself, written in a rather shaky hand, but there was no mistaking her joy.

Dear Caroline,

It is all over now. I am the happiest woman in the world. I have my baby. A little girl. Just what I wanted. Jeremy is delighted. He's forgotten all about wanting a boy. She's perfect in every way . . . the most beautiful little girl that ever was.

I have decided on the name. Jeremy wanted to call her after me, but I said it would be difficult with two

Olivias. So we've compromised. She's to be Livia. And of course she must be named after her important godmother, Livia Caroline. What do you think of that?

I did not know there could be so much happiness in the world. I long to see you and show you my treasure. The christening is going to be at the end of September.

Oh, Caroline, I do so look forward to seeing you.

With my constant love.

Your sister, Olivia.

I was relieved that she had come through the ordeal safely. She had always seemed fragile to me. I thought a great deal about Olivia and her baby. I wanted very much to see her and the child. I wondered what it would be like meeting Jeremy again. I was sure he would be discreet. Perhaps I need not see much of him.

I called on Miss Gentle who lived in one of the cottages on the Landower estate and who sewed for the two houses. She made some beautiful baby garments for me to take to London with me when I went, and for the weeks that followed my thoughts were completely occupied with what was to me a strange mixture of pleasure and apprehension.

I made my preparations, growing more and more uneasy as time passed and wondering what I should say if I came face to face with Jeremy. I would try to appear indifferent, but I wondered if my anger towards him would allow me to be so.

On the morning of the twenty-eighth of September, Joe drove me to the station in the trap and Cousin Mary came with me. She saw me into a first class compartment, kissed me briskly and told me not to stay too long.

'I shall soon be back,' I promised.

She stood on the platform waving as the train moved out.

I settled down. Always on this journey I would remember that one when I had sat opposite Miss Bell and had had my first sight of Paul Landower and Jago, who had come to play such a big part in my life.

I watched the scenery slipping past and was glad that I had a compartment to myself.

I was thinking how much the trains had changed since that first journey. Corridors had just come in and it was a great convenience to be able to walk from one compartment to another in certain sections of the train; there were now hot pipes under the floor to take the place of footwarmers, which had been in use at the time when I had travelled with Miss Bell.

So much change everywhere in such a short time.

I was looking out of the window when I heard the door leading to the corridor open. I turned sharply. A man had opened the door and was standing there. I stared disbelievingly.

'Good day, Madam,' he said. 'Would you have any objection to my sharing this compartment with you?'

'Jago! What are you doing here?'

He laughed. He looked exactly like the boy who had suggested we play ghosts to frighten prospective buyers away from Landower.

'I'm going to London,' he said, sitting down opposite me.

'I don't understand.'

'Well, I thought I'd make the most of the opportunity.'

'Jago, you really mean . . .'

'I mean that I wanted to go to London. It is such a bore travelling on one's own. How much wiser to find a pleasant companion.'

'Why didn't you say you were going to London?'

'I thought I would give you a nice surprise. I love surprising people . . . and particularly you, Caroline. You're so worldly nowadays, so knowledgeable, so learned, that it is wonderful to present you with something you hadn't thought of first.'

'You must have got on the train at the same time as I did. I didn't see you.'

'I was holding aloof while you made your fond farewells, and then . . . when you weren't looking, I slipped on . . .

and at the earliest possible moment I decided not to keep your pleasant surprise from you any longer. So here I am. Your travelling companion. Are you pleased?'

'You are so ridiculous,' I said.

'Yes. Isn't that charming? I have a delicious luncheon basket.'

'Where?'

'In the compartment where I have my seat. I am going to transfer it to here. I will leave you for a few moments.'

I found myself laughing. I felt better already.

In a short time he was back with the basket.

'I told them to make it *à deux*.'

'So you planned all this.'

'Every operation needs careful planning if it is to achieve the maximum success.'

'I still can't see why you couldn't have told me.'

'Don't you think there might have been objections? A lady of your renowned virtue travelling to London with a man of slightly less moral rectitude?'

'There might have been.'

'Well now, no one knows.'

'I suppose they know you are going to London.'

'Oh no. I'm a diplomat at heart. They think I am going to Plymouth.'

'Why the subterfuge?'

'Because I could not think of a reason to tell them I was going to London. Of course, I have a perfectly good reason.'

'I can't think why you involve yourself in all that subterfuge just to be in London when I'm there. I shan't see you. I shall be with my sister.'

'I shall call . . . as a friend of the family.'

'You are incorrigible.'

'Yes, but you know you like that.'

I began to laugh and we were laughing together.

'That's better,' he said. 'Now you look like the young Caroline. You've acquired a touch of asperity in later life. Is it due to the laggard lover?'

'What do you know about that?'

'What everyone knows. You didn't think you could keep such a piece of life in the raw from being circulated in Lancarron, did you? You couldn't have a better messenger service than that which is run by our servants. They listen at doors; they store their news; they impart it to their fellow minions – and it gets around to *us* in time. I can tell you, they know that I am the neighbourhood's Don Juan, Apollo, Lothario, whichever you care to name. This means that I have a greater appreciation of your sex than most men – and of course the feeling is reciprocated. They know that you had an unfortunate love-affair and they say you came down here to get over it. They know that Paul married poor Gwennie to get the house and he has regretted it ever since. It is no use imagining your life is a closed book. By no means. It's wide open and printed in large letters and lavishly illustrated so that all may look and learn.'

'So none of us is safe.'

'Alas none! The only defence we have against this very efficient detective agency is not to care. After all, they doubtless have their secrets. They have their amours, jiltings, *mésalliances*. It makes us all human – all the same under our skins – the rich man in his castle, the poor man at the gate. That's what they like to see. Who wants to be other than human? I think it's a very pleasant state to be in. Better a human being than, say, a butterfly or a grass-hopper – though there are some of us who resemble these feckless insects.'

I was laughing again.

'That's better,' he said. 'Now tell me, what are we going to do when you reach London?'

'I know what I am going to do. I am going to say goodbye to you and go to my sister. I shall be with her all the time. I have my duties to perform as godmother.'

'You'll be a real fairy godmother, I don't doubt.'

'I shall try to do my duty by the child.'

'I've no doubt of that. I only hope you don't get so enamoured of her and London life that you decide to desert us. I don't want to have to make constant trips to London.'

'That might be a little awkward as you are supposed to be in Plymouth now. Where will you stay?'

'I know of a hotel close to your sister's residence. You see, I have made my plans. I have stayed there on other occasions and shall go there again.'

'You know I can't see you when I'm in London.'

He grinned at me. 'I believe your sister is a charming young lady. I look forward to meeting her.'

'You will stand no chances with her!'

'Chances? What an idea! Are you suggesting that I might attempt to lure a virtuous matron from her hearth?'

'I think you would seduce any woman if you had the chance.'

'If she has a heart as cold as her sister's I shall not have a chance.'

'She has a warm heart but that warmth will not be for you.'

'Then I shall have to confine my efforts to melting the icicles which encase that of the beauteous Caroline.'

'You are wasting your time. They will never melt for you.'

'Is that an admission that they might melt for another?'

'I doubt they ever will.'

'I wouldn't take a bet on that.'

'We know you are only interested in high stakes so let's forget my icebound heart, shall we?'

'Agreed. Look. Here's Mr Brunel's bridge. Plymouth already. No one must come in here. Let's make it appear that the carriage is full.'

He put his bag on one seat and the basket containing the food on the other. He stood by the window.

'I wish they would not stay so long in these stations,' he said.

Someone was at the door, looking in. It was a man and a woman.

'I'm afraid,' said Jago, with a charming smile, 'there is no room in this compartment.' He indicated the things lying on the seats.

The woman nodded and they passed on.

It was only when the train started to glide out of the station that he resumed his seat.

'I didn't think you were going to manage it,' I said.

'My dear Caroline, I always manage everything I set my heart on. Didn't you know?'

'Not all things.'

'Oh, what do you mean?'

'Well, one thing I remember. You were going to drive buyers away from Landower and all you succeeded in doing was finding one.'

'My one failure. But it brought Landower back to us, didn't it? And that was what I was trying to do. God moves in a mysterious way.'

'Jago also, I should have thought.'

'Poor Paul. I'm afraid he wishes it had never happened.'

'I can't believe that. The most important thing was to keep the house in the family, and he did that.'

'But what a price!'

'You can't have things in life without paying for them.'

'He certainly paid. Do you know, sometimes I think he hates her.'

'He should be grateful to her.'

'Well . . . in a way, yes. It is a pity he has to pay for the rest of his life.'

'He entered into the bargain. I can't bear people who make agreements and then resent having to carry them out.'

'Don't be hard on him. He's doing his best. He's there, isn't he? He married her. He's a good sort really. A little melancholy. Who wouldn't be, married to Gwennie? He was only in his teens when he had the whole weight of the family debts thrust on him. He had to learn to take over from our father at an early age. What an inheritance! You can't blame Paul. He did his best.'

I said: 'It's his affair.'

'Alas, my poor brother.'

'I'm sure he can take care of himself.'

'Sometimes those of us who seem the strongest are the most vulnerable. He has a conscience, poor Paul!'

'You speak as though that's a pity.'

'Well, isn't it? Consciences can be a veritable plague. They rise up when one least wants them to. They torment and worry and really make life tiresome.'

'Am I to understand that you are not blessed – I mean cursed – by such an encumbrance?'

'Shall we say I put it to sleep long ago?'

'So now it permits you to behave outrageously while it slumbers on?'

'It's the best action to take against all consciences.'

'What a world it would be if everyone was like you!'

He stretched out his legs before him and laughed at me. 'What a world! Peopled by charming, insouciant, handsome, merry fellows like me, who go about having a good time and making sure that others do the same.'

'Utopia, no less,' I said.

'You should join me in it.'

I turned to look out of the window. 'I think the Devon scenery is beautiful,' I said.

I could not be sad sitting opposite him. He opened the basket and disclosed dainty sandwiches with ham and chicken and a bottle of sparkling white wine. My own luncheon was equally appetizing.

'There is enough here for two,' he said.

'I think I have more than I need.'

'It's fun, is it not, picnicking in the train, listening to the rhythm of the wheels. What are they saying? "Caroline. Caroline, Caroline, don't stay away, Caroline. Jago needs you. Jago needs you." '

'You could fit in anything you wanted to.'

'One hears what one wants to hear. That is what is so pleasant about it . . .'

He insisted that I share his wine and he poured it into the glasses he had brought with him in the basket.

'To us. Caroline and Jago.'

'To us.'

'Should have been chilled,' he said.

'Rather difficult on a train. It tastes good to me.'

'They say that hunger seasons all dishes. I would say the company, wouldn't you?'

'I think that has a great deal to do with it.'

The train was speeding on. The journey was half over. I closed my eyes and pretended to sleep. I knew he was watching me all the time.

When I opened my eyes he was smiling at me.

'How long will you stay?' he asked.

'It depends.'

'On what?'

'On many things.'

'You're uneasy, I sense.'

'Well . . . perhaps.'

'You'll have to see the false lover who is the husband of your sister. That could be quite an ordeal.'

'I know.'

'If you want any help, you know there is a stout arm waiting to defend you.'

'I don't think I shall need defending. He is mild-mannered. He will be perfectly polite, I am sure. And I shall be cold and indifferent. I'll get by.'

'You'll be that all right,' he said with a grin. 'But you mustn't let yourself get hurt.'

'As if I would.'

'Well, we all have our weak spots.'

'Even you?'

'I was talking about ordinary mortals. Life goes on no matter what happens.'

'A profound statement,' I said with irony.

'And very true. Take the Princess Mary who has recently lost her lover.'

He was referring to the death of the Duke of Clarence, eldest son of the Prince of Wales, who had died at the beginning of the year of pneumonia, soon after his engagement to Mary of Teck was announced.

'Consider,' he went on, 'she lost Eddy and now it is said

she will take George.' He raised his eyebrows almost piously. 'Of course it is a true love-match, and it was George she loved all the time. That's what we'll hear.'

I nodded.

'Very wise, you must admit. Forget what you've lost and discover that what is left is exactly what you wanted.'

'An excellent philosophy.'

'Do you know, this is the shortest journey I have ever undertaken?'

'What nonsense! We're miles on from Plymouth, which is your usual destination.'

'It is because I don't want it to end. I want to catch the golden minutes and imprison them for ever.'

'The poetic mood doesn't really suit you, Jago.'

'Not much in my line, is it? What I will say in blunt everyday prose is: It is fun to be with you.' He leaned forward and gripped my arm. 'And that is how you feel about me.'

I smiled at him. 'Yes, Jago, I admit it. It is fun to be with you.'

'Triumph! The first step is taken. Now I shall make rapid strides.'

'In what direction?'

'Surely you know?'

'I can't guess.'

He laughed and leaned towards me but I held him off.

'If you mean you are proposing to take your usual course of action, I think you should step back. We don't want to spoil this pleasant tête-à-tête, do we?'

'You're right,' he said, 'I will continue to woo you with words.'

'Words don't hurt anyone.'

'Nonsense! Words can be more effective than blows. The pen is mightier than the sword and all that.'

'Perhaps you're right. But words can't take the place of deeds, can they, and as long as you remember that . . .'

'You are prepared to go on listening to my honied tones.'

'At the moment I don't appear to have much choice.'

And so we continued in this bantering way until we came to London.

Jago took charge of the situation and we were soon driving along to the house which had been my home for so long.

I alighted at the door. Jago rang the doorbell and a parlourmaid whom I did not know opened the door.

She cried: 'It is Miss Caroline, isn't it? Do come in.'

Jago took my hand, bowed and departed, and I was taken in to Olivia.

We embraced. Both of us were in a highly emotional state.

'Oh Caroline . . . at last. This is wonderful.'

'My dear Olivia! And how well you look!'

'A little plump, eh?'

'A little, but becomingly so. Where is my goddaughter?'

'I knew you'd want to see her first.'

'May I?'

'Before anything? Before you go to your room? You must be tired out. Did you have a good journey?'

'Oh yes . . . very good. I travelled with someone from Lancarron.'

'Oh . . . who?'

I had forgotten that I had written to her very fully about the place.

'Jago Landower.'

'Oh really! Where is he?'

'He's gone to an hotel.'

'I hope I'll meet him.'

'I expect he'll make certain that he meets you.'

'Oh, Caroline . . . isn't it good to be together! And how are you? You look different . . . thinner.'

'The opposite of you.'

'Well, it's the baby. It makes you put on weight.'

'Well . . . what about this baby?'

'Come on . . . I can't tell you how beautiful she is.'

'You have already . . . at least twenty times.'

She looked happy. He must be kind to her, I thought. At least he has made her happy . . .

We went into the nursery and a familiar figure came to greet me.

'Miss Bell!'

'Well, Caroline, I am very pleased to see you.'

'Have you started preparing Livia's lessons yet?'

'I know exactly how I shall begin . . . just as soon as she is ready.'

Olivia laughed and said: 'Miss Bell can't wait for Livia to reach the schoolroom stage. Where is Nanny Loman? Oh, here she is. Nanny, this is my sister. You've heard of her. She's just arrived and the first thing she wants to do is see Livia.'

Livia was lying in her cradle curtained by thick pale blue silk. She was plump, blue-eyed and fair-haired. I fancied I saw Jeremy in her.

'She's awake,' said Nanny Loman.

'May I pick her up?' asked Olivia.

For answer Nanny Loman picked up the child and showed her to me. The baby opened her eyes and stared at me. I felt a little thrill of pleasure. I put out a hand and touched the soft cheek. She continued to stare at me. I took her tiny hand and looked with emotion at the tiny fingers tipped with miniature nails. The fingers curled round my hand.

'She's taken to you, Caroline,' said Olivia.

'She likes being picked up, that's what,' said Nanny Loman practically.

'Sit down,' said Olivia. I did so and the baby was put into my arms.

I looked up at Olivia. Yes, that was perfect bliss I saw in her face. There was no mistaking it.

Afterwards I went to my room.

'Your old one,' Olivia said. 'I thought you'd like that.'

I stood for a moment looking round. 'It feels so strange to be back,' I said.

I turned to her and she threw herself into my arms.

'Oh Caroline, I've been so worried about . . . everything.'

291

'Is something wrong?'

'For me . . . it is perfect. But it doesn't seem right when you had to suffer such . . . I often think of it. But for that I could be perfectly happy.'

'You must stay perfectly happy, Olivia. That's what I want. I'm all right. It's wonderful in Cornwall. I'll tell you all about it. We'll have such lovely talks.'

'Oh yes, we will. Caroline, it is so wonderful to have you here.'

Jeremy did not appear that evening.

'He'll be back late,' Olivia explained. 'He has to be out sometimes . . . on business. You'll see him tomorrow.'

I was relieved. At least I need not see him just yet. I was not quite sure what effect he was going to have on me; but I was taking a more kindly view of him because he was making Olivia happy.

We sat talking over dinner.

'There's so much to catch up on,' said Olivia. 'Letters are wonderful and yours bring people and places to life. I can see that place in Cornwall. But it isn't quite the same as talking, is it?'

'No. And it is wonderful to be together.'

'We mustn't be apart so long again.'

'No. It was so difficult for us to get to each other. And then there was all that time when I was with our mother.'

'Oh yes. Wasn't it wonderful about her finding that man . . . Alphonse.'

'She is still very beautiful. He was so proud of her.'

'We used to think she wasn't quite real, do you remember? When she used to come into the nursery . . . to see us . . .'

'To show herself to us,' I corrected.

Olivia did not notice the caustic tone of my voice. I reflected that I had grown bitter while Olivia was still the same simple, good person, endowing everyone with her own qualities. What did she know of the world? Perhaps it was better not to know, to go on in blissful ignorance, seeing everything through the proverbial rose-coloured glasses. Perhaps if you saw it that way, it was the way it became for you.

'Miss Bell hasn't changed,' I said.

'Well, she was worried for a time. She thought she would have to go. Then she stayed on. I said I wanted her to help me and you know that Aunt Imogen approves of her.'

'Oh, is Aunt Imogen still in charge?'

'Not really . . . now I'm married. She is very fond of Jeremy. She was so pleased when we married. But she still, as she says, keeps an eye on me. Jeremy laughs at it, but they get on very well together.'

'So Miss Bell is now in her element.'

'She was so good to us.'

'Good for us, perhaps. She certainly kept me in order. You were always the perfect pupil, Olivia.'

'Oh no. You were the clever one. That's what pupils should be if they are to be a credit to their teachers.'

'They should be well-mannered, docile . . . and good . . . and those were the things you were.'

'You're laughing at me.'

'I would never laugh at you, dear Olivia. I laugh with you.'

'I see there is a difference. Oh . . . I must tell you. Do you remember Rosie Rundall . . . or Rosie Russell as she now is?'

'Yes, indeed I do.'

'She's become a rich woman. She runs a modiste's establishment. She wrote to me asking for my patronage, so of course I went along. She is just the same . . . the Rosie we knew, but she is very important now. She sits in a sort of salon at the back of the shop . . . No, I mustn't call it a shop . . . It's an establishment. She sells the most fantastic hats to the wealthy. A hat has to be a "Rose" hat nowadays. At the races . . . garden parties . . . everywhere . . . there are Rosie's hats.'

'I am so glad. She was very helpful to us, wasn't she?'

'Oh yes. Except on that one occasion. Do you remember

when she was going to open the door to let you in? When you were Cleopatra . . .'

'I remember.' I was thinking of the first time I had met Jeremy. Rupert of the Rhine . . . the excitement . . . it was all coming back. There were too many memories in this house. Olivia was remembering too.

'She left suddenly,' said Olivia. 'She had to go away . . . some business or other. She had to leave at once and there was no time to explain. Well, I can tell you she is a very important lady now. I believe she has more than one of these . . . er . . . establishments.'

'She is a very clever woman. Did she marry?'

'No. At least not as far as I know. You must go and see her while you're here. I was there just before Livia was born and I told her you would be coming for the christening. She was very interested and said she hoped she would be able to see you.'

'I shall certainly go along to see Rosie.'

'We'll arrange it.'

We went on talking. I wished I did not feel so disturbed but now I was bracing myself for the encounter with Jeremy which must surely come soon.

I did not sleep very well that night. Too many memories were crowding into my mind. How could it be otherwise in this house where so much had happened? I thought of Jago who would doubtless be sleeping peacefully in his hotel bedroom, of Olivia in her cocoon of happiness which shut out the unpleasantness of the world. I wondered about Jeremy and what he was feeling about meeting me again; and dominating my thoughts, which was not unusual, was Paul. What was it like for him to be with Gwennie, to try to make a normal marriage out of what I believed for him was a travesty of one?

As we make our beds so must we lie on them. Olivia had made a cosy feather bed for herself, Paul one of nails.

Mine was not yet complete. Which would it be?

Olivia came into my bedroom while I was dressing.

'I couldn't wait for you to come down. Did you sleep well? It's just as it used to be. Breakfast from eight till nine. You help yourself from the dishes on the sideboard. Remember?'

'Yes, except that for most of my time we were eating in the nursery.'

'Jeremy came in late last night. After you'd retired. He asked a lot about you. I told him how well you are and how much you were liking Cornwall. He was so pleased.'

'Very good of him,' I said, and once again my irony was lost on Olivia.

'He does care about you a lot, Caroline. He was ever so upset. I think of it sometimes. You see, if it had worked out for you . . . which is perhaps what it should have done . . .'

'What nonsense! It worked out in the best possible way it could. From my point of view it was all for the best.'

'Do you really mean that?'

'I do indeed.'

'I'm so glad. I have worried quite a lot.'

I touched her brow. 'I don't like to see wrinkles there. You must be happy. You've got exactly what you need. All this . . . and Livia too.'

'But I do want you to be happy. Is there . . . anyone?'

'The trouble with all you married women is that you want everyone else to be in the same plight.'

'Not plight, Caroline. Happy state.'

'If that's how you feel I'm delighted. You will have to watch over Livia because I'm rather taken with her, and I might decide to carry her back to Cornwall with me . . . snatch her away when you're not looking.'

'Oh, Caroline, I'm so pleased you like her!'

We went into breakfast together and when we were about to leave the table, Jeremy appeared.

He seemed to be quite at ease and I tried to look the same, but I felt anger surging up within me. I wished I could forget that night at the ball, all our meetings . . . and then that cruel letter.

He was svelte.

'You look well, Jeremy,' I said. 'All this . . .' I waved my hand. 'It suits you.'

'We're happy, aren't we, Olivia?' he said.

She smiled at him. I guessed her feelings were too strong for words and I thought: She is far too good for him. And yet she loves him and he has made her happy. I must grant him that.

'Olivia was determined that you should be a godparent,' he said.

'You know you wanted Caroline for that too.'

'I knew Caroline would be the perfect godmother.'

'How nice of you to have such a high opinion of me.'

'I hope you are going to stay with us for some time and not run away as soon as you have come.'

I thought: I can't stay long here. I shall be saying something bitter to him. I shall be telling him what I think of him. I must get away as soon as I can.

'I'm learning about the management of the estate in Cornwall,' I said. 'It is so interesting. I mustn't stay away too long.'

'We shall have to insist that she comes back soon, Jeremy.'

'We shall indeed, my dear.'

'She adores Livia already.'

'Who wouldn't adore Livia?' I said. 'Livia is adorable and there is no more to say.'

We talked for a little while and Jeremy, who clearly felt the strain as much as I did, said he must be off. He had business to attend to.

When he had gone, Olivia asked what I would like to do and I said I should like to go and see Rosie.

'But of course.'

'I shan't want to buy one of her hats. I can't think what use I would have for one of her fashionable creations in Lancarron.'

'Rosie wouldn't expect you to buy a hat. She'd just be delighted to see you. But as a matter of fact I wanted to give

you a hat . . . for the christening. A present. You know
how you always liked surprise presents.'

'Oh, Olivia . . . no!'

'Oh, please, yes. Why shouldn't I give you a present? I
want to.'

'I know,' I said, 'it is such a fashionable occasion that
what I have simply wouldn't fit.'

'What does that matter? Please, Caroline, it would
please me so much.'

There was a knock on the door and a maid entered. She
announced that a gentleman was here and asking for Miss
Tressidor.

I knew who it was before he was brought in.

'This is Mr Jago Landower,' I told Olivia.

'And this is the divine Olivia. I have heard so much about
you.'

'I've heard of you, too,' said Olivia.

'I hope your sister did not malign me.'

'I think I gave a fairly true picture,' I said.

'Oh, did you? That causes me some considerable alarm.'

Olivia laughed. She clearly liked his handsome looks and
merry manner.

'She made you sound most attractive,' she said.

'And kept quiet about my misdemeanours. Caroline, I
have misjudged you.'

'You mustn't take too much notice of what he says,' I
told Olivia. 'This is his usual way of talking.'

'I trust it does not displease Mistress Olivia?'

'I like it,' said Olivia.

'And where is the blessed infant?'

'All infants, blessed or otherwise, are in their nurseries
at this hour,' I said.

'I was hoping for a glimpse.'

I looked at him in exasperation knowing that he was not
in the least interested in the baby, but trying to win Olivia's
good graces.

'Oh, if you really would like it . . .' began Olivia.

'If I left this house without seeing this wonder baby I

should consider life had cheated me.'

Olivia said: 'Come on!' and started to lead the way to the nursery.

'You are ridiculous,' I snapped at him.

'I know,' he whispered back. 'But so charming.'

We went into the nursery and he made a good job of feigning an immense interest in the baby. He even held her in his arms and Livia seemed contented that he should do so.

'You see I have her approval,' he said. 'She is already aware of my masculine charms.'

Olivia thought he was very amusing.

When we left the nursery I said: 'We were going out.'

'Allow me to accompany you.'

'I have ordered the brougham,' said Olivia.

'Then may I join you?'

'There is nothing I should like more,' replied Olivia, 'but we are going to pay a visit to a milliner.'

'To get a hat for the ceremony? My help will be invaluable. I'm a connoisseur of ladies' hats.'

'It's a hat for Caroline.'

'How interesting!'

'I suppose Rosie makes the hats. There won't be time before the christening,' I said.

'Oh, Rosie is certain to have something there. She does make specially but she has large stocks and I don't think you will be very difficult to suit.'

'What fun!' said Jago. 'What a delightful way in which to spend a morning.'

'Would you like some refreshment before we go, Mr . . .'

'Call me Jago, and I am going to call you Olivia. After all, we are not strangers, are we? We have met through our go-between, dear Caroline. I feel I know you so well.'

'It's lovely to see you,' said Olivia warmly. 'I've always wanted to meet some of the people Caroline wrote about. You're almost exactly as I imagined you.'

'But not quite. Better or worse?'

'You're much more handsome and amusing.'

'Oh, Caroline, you've been misrepresenting me, after all.'

'You don't know him yet, Olivia.'

'She has a sharp tongue, your sister.'

'She always did have that – repartee, isn't it? I was never clever enough for it.'

' "Be good, sweet maid, and let who will be clever." Your sister Caroline brings out the erudition in me . . . which I must confess is a little sparse.'

'Olivia was asking about refreshments,' I said. 'We have just had breakfast.'

'Well, so have I. Let's set about choosing this hat, shall we? I'm all agog.'

Olivia looked very pretty in her pale blue gown with a hat to match. A little matronly, yes, but how becoming that was! Happiness had changed her, even given her a little of that confidence which she had once lacked to such a large extent. It surprised me that a man like Jeremy could have done that for her. I wondered whether she irritated him as Gwennie did Paul. She was a very different person from Gwennie. There was none of that self-assertion which I believed was anathema to men. My observations told me that men liked to consider themselves supreme. In the short time I had seen Olivia and Jeremy together I realized that she was subservient to him, although she had provided him with what he needed for a life of ease. It was different with Gwennie. She never ceased to remind her husband that his residence in the house of his forefathers was only possible because of her good will.

We pulled up before Rosie's establishment. A man in livery opened the door and ushered us in. A woman in black and white came forward hastily.

'Oh, Mrs Brandon, Madam, good morning!'

Olivia said: 'Good morning, Ethel. We shall be wanting a hat for my sister, Miss Tressidor.'

Ethel clasped her hands and regarded me with ecstasy as though supplying a hat for me was a task which would please her more than anything in the world.

'But first,' said Olivia, 'we should like to see Madam Russell herself.'

'Do come in, please,' begged Ethel, 'and I will tell Madam. The gentleman will come too?'

'Oh yes, Miss Ethel. He wants to be present,' said Jago, passing a very experienced glance over Ethel's charms, which were considerable. I noticed speculation in his eyes. Ethel was aware of it, too. No doubt she was accustomed to such looks from the men who accompanied their women-folk into the establishment. She preened a little as we followed her into a small room elegantly furnished. The curtains and carpet were the colour of lapis lazuli and even had streaks of gold in them.

When Ethel had gone I whispered, 'Imagine! All this is Rosie's.'

'Rosie is very clever, obviously,' said Olivia.

'Who is the priestess of this holy temple?' asked Jago.

'She's Rosie, who has come up in the world.'

Ethel returned and asked us to follow her. We were taken to a room with the same coloured rich furnishings and I noticed that the blue and gold motif was repeated throughout the establishment.

A woman rose from a desk as we entered. She was tall, very slim and clad in black; her hair was piled high on her head and that with her high heels gave her elegance and height. But the eyes were as mischievous as ever.

'Why,' she cried, 'if it is not Miss Caroline!'

I went to her and hugged her, reacting on impulse.

'Oh, Rosie,' I said, 'I hardly recognized you amidst all this splendour.'

'It's the same old Rosie. Well, not quite the same . . . a bit older and much wiser. That's how it should be, eh? And the gentleman?'

'Mr Jago Landower. He comes from Cornwall.'

He bowed to her.

'It is so good of you to allow me to enter this holy of holies.'

'I like that,' she said. 'Holy of holies, eh? I wish I'd thought of that.'

'He thinks he can help me choose a hat,' I said.

'Is this for the christening?' asked Rosie.

I nodded.

'I have the very thing.'

'I knew you would have,' cried Olivia. 'Isn't it wonderful to see her here, Rosie?'

'It's a great pleasure.'

'What a marvellous establishment you have here,' said Jago. 'I wish I wore lovely hats with whirly feathers.'

'You would have to go back a few centuries,' I told him. 'I think they'd become you rather well.'

'Of course they would. How boring to be in this age! As far as dress is concerned, I mean.'

'I should hardly think the rest of it is boring for you, Mr Landower,' said Rosie. 'Now, I'm sending for champagne. This is a celebration. How long is it since I saw you, Miss Caroline?'

'Quite a long time.'

'And here you are in London for the christening. What a fine baby she is, eh? And you're going to be the proud godmother.'

'Yes, I'm pleased and honoured by that.'

'Of course I'd want Caroline to be my baby's godmother,' said Olivia.

The champagne was brought. Rosie asked Jago to pour it out, which he did and brought it round to us all, his eyes bright with pleasure. He was enjoying this.

I whispered to him: 'I hope you are finding your trip worth while.'

'Completely,' he answered. 'Thank you for letting me come.'

'I didn't let you. You came uninvited.'

'Nevertheless I shall be at the christening. I have already asked Olivia for an invitation.'

'Which has been granted?'

'With alacrity.'

Rosie herself presided over the selection of my hat. I was seated before a mirror and several were brought out for me

301

to try on. She wanted to know what my dress would be. It was to be the same one which I had worn for my mother's wedding and once at Landower. Cream-coloured, I explained, and I had an emerald brooch which my mother had given me.

Rosie decreed that the hat must be emerald green. It really was rather enchanting and everyone agreed that it suited me admirably. There was an ostrich feather – half green, half cream, which shaded my eyes.

'Perfect!' cried Jago.

'Yes,' agreed Rosie. 'You are right.'

Rosie wanted to give me the hat as a present, but Olivia insisted on paying for it. When I saw the price I was a little alarmed. I was clearly not rich enough to shop at Rosie's establishment.

I said I must pay for the hat myself, although I should be impoverished for some time to come; but at last Olivia won the day. She wanted to give me a present, she said, and would be very hurt if I did not accept this hat which was clearly meant for me.

Before we left I had a word with Rosie.

'I'd like to talk to you . . . sometime,' she said.

'Oh . . . what about?'

'Something . . . Could you come alone?'

'Is there something wrong?'

She lifted her shoulders. 'I'd like to talk . . . all the same,' she said enigmatically.

I said I would make sure of seeing her again before I went back to Cornwall.

We went back to the house.

Olivia asked Jago if he would care to stay for luncheon and he accepted with enthusiasm.

Two days later the christening took place. It was a solemn and moving occasion. Aunt Imogen was naturally present and she was quite affable to me though somewhat aloof. I felt a new responsibility. This little child was my god-daughter.

I was so proud and went out and paid more than I could afford for a silver porringer on which I had her initials engraved.

I spent a good deal of time in the nursery. I think Nanny Loman found me rather a nuisance but she bore with me patiently because no doubt she thought I should not be there long; but Olivia was delighted with my interest in her baby.

'It makes me very happy,' she said. 'I feel safer now. If anything happened to me you'd be there to look after Livia.'

'What do you mean . . . if anything happened to you?'

'Well, if I wasn't here.'

'But why shouldn't you be here? You're not likely to pass over Livia to her doting godmother, are you?'

'I mean if I wasn't here . . .'

'If you were to die, you mean?'

'Yes, that.'

'My dear Olivia, look at you! Plump, revelling in married life . . . with a doting husband and a perfect baby . . . what are you talking about?'

'I know I've got all that . . . but it just occurred to me.'

'That's like you, Olivia. You're always afraid good things won't last for you. I thought you'd got over that.'

'I have. Life is good. But I was just thinking . . . that was all. Forget I said it.'

I kissed her.

'It's done me a lot of good to see you, Olivia. Things have worked out well for you and you deserve all the happiness there is. May you always be as happy as you are now.'

'I'd like you to be happy too, Caroline,' she said wistfully. 'Jago is very attractive. I think he likes you.'

'He does . . . along with the entire female population that is not too old or ill-favoured.'

'You are cynical.'

'It suits me to be.'

'Your time will come.'

I patted her hand. I thought the conversation was drifting towards danger.

303

I said: 'I shall have to think of going fairly soon.'

'Stay,' she begged; and I said I would for a few more days.

I did go to see Rosie. I was determined to do that. Ethel knew me now and I was taken straight to Rosie's room.

She greeted me warmly. She made me sit down and once more she sent for wine.

She talked a little while before getting down to the reason why she had asked me to come.

She had progressed rapidly since she had seen me, and she had been moderately comfortably off then. She had told me that Robert Tressidor had been obliged to help her to independence but that was not good enough for Rosie Rundall nor Rosie Russell. She had had good friends. They had invested for her. They were men who really knew what they were doing and her capital had increased. She had had a gentleman friend who had advised her and helped to set her up in business.

'No strings for Rosie,' she said. 'I wanted everything my way and in time I bought him out. This is my empire now. I've another place like this one . . . or almost. Not quite as grand yet, but that'll come and I've got plans for another. Dresses as well as hats . . . accessories and things.'

'Rosie, you have genius!'

'Not me. I've got loads of common sense, though. Oh . . . and something else . . . energy. I say to myself, "You're going to do this, Rosie. No matter how hard it is, you're going to pull it off." And then I have to. It's the way I've always worked.'

'I am so pleased for you. Do you ever see any of the people who were in the house when you were a parlour-maid?'

'Oh yes. I keep in touch. That's how I know what I know. I have other sources, though. In the beginning I had to keep a few things dark – just till I got going. Then I thought: To hell with it. I'm myself and that's what I'm going to be. Where I am, nobody's going to pull me down. Oh yes, I prefer to keep in touch with the people I knew in my less comfortable days. That's how I get to know what's what.'

'What do you know?'

She hesitated. 'I wondered whether I should talk about this. I'm not sure. I don't know what can be done about it either.'

'What are you trying to tell me, Rosie?'

'Well, Robert Tressidor must have left Miss Olivia well off.'

'He did. Most of the money went to her.'

'There were charities and things. They got a good share.'

'Yes, they did. But Olivia had the bulk. She is quite rich, of course, and she has the house and the house in the country. She runs a big household . . . just about the same, I imagine, as when her father was alive.'

'Well, I have friends. They come and see me now and then. I'm the sort who's been able to keep my friends. I always liked the independent life. Some of those jaunts of mine I used to enjoy but most of them were a matter of business. I don't need that sort of business now. Sometimes I have a steady gentleman friend . . . but it doesn't mean all that much to me. What I was saying was, I have kept a lot of my friends and that's how I hear things.'

'It's not like you to take so long to get to the point, Rosie.'

'I know. I'm just wondering . . . I don't want to put a word out of turn. I could be quite wrong. Well, the fact is, that husband of your sister's . . . he's playing the tables pretty recklessly. I heard that he'd got to be pretty rich to keep up that sort of play.'

'Oh . . . I see,' I said blankly.

'I know what can be lost in some of those clubs in a night. It's a mug's game. I couldn't speak to Miss Olivia about it. I thought you might be the one to mention it.'

'It's a horrible situation. Jeremy Brandon . . . gambling her fortune away. What will become of Olivia?'

'I don't suppose it would get all that bad. She may have money of her own which he can't touch.'

'He'd get round Olivia. She couldn't keep anything back from him. I feel rather alarmed.'

'It may be only a rumour.'

'What can *I* do about it, Rosie?'

'I don't know. I wondered if you might speak to him.'

'Me! Speak to him! You know what happened between us.'

'He threw you over when he knew there was no money. I reckon he's a real gambler.'

'I couldn't bear it if anything went wrong for Olivia. She's so happy.'

'Well, perhaps it's one of those storms in a teacup. I just thought I'd put you in the picture.'

'Olivia doesn't seem to be short of money, does she? I mean . . . she pays her bills to you?'

'On the dot. I wish there were more like her. I expect I've raised something where there isn't anything. Forget what I said. It was just that it was on my mind. I always had a special soft spot for you and Miss Olivia. See if you can find out whether she's anxious. She might know . . . If he's asked for something . . . selling out bonds and shares and things. She ought to stand firm. I know a bit about finance myself and how easy it is to come a cropper.'

'I'll see if I can probe a bit. But I don't see how I can ask outright.'

'Of course not. Don't let her know that I've put you up to it.'

'I won't, Rosie. It's good of you to be so concerned.'

'Money has to be handled with care. There's some like me who started with none. We make it and have a special reverence for it. But there are others who have to get it somehow and they seem to think it's just there for throwing away.'

'A pity they're not all wise like you, Rosie.'

She winked. 'I wouldn't want too many rivals. But having laid my hands on a bit, I'm not letting it go. With men like Jeremy Brandon it's "Easy come, Easy go." Perhaps it's because he's so different from me that I'm suspicious of him. He might win it all back one day. There's good luck around as well as bad and somebody's got to get it sometime.'

'So it's the money. I was really rather afraid it might have been another woman.'

Rosie was silent and I looked at her sharply.

'Is there?' I asked.

She shrugged her shoulders. 'I know nothing definite. There's always talk. There is a woman . . . Flora Carnaby . . . rather a flashy sort. He's been seen with her. Nothing serious, I imagine. She's just there at one of the clubs, working there, I think.'

'Oh dear. Poor Olivia!'

'She wouldn't have an inkling.'

'People might tell her. You know what they are. All her illusions would be shattered. One of the things which has made all this acceptable to me is Olivia's belief in the goodness of life and him and everything.'

'She'll go on believing in it all. It's common enough, you know. I couldn't tell you the number of model husbands I've come across in the course of my life.'

'It's horrible. I want none of it. Wise women like you and my Cousin Mary keep out of it. They know what they are doing. They are dignified and independent. Oh dear, I do hope Olivia never finds out . . .'

'She won't. I tell you, it's commonplace. She's not the probing sort and Flora's not the girl any sensible man would leave home for. Forget it. I'm sorry I told you. I've worried you. It was the money that I was concerned about . . . more than the girl.'

'I feel I want to look after Olivia, protect her.'

'Yes, I know. One feels like that with Olivia. But in the long run it often seems people like her are better able to look after themselves than the rest of us. They are protected by their innocence.'

'Rosie . . . if anything happens . . . will you tell me? Will you write to me?'

'Honour bright, I will do that. Now stop fretting. How did you like the hat?'

'Very much.'

'You looked a picture in it, I bet. I expect everyone was

307

saying, "Who is the girl with the green eyes?"'

'I think most of them were concentrating on the smaller girl with the blue eyes. It was Livia's day. There was no doubt of that.'

'That fellow who came with you. Now he was something.'

'You mean Jago Landower.'

'He'd got his eye on you.'

'Among others.'

'One of the rovers. Oh, I saw that. He'd need a firm hand.'

'I've no intention of supplying it.'

'Yes, I see he's too much every woman's man to be any one's in particular.'

'You should know. You're the connoisseur of the sex.'

'Men are like hats. Either they suit you or they don't.'

'I can hardly believe that any of them would be flattered by the comparison.'

'Remember I have a great respect for hats,' said Rosie. She lifted her glass. 'To you, dear Caroline and Olivia. All the very best that life can offer, and that's quite a lot.'

I raised my glass.

'And the very same to you, dear Rosie.'

That evening I found myself alone with Olivia and I said: 'I suppose you are very rich, Olivia?'

'I suppose so,' she answered.

'This is a costly household. It is just the same as it was when your father was alive.'

'There are very few changes. I don't have to worry about money.'

'Does anyone do the worrying for you then?'

'Jeremy, of course.'

'I see,' I said. 'And he's quite happy with the arrangements? I mean . . . it doesn't worry him?'

'Not in the least. He understands about money.'

I thought: I know he has a great appreciation for it, but

does he know that even a large fortune can be squandered in a short time?

She looked so trusting and contented, how could I arouse suspicions in her mind? Moreover, it was only conjecture. How could I say, 'Rosie has heard rumours that your husband is losing money at the gaming tables . . . money you brought to him?' Perhaps it was only a rumour. He could have been seen to lose a little and people would start fabricating all sorts of stories about him.

There was nothing I could do.

I said to her: 'Olivia, you would write to me . . . if you needed to confide anything?'

'But of course.'

'Don't forget I shall want to know all about my god-daughter.'

'You shall,' said Olivia, dimpling.

'And . . . about you yourself,' I added.

She nodded. 'And in return I want to hear about those amusing people you meet down there.'

'And don't hesitate to write about anything . . . just anything. If something goes wrong . . .'

'What do you mean?'

'Well, you never know. You often used to keep things to yourself. I want you to tell me if anything worries you.'

'Nothing is going to worry me.'

'But if it should, you will?'

'Yes, I will.'

'And write and let me know everything that Livia does. First smile. First tooth.'

'Too late for the first smile.'

'All the rest, then.'

'I promise. And do come again soon.'

'Yes, I will. And wouldn't it be fun if you came to Cornwall?'

'Perhaps when Livia is older.'

So we talked and I consoled myself that Jeremy could not be losing a great amount of money, otherwise she must surely know.

Jago left at the same time as I did and the journey back passed speedily and pleasantly. Joe was waiting for me.

'Miss Tressidor 'ave missed 'ee something terrible, Miss Caroline,' he told me. 'She have been as touchy as a bear with a sore head. You can guess what she's been like.'

'I have never known a bear . . . let alone one with a sore head.'

'You're a funny one, you are, Miss Caroline. Proper touchy, she's been. All happy today, though. I see Mr Jago was on the train with you. He's been away as long as you have.'

'Oh?' I said noncommitally.

I wondered how soon that information would be passed round.

'Reckon he's been to Plymouth. Still a bit of to-ing and fro-ing with them Landowers. Mind you, it ain't like it was afore they come into the money.'

I thought: I am indeed back, back to local speculation and gossip, back to a situation which I must keep in hand.

As we passed Landower I wondered whether Paul had noticed my going and how he had felt about it. Suppose I went back to London. Perhaps I could help Rosie sell her hats. I should think that would be an eventful career.

How amusing . . . the daughter of the house – who had turned out to be no true daughter – going to work for the parlourmaid – who was no true parlourmaid.

Things were not always what they seemed.

Did I want to go away. No. I should hate to. I wanted to be free with Cousin Mary, and why not admit it? With the chance of seeing Paul Landower and dreaming – and hoping – that we could pass together out of this unsatisfying state in which we found ourselves.

Cousin Mary was waiting for me.

There was no mistaking her joy in my return.

'Thought you were never coming back,' she grumbled.

'Of course I came back,' I said.

'No Longer
Mourn for Me'

———❦———

Memories of Olivia stayed with me after I had returned.

Cousin Mary wanted to hear all about my visit and I told her. I mentioned that Jago had travelled up with me.

She laughed. 'One can't help liking Jago, eh?' she said. 'No, of course one can't. He's a bit of a rogue but a charming one. I dare say he'll be marrying soon.'

'He won't have to be so concerned with bolstering up the family fortunes as his brother was.'

She looked at me sharply. 'It's a pity. Jago ought to have been the one to have done it. It wouldn't have affected him half so much. He would have just gone on in his old way.'

'Would he have looked after the estate?'

'Ah, there you have a point. Well, it's worked out the way it has and Jago will, I dare say, settle down in due course.'

She was looking rather slyly at me.

'He won't with me,' I said, 'even if he had the inclination – which I doubt.'

'I think he's fond of you.'

'As I have said: and of every member of the female population under thirty and perhaps beyond.'

'That's Jago. Well, well, it'll be interesting. But he did go up to London, remember. What did Olivia think of him?'

'Charming. But then she would be inclined to think everyone charming – and he was very pleasant.' I told her about Rosie and her comments.

She looked grave. 'It would be in character, wouldn't it? Yes, indeed it would. Well, there's nothing you can do about it. Perhaps it's a temporary embarrassment. I suppose people sometimes win. Otherwise they wouldn't do it, would they? As for that woman . . . some night-club hostess . . . that wouldn't be serious, and it's inevitable, I reckon, with a man like that.'

Enthusiastically I described the baby. She gave me some oblique looks which I knew meant she thought I was hankering after one of my own.

I answered her as though she had spoken. She was accustomed to my reading her thoughts. 'Being a godmother is quite enough for me.'

'You might change your mind.'

'I hardly think so. Unfortunately one can't have a family without a husband, and that is something I really can do without.'

'You'll grow away from all that.'

I shook my head. 'There are too many about like Jeremy Brandon.'

'Oh, but they're not all like that!'

'My circle is rather limited, but in it there are two who sold themselves for a mess of pottage. Very nice pottage in both cases, I must admit. A fortune and a grand old house. Well worth while both. No. I have nothing to offer so there will be no suitors for my hand.'

'I wouldn't be too sure of that.'

'I'm sure enough . . . and of my own feelings.'

'I've often thought that you could get rather bitter, Caroline. People do, I know . . . when these things happen to them. But it doesn't do to judge the whole world on one or two people.'

'There is my mother. I doubt whether she would have found Alphonse so appealing without his money. Poor Captain Carmichael couldn't stay the course, could he? He was handsome and charming . . . more than Alphonse.'

'You shouldn't dwell on those things, dear.'

'I have to see the truth as it is presented to me.'

'Forget it all. Stop brooding on the past. Come out now. I want to go along to Glyn's farm and then I want you to

312

have a look at the books with me. Everything is getting very profitable. Very satisfactory, I can assure you.'

She was right. I threw myself into the work of the estate. I was becoming absorbed in it, and I realized how I had missed it while I had been away.

There came the occasional postcard from my mother. Life was wonderful. They were in Italy, in Spain and then back in Paris. Alphonse was such an important business man. She was in her element. There were so many people who had to be entertained. Alphonse wrote to me and said he would be delighted for me to join them. There was always a home for me with them if I wished it. But at least why not come for a visit? He was as enamoured of my mother as ever and I imagined she was of use to him in his business. She certainly knew how to entertain and there was no doubt of his delight in his marriage. My mother was less pressing in her invitation and I gathered she did not want a grown-up daughter around to betray her age.

I would not wish to go with them. While I was working here with Cousin Mary I could forget so much which was unpleasant.

Soon after my return I rode out to the moors. It was my favourite spot. I loved the wildness of the country, the wide horizons, the untamed nature of the place, the springy grass, the clumps of gorse, the jutting boulders and the little streams which seemed to spring up here and there from nowhere.

The country was colourful – its final splash of colour as the year was passing. The oaks were now a deep bronze; very soon the leaves would be falling. There were lots of berries in the hedgerows this year. Did that mean a cold winter?

I rode almost automatically in the direction of the mine. It fascinated me. It looked so desolate and grim. How different it must have been when the men were working there!

I dismounted and, patting my horse, asked him to wait awhile; but on second thoughts, fearing he might not be able to resist the wild call of the moor, I tethered him to a bush and I went close to the mine and looked down.

It was eerie – due to the loneliness of the moor, I told myself. I took a stone and threw it down into the shaft. I listened to hear it hit bottom, but I heard nothing.

Paul was almost upon me before I heard the sound of his horse's hoofs. He galloped up, dismounted and tied his horse to the same bush as mine.

'Hello,' I said, 'I didn't hear you approach until you were almost upon me.'

'I thought I told you not to go near the mine.'

'I believe you did. But I don't have to do as I'm told.'

'It is as well to take advice from people who know the country better than you do.'

'I can see no danger in standing here.'

'The earth is soft and soggy. It could crumble under your feet. You could slide down there and call till you'd no voice to call with, and no one would hear you. Don't do it again.' He had come close and he caught and held my arm. 'Please,' he added.

I stepped backwards so that I was nearer to the edge of the mine. He caught me in his arms and held me.

'You see . . . how easy it is.'

'I'm perfectly all right.'

His face was close to mine. I felt weak, forgetting that he had married a woman for what she could bring him and that he was as mercenary in his way as Jeremy was in his.

He said: 'I have wanted to talk to you for so long.'

I tried to release myself but he would not let me go.

'Come away from the mine,' he said. 'I feel alarmed to see you so reckless.'

'I'm not in the least reckless, you know.'

'You were dangerously close. You don't understand these moors. You should come here with people who know the country.'

'I've been here quite a while now. I am becoming as sure-footed as a native.'

He was still holding me, looking at me appealingly. Then

suddenly he held me tightly against him and kissed me.

For a moment I did not struggle. In spite of everything I wanted this . . . for so long I had wanted it . . . ever since the days at school when I had dreamed about him.

Then all my anger came sweeping back. It was anger against him . . . against Jeremy . . . and all arrogant men who thought they could use women as it suited them . . . becoming engaged when they thought there was a fortune, casually saying goodbye when there was not, marrying to retrieve their fortunes and then afterwards attempting to make love to someone they preferred to the one who went with the bargain.

Yes, I was angry, bitterly angry, because there was nothing I wanted more than to be with Paul, to love him, to spend my life with him.

'How dare you behave in this way!' I cried.

He looked at me sadly and said simply: 'Because I love you.'

'What nonsense!'

'You know it's not nonsense. You know I loved you when we were in France and I felt you were not indifferent to me then. That's true, isn't it?'

I flushed. I said: 'I did not know you then, did I?'

'You knew how you felt about me.'

'But it was not *you*. It was someone I mistook for you. Then I discovered my mistake. You've forgotten I've already learned something about men and their motives.'

'You saw that man when you were in London?'

'Yes, I saw him.'

'Something happened . . .'

'What do you think happened? He is married to my sister. I was godmother to their child.'

'But you and he . . . How were you?'

'*He* behaved like the exemplary husband. Why should he not? He achieved his ends. An impecunious young gentleman, he now lives the life of a very wealthy one. You will understand that. As for myself I was aloof, cool, dignified . . . indifferent. How did you expect me to be?'

'Caroline, listen. I want you to understand. Please . . . let us move away from this mine.' He put his arm round me and held me tightly against him. I made a pretence of trying to escape but he held on firmly and I allowed him to lead me over the grass.

He indicated one of the boulders. 'Sit down,' he said. 'They make good back rests.'

'I really don't want to sit.'

'I think you are afraid of me.'

'Afraid of you! Why should I be? Are you a monster then, as well as . . .'

He drew me down beside him. 'Go on,' he said, 'as well as what?'

'A fortune-hunter,' I said.

'You are talking about my marriage. I want to talk to you about that. I want to explain.'

'There isn't really anything to explain. It is all very clear.'

'I don't think it is.'

'It is not really so profound, surely. You saved the house for the family. It was a noble act. Landower was passing into alien hands and for the honour of tradition, the family, the ancient ancestry in general, you sacrificed your own in particular.'

'You are so bitter. It tells me a good deal.'

He turned my head to look at me; then he took my face in his hands and kissed me, angrily, wildly, over and over again.

I tried to escape but it was impossible. In any case I did not really want to. I wanted to stay here, leaning against him. It was a kind of balm to my wretchedness, because I knew now more certainly than I had ever done that I wanted to be with him always and for ever . . . and that I could never be.

'If I could go back,' he said, 'I would not do it. I would face anything . . . rather.'

'It is easy to say that . . . when it is too late.'

'If I could be here with you and all that had not happened . . . I could be happy . . . so happy . . . happier than I have

316

ever thought possible . . . because of you, Caroline. When I am with you everything seems different. I'm alive as I never have been before. I just don't care about anything. I just want to be with you.'

I wanted to believe him. I wanted to lie against him and say: 'Let's forget it happened. Let's pretend.'

I heard my voice, hard and brittle, because of my wretchedness and my need to disguise my true feeling: 'It's an old complaint. When things haven't turned out as we expected . . . we want to go back and live our lives over again. We can't go back . . . ever. We ought to remember that when we take these actions. No, Paul. You'd do the same thing over again. That house . . . it's important to you . . . more important than anything. Just consider. You'd be living in the farmhouse. You'd see Landower stretched out before you . . . all that land which used to be yours for all those generations . . . now belonging to someone else. That would have been hard to bear.'

'I could have borne it,' he said, 'if you had been there. And I would have got it back . . . decently . . . honourably . . . in time.'

'How is a farmer going to find the money to buy a big estate?'

He was silent.

'You can't go back, Paul,' I said.

'No. That's the pity of it. It's a mistake, I know now, to live for bricks and stones. If you had been there it wouldn't have happened. I should have known.'

'I was there.'

'A child. But there was something special about you even then. I saw you in the train. Often . . . during those magic days in France . . . it seemed as though you and I were meant for each other. You must have felt that.'

'I was pleased to see you. Life was rather dull there.'

'You mean I relieved the tedium.'

'You did, of course.'

'But you seemed . . .'

I turned to him and said coolly: 'I did not then know about your bargain.'

'Don't call it that.'

'Your transaction, then.'

'That sounds worse.'

'It is what it is. It was a sordid bargain and there is no disguising that. You should have told me then that you had saved the house . . . by marrying.'

'I wanted to get away from it all. I was trying to behave as though it had never happened. When Miss Tressidor asked me to look for you I was excited . . . and then I found you . . . the same girl and yet . . . different. I just snatched at those few days and tried to forget.'

'It was foolish of you.'

'When you fell from your horse and I thought for a moment that you might have been badly hurt . . . killed even . . . I knew then that if anything happened to take you from me I should never be happy again. I should be living my life in a sort of twilight . . . which is what I have been doing until you came. It's different now you're here, Caroline; and somehow that gives me hope.'

'I cannot think what you hope for,' I said gravely.

'When I kissed you just now, for a moment – just for a moment – I knew that you could love me.'

I was silent. I wanted to deny it, but I could not. My voice would shake and betray me. This was different from anything I had known before, but I must be strong. I would not be hurt again.

I said: 'I don't think you should talk in this way.'

'I want you to know my feelings.'

'You have explained them. Whether I believe you or not is another matter.'

'You believe me, Caroline.'

'I do not see what purpose these revelations serve.'

'If I thought that you cared for me . . . just a little . . . I should hope.'

'Hope for what?' I asked sharply.

'I should hope that I might see you sometimes . . . alone. That we could meet . . . be together . . .'

'It would be unwise for a husband to make assignations with a woman not his wife. They would have to be secret. If we met in public places the Lancarron gossips would make a good deal of it.'

He moved nearer to me and put his arms about me. 'Let me hold you for a moment, Caroline my darling.'

We were silent for a few moments. I tried to draw myself away. I tried to deny the truth, but it was too strong for me. Whatever he had done I loved him.

He kissed me. He threw off my riding hat and ran his hands through my hair.

'Caroline,' he said. 'I love you.'

This is madness, I thought. It can only lead to one thing. I had been humiliated once. Was I going to let it happen again? I knew what he was implying. I should be his mistress. Secret, clandestine, sordid . . . and in time he would grow tired. Goodbye. It was nice while it lasted. I had been wooed once for the fortune I was thought to have; and then discarded. Was I going to give way to my emotions? Was I going to allow myself to be used again?

I withdrew myself and said: 'There must be no more meetings.'

'I must see you,' he said.

I shook my head.

'Let us take what happiness we can.'

'What of Gwennie?'

'She cares for the position. She is in love with the house and all it entails.'

'And not with you?'

'Certainly not with me.'

'I think she is in a way.'

'You don't mean that.'

'I do. I have seen her look at you. She loves the house, true. Why should she not? She bought it . . . but she bought you with it.'

319

'Please don't talk of it in that way,' he begged. 'Shall I tell you how it came about?'

'I know how it came about. It is a simple story. The house was falling about your heads. It needed a fortune spending on it. The family couldn't save it. Moreover, there were enormous debts. Mr Arkwright came along and bought the house and then thought it was a good idea to buy the squire as well. It's not a particularly original story.'

'That's the bald outline. Shall I tell it my way? What you said is right about the house needing repair and the debts. Up to the time the Arkwrights came. But for one incident they would have gone away and it might have been that we should never have sold the place. Then I suppose we should have patched it up in some way. I would have set about improving my fortunes. I might have succeeded, who knows?'

'But it didn't work out like that.'

'No, because of a certain incident. Gwennie said, "I must see that wonderful old minstrels' gallery." She went up there on her own. I was in the hall with her father . . .'

'Yes,' I said faintly.

'Something happened in the gallery. Two people played a trick.'

'Oh?'

'Yes. I was in the hall, remember. When she screamed, I looked up. I was just in time to see what Gwennie saw. There *was* someone there . . . someone whom I recognized.'

I felt my heart begin to beat very fast. Paul leaned towards me and put his hand on it.

'It's racing,' he said. 'I know why. Do you know, if that incident hadn't happened the Arkwrights would have gone away. They told me this afterwards. They liked the house but were appalled by its condition. He was too shrewd to see it as a good proposition. Yes, they would have gone away and we should never have seen them again . . . but for the ghosts in the gallery. The ghosts are not blameless in this.'

'So . . . you knew . . .' I said.

'I saw you . . . you particularly. I know now that Jago was with you. I know what your motives were . . . his rather, and you were helping him. I have been up to the attics and seen the clothes you wore. You see, even then I was very much aware of you . . . dancing in and out of my life, the mischievous little girl indulging in a prank with my young brother. But for you . . . it would have been different.'

'I didn't force you into marriage.'

'But you were in a way responsible for bringing it about.'

'Does Jago know . . . you know?'

'No. There's no point in telling him. Moreover, at the time we didn't want the Arkwrights suing us – with even more reason than they had already. We looked after Gwennie and she and her father stayed at the house. They became enamoured of it and then they had to buy it and the idea came to them that . . .'

'They should buy the squire as well. A bonus with the house.'

He put his hand over mine and held it fast. 'I'm telling you that you are in part responsible. You are involved in this, Caroline. Doesn't it show how we can all do foolish things and wish we could have another chance. Knowing what you know, would you have gone up to the attics and played ghosts?'

I shook my head.

'Then understand. Caroline, understand me, the position I was in. My home . . . my family . . . everything I have been brought up with . . . it all depended on me.'

'I have always understood,' I said. 'I have always known it was the way of the world. But I want to get away from it. I don't want to be involved. I've been hurt and humiliated once and I am determined that it shall not happen again.'

'Do you think I would hurt or humiliate you? I love you. I want to care for you, protect you.'

'I can protect myself. It is something I am learning fast.'

'Caroline, don't shut me out.'

'Oh Paul, how can I let you in?'

'We'll find a way.'

I thought: What way is there? There is only one, and I must never allow my weakness, my passion for him, my love perhaps, to lead me down that path.

Yet I sat there and he kept my hand in his. I looked to the horizon where the stark moorland met the sky and I thought: Why did it have to be like this?

We were startled by the sound of horse's hoofs in the distance. We scrambled to our feet. A trap drawn by a brown mare was coming across the path not far from us. I recognized the trap and horse and then the driver.

I said: 'It's Jamie McGill.'

He saw us and brought the horse to a standstill. He descended and the Jack Russell leaped out of the trap and started to scamper across the moor.

Jamie took off his cap and said: 'Good day, Miss Caroline . . . Mr Landower.'

'Good day,' we said.

'I'm just coming from the market gardens,' he went on. 'I've been buying there for my garden. Miss Tressidor gives me leave to take the trap when I've a load to carry. Lionheart looks forward to a run on the moors when I come this way. He's been asking for it as soon as we touched the edge of the moor.'

I said: 'Mr Landower and I met by chance over there by the mine.'

'Oh, the mine.' He frowned. 'I always say to Lionheart, "Don't go near the mine." '

'I hope he's obedient,' said Paul.

'He knows.'

'Jamie believes that animals and insects understand what's going on, don't you, Jamie?'

He looked at me with his dreamy eyes which always seemed as though they were drained of colour.

'I know they understand, Miss Caroline. At least, mine do.' He whistled. The dog was dashing along not far from

322

the mine. He stopped in his tracks and came back, jumping up at Jamie and barking furiously.

'He knows, don't you, Lion? Go on . . . five minutes more.'

Lionheart barked and dashed off.

'I wouldn't go riding too near that mine, Miss Caroline,' said Jamie.

'I was giving her the same advice,' added Paul.

'There's something about this place. I can feel it in the air. It's not good . . . not good for beast or man.'

'I have been warned about the ground close to the mine being unsafe,' I told him.

'More than that, more than that,' said Jamie. 'Things have happened here. It's in the air.'

'They were mining tin here until a few years ago, weren't they?' I asked.

'It's more than twenty years since the mine was productive,' said Paul. I sensed his impatience. He wanted to get away from Jamie. 'I dare say the horses are getting restive,' he said. He looked at me. 'I think I am going your way. I suppose you are going back to the Manor?'

'Well, yes.'

'We might as well go together.'

'Goodbye, Jamie,' I said.

Jamie stood with his cap off and the wind ruffling his fine sandy hair, as I had seen him so many times before.

As we walked away I heard him whistling his dog.

Then his voice said: 'Time for us to go, Lion. Come on now, boy.'

Paul and I rode on in silence.

Then I said: 'I don't think Jamie will talk.'

'About what?'

'Seeing us together.'

'Why should he?'

'Surely you know that people thrive on gossip. They will be inventing scandal about you and me . . . and I should hate that.'

He was silent.

'But I think Jamie is safe,' I went on. 'He is different from everyone else.'

'He's certainly unusual. There's something almost uncanny about him . . . coming along like that.'

'It was a perfectly reasonable way of coming along. He'd been to get things for his garden and was using the trap to bring them back.'

'I know . . . but stopping like that.'

'I was because he saw us and was being polite. He has good manners. Besides, he'd promised the dog he should have a run.'

'All that talk about the mine . . . and then letting the dog run loose there.'

'He thinks the dog would sense anything strange before we did. Is that what you mean by uncanny?'

'I suppose so. Heaven knows there's been enough gossip about the mine. White hares and black dogs said to be seen there.'

'What are they?'

'They are supposed to herald death. You know what people are. I always thought it was a good thing to scare people off going there. There could be an accident.'

'Well, then Jamie is doing what you wish.'

As we rode on Paul said: 'I must see you again . . . soon. There is so much more to say.'

But I could not see that there was anything more to say.

It was too late. And nothing we could say could alter anything that had gone before.

I loved Paul, but I had no doubt now that my love must be put aside.

I had begun to believe that happiness was not for me.

Everything had changed now that Paul had revealed his feelings to me and I was afraid that, in spite of my resolve, I had been unable to hide my response.

I was excited and yet dreadfully apprehensive. I dared

not think of the future and more and more I told myself I ought to get away. I even thought of writing to the worldly-wise Rosie and putting the case to her and perhaps hinting that I might come and work for her. Oh, what use would I be among the exquisite hats and gowns? I could learn, perhaps. I even thought of taking up Alphonse's invitation. It was not really very appealing. Moreover, I knew that Cousin Mary was relying on me more and more. I very often went out alone visiting the various farms, and Jim Burrows had a great respect for me. There was a great deal to learn about the estate, of course, but as Cousin Mary said, I had a knack of getting on with people, a quality for which the Tressidors were not renowned. She herself, with the best of intentions, was too brisk, too gruff; but I was able to hold the dignity of my position and at the same time show friendliness. 'It's a great gift,' said Cousin Mary approvingly, 'and you have it. People are contented, I sense that.'

How could I leave Cousin Mary when she was 'like a bear with a sore head' when I was away?

It was comforting to be wanted, to know that I was becoming a success in the work I had undertaken; yet at the back of my mind was the nagging certainty that by staying I was courting disaster.

I must think about it, I told myself, and the weeks passed.

I often went to Jamie's cottage. I found such peace there. He now was tending a broken-winged bird which he had found and which he was looking after until it was recovered.

I also watched him preparing winter supplies for the bees, stirring sugar in a saucepan over the fire. He was very anxious to make sure that he had ample supplies to keep his colony going through the winter.

'Winter can be a sad time for animals and insects,' he mused. 'Nature doesn't always make provisions.'

'It is a good thing that there are people like you in the world to take up where nature leaves off.'

'They're my friends,' he said. 'There's no virtue in what I do.'

'I should think there is great virtue in it. Any of those living things who cross your path should be considered very lucky. Have you always been like that . . . caring for things?'

He clasped his hands together and was silent for a moment.

Then he looked at me and smiled. 'I've always cared for the wee creatures,' he said. 'I've been a father to them.'

'You never had any children of your own, Jamie?'

He shook his head.

'But you were married, weren't you?'

'That was long ago.'

'Did she . . .?' I wished I hadn't spoken because I realized at once that the subject was very painful to him.

'Aye,' he said. 'She died. Poor wee creature. She dinna make old bones.'

'It's very sad. But then life can be sad. And now you've settled down here and you have the bees and Lionheart and Tiger . . .'

'Oh, aye. I'm not lonely any more. It was a happy day when I came to work for Miss Tressidor.'

'I'm glad you came. She is a wonderful woman. She has been good to me, too.'

'There's sadness all around. Up at Landower there's sadness. We're happier here . . . at Tressidor.'

I wondered if he had heard gossip. He was not the sort to whom the servants would talk. It was only rarely that I could get him to talk to me as he was now, and we had taken some time to reach this stage in our relationship.

He paused with the spoon held over the syrupy mass in the saucepan.

'Yes,' he went on, 'there's a lot of unhappiness there. It is not a happy home, that I know.'

'You don't have much to do with them, do you?'

'No. There's one of them comes up to buy honey now

326

and then. It's someone from the kitchens.'

'The whole neighbourhood wants your honey, Jamie. And does whoever comes talk to you about the unhappiness up at Landower?'

He shook his head. 'No one tells me. It's what's in the air. I know it. When I pass the house I feel it. When I saw Mr Landower with you, I knew it. I feel these things.' He tapped his chest. 'It makes me sad. I say, there'll be tragedy there one day. People stand so much and then there can be no more. The breaking-point comes . . .'

He was staring straight ahead of him. I had a strange feeling that he was not in this room with me. He was somewhere else . . . perhaps in the past . . . perhaps in the future. I had the impression that he was looking at something which I could not see.

'It was really a very satisfactory arrangement,' I said. 'The marriage saved the house for the family.'

' "What shall it profit a man if he shall gain the whole world and lose his own soul," ' he said slowly.

'Jamie,' I said, 'you're in a strange mood tonight.'

'I'm like that when the bees are quiet. There's a long winter ahead, dark nights. There's a stillness over the land . . . It's the spring I like when the sap rises in the trees and the whole world's singing. Now the country's going to sleep for the winter. It's a sad time. This is when people want to break out and do what they wouldn't dream of doing on a bright summer's day.'

'The winter isn't really with us yet.'

'It will be soon.'

' "And if winter comes, can spring be far behind?" '

'Winter has to be lived through first.'

'We'll manage . . . just as the bees will with all that stuff you're concocting for them.'

'Don't go near . . .' he began and stopped abruptly. He was staring at me intently.

I felt the colour flood into my face. He was thinking of the time he had come upon Paul and me on the moor. He was warning me.

He finished: 'Don't go near that mine.'

'Oh, Jamie, it's perfectly safe. I wouldn't dream of standing right on the edge.'

'There's a bad feeling there.'

'You talk like the Cornish,' I chided. 'I don't expect that from a canny Scot.'

'We're all Celts,' he said. 'Perhaps we can see more than you Anglo-Saxons. You're practical. You see what's happening all round you . . . but you can't see back and you can't see forward. Keep away from that mine.'

'I know it's supposed to be haunted. I think that is probably why it has an attraction for me.'

'Don't go near it. I know what happened there once.'

'Do tell me.'

'It was a man who murdered his wife. He couldn't stand her going on and on. They'd been married for twenty years and he hadn't noticed much at first, but it got worse and worse. It was his nerves. They jangled . . . first a little . . . then more and more and then one day they snapped. So he murdered her and brought her to the mine and threw her down.'

'I've heard something happened like that. How did you get all the details?'

'I just knew,' he said. 'He said she'd left him. All knew the terms they were on and she'd said often that she'd leave him, so they believed him when he said she'd gone away . . . gone back to her family in Wales. But he couldn't keep away from the scene of the crime. That was foolish. He should have gone right away but he was a fool and stayed and he went back to the mine again and again. He couldn't stay away . . . and one evening . . . it was dusk . . . he heard voices calling him – hers among them – and he followed them and went down and down into the mine shaft to lie beside her. They searched for him. Clues led them to the mine. They found them down there together . . . him and his wife.'

'I have heard something of that. It was a misty night, so they said, when a man was lost on the moors, wandering round and round in circles. He had upset a witch or something. He must have been someone else.'

'It was the voices that lured him. They said it was the mist. They always would say those things . . . the Anglo-Saxons . . .'

'And it is only the Celts who have this special understanding. You and the Cornish, Jamie.'

'We have it more than most. It was the voices he couldn't resist. He had to follow her down . . . down . . . into the mine.'

'All right, Jamie. You have it your way. I don't mind. It's a morbid subject anyway. And don't worry. If I hear the voices I'll get as far away from the old mine as fast as I possibly can. I think that stuff in the saucepan is sticking, I smell burning.'

He turned his attention to the saucepan and when he was satisfied with the state of the concoction he took it away to cool. Then he began to talk about the bees and their yield, and how he was seriously thinking of getting another hive.

Now he looked at peace and quite different from the seer who had talked of supernatural matters.

I felt better after the visit and forgot the clouds which were building round me . . . even if it was only for a little while.

The weeks slipped by. I forced myself into a routine and continued to feel very uncertain about the future. Cousin Mary was relying on me more and more. We talked constantly of estate matters in which I was becoming very deeply involved.

I tried not to see Paul alone. Of course we met socially, and I thought he looked strained, enigmatic, secretive. His eyes would change when he saw me; they could become animated and he would make his way to my side and indulge in light conversation – the sort any guest would make if he were at Tressidor or host at Landower.

Sometimes I had a feeling that Gwennie was watching him. She seemed to be more ostentatious than ever. She continually stressed that this was *her* home, that she had made the renovations, discovered how something could be improved and as good as it was in the fourteenth century.

Gwennie was a strange woman. I would have thought she would have been devoted to her child. He was a beautiful boy with deep-set dark eyes and abundant dark hair which sat like a cap about his well-shaped head. One day when I was calling at Landower I found him with his nanny in one of the lanes and I stopped to speak to them. There was something very appealing about him and what struck me at once was how grateful he was for a little adult attention, which signified that it did not often come his way. I sat on the grass with him and asked him about himself. He was shy at first and his dark eyes surveyed me solemnly, but after a while he became friendly. I told him about my nursery where I had been with my sister and he listened intently.

'You mustn't let him bother you, Miss Tressidor,' said Nanny.

I replied that far from being bothered I was being delightfully entertained.

I told him one of the stories I remembered from nursery days. Supervised by Miss Bell, it naturally had a moral. It was about two children who helped an ugly old woman with her burden through the woods and after they had staggered along with the heavy load they had been amazed to find that the old woman turned into a fairy who gave them three wishes. I could hear Miss Bell's voice: 'Virtue is always rewarded in some way. Perhaps not with three wishes, but it brings its own reward.' I left that bit out, and I was very gratified that Julian was so interested and I saw the look of regret on his face when I said goodbye.

There was another occasion which gave me an inkling of his parents' indifference. It was when I saw him in the stables. He was looking with delight on young puppies who were gambolling and indulging in a mock fight against each other. One of the stablemen's children was with him – a little boy of his own age. They were laughing together and the stableman's wife came to collect her child.

She stood watching the children's pleasure for a few moments and then she said quietly to me: 'Poor little mite. It's nice for him to have a companion sometimes.' I realized she was speaking of Julian. 'I often think my own little Billy's got a better time of it than he has, for all he's squire's son.'

I said Billy looked as though he were a very happy little boy.

'There's no big fortune waiting for him. But it's not big fortunes little 'uns be wanting. It be love . . . that's what it be. And our Billy's got that an' all. Poor little Master Julian.' Then she froze. 'I be talking out of turn. I reckon you won't want to repeat what I have said.'

'Of course I won't,' I assured her. 'I agree with you.'

I thought: So they are sorry for him! Poor little unloved one! And I felt a great anger against people who allowed their own affairs to overshadow the lives of their children.

I knew from my own experience the lack of parental affection; but I had had Olivia. This poor little boy was alone really – left to the tender mercies of his nanny.

She was a good woman, I was sure, and carried out her duties according to the rules. But I had recognized at once that Julian was a child who needed tenderness and lacked it.

I had never thought much about children before. Now my anger against Paul and Gwennie grew. Gwennie was obsessed by getting value for her money; Paul was equally obsessed by his hatred of the bargain he had made.

I understood them both – Paul taking the easy way out, Gwennie angry because now he had made the bargain he was deeply regretting it. What I could not forgive was what they were denying this innocent child.

Julian was the heir – highly desirable, of course, for he would carry on the name of Landower. They did not appear to think of him as a child born into a strange world with no one but paid servants to guide him.

I became obsessed by Julian. I went often to see him and

he began to watch for my visits. It would be noticed soon, I guessed; and I wondered what construction the watchers would put on that.

In the meantime the tension in the house did not decrease. Gwennie seemed to go out of her way to stress what she had done. I could see how Paul tried not to look at her and how his eyes would darken when he did. I thought of a conversation I had had with Jamie. 'It jangled on his nerves . . . first a little bit . . . and then more and more until one day it snapped.'

Yes, I could see the dangers. I was aware of the warning voices within me. Get away. There will be trouble. Do you want to be involved in it? You should get away . . . while there's time.

But still I remained.

I saw Jago frequently. He did me a great deal of good. I could indulge in frivolous, flirtatious repartee with him and we could laugh together. His sunny nature, his casual acceptance of life, were in complete contrast to Paul. Jago would make a joke out of every situation. He pretended to be in love with me in the most light-hearted way. He said I was cruel to repulse his advances, to which I retorted that he seemed to endure it very well – in fact to thrive on it. He retorted that he could not fail to thrive in my company.

Sometimes I met him when I rode out. I did not think it was design exactly. If he had met a personable young woman on the way he would have been pleased to dally for a while. That was how it was with Jago – and it suited my mood at the time.

Cousin Mary said: 'Yes, certainly he ought to have been the one to marry the Arkwright girl. He would have taken it in his stride and they would have lived happily ever after.'

'She might have caught him in his infidelities,' I suggested, 'and that would very probably have marred the connubial bliss.'

'He would have had explanations, I've no doubt.'

'Well, it didn't work out that way.'

'More's the pity,' said Cousin Mary sadly, and I wondered how much she knew and if she were thinking of me.

As for myself, I had become quite a different person from that one who had dreamed of romantic heroes. I told myself that now I saw men as they really were; and it did not give me a great deal of faith in human nature.

I thought of my mother and her husband and Captain Carmichael; I thought of Jeremy desperately seeking the main chance and when he had achieved it setting about using my sister's fortune and spending it on someone called Flora Carnaby. And even Paul, who had sold himself in marriage, was now looking at me pleadingly, begging me to share my life with him in secret.

I want to live my life without men, I told myself.

But that was not quite true. I dared not be alone with Paul because I was weak and I was afraid that my passion, my love for him, might betray me, make me throw aside my principles, my independence, my inherent awareness of what was right. I felt he would be weaker than I was in this respect and that it was I who must act decisively.

So I made sure that I saw him only in company and I encouraged this mock flirtation with Jago which could, for a time, restore a certain light-heartedness, and make me laugh with real merriment.

Christmas came and went. Gwennie insisted that the day itself should be celebrated at Landower and we, among many other guests, were invited.

She had followed all the old Cornish customs. She had Christmas bushes hung over the doors. I had never seen them before. They were two wooden hoops fastened into each other at right angles and decorated with evergreens. They were called 'kissing bushes' because if any man caught a girl under them he was allowed to kiss her. It was rather like the old custom of the mistletoe, of which there was ample hanging from convenient places. The yule log had been ceremoniously hauled in; the carol singers had come while the guests were assembled at midday; and we sang carols we all knew: *The First Nowell, The Seven Joys of Mary, The Holly and the Ivy*. The voices, a little out of tune, echoed through the old rafters. 'Born is the King of Israel . . .' while the punch bowl was brought in and the mixture ladled out. 'God rest you merry, gentlemen,' sang the carollers.

Gwennie was beaming.

'Just think,' she said to me, 'this was exactly how it must have been years and years ago. I don't ever regret what it cost to keep this place from tumbling down. No, I don't regret a penny.'

Jago who was standing by, winked at me and said: 'Just think of all those pretty pennies . . .'

And I saw Paul's lips tighten, hating it, and again I remembered Jamie's words.

The great hall table was groaning under the weight of joints of beef and lamb, geese, and pies of all descriptions.

'The Cornish are great lovers of pies,' said Gwennie from one end of the table. 'I think it is our duty to uphold the old customs . . . at all cost.'

Musicians played in the gallery. I would never forget that fateful moment when Gwennie had seen Jago and me standing there and how she shrieked before grasping the rotten rail and falling.

Gwennie was beside me.

'The musicians are good, don't you think? They asked a big fee but I thought it was worth while to have the best.'

'Oh yes. They're very good.'

She looked up at the gallery. 'The rails have been well reinforced,' she said. 'Fancy letting the place go as they did. I've had to have it all strengthened up there. It needed a new rail, and they had to find something old . . . but not worm-eaten . . . if you know what I mean.'

'Yes,' I said, 'you mean not worm-eaten.'

'It's not easy to find. You have to pay through the nose for that sort of thing.'

'A pretty penny, I'm sure.'

I was feeling too annoyed with her to be polite; but she merely agreed, the irony lost on her.

I could understand Paul's exasperation. I tried to imagine what they must be like together. I was becoming very sorry for him and that was something I must not be. I must keep reminding myself that he had agreed to the bargain, and he must not expect sympathy because he had to pay for what he had acquired.

Cousin Mary had a dinner party on Boxing Day. The Landowers came – among others. Conversation was general and there was no obvious friction between Paul and Gwennie. Jago was bright and amusing – what was called the life and soul of the party; and I had to admit he was a very useful person to have around.

He told us he had a plan for introducing special machinery which might be helpful on the farms of the estate. He was going to London in the New Year to investigate. I said to him, when I had a chance to speak quietly to him, that I was surprised to see him so interested in estate affairs.

'I am enormously interested in this project. Why don't you pay a visit to your sister? We could travel up together.'

'I am afraid you must go on your own this time.'

'I shall miss you. Travelling won't be the same without you.'

'I dare say you will contrive to make it interesting, nevertheless.'

When the guests had departed Cousin Mary said: 'Well, that's over. I deplore these duty entertainments. I often wonder how things are at Landower. Gwennie must be a trial. And what of Jago? Going up to London to investigate machinery! Female machinery, I shouldn't wonder. He must have got tired of that woman in Plymouth.'

'Dear Cousin Mary, how cynical you are! Perhaps he really is going to investigate this machinery.'

'I saw the look on his brother's face when he was talking. I think he had a pretty shrewd idea.'

'At least,' I said, 'he knows how to enjoy life.'

'He's the sort of man who will let others carry the burdens.'

After I had said goodnight to Cousin Mary, I went to my room and there I brooded on the evening and I thought again that if Cousin Mary would not be so upset, I would start making plans to leave.

The New Year had come. We had had the south-west gales, which had been fierce that year. Several trees had been blown down; but now the wind had changed to the north. The sky was bleak with snow clouds and the wind seemed to find its way into the house itself, and even the great fires could not keep it warm. We shivered.

I had a letter from Olivia which disturbed me. There was a hint of uneasiness in it and I kept thinking of what Rosie had told me.

Dear Caroline,

I think about you all the time. I loved your account of Christmas and the carol singers and all that wassailing. It must have been very amusing. I dare say Jago Landower made it all very merry. What a delightful young man he is!

I have some news for you. I am going to have another baby. It is very soon . . . too soon perhaps . . . but I am very excited about it. Livia is well and getting plump. She is very bright. I wish you could see her.

Caroline, I do wish you'd come. It's wonderful to get your letters but it is not the same, is it? I want to talk to you. There are so many things one can only say. It isn't the same writing them down.

Please come, Caroline. I have a feeling that I must see you. It's just that I miss you very much. Miss Bell is good, but no one can talk to Miss Bell. You understand that. It's *you* I want to talk to.

The baby is due in June. Yes, I know it will be only a year since Livia was born. That is a bit soon. And being in this condition does cut one off from people. You know what I mean.

Please, Caroline, do come.

Go on writing to me and I shall hope in your next letter you will tell me you are coming.

Your loving sister who needs you,

Olivia.

I read and reread that letter. It meant something. It was a cry for help.

'What's wrong, Caroline?' asked Cousin Mary.

'Wrong?'

'You're withdrawn, thoughtful. Something's happened, hasn't it?'

It was impossible to keep anything from Cousin Mary. 'It's a letter from Olivia. I don't know what it is . . . but it seems like a cry for help.'

'Help . . . help from what?'

'I don't know. She's going to have a baby in June.'

'In June? How old is the other one? Not a year yet. It's too soon.'

'Yes, that's what I think. She's frightened. I sense it.'

'It can be something of an ordeal.'

'She was delighted when she was going to have Livia.'

'I should imagine it is a procedure which it is not convenient to repeat too often.'

'Yes . . . but I think it is more than inconvenience. I think she's frightened.'

'Would you like to show me the letter?'

I did, and she said: 'I see what you mean. She's not very explicit, is she?'

'No, but in view of what Rosie told me . . .'

'I see. You think he may be playing ducks and drakes with the money?'

'Or perhaps . . . what would hurt her more . . . she knows he has someone else.'

'Poor child! I suppose you want to go to her.'

'I believe I should . . . just for a short visit to satisfy myself.'

'I should wait until the spell of bad weather is over.'

'I'll write to her at once and tell her I'll come . . . perhaps

337

at the beginning of March. The days will be longer then and March can be mild.'

' "The March winds do blow and we shall have snow . . ." '

'How often have you had snow here?'

'Once in ten years. But you're leaving balmy Cornwall, you know.'

'I'm not going to the north of Scotland. I think I'd chance the weather in March.'

'You might have travelled with Jago Landower who, I believe, is on one of his machinery inspections.'

We laughed. I was glad she had taken the prospect of my visit to London with equanimity. She did not want me to go but she sensed the appeal in Olivia's letter.

I wrote to Olivia at once and said I was planning a visit for the beginning of March. She wrote back enthusiastically. She was so delighted.

'I feel better already,' she wrote.

Oh dear, I thought, then she had been feeling bad before.

February had come and the cold weather was still with us. I found it stimulating riding round the estate. Sometimes Cousin Mary came with me.

It was the middle of February. In two weeks I was due to set out for London. That morning Cousin Mary said she would come with me. She wanted to go out to the Minnows' farm. There was trouble with the roof. She would get Jim Burrows to meet us there.

We were riding along past the fields and Cousin Mary was discussing the progress of the wheat and barley. The roads were rather treacherous. There had been ice on them in the early morning, but a thaw had set in and the ice in some places was only half melted.

I did not understand exactly how it happened until later. Her horse slipped and she was jolted forward. She was an excellent horsewoman and the incident would have been hardly worthy of mention, but for some reason the horse took fright and started to bolt.

I stared after her in dismay, but she had him under control. I expected her to pull up suddenly and I followed. Then I saw the tree lying across the road. It must have been brought down in the recent gales. The horse was galloping wildly, head up and . . . there was the tree. I saw Cousin Mary thrown high in the air and then fall. The horse was rushing on.

I felt sick with fear. I dismounted and ran to her. She was lying still, her hat beside her.

'Cousin Mary,' I cried helplessly. 'Oh . . . Cousin Mary, are you hurt?'

It was a stupid thing to say, but I was frantic. What could I do? I could not move her. She was obviously not aware of me.

I must get help. There was nothing I could do by myself. Trembling, I mounted my horse and galloped along the road. I was some way from the Manor and was greatly relieved to see two riders in the distance. It was Paul and his manager.

I cried: 'There's been an accident. My cousin . . . She's lying . . . there, in the road.' I pointed wildly back the way I had come.

'It's that tree,' said Paul. 'It should have been moved yesterday.' He turned to the man beside him. 'Go and get the doctor right away. I'll go with Miss Tressidor.'

My relief in finding him was overcome by a terrible fear that Cousin Mary might be dead.

Paul was wonderful. He took complete charge. He knelt beside her. Her face was like a piece of parchment, her eyes shut. I had never seen her look like that before. I kept thinking: She's dead. Cousin Mary is dead.

'She's breathing,' said Paul. 'Landower is nearer than Tressidor. They'll bring a stretcher, but we shouldn't move her until the doctor has seen her.'

'It happened so suddenly. We were laughing and talking and then . . . the horse bolted. Where is he? He just went off.'

'He'll probably return to your stables. Don't worry

about him now. There's little we can do to help. I'd be afraid to touch her. Something may be badly broken. Perhaps I could put something under her head.'

He took off his coat and rolled it up.

I closed my eyes and knelt beside Cousin Mary. I was praying: 'Don't take her away from me . . .'

I realized all she meant to me and how she had taken me in and given me a new life.

It seemed hours that we stayed there on that road but there was a little comfort for me because Paul was there.

We took her to Landower which was nearer than Tressidor. When the doctor had made a cursory examination, they brought a stretcher and she was carried with the utmost care.

She was badly injured, but she was not dead. I clung to that fact. A room was made ready for her and another for me, as I wanted to stay with her. She was unconscious for two days and even then we did not know the extent of her injuries. Both legs were broken and there was a hint that she might have injured her spine; there was only one thing I could be thankful for: she was still alive.

The next few days seemed unreal to me . . . like something out of a nightmare fantasy. I was aware of people round me. Gwennie was determined to do everything she could for us – and I was grateful for that. I thought fleetingly that adversity brought out the best in people. Paul was there; he represented strength to me – just as he had come to me on the road when I needed help; he was there now and I felt that I should have the courage to face whatever had to be if he were there.

I scarcely slept; I did not notice the passing of the days. I was constantly at Cousin Mary's bedside, for that seemed to comfort her. She wafted in and out of consciousness and on those occasions when she was aware, I wanted her to know that I was beside her.

Paul was often with me. He held my hand and whispered words of comfort, and yet at the same time he did not attempt to hide the truth concerning the gravity of Cousin Mary's injuries. I wanted to know all, however bad; I wanted nothing held back.

It was Paul who said he should be with me when the doctor talked to me, and it was he who said to the doctor: 'You must be frank with Miss Tressidor. She wishes to know exactly what the position is.'

The doctor said: 'She will never be the same again. She has sustained multiple injuries. I can't say exactly how bad they are yet, but they are considerable. I doubt she will ever walk again. She is going to need nursing.'

'I shall nurse her,' I said.

'That is excellent, but you may need help. I think I should send a professional nurse.'

'Only if I need it,' I said. 'Let me try first. I am sure she would prefer that.'

The doctor hesitated, then nodded.

'There is another thing,' I went on. 'She would prefer to be in her own home. Mr Landower has kindly offered us wonderful hospitality here, but naturally . . .'

'Naturally,' said Dr Ingleby. 'But let her rest here for a few more days yet. Perhaps in about a week she could be moved. We'll have to see.'

Paul said: 'You must stay here as long as is necessary. Please don't have any qualms about that.'

'Let us wait and see,' said the doctor.

So we waited, and to my joy after two days Cousin Mary was able to talk a little. She wanted to know what happened. 'All I remember is Caesar's bolting.'

'It was a tree-trunk, right across the road.'

'I remember it now. I saw it too late.'

'Don't talk, Cousin Mary. It tires you.'

But she said: 'So we're here at Landower.'

'I found Paul and he helped me. We'll be home soon.'

She smiled. 'It's good to have you here, Caroline.'

'I'm going to stay here . . . right beside you until you're well.'

She smiled again and closed her eyes.

I felt almost happy that day. She's going to get better, I said to myself over and over again.

That evening I wrote to Olivia.

Dear Olivia,

Something awful has happened. Cousin Mary has had a terrible accident. She was thrown from her horse and has injured herself very badly. I must stay with her. You'll understand I can't leave her for some time. That means postponing my visit.

I am so sorry not to see you but you will understand. Cousin Mary needs me. She is very bad and my being with her comforts her. So . . . it will have to be later. In the meantime, do write to me often. Tell me what you want to by letter. Then I shall be as close as if I were with you.

I then went on to give her an account of the accident and to tell her that we were staying at Landower and why.

She intruded on my anxieties for Cousin Mary, because the feeling that something was wrong with her would persist.

Cousin Mary improved during the next few days . . . in spirit, that was. She felt little pain and the doctor told us that probably meant that her spine was injured, but apart from her inability to move she seemed not to have changed very much.

I knew the reverse was the case. She had great spirit and that was evident; but I wondered what effect her condition would in time have on an active woman who had always been independent of everyone – and I shuddered to contemplate that.

In the meantime I was very much aware of the atmosphere which pervaded the house. Living in the midst of it brought it home to me more strongly. It was like a cauldron, murmuring, rumbling, seething, all set to boil over.

As the days passed it became clear to me that my presence did not help. I had no doubt of the strength of

Paul's feelings for me and I was sure that Gwennie was becoming increasingly aware of this. The house seemed to be closing about me, holding me, charming me in a way, claiming me for its own.

I spent a little time with Julian. He looked so delighted when I crept in to his nursery at bedtime. I would read a story to him from the book I had bought him for Christmas and he would avidly watch my lips as they formed the words, sometimes repeating them with me.

There were occasions, too, when I saw him out in the gardens and I would then go and play with him.

Gwennie said: 'You and my son seem to be good friends.'

'Oh yes,' I replied. 'What a delightful little boy! You must be proud of him.'

'There's not much Arkwright in him. He looks just like a Landower.'

'I expect there is something of you both in him.'

She grunted. I wondered afresh about her. He was a possession – one would have thought her greatest – but she did not regard him as she did the house. 'Pa thought the world of him,' she said.

'Poor Julian! I dare say he misses his grandfather.' I was glad there had been one member of the household who had loved him.

'It's secured the family line,' said Gwennie. 'I don't think there's likely to be any more.'

I found this conversation distasteful. I think she knew it and for this reason pursued it. There was a malicious streak in Gwennie. 'There had to be some pretence at first, of course,' she said. 'That sort of thing's all over now.'

I said: 'You don't mind my going to see Julian, do you?'

'Why, bless you, no. You go when you like. Make yourself at home. That's what I say.'

She was looking at me slyly. Did she know that my relationship with Julian was one of bitter sweetness? Did she know that when I was with him, I thought I might have a child of my own . . . one rather like this one . . . dark hair, deep-set eyes, a Landower? Did she understand how I longed for a child of my own?

Gwennie knew a great deal. She was not one of those people – like so many – who are completely absorbed in themselves; she could not resist probing the lives of other people; she liked to discover their secrets, and the more they tried to hide them the more eager was she to know. It was, in a way, the driving force of her life. She knew about my broken love-affair, the marriage of my one-time lover with my sister. Such matters were of the utmost interest to her.

I often thought of those servants who watched our actions. Their endeavours were mild compared with those of Gwennie. She was an unusual woman.

Then there was Paul. He was finding it more and more difficult to veil his feelings.

I wondered why he was so indifferent to his son. One day, on a rare occasion when I was alone with him, I asked him. We were in the hall and I had just come in. It was dusk and a blazing fire in the great fireplace threw flickering shadows over the gilded family tree. He said: 'Every time I look at him, I think of her.'

'It's unfair.'

'I know. Life is unfair. I can't help it. I'm ashamed it ever happened. I don't want her and I don't want the child.'

'All you wanted was what she could bring you.' It was the familiar theme. I had harped on it so many times before. I said: 'I'm sorry, but it is cruel to a little child who is in no way to blame for what his parents are.'

'You're right,' he said. 'If only *you* were here . . . how much happier we should all be.'

He meant if only I were the mistress of this house and mother of his children. It could not be. The house itself prevented that. Time and weather had taken its toll and the house had cried out for the Arkwright fortune – and so the present situation had been created.

'I must go,' I said. 'I see that. Soon I must go.'

'It has been wonderful to have you here,' Paul told me. 'Even in these circumstances.'

I only repeated that I must go.

I often wondered of how much Cousin Mary was aware as she lay in her bed. She slept for the greater part of the time, but when she was awake I contrived to sit by her bed.

'I shan't be like this for ever,' she said to me.

'No, Cousin Mary,' I replied. But I wondered.

We seemed to be settling into a routine. I walked a little in the gardens. Paul used to watch for me, I believe, for he often came out to join me. We would walk among the flowerbeds.

He said: 'What is going to be the end of all this?'

'I don't know. I can't see into the future.'

'Sometimes we can make the future.'

'What could we do?'

'Find some means . . .'

'I used to think I should go away . . . but now I know I must stay with Cousin Mary as long as she needs me.'

'You must never go away from me.'

I said: 'There is nothing we can do.'

'There is always a way,' he said.

'If only one could find it.'

'We could find it together.'

Once I thought I saw Gwennie at a window watching us and later that day when I passed through the gallery she was there. She was standing beside one of the pictures. It was a Landower ancestor who bore a resemblance to Paul.

'Interesting, these pictures,' she said. 'Fancy them being painted all those years ago. Clever, these painters. They bring out the characters. I reckon some of them got up to something in their time.'

I did not answer but gazed at the picture.

A look of cupidity came into her eyes. She said: 'I'd like to find out. I reckon there'd be some tales. But most of them are dead and gone . . . I'd rather know what goes on among the living. I reckon there'd be some revealing, don't you?'

I said coolly: 'I dare say you have some records of what happened in the family.'

'Oh, it's not the dead ones I'm so interested in.'

There was a gleam in her eyes now. What was she hinting? I had heard that she was insatiably curious about the affairs of the servants. How much more so would she be concerning her own husband!

I must get away from Landower.

Cousin Mary seemed to sense my feeling.

'I want to go back,' she said.

'I know,' I answered. 'I'll speak to the doctor.'

'I'll speak to him now,' said Cousin Mary.

She did, and as a result he had a conference with Paul and me.

'I think she had better be moved,' said the doctor. 'It's a bit tricky, but she is fretting for her home and I think she should be at peace with herself.'

Paul protested. He wanted us to remain in the house. He insisted that it would be highly dangerous to move her.

The doctor, however, said: 'There is nothing to be done for her. We can at least give her peace of mind. That will be best for her.'

So it was arranged.

They put her on a stretcher, which seemed to be the best way of carrying her, and they took her back to Tressidor.

Cousin Mary's condition improved a little. She could not move from her bed but she was becoming more like her lively self. Whatever had happened to her body had not impaired her brain.

I was constantly with her. The days were taken up with work and I was glad of this because I did not want time to think of the future. I knew she would never walk again and I wondered what effect that would have eventually even on her spirits. In spite of myself I was getting more and more involved with Paul. He called often to ask after Cousin Mary and he always contrived to be alone with me.

I was glad to see Jago. He supplied the right sort of balm

which I needed. He could never be morbid and it was good to be able to laugh now and then.

When I asked him about the machinery he said: 'It's all in the melting-pot. But I have my hopes. You'll hear in due course.'

I didn't believe him, but before long he was away again, looking mysterious, and even more pleased with himself than he usually was.

Spring had come. Olivia wrote often and I still detected a note of something like wistfulness in what she wrote, and occasionally I fancied I caught a whiff of fear. If I could have left Cousin Mary, I should have gone to her.

April was a lovely month, I always thought – particularly in Lancarron. There was a great deal of rain, showers which would be followed by brilliant sunshine, and I liked to walk in the gardens after the rain had stopped. I rode often and sometimes walked. I went past fields of corn where the speedwells grew a vivid blue and in the lanes where the horse-chestnuts were in flower. Another year had gone. It was nearly six since that Jubilee which had been so fateful for me. I was now twenty. Most young women were married at my age.

It was a thought which must have occurred to Cousin Mary, for as I sat by her bed she said: 'I should like to see you married, Caroline.'

'Oh, Cousin Mary. I thought you extolled the joys of single blessedness.'

'It can be blessed, of course, but it is, I suppose, an alternative.'

'You're weakening. You really think marriage is the ideal state?'

'I suppose I do.'

'For example, take my mother and your cousin. Think of Paul and Gwennie Landower . . . and perhaps my sister Olivia and Jeremy. What an ideal state they have worked themselves into!'

'They're exceptions.'

'Are they? They are the people I know best.'

'It does work sometimes. It would . . . with sensible people.'

'You think I would be sensible?'

'Yes, I think you would.'

'I'm not sure of that at all. I nearly married Jeremy Brandon, being completely deluded into thinking I was what he wanted. It never occurred to me that I was an investment. What a lucky escape! And that was entirely due to my good fortune rather than any good sense I possessed.'

'You wouldn't make the same mistake again.'

'People are notoriously foolish in these matters.'

'I wish things could have been different here.'

'What do you mean? You have done so much for me.'

'Nonsense! I've had you here because I wanted you to be here. Look at me now . . . a burden to you.'

'Don't dare say such a thing! It is ridiculous and quite untrue.'

'Just at the moment perhaps you feel like that. But how long am I going on like this, eh? You don't know. It could be for years. I don't want to tie you to an invalid.'

'I am here because I want to be here.'

'I wish the right man would come along.'

'I wouldn't have believed that of you, Cousin Mary. Are you still thinking of shining knights on chargers? I'm happy here. I love the work I am doing. I feel . . . useful. You've done everything for me, Cousin Mary. Now no more of this talk, please.'

'All right,' she said. 'But I really do think you would have made a success of marriage.'

'It takes two.'

'It should be easy enough. Two people make up their minds that it is going to work, then it couldn't fail. People are too absorbed in their own wants – that's it.'

'People are human.'

'I like the Landowers,' she went on. 'It's funny . . . the rivalry between the families. Still there, perhaps. It's a pity

348

we didn't have our Romeo and Juliet . . . but with a happy ending, of course. I like Jago.'

'Everybody likes Jago.'

'He could be tamed.'

I laughed. 'You talk as though he is some wild beast.'

'I thought he might have some fine feelings under all that froth.'

'He'd never change.'

'I think some woman might change him . . . make him serious . . . make him settle down.' She looked at me wistfully.

'Dear Cousin Mary,' I said, 'I'm no Juliet and he's no Romeo. It's quite incongruous.'

'I dare say you are right.'

When I left her that night she seemed much as usual.

Next morning when I was getting up there was a knock on my door. It was one of the maids. She was white-faced and trembling.

'Miss Caroline,' she said, 'I went in to wake Miss Tressidor with her tea and . . .'

'What? What?' I cried.

'I think something's wrong.'

I hurried along to Cousin Mary's room. She was lying back on her pillows, white and still. I went to her and touched her cheek. It was cold.

A terrible desolation swept over me. Cousin Mary had died in the night.

As soon as the doctor came I took him to her room. He shook his head.

'She's been dead some hours,' he said.

'She was as usual last night.'

He nodded. 'But it was inevitable,' he said, 'and she would not have wished to go on as she was.'

'But I thought she was going to get better.'

'She was too badly injured for that. It was her spirit that kept her alive, her determination to set her house in order. I guessed that. It couldn't have lasted. You have made her

349

final weeks happy, Miss Tressidor. There was nothing else that could have been done.'

I felt stupefied. I was going about in a dream.

I could not bear to think of Tressidor without her. I could not believe that I should never see her again.

I had to rouse myself from my stupor. There was a great deal to be done, the funeral arrangements to be made, people to be notified.

The day after Cousin Mary's death, her lawyer came to see me; he expressed his deep concern and he said he hoped I would regard him as my friend, as Miss Tressidor had done.

'I have a letter which she left with me and which was to be delivered to you on her death. She wrote it after the accident and it is in my keeping. It will explain the will, I think, but she wanted you to be prepared and to tell you in her own words.'

I took the letter. I knew she had done a certain amount of writing in bed and that some of these communications had been to her solicitor. She must have known that she could not live long. She was fully aware of how badly damaged she was. She had often said that she was lucky that her injuries caused her the minimum of pain, but she knew that what had been done to her body had rendered part of it insensitive.

I took the letter to my room, for I knew that reading it would be an emotional experience – and indeed it was.

My dear Caroline, [she had written]

When you read this I shall be dead. The last thing I want you to do is grieve for me. I'm better off like this. You don't think I could have endured months – perhaps years – incapacitated as I was. It wouldn't have been in my nature. I should have been a horrible, crotchety old woman – ungrateful, irritable, biting the hand that fed me . . . which would have been yours, for you, my dear, are the one who has brought the most joy into my life. Yes, from the moment you came, I took to you.

Well, now I'm going and what I want more than anything is to make sure that you are all right . . . as far as I can make you, I mean . . . for mostly it depends on yourself.

You have worked for Tressidor and you have a good knowledge of the estate. So I am leaving you Tressidor . . . lock, stock and barrel, as they say. It's all drawn up legally. I dare say Imogen might try to put her spoke in, but I've dealt with that. She'll say she's the nearest blood relation and the place is hers by right. Can you see her here? What would she do with it? Bring it to ruin in next to no time . . . or rather, sell it. That's what it would mean to her . . . hard cash. No, that's not to be. Tressidor is mine and I say it is going to be yours.

I know we found out that there was no blood tie between us, but you're like me, Caroline. You're strong. You care about the place. You're a Tressidor by adoption. Blood's thicker than water, they say. It's true about blood and water but that doesn't mean it's true about people. You're closer to me than any of the family have been.

Well, there it is, Tressidor will be yours. You know something about the management and you'll learn more. When they read my will you'll see how it's worked out. Jim Burrows is to be looked after if he stays to help you. He's a good worker and loyal, I know. You'll do well. I'll prophesy the estate will prosper under you. You've got the touch.

I know you've always been uneasy about what you should do with your life and thought about getting posts and so on. Well, there's no need. You'll be mistress of Tressidor.

The lawyers will explain everything. They'll help you when you need help. With them and the bank and Jim Burrows you can't go wrong. You'll find everything in order. Tressidor is yours and everything you need to keep it in the state in which it comes to you.

Now a word about you. I know it was a terrible shock when that silly young man turned from you. I think it did something to you. It embittered you. That was natural. Then I believe there might have been happiness for you in another direction . . . and that's a blind alley. Sometimes I fancy there is a little canker in your heart, Caroline, a seed of bitterness which gives you a jaundiced view of some aspects of life. If I say to you, Cut it out, you might say you cannot. I know it is hard, but you won't be completely happy until you are free of it. Take what comes to you, Caroline, and be grateful for it. Sometimes life is a compromise. It was with me. I made the best of what I had and on the whole it was a good life.

We have talked of marriage now and then. I should have liked to see you a happy wife and the mother of children. I suppose that would be reckoned the ideal state. You need a very special sort of man. One, if I may say so, who will direct you to a certain extent and to do that he will have to be very wise and strong as well. He will have to be someone you can respect. Remember that, dear Caroline.

Now I have finished sermonizing.

Goodbye, my child. That is how I think of you . . . the daughter I never had. If I had had one I should have liked her to be exactly like you.

I thought you should be prepared for all this when they read the will. It might have been a shock to you.

There is one other thing I have to say to you and that is, don't grieve for me. Remember this is the best thing that could have happened since poor old Caesar tripped over that tree-trunk. I couldn't have gone on like that. Much better for me to go while I could do so with some dignity and a certain self-respect.

Thank you for being to me what you have. Try to be happy. I'm not much given to poetry, as you know, but there is something I came across the other day. Shakespeare, I think – and it expressed more beautifully, more poignantly than I could have believed possible, all that I want to say to you about my passing. This is it:

No longer mourn for me when I am dead
Than you shall hear the surly sullen bell
Give warning to the world, that I am fled
From this vile world, with vilest worms to dwell.

Nay, if you read this line, remember not
The hand that writ it; for I love you so
That I in your sweet thoughts would be forgot
If thinking on me then should make you woe.

Your Cousin Mary

I was in a daze of misery. I knew I should have been prepared for Cousin Mary's death but it was a bewildering shock. I was grateful that there was so much to do and the weight of my new responsibilities in some measure helped me through the days.

The dismal tolling of the bell on the day they laid her in her grave seemed to go on and on in my head; and what it signified filled me with utter despair. I missed her in so many ways. I wanted to talk to her of things which happened. Sometimes it was hard to believe that I should never see her again. I went over little incidents in my mind from the first day when I had arrived from London with Miss Bell and remembered in what awe I had held Cousin Mary until I had understood those human qualities and the friendliness which had reached out to a lonely child.

I did not weep for Cousin Mary. Sometimes I thought my grief went too deep for tears. I went through it all as though in a hideous nightmare; the falling of clods on the coffin, the mourners round the grave, the return to the house and the solemn reading of the will, the new way in which people now regarded me.

I was Mistress of Tressidor – but there was little joy in that.

That would come. It was almost as though Cousin Mary was commanding me. I kept saying over and over to myself the lines she had quoted. She meant that. I must try to stop grieving. I must give my attention to what really mattered. It was her life and she was passing it on to me.

Jim Burrows came to see me and very movingly pledged himself to support me and to work for me in the wholehearted manner in which he had worked for Cousin Mary.

I rode round the estate and saw the tenants.

It was gratifying. Many of them said, in various ways, that they welcomed me as the new mistress. They knew everything would go on as before. They would have been apprehensive of a newcomer.

I thought then of Aunt Imogen and the terror she would have struck into them, and for the first time since Cousin Mary's death I managed to smile.

The estate was my salvation. I would work for it and it would soothe my sorrows. I would make sure that Tressidor prospered and that Cousin Mary, if she could know what was happening, would not be displeased with me.

Gwennie came over to condole. 'My word,' she said, 'you've come into a nice little packet.'

Her eyes glistened acquisitively, as I was sure she tried to calculate the value of the estate.

I was cool with her and she did not stay long.

Paul's reaction was different. 'It means,' he said, 'that you can't go away. You'll stay with us now . . . forever.'

Yes, I thought. That was what it meant. My grief had thrust the thought of my future – except with the estate – right out of my mind. I wondered what it could possibly hold for Paul and me. Years of frustration . . . or perhaps slipping into temptation. People are frail. They mean to behave honourably but they are caught off guard and the barriers are down. What then?

Who could say?

Jago was more solemn than I had ever seen him. He seemed to understand my grief but he did not dwell on it.

His comment was similar to that of Paul. 'It's good to know we've got you here for keeps. It was right that she should leave it all to you. You deserve it.'

I was very eager that everyone on the estate should be assured that the future should be as safe for them as I could make it. I visited them all and, of course, Jamie McGill at the lodge.

I said: 'I want you to know, Jamie, that I am not making any changes. I want everything to go on as before.'

'I knew it would be like that, Miss Caroline. I reckon this is the best thing that could have happened since we had to lose Miss Tressidor. We've got another Miss Tressidor who is as good a lady as the first one.'

'I'm glad you feel that.'

'And it is right and proper the way it has worked out.'

'Thank you, Jamie.'

'I told the bees. They know. They know there's death about and they're glad the place has come to you.'

I smiled at him wanly.

'There's a terrible sadness all around,' he said. 'I canna see for it. I saw death coming. I knew there'd be a death.'

'So you see these things, Jamie?'

'Sometimes I see them. I don't talk of them. People laugh and say you're crazy. Perhaps I am. But I saw death as plain as you're sitting there. And I feel it still.'

I said: 'Death is always somewhere . . . like birth. People come and go. That's the pattern of life.'

He nodded. 'Sometimes it goes in threes,' he said. 'I've seen it work that way. Miss Tressidor she was here . . . her lovely self one day and then . . . her horse throws her and that's the end.'

'That is life.'

'And it's death, too. I go cold thinking of death. Where will it strike next? Who can say?'

He looked dreamily into the future.

I rose and said I must go.

He came to the door with me. He had changed. He looked happier now.

The flowers in the garden made a riot of colour and the air was filled with their scent and the buzzing of the bees in the lavender.

There was a letter from Olivia. She was so sorry about Cousin Mary's death, for she knew how much I had cared for her, and she was amazed that Tressidor had been left to me.

I'm sure you deserve it [she wrote], and I am sure you will make a success of it. But it does seem an enormous inheritance. You're clever, though, different from me. You'll be as good managing it as Cousin Mary was. Aunt Imogen says it is madness and ought to be stopped. She has been to solicitors and they have warned her against taking action. She is furious that nothing can be done about it. But I am glad, for I am sure it is best the way it is, although I know how you must be grieving for Cousin Mary.

I am getting near my time. Do try to come and see me, Caroline. I do particularly want to see you. I have a reason. Could you come soon? It is rather pressing. It means a great deal to me.

Your loving sister, Olivia.

Again that plea. I knew there was something she had to tell me. Why did she not write it? Perhaps it was too intimate. Perhaps it was something she did not want to put on paper.

I had a conference with Jim Burrows. I told him that I was worried about my sister and I wanted to go to her. I could postpone it until after the birth of her child but I rather fancied she wanted to see me before.

Jim Burrows said everything would be in order and I could safely leave him in charge.

I should make my arrangements and go.

The Revenge

—❧—

When I arrived in London there was a great deal of excitement over the coming wedding of the Duke of York to Princess Mary of Teck who had been betrothed to York's brother, Clarence.

Everyone was talking about the 'love-match' which had been switched to the living prince when his elder brother had died – some with innocent conviction, others with wily cynicism.

But whatever they felt, everyone was determined to make the most of the royal occasion. London was crowded with visitors and the street vendors were already out in force to sell their souvenirs of the wedding.

I could never enter the house without a certain emotion. So much of my childhood was wrapped up in it. Miss Bell met me at once.

She said: 'I'm glad you've come, Caroline. Olivia is longing to see you. You will find her changed a little.'

'Changed?'

'She has had a bad time during her pregnancy. It was too soon.'

'Well, it will soon be over now. The baby is due.'

'Any time now.'

'Shall I go straight to her?'

'That would be the best. You can go to your room after . . . your old room, of course. Lady Carey is in the house.'

I grimaced.

'She has been here for some weeks. So has the midwife.'

'And – er – Mr Brandon?'

'Yes, yes. We're all a little anxious, but we don't want Olivia to know.'

'Is there anything wrong?'

'It is just that she didn't really have time to recover from having Livia. It was unfortunate that it should be so soon, and I don't think she was ever very strong . . . as you were. However, we're taking great care.'

'I'll go to her,' I said.

She was lying in her bed propped up with pillows. I was shocked by the sight of her. Her hair had lost its lustre and there were shadows under her eyes which looked bigger than usual.

They lit up with joy at the sight of me. 'Caroline, you've come!'

I ran to her and hugged her.

'I came as soon as I could.'

'Yes, I know. It must have been terrible . . . Cousin Mary . . . and all the things that happened.'

'Yes,' I said. 'It was.'

'And she has left you Tressidor.'

'I must tell you all about it.'

'You're so clever, Caroline. I was never clever like you.'

'No . . . I'm not clever . . . very foolish, often. But let's talk about you. How is my goddaughter?'

'Asleep now, I fancy. Nanny Loman is in charge and Miss Bell, of course.'

'I saw Miss Bell as I came in.' I looked at her anxiously. She was in the last stages of pregnancy and I knew that women change at such times, but should her skin look so waxy, her eyes so enormous with that haunted expression in them. My concern for her was making me forget my grief at the loss of Cousin Mary.

'You must be exhausted after your journey.'

'Not a bit. Just a little grubby.'

'You look wonderful. I always forget how green your eyes are and when I see them they startle me. Caroline, you won't hurry away, will you?'

'Oh no. I'll stay as long as I can.'

'Go to your room now . . . wash and change. I am sure you want to, and we'll have supper together up here.'

'That would be lovely.'

'All right. Go now, but come back soon. I've such lots to say to you.'

I left her and went to the room I knew so well. I unpacked my case and washed in the hot water which had been brought up. I changed and went back to Olivia.

'Come and sit by my bed,' she said.

'I'm sorry I couldn't come before. I was all ready to depart and there was the accident . . .'

'Yes, I know. It's just that I'm worried.'

I looked at her steadily and said: 'Yes, I gathered that you were.'

'It's about Livia.'

'What about her?'

'I want to know that she's all right.'

'Is there anything wrong with her?'

'No. She's a healthy, lively child. There's nothing wrong with her. I just wanted to make sure that if anything happened to me she'd be all right.'

'What do you mean . . . if anything happened to you?'

A terrible fear was clutching at my heart. I had just come face to face with death. I did not want to meet it again . . . ever.

'I just meant that . . . if anything happened to me.'

I was angry suddenly, not with her, but with fate. I said: 'When people use that expression they mean Death. Why don't they say what they mean?'

'Oh, Caroline, you are so vehement. You always were. You're right, though. I mean, I'm worried that if I died . . . what would happen to Livia?'

'How absurd to talk about dying. You're young. There's nothing wrong. People have babies every day.'

'Don't be angry. I just want your assurance. You're her godmother. I should want you to take her. Now that you own all that property . . . now you're a rich woman . . . you could do it. In any case I would have made provisions for her . . . and for you . . . so that you could be together. I've had it all done by the solicitors, but I'm glad you're rich now, for your own sake.'

'Is that what you wanted to say to me?'

She nodded.

I was dumbfounded. I had known there was something, but I had thought it was Jeremy's extravagances. This as quite unexpected.

'Oh, Olivia, what gave you this idea?'

'Child-bearing is an ordeal. I just thought . . .'

'Don't hedge with me,' I said sternly. 'Tell me the truth.'

'I've had a bad time, Caroline. They say it shouldn't have happened . . . so soon. I've spent most of the time in bed. I just have a feeling that something is going to happen . . . I mean, that I might die.'

'Olivia, that's no way to face all this.'

'I thought you believed in facing up to reality.'

'But what makes you say this?'

She touched her breast and said: 'Something in here.'

I stared at her in dismay and she went on: 'I wouldn't have any qualms about leaving Livia to you. I have complete confidence in you. You'd be better for her than I . . .'

'Nonsense. No one's as good as a mother.'

'I don't think that is always so. I'm too tired to be with her. I'm soft and foolish. You'd be better for her and you would love her too. She is very lovable.'

'Stop it,' I cried. 'I won't listen. All this talk of death is silly. I've had enough of death. I've lost someone very dear to me. I won't consider losing another.'

'Oh, Caroline, I'm so glad you've come and we won't talk about it any more. Just give me your word. You will take Livia, won't you?'

'I don't want to talk of such . . .'

'Promise and I'll say no more.'

'Well, of course, I would.'

She took my hand and pressed it. 'I feel contented now. Tell me about Cornwall. Not about the funeral, but after and before all that. All those people . . . Jago and Paul Landower and the man with the bees.'

I sat by her bed talking. I tried to be amusing. It was not easy, because when I thought of the light-hearted days before Cousin Mary's death I was reminded forcibly that she was no longer there.

But Olivia delighted in my presence and that comforted me. We had a little supper in her room and when her face was animated she looked more like her old self.

I said good-night to her and went down to see Aunt Imogen, who was asking for me.

She greeted me with a little more respect that I remembered before and she looked less formidable than she had in the past. Whether this was because she was getting older or because I was a person of consequence now, I was not sure. Uncle Harold was with her – self-effacing as ever and very cordial.

'How are you, Caroline?' asked Aunt Imogen. 'You must be very pleased with the way everything has turned out.'

'I am still mourning Cousin Mary,' I reminded her coldly.

'Yes, yes, of course. So you have become a very rich woman.'

'I suppose so.'

Uncle Harold said: 'I believe that you and Cousin Mary were very fond of each other.'

I smiled at him and nodded.

'She was a forthright woman,' he said.

'She had no right to Tressidor, and of course it should have come to me,' said Aunt Imogen. 'I am the next of kin. I could, of course, contest the will.'

Uncle Harold began: 'No, Imogen. You know . . .'

'I could contest the will,' she repeated. 'But, well . . we have decided to let sleeping dogs lie.'

'It was Cousin Mary's wish that I should inherit,' I said. 'She taught me a great deal about the management of the estate.'

'It seems wrong for a woman,' put in Aunt Imogen.

'For you too, then?' I asked.

'I have a husband.'

Poor Uncle Harold! He looked at me apologetically.

'I can assure you, Aunt Imogen, that the estate, far from suffering under the management of Cousin Mary, improved considerably. I intend that it shall continue to do so under mine.'

I thought Uncle Harold was going to break into applause, but he remembered the presence of Aunt Imogen in time.

I said: 'I am anxious about Olivia. She does not seem well.'

'She is in a delicate condition,' Aunt Imogen reminded me.

'Even so, she seems rather weak.'

'She was never strong.'

'Where is her husband?'

'He will be here soon, I imagine.'

'Is he out every night?'

'He has business.'

'I should have thought he would have wanted to be with his wife at such a time.'

'My dear Caroline,' said Aunt Imogen with a little laugh, 'you have lived with Cousin Mary, a spinster, and you are one yourself. Such do not know very much about the ways of husbands.'

'But I do know something about the consideration of one human being towards another.'

I enjoyed sparring with Aunt Imogen and having Uncle Harold looking on like some referee who would like to give the points to me if he dared.

Her attitude towards me amused me. She disapproved of me, but as a woman of property I had risen considerably in her estimation; and although she deplored the fact that I had taken Tressidor from its rightful owner, she admired me for doing so.

But I could see that I should not get any real understanding of Olivia's state of health from her, and I decided that in the morning I would question Miss Bell.

I retired to bed soon after that, but I did not expect to sleep.

I could not throw off my melancholy.

I had just emerged from the tragedy of Cousin Mary's death to be presented with the possibility of Olivia's. But she had let her imagination run on, I tried to assure myself. She just had pre-confinement nerves, if there were such things, and I was sure there were. To face such an ordeal after having gone through the whole thing such a short while before was enough to frighten anyone . . . especially someone as nervous as Olivia.

I tossed and turned and found myself going through all the drama of Cousin Mary's accident, and then coming back to Olivia.

It was a wretched night.

In the morning I came face to face with Jeremy. He looked as debonair as ever.

'Why, Caroline,' he cried, 'how wonderful to see you!'

'How are you?' I replied coldly, implying that the question was merely rhetorical and that I had no interest in the answer.

'Much the same as ever. And you?'

'The same. I wish I could say that of Olivia.'

'Oh well, in the circumstances . . . She'll be all right.'

'I feel uneasy about her.'

'Well, I suppose you wouldn't know much about these occasions, would you?'

'No. But I do know when people look ill.'

He smiled at me. 'It is so sweet of you to concern yourself. Congratulations, by the way.'

'On what?'

'On your inheritance, of course. What an extraordinary thing! Who would have thought . . .'

'Certainly not you. I confess it was a surprise to me.'

'To fall right into your lap like that.'

His eyes were shining with admiration as they looked at me and I was carried right back to the days of our courtship. With the aura of affluence I now must look as desirable to him as I had then, when he had thought of my fortune as well as my person.

'Cousin Mary and I were very close to each other,' I said. 'Her death has been a great blow to me.'

'Of course.' His expression changed; now he was all concern and sympathy. 'A great tragedy. Riding accident, wasn't it? I do feel for you, Caroline.'

He was adept at expressing emotion. His face fitted into the right lines. Now he was very sympathetic, but in my newly acquired wisdom I saw the acquisitive light shining through.

It amused me to think that he was contemplating my fortune and I wondered how Olivia's was faring in his hands.

'I hear you enjoy the gaming tables,' I said maliciously.

'How did you hear this?'

'Oh, I have friends.'

'You heard that in Cornwall!'

'No. Well, visitors from London, you know.'

'Oh.' He was puzzled. 'Who doesn't like a flutter? I could take you along while you are here.'

'It is not the sort of thing that appeals to me. I like to keep what I have.'

'You could add to it.'

'I might not have that success and I should not care very much if I won; on the other hand I should hate to lose. You see, I should be a very poor gambler.'

'All the same, I'd like you to come along . . . just for once.'

'I'm here to see Olivia. I shouldn't have time. I shan't be able to stay very long.'

'No. You have your responsibilities. Shall you keep the estate?'

'What do you mean?'

'I wondered if you might sell out and come back to London.'

'The whole point of my having it is for me to carry on as before.'

'Well, who knows? I'm so glad you're here, Caroline. I have been thinking a lot about you.'

'I am sure you have been . . . when you heard of my inheritance.'

'I always did.'

'Well, I must go now to Olivia.'

I passed on. And I thought: He hasn't changed. He is very good-looking, very charming – and very interested in my inheritance.

A few days passed and I was with Olivia most of the time. I found comfort being with her as this took me away from memories of Cousin Mary's death. I found I could laugh a little. She was very interested in Jamie McGill and asked many questions about him. I tried to remember all I could of his eccentric ways and I talked at some length about the bees and the animals he looked after.

She said: 'How I should love to see him.'

'You shall come down and stay . . . you and Livia and the new baby. You shall spend the whole of the summer there. Why not? It's mine now. Not that Cousin Mary wouldn't have welcomed you.'

'Oh, I should like that, Caroline.'

Then I talked about what we would do. I told her of the old mine and the legends about it and how it was said to be haunted. 'We'd ride out to it, Olivia. You'd love the moor. It's wild . . . in a way, untamed. I suppose it is because it can't be cultivated . . . the stones, and the little streams and the gorse and all the Cornish legends – knackers and piskies and ghosts. We'd have a wonderful time. Oh, Olivia, you are going to come. Perhaps I'll take you back with me.'

'I should love it, Caroline.'

'What about your husband?' I looked at her sharply. I had scarcely mentioned him since my arrival. Nor had she. Perhaps she thought that as I had once nearly married him, he was not a subject I should care to discuss.

'Oh, Jeremy . . . he wouldn't mind, I'm sure.'

'He wouldn't want to lose his family, would he?'

'He'd be all right.'

'Perhaps he would want to come, too.'

'Oh . . . he's not really a country person.'

No, I thought. He likes the gaiety of town, the gaming clubs, the hostesses . . . Oh, definitely not a country person.

I went on planning what we should do. 'Too late for the midsummer bonfires,' I said. 'Well, that's for next year. You're going to make an annual thing of your visits, you know.'

Nanny Loman brought in Livia and she and I played on the floor together. Olivia watched us with shining eyes.

'You're better with her than I am,' she said. 'Well, I suppose all the time she's been growing up I've been pregnant.'

'You'll feel better soon. The Cornish air will work wonders. There's a little boy . . . The Landowers' . . . I'm rather fond of him. He'll be a playmate for Livia.'

'I long for it, Caroline.'

'It's something to look forward to.'

When I was alone with Miss Bell, she said to me: 'Olivia has been much better since you came.'

'I'm worried about her,' I replied.

She nodded. 'Yes. She is far from well. She was never as strong as you were and she suffered a lot with Livia. This was too soon . . . too soon.' She pursed her lips and put her head a little on one side. I knew she was expressing disapproval of Jeremy and I wondered what she knew. I resisted the temptation to ask, for I was sure she would consider it was disloyal to discuss her employer; and being Miss Bell, with ingrained ideas of the supremacy of the male, she would doubtless consider Jeremy, rather than Olivia, her employer.

A few days later Olivia's pains started and the household was in a turmoil. Her labour was long and arduous and I was in a state of deep anxiety.

Miss Bell and I sat together waiting for news. I felt very

melancholy. I kept thinking of Cousin Mary and how quickly death can take away.

I was trembling with anxiety and the hours of waiting seemed like an eternity.

At last the child was born – stillborn. I felt myself enveloped in terrible depression, for Olivia was very seriously ill.

I could not rest. I went to see her. She was lying back in her bed – pale and hardly aware of anything. She did open her eyes and smile at me.

'Caroline.' She did not exactly speak but her lips shaped the words. 'Remember.'

I sat beside her for a while until she appeared to be sleeping. I tiptoed out and went to my room because the sight of her so wan, so lost to the world, was hard for me to bear.

I did not undress. I sat there with my door open – for my room was next to hers and I had a feeling that she might wish to see me and if she did I wanted to know and be there.

It was past midnight and the house was quiet. I could not resist the impulse to go to her. It was almost as though she were calling me.

She was lying on her bed, her eyes open. She looked at me and smiled.

'Caroline . . .'

I went to the bed, sat down and took her hand.

'You came . . .' she said.

'Yes, dear sister, I'm here.'

'Stay. Remember . . .'

'Yes, I'll stay and I'll remember. You're worried about Livia. There's no need. If it were necessary, I would take her. She would be as my own.'

She moved her head slightly and smiled.

We sat there for some time in silence.

Then she said: 'I'm dying, Caroline.'

'No . . . no . . . You'll feel better tomorrow.'

She shook her head. 'The baby died. He'll never know anything. He died before he was born.'

'It happens now and then,' I said. 'You'll have more . . . healthy ones. All will be well.'

'No more . . . never again. Livia . . .'

'Livia is all right. If . . . it happened, I will take her. She'd be mine.'

'I'm happy now. I'm not sorry . . .'

'Olivia, you've got to think of living. There's so much to live for.'

She shook her head.

'Your child . . . your husband . . .'

'You'll take Livia. Him . . .'

I put my face close to her lips.

'He . . . the money . . .'

I thought: Rosie was right. And Olivia knows.

'Don't worry about money.'

'Debts,' she whispered. 'I hate debts.'

'You haven't anything to worry about. You've got to get well.'

'Flora . . . Flora Carnaby . . .'

I felt sick. She knew, then. Was this the reason for her apathy? Olivia had discovered the perfidy of men . . . just as I had. But whereas I had hated fiercely, she had given up hope and looked forward to death.

As I looked at my sister I felt the old bitterness well up within me. How dared he use her like this! Take her money and waste it on gaming tables and other women. I felt an overwhelming desire to hurt him as he had hurt her.

My voice was shaking as I bent over her and spoke to her.

'Olivia, there's nothing to worry about. Don't think of anything but getting better. You've got me and I'll look after you. You'll come to Cornwall. You'll meet the people who interest you so much. We'll be together . . . the three of us, you, me and Livia. We'll shut out the rest of the world. Nobody's going to hurt you or me any more.'

She was clinging to my hand and a certain peace seemed to come into her face.

I sat there for a long time holding her hand, and I knew that my presence comforted her.

She never spoke to me again.

The doctor was at the house all next day. There was a hushed gloom everywhere. I could not believe it. Death could not strike twice so soon.

But it could. Olivia was dead. She lay white and still, her face surprisingly young, the lines of anxiety and pain wiped from it. She was the Olivia of my childhood, the sister whom I had patronized, looked down on in some ways although she was older than I. Nevertheless I had loved her dearly.

If only she would come back, I would take her to Cornwall with me. I would make her forget her perfidious husband, her disillusion with life.

I shut myself in my room. I could not speak to anyone. I felt a deep-rooted sadness which I feared would be with me for the rest of my life.

She must have known she was going to die. I remembered the way she had spoken of death; the certainty with which she had faced it. It was why she wanted to see me; why she had been so insistent that I look after her child.

She had not wanted her to be left to the mercy of a father who might remarry someone who would not care for the child. How much did he care? Was he capable of caring for anyone but himself? Had she feared that Aunt Imogen might take the child? Poor Livia, what a life she would have had! She would be left to the care of Nanny Loman and Miss Bell – kind, worthy people – but Olivia had wanted the equivalent of a mother's love for her daughter, and she knew there was only one place where she could be sure of that. With me.

As I realized the weight of my responsibility, my terrible melancholy lifted a little. I went to the nursery. I played with the child. I built a castle of bricks with her. I helped her totter along; I crawled on the floor with her. There was comfort there.

The funeral hatchment was placed on the outside wall as it had been at the time of Robert Tressidor's death, and the ordeal through which I had recently passed in Cornwall had to be faced again here. There were the mutes in heavy black, the caparisoned horses, the terrible tolling of the bell and the procession from the church to the grave.

I caught a glimpse of Rosie as I went into the church. She smiled at me and I was pleased that she had come.

I walked beside Jeremy. He looked sad and every bit the inconsolable husband, and I think my contempt for him helped me to bear my own grief. I wondered cynically how deep his sufferings went and whether he was calculating how much of her fortune would be left to him.

I stood at the graveside with him still beside me and Aunt Imogen on the other side with Uncle Harold. Aunt Imogen was wiping her eyes and I asked myself how she managed to produce her tears. I myself shed none.

Back at the house there was food and drink – the funeral meats, I called them – and after that the reading of the will. Olivia's wish that I should have the custody of her child was explained.

Everything passes, I consoled myself. Even this day will be over . . . soon.

There were several family conferences. Aunt Imogen usually took control. She thought it was rather unseemly for an unmarried woman to have charge of a child. What would people say? Whatever explanation was given, they would think . . .

I said: 'They may think what they will. But as it is a matter of concern to you, Aunt Imogen, let me remind you that I intend to take Livia with me to Cornwall, and if it is any consolation to you and soothes your fears, there they will all know that it is impossible for her to be my child. I was very much in evidence among them at the time of her gestation and birth, and I am sure that even the most suspicious and scandal-loving would find it very hard to explain how a young woman managed to bear a child while going about the countryside, keeping its existence a secret and somehow smuggling it to London.'

'I was thinking of your future,' said Aunt Imogen, 'and however you look at it, it is unsuitable.'

All the same, her protests were half-hearted, for she herself did not want to be burdened with the care of Livia.

'And another thing,' she went on, 'it seems to be forgotten that Livia has a father.'

'When Olivia asked me, just before she died, she did not mention Livia's father.'

Jeremy said: 'There is no one to whom I would rather trust my daughter than Caroline.'

'I still think it is irregular,' added Aunt Imogen.

'I shall be leaving for Cornwall very shortly,' I said firmly. 'I have written asking them to prepare the nurseries there.'

'They can't have been in use for ages,' said Aunt Imogen.

'Well, it will be pleasant to use them again. I shall take with me Nanny Loman and Miss Bell . . . so Livia will not find everything very different around her.'

'Then,' added Aunt Imogen, and I fancied I detected a note of relief in her voice, 'there is nothing more we can do.'

I overheard her say to her husband that I had a very high opinion of myself, and I was Cousin Mary all over again. To which he replied, rather daringly, that that was perhaps not such a bad thing in view of my responsibilities. I didn't wait to hear her comments. I was not interested in Aunt Imogen's view of me.

I spent a great deal of the rest of my time in London with Livia. I wanted her to get used to me. She did not appear to be aware that she had lost her mother, which was a blessing. I was determined to give her a substitute in myself, in the hope that she would never really know what she had missed.

I played with her; I talked to her; she had a few words; I showed her pictures and built more castles. I crawled about the floor and I was rewarded by the smile which appeared on her little face every time I appeared.

371

She was helping me to overcome my grief. I did not want to think of death. It seemed to me so cruel that two loved ones should have been taken from me within a few months.

I clung to Livia as I had clung to Tressidor. Worthwhile work was the only solace I could find.

Nanny Loman and Miss Bell were eager to accompany me to Cornwall. They both thought it would be best to get right away.

'She doesn't know her mother's gone yet,' said Nanny Loman. 'She didn't see so much of her while she was ill . . . but she might remember . . . here. New surroundings are what she needs.'

I believed Nanny Loman was a very sensible woman; and I knew the worth of Miss Bell.

'Death in childbed,' she said, 'is no uncommon occurrence, alas. Olivia should never have undergone another pregnancy so soon. It was most unfortunate.'

'She knew, I think.'

'She was not really happy towards the end,' said Miss Bell.

No, I thought, indeed she was not. She must have known he was losing money, for she had murmured something about debts. And Flora Carnaby . . . she knew of that too. Servants whisper, I supposed. Those things which were not intended for her ears reached her in some way. It could so easily happen.

Before I left Jeremy talked to me.

'Thank you, Caroline. Thank you for all you are doing for Livia.'

'I am doing what Olivia asked me to before she died.'

'I know.'

'She was aware that she was going to die.'

He hung his head, implying that his grief had overcome him. I was sceptical. All the old hatred I had felt for him when he had told me he did not want me without a fortune, swept back.

'I don't think she was very happy,' I said pointedly.

'Caroline . . . I shall want to see my daughter some-times.'

'Oh, shall you?'

'But of course. Perhaps you will bring her to me . . . or perhaps I will come to see you.'

'It's a very long journey,' I reminded him. 'And you would find it rather dull in the country.'

'I should want to see my daughter,' he said. 'Oh, Caroline, I'm so grateful to you. To be left with a young daughter . . . I feel so inadequate.'

'You couldn't be expected to excel in the nursery as I am sure you do in other fields.'

'Caroline, I shall come.'

I studied him intently and thought: Oh yes, he will come.

Was that a certain gleam I detected in his eyes? Now he was looking at me as once he had before. He would see me against the background of a country mansion, and I could see that he found the picture as attractive as it had been once before against another setting – which had, however, proved without substance. This one was undoubtedly real.

I was amused. Oddly enough, he helped to assuage my grief a little. Thinking of him and his motives made me forget for a while the memory of my sister lying cold and lifeless in her grave.

There was great excitement when I arrived in Lancarron with my nursery cavalcade. It was the talk of the place for at least a month.

People called to see the child, to hear the latest about the new arrangements at Tressidor. The nurseries were more spacious than those in the London house and although they had been cleaned and made ready there were new acquisitions needed. I plunged feverishly into the buying of new curtains and equipment, everything that was wanted for a modern nursery. To work hard all day, to go to bed tired so that I was too exhausted to brood, was the best thing possible.

My life was doubly full. There were the estate matters

which had fully occupied me before, but now there was the child as well and I was determined to be the sort of mother to Livia that Olivia would have wished.

I had the excellent Nanny Loman and the ever-watchful Miss Bell; but I wanted Livia to have a mother in me, and I spent every possible moment with her. I arranged a meeting between Nanny Loman and the guardian of Julian's nursery, and it was fortunate that the nannies – as Nanny Loman put it – immediately took to each other. There was hardly a day when Julian was not at Tressidor, or Livia at Landower.

I saw less of Paul because when I rode out I was usually in haste on some mission or other. I had no time for dallying on the moors or in the lanes.

Jago was amused. He called me the New Woman. Caroline, the clucking hen with her one chick. He was still making mysterious trips to London and talking vaguely about machinery, and wheels within wheels and contracts which were pending.

'Why do you bother?' I asked. 'We all know there is only one reason for these mysterious trips.'

'And what is that?' he asked.

'A secret woman.'

'You'll be surprised one day,' he retorted.

I didn't think very much about him; but I did think a great deal about Livia.

I was getting more and more fond of Julian, who was delighted by the turn of events. He looked happier and asserted himself quite vigorously and adopted a somewhat protective attitude towards Livia. I longed for a child of my own. The nursery was big. I had daydreams of seeing it full of my own sturdy little ones. But I should need a husband. Was I going on frustrated for ever?

In spite of my desire to shut him out, Paul would creep into my thoughts. He was a sad man nowadays, but he could be so different. I often thought of him as he had been when I had first seen him on the train. Powerful. In charge, that was how I had thought of him. Master of his fate. But even then he had been worried about the estate and had been returning from Plymouth where he had possibly been to arrange a loan to bolster up the old place. But he had still had his dignity then, his honour.

That marriage had been like a net around him. I dreamed that we were free. But how could we be free? Yet in my dreams some miracle happened and he was there with me at Tressidor. The two estates were as one.

What a wild dream! But dreaming has always been a consolation when one wants to escape from reality. The loss of two people whom I had loved very dearly was too hard to bear without some solace. One had brought me Tressidor, the other Livia, it was true. That was the way one must look at life. One must remember the consolations.

Gwennie came to see me often. I wished she wouldn't. Her inquisitive eyes seemed to probe into my mind.

'What a tragedy!' she cried. 'They say the number of people who die having babies is more than you'd think. Your poor sister . . . and she left the little girl to your care. I said to Betty' – that was the lady's maid with whom I understood she gossiped a great deal – 'I said, I reckon Miss Tressidor will be a mother to that little girl. She ought to have some of her own. I've often wondered why you haven't married, Caroline. But then, of course, it's a matter of finding Mr Right. If he doesn't come along . . . well, what's a girl to do?'

Her bright eyes studied me intently. What of you and my husband? I imagined she was thinking. How far has that gone?

I wondered what she knew. It was a fact that one often betrayed one's feelings when one was quite unaware of doing so.

Time passed quickly. Livia was growing into a person. She was walking rather than stumbling; she was beginning to talk; she used to run to me every time I went to the nursery and I was thinking about getting a pony for her when she was a little older. There was some time to go but I took her for rides on my horse round the paddock, holding her tightly while she squealed with delight.

Nanny Loman said to me one day: 'That child is happier than she ever was in London. Oh, I know she was young but she wasn't getting the attention. Her mother w⁓ ill all the time. We did what we could but there's nothing like a mother, and you're being that, Miss Tressidor.'

It was the highest praise I could have and for a few hours my melancholy lifted and during that time I did not think of how much I missed Cousin Mary and that I should never see Olivia again.

Within a month of our arrival Jeremy wrote that he wished to see his daughter.

I could not refuse him. I made up my mind to see as little of him as possible, but when he came I felt I wanted to taunt him. I knew it was unkind of me; I knew that I should not have revelled in revenge; but I had to do it. I had to soothe my own sorrow and I could not allow him to flaunt his role of grieving husband, devoted father and would-be friend, for those were the roles he was determined to play. He was false and I could see clearly what lay behind that façade of charm; but I wanted to trick him as he had tricked me . . . and Olivia.

I took him riding round the estate. I spread it out before him, as it were, in all its affluence. He could not keep the excitement out of his eyes.

'I'd no idea it was so extensive,' he said.

I thought: Then you have now, my worldly Jeremy. What plans are being formulated in that greedy little mind of yours?

I took him to call on the Landowers. Gwennie liked him, for he charmed her with the utmost ease. Paul was suspicious and, of course, jealous, which did not displease me.

He stayed for a week and during that period he spent a certain amount of time in the nursery. He had brought a novel toy for Livia. A doll on a swing which could be made to rock back and forth.

I was a bit hurt to see how easily she was charmed by him,

but he was playing a part for her as well as for the rest of us.

When he left he held my hands for a long time and said: 'How can I thank you, Caroline, for making my little girl so happy here?'

I said: 'Olivia wished it. Before she died she spoke to me. She wanted to make sure that I and no one else had the child.'

'She knew what was best. Thank you, my dear. Thank you.'

It could have been very touching, but I told myself I knew him too well to believe in his gratitude.

He kissed me swiftly. 'I must come again,' he said. 'Soon.'

And I fancied I saw the plan which was beginning to form in his mind.

He did come again before another month had passed. There were more presents for Livia. He himself took her on a horse round and round the paddock. She demanded that we both hold her – one on either side.

He looked across at me. 'This is fun, Caroline,' he said.

I nodded.

He was trying to make me look at him. I knew what was in his mind.

And then the plan came to me and once it had come I could not rid myself of it.

I used to think of it at night. When the melancholy descended upon me, when I was going over and over the early days with Olivia, when I remembered that Cousin Mary was gone forever, when I thought of Paul and how everything might have been different, I brooded on what I thought of as The Plan and my spirits rose.

It was an indication of my nature, I supposed, which was not a very admirable one, that this was the only thing which could assuage my grief.

He came for Christmas, which I gave over entirely to Livia. I did not entertain. It was not expected of me as

Cousin Mary had not been dead a year. I told Jeremy that he should not have come. He would find it dull in the country, especially in a house which was still in mourning.

He, too, was mourning, he told me, at which I wanted to laugh aloud; but I did not. I looked suitably sad and sympathetic.

I was playing my part carefully – softening, not too quickly but gradually.

We both knelt on the floor and played games with Livia. She was delighted with him – and again I felt that twinge of jealousy. Nanny Loman said: 'They always feel that for a parent. No matter how neglected they are, they seem to know their father or mother. That's when they're very little. After four or five it changes. Then they love those that love them.'

Miss Bell was a little abrupt with him. She blamed him for Olivia's pregnancy which she had maintained more than once, with pursed lips, should never have been allowed to happen.

How time was passing and how glad I was that it did so with such speed! Olivia had been dead for six months and Livia had been mine for that time.

It was during that Christmas that Jeremy made his first approach – tentatively, of course, but with a skill which I would have expected of him.

He said he thought Livia was lucky in spite of having lost her mother. She had found a new one in me . . . and none would have guessed she was a semi-orphan.

'When I see you with her I rejoice, Caroline.'

'I do my best to carry out my promise to Olivia and it is not difficult. I love Livia.'

'I can see you do. It warms my heart. It's a great privilege for me to be able to come here.'

'I am sure you would rather be in London.'

'How wrong you are! It is the greatest pleasure for me to be where you are, Caroline. I often think of the fancy dress ball. Do you remember?'

'Vividly,' I said.

'Cleopatra.'

'And Rupert of the Rhine.'

He looked at me, his eyes shining, and we laughed.

He was too clever to pursue it from there but I was aware of his intentions.

He said: 'I shall come again . . . soon, Caroline. You don't mind, do you?'

'I understand you wish to see your daughter.'

'And . . . you.'

I bowed my head.

He was there again before the end of January. He was no laggard once he had made up his mind on the course to take. I had to grant him that. He wrote frequently, begging for news of Livia's progress. He was the ideal father.

In February he was with us again, facing the rather cold train journey and some delays due to ice on the line.

'What a devoted father you are!' I said when he arrived.

'Nothing would have kept me away,' he replied.

During that visit he made more steps forward.

We were on the nursery floor fitting together some simple jigsaw of animals in which Livia indulged with great delight.

He said: 'This is how it should be . . . the three of us. It's like a home.'

I didn't answer and he put his hand over mine. I let it lie there. Livia leaned against him and he put his arm about her.

Before he left he found me alone in the little winter parlour and he said: 'Perhaps it's a little too soon, Caroline, but I always felt this was how it was meant to be. I am sure Olivia will understand if she can look down on us. You see . . . I always loved you.'

I opened my eyes wide and looked at him.

'It was a mistake,' he went on. 'I realized almost as soon as I had broken it off.'

'A mistake?' I said. 'I thought you showed great wisdom . . . pecuniary wisdom.'

'A mistake,' he went on. 'I was young and ambitious . . .

379

and foolish. I soon realized that. It's different now. I'm wiser.'

'We all grow wiser, Jeremy.'

He took my hand in his and I did not remove it.

When he left I went with him to the station.

He said: 'I shall be back again very soon. Caroline, you're here in this place. It is not the life for you. You should have children. You're so wonderful with Livia. I feel I could be a good father . . . when you're around. It makes a happy little circle. Don't you agree?'

'Oh yes,' I said.

'It's too soon to make plans yet, perhaps . . . but for the future . . . We could be happy, Caroline. It's how it was meant to be.'

I was silent.

He construed that as agreement.

Riding back in the trap I felt more alive than I had for a long time.

It was a lovely spring. I felt my sadness was passing a little. The earth was waking to a new life – it was the buds on the trees and the song of the birds. Myself too.

I felt I might put the past behind me and I could make some sort of life for myself.

April was a lovely month. 'April showers bring forth May flowers,' I quoted to myself. I was beginning to live again.

When Jeremy arrived he took both my hands in his. 'You look wonderful, Caroline. Your old self. You're Cleopatra once more.'

'One grows away from sorrow,' I said. 'It's no use nursing grief.'

'How wise you are! You were always wise, Caroline. I think I am the luckiest man on earth.'

'And you a widower of less than a year!'

'I am going to put grief behind me. That is what Olivia would wish. I *know* this is what she would wish.'

380

'It is always comforting to have the approval of the dead,' I commented.

'I think she knew . . . that was why she wanted you to have Livia. She was quite wise in some ways.'

'I am sure she would be most gratified, if she is looking down, at such faint praise.'

'I always liked that touch of asperity in you, Caroline.'

I was silent.

He went on: 'I can't tell you how happy I am. It is like seeing a light at the end of a tunnel.'

'A rather well-used simile,' I said.

'But so apt.'

'I suppose that is how these comparisons become clichés.'

'Why are we talking like this? There are so many more important things to discuss. I suppose we shall have to wait for a year. I do think conventions can be tiresome.'

'Very tiresome,' I agreed.

'We'll have to have a quiet wedding. Never mind. I rather fancy we shall have the approval of Lady Carey.'

'I have never worried very much about Aunt Imogen's approval – which is as well, for it rarely came my way.'

'You're so amusing. I can see life is going to be fun for us. Livia and I are two very lucky people.'

I smiled at him.

He went on talking of the future. He felt that the country was no place for me. There would be a great deal to clear up. He thought about making enquiries about the actual market value of great estates. He was sure he would have a very agreeable surprise for me.

I was aghast, but I merely smiled at him and he went on talking about life in London, the amusing people I must be missing.

'Dear Caroline,' he said, 'you were whisked away just as life was beginning to get interesting for you. What fun that ball was! You just had a brief taste and that was all. We are going to alter that!'

I was surprised at myself. I was more silent than usual,

for I could not entirely trust my tongue. I listened to him and he must have thought how much love had softened me. He preened himself a little. He was exceptionally handsome.

There was a great deal of talk in the neighbourhood. I imagined Gwennie was having a very busy time.

I gleaned a little from the servants and I could guess how tongues were wagging.

One day Paul came over to Tressidor. I was in the flower room which was just off the hall. It was a very small room, rather like the one we had had in the London house, in which there was a tap and a sink and some benches and vases.

Daffodils and narcissi which I had just gathered lay on the bench, and he walked in looking very angry.

I said: 'What is wrong?'

'Is this true?' he demanded.

'What do you mean?'

'Are you going to marry this man? You must be mad.'

'Marry?' I queried.

'This man who gave you up once and has now decided you are rich enough to suit him?'

'Oh . . . you mean Livia's father.'

'He may be Livia's father but he is also a fortune-hunter. Can't you see that?'

'I see a great deal, but there is one thing I fail to see and that is why it should be a concern of yours.'

'Don't be absurd. You know it is a concern of mine. I thought you were a sensible woman. I've always had a great respect for your intelligence, but now . . .'

'You're shouting,' I said.

'Tell me this isn't true.'

'Tell me what you would do about it if it were?'

He looked at me helplessly. Then he said: 'Caroline, you must not . . .'

I turned away from him. I could not help the joy which came to me to see his concern and I did not want him to know how deeply it affected me. He was beside me. He took me by the shoulders and turned me round to face him. 'I'd do anything . . . anything . . . to stop it.'

I put up my hand and touched his hair gently. 'There isn't anything you could do,' I said.

'I love you,' he answered. 'I shall not go on like this. I shall find some way. We'll go away together . . .'

'Go away! Leave Landower. That was what it was all about, wasn't it?'

'I wish I could go back. What a silly thing to wish! As if one ever can. But you must not do this, Caroline. Think what it means. You've always been so independent, so much a person in your own right. Don't change. Don't give way to this. I suppose he is very attractive, isn't he? Good-looking . . . saying what women want to hear . . . But can't you see what he's after? This child is here . . . and you're obsessed by her, obsessed by the prospect of motherhood. Oh, Caroline, you can't do this. I won't let you.'

'What would you do to prevent me?'

He had bent me back and was kissing me passionately on my throat and my hair and my lips. I felt I wanted this moment to go on forever. I would remember it always, the scent of daffodils and Paul there expressing his love for me . . . desperately, ready to do anything . . . just anything so that we could be together.

I withdrew myself. I said: 'You shouldn't be here like this. Any moment one of the servants might see you.'

'I'm tired of this,' he said. 'Something must be done. I shall never let you go. I've got to do something. I'm desperate, Caroline. I've never let life get the better of me yet and I never will. And this is the most important thing that has ever happened to me.'

'As important as saving Landower for the Landowers?'

'More important than anything in my life.'

'You can't do anything about it, Paul. It's too late. You saved the house. I know how you felt. It had to be done . . . that was how you saw it. It can't be undone now.'

'There must be a way out. I'll ask her to release me.'

'She never would. Why should she? It's part of the bargain. She loves Landower. She loves her position. She bought it. It's hers and she will never give it up . . . any of it.'

'There will be a way . . . and I will find it.'

'Paul, you frighten me a little when you talk like that. There's a look of fanaticism in your eyes.'

'I am fanatical . . . about you.'

'You are jealous because you think I will take someone else.'

'Yes, I'm jealous. I won't stand by and see you do it. It's the child, isn't it? That's changed you. You want to make it right for her . . . or what seems right and cosy. You want children. Of course you do. You're seeing everything differently. I've noticed the change in you since you came back from London.'

'Wouldn't you expect me to change? I loved my sister. I know I didn't see her often but she was always there. We were very close to each other and she has left me her dearest possession . . . her child. Wouldn't you expect me to change?'

'Caroline, my love . . . of course I understand. But it's too big a price to pay. You think it will all be neatly rounded off, but it won't be like that. A marriage that is wrong for you is just about the biggest tragedy that can happen, and it doesn't make it any easier to bear because you have brought it on yourself. Don't seek an easy way out . . . as I did. Learn from me. I have seen you and him and the child together. It looks idyllic and you think it is the answer. It isn't, Caroline. My darling, I am not going on like this. I've been thinking of it . . . I've thought of nothing else . . . night and day. We're being foolish. We've got to do something. This love of mine for you . . . and I believe you could feel deeply for me too . . . it can't be ignored any longer.'

'My dear Paul, what are you suggesting?'

'If you can't have exactly what you want . . . take what you can?'

384

'What does that mean? Furtive meetings? Where? In some inn a few miles away . . . holding secret meetings . . . I don't think either of us would be very happy.'

'How can we be happy now? I want you with me at Landower. I want our nurseries opened up. I want a happy life with you.'

'It's something we can't have,' I said. 'It's crying for the moon.'

'It's nothing of the sort. Who wants the moon? And you and I could work out something. Instead of which, you are getting ready to plunge into disaster . . . as I did . . . because it seems an easy way out.'

I heard the sound of footsteps in the hall and I sprang away from him. I said in a loud voice. 'It was good of you to call.'

I stepped into the hall. One of the maids was just going up the staircase. I walked towards the door and he followed me.

I said: 'There is so much gossip. I believe the servants watch our movements. Moreover, I think they listen at doors. Information gleaned passes through the ranks and it sometimes comes to the ears of the master and mistress of the house.'

We came out into the courtyard.

I said: 'You must not be so vehement, Paul.'

'How can you do this?' he demanded.

'I have to live my life. You have to live yours.'

'I won't let it happen.'

'I must go,' I told him. 'I promised Livia I would take her for a ride in the paddock.'

He gazed at me in despair; and then I saw a look of determination in his eyes.

I felt a thrill of pleasure, and I had to admit to myself that I had enjoyed his passionate declaration. His jealousy was balm to me and for a while I could gloat over his love for me.

It was wrong, of course; it was dangerous; but it was only later that I began to think about that.

It was May and Jeremy was coming as frequently as ever and staying longer. He showed an enormous interest in the estate. He had become quite knowledgeable about it and I was interested to hear him assessing its worth.

'That manager of yours is quite good,' he said. 'I had a chat with him this afternoon.'

'The job is his life. He served Cousin Mary well and now he does the same for me.'

'I was talking to a man in Town. He was quite interested.'

For a moment I went cold with fear. 'You talked to him . . . about what?'

'Well, about the sale of the estate.'

'Sale of the estate!'

'I know that you won't want to stay buried in the country. I thought it would be a good idea to put out a few feelers . . . just tentatively.'

'Isn't that a bit premature?'

'Of course . . . of course . . . Nothing definite. But these things always take time, and it is as well to know what we are about.'

'What we are about!' I was repeating his words after him.

'My dear Caroline, I want to take the burden of everything off your shoulders.'

'As you did off Olivia's?'

'I did what I could for her.'

'Olivia was left very wealthy.'

'Well, less than she had thought, poor girl. And things didn't go very well.'

'How was that?'

'Markets and things. I wouldn't want to bother you with them, Caroline.'

'I would not want anyone here to know that enquiries were being made about selling the estate. There would be panic. These people's homes are here . . . their work . . . their lives.'

'Of course . . . of course . . . Only tentative enquiries, I assure you. I shall just want to get everything settled. I have spoken to Lady Carey. She is delighted. She thinks it is an excellent idea. She's so relieved about Livia.'

'I didn't know she gave much thought to Livia.'

'Oh, she likes to see everything settled as it should be. She thinks that it will have to be quiet. And she thought you should come up to London. She'll take charge of everything. A very quiet ceremony. I agreed with her.'

'You and she seem to work out everything between you.'

'We're both concerned about you, Caroline.'

I thought: He's getting a little careless, a little too sure. Perhaps the time has now come.

He went on to say that he thought he should arrange it for the first of July.

'The year will be up then,' he added. 'No one can carp about that. Why don't you come up in June . . . about the middle, say. There will be a lot to do.'

'What about Livia?'

'She's all right with Loman and that Miss Bell.'

'Of course,' I said.

I saw him off on the train, very jaunty, very sure of himself.

Then I went home to write the letter.

Dear Jeremy,

You wrote to me once explaining why we should not marry and it is now my duty (by no means painful) to tell you why I have no intention – or ever had – of marrying you. How could I marry a man who had such a low opinion of my intelligence that he thought I could be deceived by such puerile blandishments? You are a great lover, Jeremy – of money. Yes, the estate is a very fine one; it is mine and I am rich . . . possibly more so than Olivia was before you squandered the greater part of her fortune.

You broke your promise to me when you discovered I had nothing. Well, now I am paying you back in your own coin, as they say.

You will now know what it feels like to have to go

among your acquaintances – the one who was turned out, refused, jilted.

Caroline Tressidor.

I sent off the letter at once and I gave myself up to the pleasure of contemplating his reception of it.

A few days passed. I was surprised when he arrived in person.

He came in the early evening. I had been with Livia, seeing her into bed, reading a story to her; and had just gone to my room when one of the maids knocked on the door.

She began: 'Miss Tressidor, Mr Brandon . . .'

He must have been immediately behind her because before she got any further he burst into the room.

'Caroline!' he cried.

The maid shut the door. I wondered if she were listening outside. 'Well,' I said. 'This is unexpected. Did you not get my letter?'

He said: 'I don't believe it.'

'Just a moment,' I said. I went to the door. The maid sprang back a few paces.

'There is nothing I need from you, Jane,' I said.

'No, Miss Tressidor,' she said, flushing and hurrying away.

I shut the door and leaned against it.

He repeated: 'I don't believe it.'

I raised my eyebrows. 'I thought I had made it perfectly clear to you.'

'Do you mean you were playing games . . . with me?'

'I was following a certain course of action, if that is what you mean.'

'But you implied . . .'

'It was you who implied. You implied that I was a complete idiot, that I couldn't see through you. You must have thought I was the biggest fool imaginable. Oh come, Jeremy, you really did put up a very poor show. Not nearly as good as you did all those years ago. You were quite credible then. Of course you didn't have your past to live down.'

'You . . . you . . .'

'Say it,' I urged. 'Don't be afraid. You have nothing to lose now. You have already lost. I doubt your feelings for me are one half as contemptuous as mine for you.'

'You . . . scheming harridan.'

I laughed. 'Spoken from the heart,' I said. 'And I will retaliate by telling you that you are a blatant fortune-hunter.'

'So this is revenge . . . because I refused to marry you.'

'Look upon it as a little lesson. When you go out on your next treasure hunt, I should try to be a little less blatant. You should have shown a little discretion. Olivia is scarcely cold in her grave.'

He was looking at me as though he could not believe what he saw and heard. He had been so conceited, so completely sure of himself, he had thought he had only to beckon and I would willingly follow. It was a hard and bitter lesson for him.

I was ashamed of my feelings, but I was almost sorry for him.

I said rather gently: 'You couldn't really have thought I was such a fool, could you, Jeremy? Did you really think I would sell my estate . . . my inheritance . . . to provide you with the money you needed for the gaming tables and entertaining your friends there? I dare say the ladies of the gaming clubs thought you were a very fine fellow.'

'You don't know what you are talking about.'

'I know more than you give me credit for. Have you replaced Miss Flora Carnaby or does she still reign supreme?'

He turned pale and then flushed hotly. 'Have you set spies on me?'

'Nothing of the sort. The information leaked out. It is amazing how these little facts come to light. Olivia knew. That's what I can't forgive. Olivia thought you were

389

wonderful until you impoverished her to indulge your weakness for gambling and the Flora Carnabys of your superficial world.'

'Olivia . . .'

'Yes. You made the last months of her life unhappy. She knew and she was completely disillusioned. That was why she wanted me to take Livia. She was afraid to leave her with you. Now you know. I see no reason why you should be shielded from the truth.'

'You wanted to have your revenge on me because of what I did to you.'

'How right you are! I wanted that . . . among other things. Now you must tell your friends . . . and possibly your creditors . . . that the rich marriage is off. The lady knew all the time what her prospective bridegroom was after and she has told him in no uncertain terms to get out.'

'You're a virago.'

'Is that an improvement on a harridan? Yes, I am one, and I am revelling in your discomfiture. I shall laugh when I think of you confessing to your cronies, and to my Aunt Imogen, that the marriage will not take place. You'll make a good story of it, I don't doubt. You'll wonder at the wisdom of marrying your late wife's sister. Whatever you say, it makes no difference. This is the fortune which will not fall into your lap.'

'You forget you have my daughter here.'

'I'm sorry she has such a father.'

'I shall not allow you to keep her.'

I felt a sudden fear in the pit of my stomach. What could he do? He was, after all, her father.

As usual when I was afraid I was immediately on the defensive.

'If you attempted to take her from me I should probe into your financial affairs. I should discover the details of your liaison with Flora Carnaby – and doubtless others. I should provoke a scandal which would kill off all your future chances of securing an heiress. You would be finished,

Jeremy Brandon. I have the money to make sure of that – and I should not hesitate to use it.'

He was white and trembling and I saw that he was frightened.

'I will give you a word of advice although you don't deserve it,' I went on. 'Go away . . . and never let me hear of you again. I don't know how much of Olivia's money you have left. I should salvage what you can. You'll probably lose it all at one stroke at the gaming tables. But who knows, you might be lucky. Whether you rise out of the ashes or are ruined, I don't want to know. All I ask is that you go away from here and I never see you again.'

He stood looking at me – lost and beaten.

I saw him differently, shorn of his bravado. I imagined his coming on to the London scene, a younger son with very little money but outstanding good looks and an undoubted grace and charm. I could imagine his dreams, his ambitions.

Now he had been utterly humiliated and I had done this.

I couldn't help feeling the tiniest glimmer of remorse which I suppressed immediately.

This was my triumph and I was going to savour it to the full.

He left me.

He must have stayed the night at an inn and gone back to London the next day.

The news spread rapidly. How did they learn such things? How much of my scene with Jeremy had been overheard, how much guessed at?

Paul was waiting for me next morning when I rode out to visit one of the farms where there was a little trouble over some land. There was no mistaking his relief.

'So it is over!' he cried.

'How did you know?'

'Heaven knows. Gwennie talks of nothing else.'

'I expect she got it from one of your servants who got it from one of ours.'

'Where is unimportant. All that matters is that it is over.'

'You couldn't have thought seriously for a moment . . .'

'You let me believe.'

'Because you knew me so little as to imagine it could possibly be true.'

'And all the time . . .'

'All the time I intended to do just what I did.'

'You didn't tell me.'

'I had to live the part while I was playing it. Besides, I liked to see you jealous. I liked you to feel that you had lost me.'

'Caroline!'

'I'm realizing I'm not a very admirable character. I hurt him terribly . . . and I revelled in it.'

'He had hurt you.'

'Still, I delighted in . . . revenge.'

'And you are repentant now?'

'Sometimes we don't know ourselves very well. I thought I was going to enjoy hurting him . . . turning the knife in the wound as it were . . . and when the time came, I did it. I blazed at him. I wounded him, humiliated him, far more than he ever had me. He let me down lightly. He was courteous all the time. I just went for him like a harridan . . . a virago.'

'My dearest Caroline, you had been provoked. And he was after your fortune now as he had been before.'

I said bitterly: 'He would not be the first man to marry for money, for what his wife could bring him.'

He was silent and I went on: 'But who are any of us to judge others? I feel drained now . . . just rather sad. I was buoyed up by my plans to hurt, to wound, and now it's over and I don't really feel any great satisfaction.'

He said: 'When I thought you were going to marry him, I was desperate, ready to do anything to stop it. I was making plans . . . wild plans . . .'

'Paul,' I said, 'if only it could be . . .'

'Perhaps . . . something.'

'What?' I cried. 'What can ever happen?'

'I won't go on like this. This has made me realize that I shall not.'

'I can see no way out . . . except what you have suggested before. It might give us temporary satisfaction, but it's not what we really want . . . not what you want or I want . . .'

'That's true. But we could snatch what happiness we could and who knows . . . one day . . .'

'One day,' I said. 'One day . . . I should never have stayed here. It would have been better if I had gone. I believe I might have, if Cousin Mary hadn't had her accident. I was thinking of it . . .'

'Running away never helped.'

'This is one case where it might. If I had gone you would have forgotten me in time.'

'I never should. I should have lived my life in shadow. At least now you're here. I can see you.'

'Yes,' I said. 'Those are the good days when I see you.'

'Oh . . . Caroline!'

'It's true. I don't want to hide anything any more. One cannot go on pretending. We were doomed from the beginning. We are the star-crossed lovers. Cousin Mary used to say that there should have been a Romeo and Juliet in our families, but with a happy ending so that Landower and Tressidor could flourish side by side. But you see our story hasn't a happy ending either.'

'At least we are here and we are neither of us people to accept defeat.'

'There is no way out of this. You could not leave Landower. And Gwennie has a stake in it. She bought it. She will keep what she has. There isn't a way.'

'I shall find a way,' he said.

And I remembered later. I kept on remembering how he had looked when he said that – and I could not forget, however much I tried.

Jago's Lady

Summer was hot and sultry. Livia was now a lively two-year-old. She was a great comfort to me; she helped me through my days, which were so full that there was little time for dreaming.

I had bought a pony for her – a tiny creature – and I let her ride round the paddock on a leading rein. This was what she loved more than anything else. I had bought the pony soon after Jeremy left, hoping to divert her attention from him. I was greatly relieved when she did not appear to miss him.

Sometimes I would lead her out and take her down the drive a little way – sometimes as far as the lodge and Jamie would come out to applaud.

He was very fond of Livia and she had taken a fancy to him. He would invite us into the cottage and Livia would be given a glass of milk and pieces of bread cut into diamond shapes covered in honey, which he told her was made especially for her by his bees.

One day when we called Gwennie arrived. She had come to buy some honey. She was invited in and offered a glass of mead – Jamie's own very special brand.

She asked how he made it but he would not tell her. It was his own secret, he said.

'It's delicious,' I said, 'and surprisingly intoxicating.'

Gwennie smacked her lips and said she would buy some. 'It's really an old English drink,' she added. 'I like to keep to the medieval customs. Did you learn to make honey in Scotland? And did you have special bees there, Mr McGill?'

'Bees know no borders, Mrs Landower. They're the

same the world over. It wouldn't matter to them whether they were in England, Scotland or Australia. They are bees, and bees are bees the whole world over.'

'But I asked you if you learned about them in Scotland. You do come from Scotland, don't you?'

'Oh aye.'

'You must find it very different down here?'

'Oh aye.'

'I suppose sometimes you're a bit homesick?'

'No.'

'That's funny. People usually are. Sometimes I think of Yorkshire. How long is it since you left Scotland, Mr McGill?'

'A long time.'

'I was wondering how long.'

'Time passes. You lose count.'

'But surely you remember . . .'

I saw that Jamie was getting restive under this cross-examination and I put in: 'One week is so like another. I must say I am just amazed how quickly time passes. Livia, darling, have you finished your milk?'

Livia nodded.

'I've never been to Scotland,' said Gwennie, who did not seem to understand what I had very early in my acquaintance with Jamie, and that was that he did not like direct questions. I had always respected the fact that he did not wish to talk about himself. Gwennie, of course, was heedless of his reticence – or if she was not, decided to ignore it.

'What part did you come from, Mr McGill?'

'Oh, just above the Border. I must go and see to the bees. They're angry about something.'

'Well, mind they don't turn on you,' said Gwennie with a little laugh.

'They won't,' I said. 'They always respect Jamie. Well, we had better be going. Thank Jamie for the honey diamonds and the milk, Livia.'

Livia said thank-you and I wiped the honey from her fingers. 'Well, now we're ready,' I said.

We all came out of the lodge together.

'I'll walk with you up the drive a little way,' said Gwennie. 'I can take the short cut across Five-Acre Field.'

I sat Livia on her pony and walked along beside her. Gwennie was on the other side of me.

'He's a queer customer,' she said. 'Something funny about him.'

'You mean Jamie. He's rather unusual.'

'Doesn't give much away, does he?'

'He's very generous with his milk and honey and mead, I thought.'

'I don't mean that. He doesn't *tell* you anything.'

'Well, you can't be surprised that he doesn't want to tell you how he makes his mead.'

'You know I wasn't thinking of his mead. I mean he won't tell us anything about himself.'

'He likes to keep his life private.'

'I wonder why.'

'Many people do, you know.'

'When they've got something to hide. We don't really know anything about him, do we?'

'We know he's a good lodge-keeper. He supplies us with honey and many of the flowers we have in the house come from his garden. He grows some very fine blooms.'

'But I mean what do you really know about *him*?'

'That he's pleasant and contented.'

'He's odd. There's no doubt about that. Some of the servants think he's not quite all there.'

'All where?'

She burst out quite angrily. 'You're on your high horse again, Caroline. You know exactly what I mean but you're playing the grand lady to the little upstart from the north. I know. Paul's the same. I don't belong here. I'm not one of you. I always say to him . . . when he takes up that attitude. This is where I belong. It was my father's money that bought this place. That's what I have to remind him.'

'I think he remembers what happened.'

'And I see he doesn't forget it either.'

'And all this has grown out of poor old Jamie.'

'Silly old fool! With his garden and his bees! He's hiding something. I'll find out, though. You see.'

We had come to that part of the drive where she would leave me to cross Five-Acre.

I said *au revoir* gladly. There were times when I found her company intolerable.

It was about a week later when Gwennie came to Tressidor in a state of great excitement.

'I had to come over right away,' she said. 'Such news! What do you think has happened? I can't wait to tell you. You could have knocked me down with a feather.'

'What is it?'

'It's Jago. He's coming home on Saturday.'

'Well, what's so special about that? He's always going to London and now he's coming home for a spell.'

'This is different. Guess what?'

'You seem determined to keep me in suspense. It's not like you.'

'It's such news. I never would have guessed. Jago is married. He's bringing home his bride.'

'Really!'

'I knew you'd be surprised. This is an occasion, isn't it? Jago married. All this time he's been holding out on us.'

'Whom has he married?'

'That's the point. He doesn't say. He just says he's bringing his wife to see us. He was married last week. Isn't it exciting?'

'Very.'

'He seems very pleased with himself. I imagine she has plenty of brass.'

'Did he mention . . . the brass?'

'No . . . not exactly.'

'What do you mean . . . not exactly?'

'Well, not at all. The Landowers are like that. It's something you're not supposed to talk about. They want it but they pretend they don't. That's their way. Well, I hope she's nicely gilded, as Pa used to say. And I can't wait till Saturday.'

I felt as eager myself.

All day on Saturday I was thinking about Jago. It was difficult to imagine him married. I supposed he would live at Landower with his new wife. I wondered how she and Gwennie would get on together. I should be very interested to see and promised myself that the next morning I would ride over to meet the new wife.

I did not have to wait until then. In the evening of the Saturday I had a caller.

I heard a slight commotion and went down to the hall to see what was happening.

Jago was there. He was whispering to one of the maids.

'Jago!' I cried.

He ran to me, picked me off my feet and twirled me round and round.

'I had to come and see you,' he said.

' "Behold the bridegroom cometh," ' I said.

'That's it. Benedick himself. Wasn't he the one who hesitated before taking the plunge?'

'Exactly. Oh, Jago! You – a husband!'

'Well, it had to happen sometime, didn't it? And as you wouldn't have me I had to look elsewhere.'

'I'm bitterly hurt,' I said, laughing.

'I guessed you would be.'

'All this machinery and plans for improvements and contracts . . . it was this, was it?'

'Right first time.'

'Jago, you are machiavellian in your cunning.'

'Of course,' he said modestly.

'And why did you not bring your bride to meet me?'

'As a matter of fact, she was the one who insisted on coming over this evening. She wouldn't wait until the morning.'

'*She* insisted. But why didn't she come?'

He put his face close to mine. 'She's very anxious for your approval.'

'Mine?'

'Oh, she knows a lot about you. Just a minute.' He went to the door. 'You can come in now.'

She came in and I stared at her disbelievingly. Then we ran to each other and she burst into laughter in which I joined.

We hugged each other.

'Rosie!' I cried.

'I thought you'd be surprised.'

'*You* . . . married Jago!'

'Yes. Don't look so bewildered. I have him in tow.'

'But you . . . of all people.'

'Don't worry. We've worked it all out.'

'All that machinery,' said Jago.

'I had no idea.'

'Nor did Jago until he was caught.'

'She doesn't always tell the truth, my wife,' said Jago. 'To let you into a secret, I was the one who caught her.'

'I am so surprised,' I said, 'that I am forgetting my duties. Come on. We're going to drink to this.'

Rosie had always been the most unpredictable person I had ever known and she lived up to that reputation.

The following day she came to see me and we talked for a long time. Contrary to custom, they were not going to make their home at Landower.

'What!' said Rosie. 'Give up my business . . . just when it's beginning to expand! Why, in three months' time we're opening in Paris.'

'What about the estate . . . Landower and all that? Jago helps in the management.'

'Half-heartedly, I gathered. His heart's not in it and I couldn't see that that brother of his is all that put out at the thought of him giving up. Jago's known for a long time that it's not his bent. Whereas you'd be surprised how good he is

with me and my enterprises. All that charm and merriment
. . . it goes down well with everybody and he is beginning
to learn something. I didn't expect he'd ever be any good in
that direction, but he has a sort of appreciation of beautiful
women and what they should wear follows from that. I saw
his possibilities right from the start. He kept calling, you
know, after that first time. We suit each other.'

'Yes, I suppose you do.'

'I'm certain we do. I wouldn't have entered into this if I
wasn't sure it was the right thing.'

'You never married before. You must have had lots of
opportunities.'

'Opportunities which did not often include marriage.
No, when he started to call and we had such a lot of fun
together. he began to show this interest in what I was
building up. It started then.'

'Oh, Rosie, it's so funny!'

'Yes, it is, isn't it?'

'Does Jago know about . . .?'

'About my parlourmaid days and my early strivings?
Yes, he knows. I haven't the time or the inclination to be
burdened with secrets. One wastes so much time covering
up. I am myself, to be taken as I am or not at all. He's not
exactly been a model of virtue himself. He understood my
need to get away from my origins. He admired that. Well,
there we are. You see me, Mrs Landower . . . Rosie
Rundall, Rosie Russell that followed and now Rosie Landower, respectably married to a gentleman of good family.
It's rather a joke, don't you think?'

'No,' I said. 'I think it's wonderful. I think Jago is the
luckiest man and I'm going to tell him so.'

'Thank you. I'm glad, too, that I shall be closer to you.
You must come up to London to stay with us, and I dare say
we shall come down here now and then to visit the ancestral
home.'

'Rosie, I'm so pleased.'

'I thought you would be. That's why I insisted we come
right over to see you as soon as we arrived. We're going to

stay here for two weeks. We can't take longer away than that.'

'What do you think of Landower?'

'Spectacular. I've never been in a place like that. It creaks with the olden days, doesn't it? Fancy being born in a place like that. And this is yours now! I'm glad Cousin Mary did the right thing. You suit this place. And how is the little one getting on?'

'Very well.'

'And you're getting over it?'

'One does forget . . . at times, and then one remembers with a terrible sadness. But it does become muted with time.'

She nodded.

'I saw you at the funeral,' I said.

'Yes. I had to go. Poor Olivia, she was too frail to fight for herself. It was a great pity Jeremy Brandon ever came into your lives.'

'Oh, he was a weakling really. I think about him now and then. You know what happened?'

'There was talk at the time. I think he was in a bit of a mess. The creditors descended on him when they knew there would be no rich marriage. I was horrified when I heard you had accepted him. I couldn't believe my ears.'

'I was very cruel, really. I planned it, Rosie. I wanted revenge . . . for myself mainly, I suppose, but for Olivia too.'

'Well, he got his deserts.' She looked at me rather sadly. 'And there's no one else?'

I hesitated and she did not press the question.

'Here I suppose you meet the same people all the time.'

'You could say that.'

'You must come to London for a visit. Bring Livia. She ought to see something of the big city.'

I could see the thoughts in her mind. She would try to find a suitable husband for me. I laughed at her and tried to sound light-hearted.

'Why is it,' I asked, 'when people marry, they feel everyone else ought to be in the same state?'

'A good marriage is the best way of life.'

'You hesitated for a long time.'

'I waited until I was absolutely sure. That is what every wise woman should do.'

'But how can one be absolutely sure?'

'By making up your mind that such and such is for you and once you have made up your mind on that, make it up again. You are going to see that it works.'

'All are not as far-sighted as you, Rosie.'

'I admit I have had some experience of men . . . and women.'

'And when you look round do you find the failures exceed the successes?'

'We hear of the failures. The successes are not talked of.'

I said: 'I think of Robert Tressidor. What sort of marriage was that? I think of my mother and Captain Carmichael . . . of Olivia and Jeremy . . .' I hesitated and she waited. But I could not speak of Gwennie and Paul.

She was watching me with serious eyes; but she remained silent.

After a while she said: 'While I am here you and I must see each other . . . often.'

We did. I had many talks with Rosie. She was so interested in everything about her. She created a furore of excitement in the countryside and quickly became known as Mr Jago's Lady. Her clothes and her general appearance were stunning. Her statuesque good looks made her seem like a goddess come down from the Olympian heights to our community.

She was by no means an expert horsewoman but she looked like Diana on horseback with her beautifully cut riding habit in silver grey with top hat of the same colour and a cravat flecked with mauve stars on grey silk.

Jago was very proud of her. I did not suppose for a

moment that he would be converted to a completely faithful husband, but Rosie would know how to cope with that. She understood well the vagaries of men and the reason for her success was that she knew how to compromise. She took what life offered and then set about moulding it to her own needs and desires. I felt there was a great deal to be learned from Rosie.

She showed an immense interest in the people – however humble. She delighted in Jamie and his bees. We spent a very pleasant hour in the lodge.

'Presumably,' I said, 'the bees approve of this marriage.'

She was very discerning and had quickly summed up the situation at Landower; and it did not take her long to realize that I was caught up in it.

She was rather grave about that.

She said: 'Gwennie isn't a bad sort. She is just obtuse. She can't forget that she's paid for something and she wants full value. She can't understand that she can't have what she wants just by paying. One couldn't explain to her. She would never listen. The Gwennies of the world just think they know it all. That's their mistake. She wouldn't listen to advice. She would never be diverted from her course. You could cut the tension in that house with a knife. It'll break. I reckon it's near breaking-point now.'

'You mean . . . with Paul?'

'He hates her. Even when she's not being offensive about paying for the house and so on. He can't bear the sight of her. Every little thing she does irritates him . . . the sort of thing he wouldn't notice with other people. I don't like it, Caroline.'

'What does Jago think?'

'Jago says it has always been like that. But I feel it's rising . . . perhaps because I'm new to it. I knew the situation, of course. Jago had told me. But I didn't realize that it was so far gone.'

She looked at me steadily. 'Is it because of you?' she asked.

I tried to look surprised but she went on: 'He's in love

with you, and you with him. What are you going to do about it?'

I could see it was no use trying to hold anything back from Rosie. 'Nothing,' I said. 'What can we do?'

'It's difficult . . . You've got this place. He's got that place. The children . . . The responsibility to the tenants.'

'You see how impossible it is.'

'Are you going on like this . . . till the storm breaks?'

'What would you do, Rosie?'

She hesitated for a moment, then she said: 'I'm myself and you are yourself. There could be secret meetings, but how would that end? You'd be discovered sooner or later. That might make things worse. You're in a trap, both of you. If it weren't for all this –' She waved her hand '– I'd say, Get out. Go away. Try to make a new life.'

'And what of the estate?'

'Go away for a while. Even a month or so. Come to London. Stay with us. That manager of yours could look after everything, couldn't he? Yes, that's the solution. Get away. Sort out your own thoughts. You can't see these things clearly when you're right on top of them. That's my advice, Get away. Look at yourself. Look at the future. See what can be done. At the moment you're sitting on a powder keg. Anything could happen.'

'Do you think it is as dangerous as that?'

'I've been in and out of tricky situations. I do have a nose for these things.'

'It's wonderful to talk to you, Rosie.'

'I'm at your service. Another good thing about this marriage . . . it has brought us closer together.' She was silent for a moment, then she went on. 'In a place like this you live close to people. Everyone seems to know a great deal about everyone else, and with a woman like Gwennie . . . well, she's insatiably curious. I suppose her own life is unsatisfactory, so she has to probe into those of others to find the flaws.'

'Not satisfactory! She thinks she has bought herself a wonderful life.'

'And a husband who can't bear the sight of her. She's aware of that and she blames him.'

'People always blame others for their own shortcomings.'

'I've got to know her quite well. She has a passionate interest in people around her. It's an unhealthy sort of interest because it is the scandals and the shadowy side which interest her. She told me of your engagement to Jeremy and its ending with the utmost relish. She's absolutely obsessed by that man with the bees. She knows that it was exactly eight months after her marriage that one of the servants had her baby and that it was not premature. These are the kind of details which absorb her. I think it's a sort of compensation for shortcomings in her own life which make her rejoice in the frailties of others.'

'You understand her. I think she likes you. I heard through one of the servants that she was delighted with Mr Jago's Lady.'

'I'm with her a good deal. I can't avoid it, being in the house.'

'Does she confide in you?'

'Not about herself. Only about others . . . what she discovered . . . what she hopes to discover. Poor Gwennie, I'm sorry for her in a way. She's not a bad sort. She's just blind and won't see. I shall invite her to London, too. But what we want most is for you to come and be with us. Think about it. I am sure it is what you need.'

'It's wonderful to have you here, Rosie. I shall miss you so much when you have gone.'

How right I was. I felt very lonely after she and Jago left.

The Secret of the Mine

———————————

After Rosie had gone there seemed to be an anticlimax until one day when I met Paul in the lane leading to Tressidor just as I was going to one of the farms.

I noticed the change in him.

I said: 'Something has happened.'

'She's gone away,' he told me.

'Your wife?'

He nodded and a smile spread across his face. 'You can't imagine . . . the relief.'

'I think I can. Where has she gone? For how long?'

'She's gone to Yorkshire . . . visiting an aunt.'

'I didn't know she had an aunt.'

'Oh yes. They've corresponded apparently . . . spasmodically. She suddenly took it into her head to go and see her.'

'For how long?'

He lifted his shoulders. 'Who knows? Not a brief visit . . . I hope.'

'She must have decided suddenly.'

'Yes. It was after Jago and Rosie left. She didn't waste much time once she'd decided. I drove her to the station myself. She had to go to London first and take the train to Yorkshire from there.'

'She has never been away before.'

'All those years . . .' he said wearily. 'At least this is a respite. I have wanted to talk with you so often . . . to be with you.'

I was silent and he went on: 'What are we going to do, Caroline?'

'Much the same as we have been doing, I suppose,' I answered. 'We seem to go on in the same way. What else can we do?'

'We must see each other sometimes . . . alone. We have to face up to facts. Here we are . . . in this impasse. We can't go forward and we can't go back. Are we going to deny ourselves forever? Are we going to live here like this, frustrated all our lives?'

'I had thought of going away for a while . . . going to London. Rosie suggested I should visit them.'

'Oh no,' he said.

'I thought it was a good idea. I need to get away . . . to think about everything.'

'You can't leave Tressidor any more than I can leave Landower.'

I said: 'I have Livia now. It makes me think very seriously about what I can do. Before, I had a sort of freedom. There was a time when I had almost decided . . .'

'Decided what?'

'That I would risk everything to be with you.'

'Caroline!'

'Oh yes, I did. I almost did. I saw it all clearly . . . this liaison between us . . . secret meetings . . . living in fear of discovery . . . asking myself what discovery would mean. And there were times when I told myself that I did not care what the consequences would be, I would risk everything. Then I had my responsibilities . . . just as you have.'

He said: 'We could go right away. God knows I've thought of it often enough. We could live abroad. France . . . do you remember France? What a long time ago that seems. I was so afraid for you then. I learned what you meant to me in those few days . . . and I learned it forever. I came to look at you when you were sleeping. I stood at the glass doors leading to the balcony.'

I said: 'I was not sleeping.'

'I . . . almost came in. I often wondered if things would have been different if I had.'

'Yes, I wondered that too.'

'You would have taken me in then.'

'I did not know that you were married . . . married to save Landower. I thought you had worked some miracle. I believed you were capable of miracles.'

'What a sordid miracle! A miracle that brought with it a lifetime's bitterness.'

'Do you hate her so much?'

'I hated her for all sorts of reasons. I hated her for a hundred irritating habits. I hated her because she was herself and I hated her most of all because she stood between us.'

I said: 'You are talking of her as though she were no longer there.'

'Let us think of her as gone.'

'She will be back soon.'

'Not yet . . . Let's hope not yet.'

'It's only a visit.'

'Let's hope she stays away.'

'But when she comes back . . .'

'Let us not think of her.'

'How can we do anything else? She's there and, as you said, she is between us.'

'Not at this moment. Forget her. Talk of us.'

'There is nothing more to say.'

'We are not going on like this.'

'But what is the alternative?'

'You know. And perhaps . . . one day . . . everything will come right for us.'

He leaned towards me and laid his hand over mine. Then he took it and held it to his lips.

'Caroline, the future is ours to make. Let us forget all this. Let us go away . . . somewhere where we are not known . . .'

I shook my head and turned away.

I left him then but all that day I kept thinking of him and I wanted to be with him, to explore those avenues which he was begging me to travel with him.

Yet still I hesitated.

I was not quite sure when the rumours started.

Someone said he saw a black dog at the mine; then someone else immediately saw – or thought she saw – a white hare.

These were the harbingers of death. In the old days they had been said to foretell a disaster in the mine; now it was just the warning of death . . . but in the mine.

Old rumours were recalled. At the time when a man had murdered his wife and put her in the mine, people had seen a black dog; at the time when the man himself had gone down the shaft the dog had appeared again – and with it the white hare.

Now the sightings had begun again.

Something was due to happen at the mine.

I rode out there on one occasion and was surprised to see several people. Some were sitting about on the grass . . . others walking, and there was a rider or two.

I saw one of the grooms from the stable and greeted him.

'Don't 'ee go too near the mine, Miss Tressidor. They do say the black dog have been seen again.'

'I thought that was last week.'

'And again this, Miss Tressidor. There be something going to happen at the mine, sure as God made little apples. Aye, you can be sure of that.'

'I expect everyone is taking special care.'

' 'Tis a bad thing to see the black dog.'

'I should have thought it would have been good to be warned.'

' 'Tain't like that, Miss Tressidor. If the black dog 'ave come for you, 'tis no use trying to escape from 'un.'

'Well, there are quite a few people here. Aren't they tempting fate?'

'Oh, I don't know about that, Miss Tressidor. You'm not been in these parts long enough to pay proper attention, like. But things happen here in the Duchy as perhaps don't happen in other places.'

'I'm sure they do,' I said.

I rode home thinking about Paul and wondering what he was doing at this moment.

There were times when I almost went to him but something made me draw back. Then I would go and play with Livia. But for her perhaps I should have considered giving up everything, for I believed he had that in mind too. Landower was not the same to him since his marriage. It had had to be too dearly bought.

Then the terrible fear came to me.

It happened when I went to my room to find Bessie, my personal maid, dusting there. She apologized and said that there had been such a lot to do this morning that she was behind with her work.

I said: 'That's all right, Bessie. Just carry on.'

'I was wondering, Miss Tressidor,' she said, 'if you'd heard from Mrs Landower.'

'Heard from her? Why? She's away. In Yorkshire . . . visiting her aunt.'

'Well, there be some as says . . .'

I said: 'What do they say?'

'Well, there's some as asks whether she did go to Yorkshire. She left . . . sudden, like.'

I wanted to close the conversation but I had to know what lay behind Bessie's words.

'I suppose she suddenly made up her mind,' I said. 'She comes from Yorkshire, you know.'

'It's Jenny . . . her maid . . . lady's maid. She said she knew her mistress well and she didn't say nothing to her about going to Yorkshire.'

'That was a matter for Mrs Landower to decide, surely.'

'Jenny said it was funny, like . . . her not saying . . . and she's left her comb behind.'

'Comb? What on earth are you talking about, Bessie?'

'Well, according to Jenny, she always used this comb when she was dressing up, like. For her hair. You know what her hair was like. It was all over the place if it wasn't held . . . like. This comb used to be stuck in the back. She

410

was hardly ever without it.'

'It seems to me that Jenny's trying to tell us something. What?'

Bessie looked embarrassed and said: 'Well, I don't want to talk out of turn, Miss Tressidor.'

'But you want to share this gossip with me. You know that I am outspoken and like others to be the same. So tell me quickly, please, what is Jenny hinting?'

'Well, I don't rightly know. She said she thought Mrs Landower might not have gone to Yorkshire after all.'

'Well, where does the all-knowing Jenny think she went?'

'That's what she's worried about. She's gone . . . and she's left the comb.'

'I cannot imagine that a comb should play so big a part in Mrs Landower's life.'

'Well, seeing as how things are . . . up at Landower, I mean, Jenny just thought it was funny, like.'

'I should think Jenny probably hasn't got enough to do now that her mistress is away.'

Bessie was silent.

'She writ a letter. Jenny can write a good hand. She likes to show it off a bit, I think.'

'So she has written, you say . . . To whom?'

'She's writ to Mrs Landower's aunt. She knew her address because Mrs Landower had it in a little book, and Mrs Landower talked to Jenny a lot. She tells her things . . . and Jenny says they always talked together . . . like friends. It wasn't like a mistress and maid, if you know what I mean.'

'Yes, I know.'

'Mrs Landower liked to hear about everybody, and Jenny used to tell her what she knew. Well, Jenny have writ this letter to her aunt with a letter inside for Mrs Landower . . . care of Miss Arkwright. Jenny knows how to do these things. Jenny reckoned she'd be missing that comb and perhaps sending for it and Jenny thought she'd ask her. That's if she's there . . .'

411

'If she's there?'

'Jenny thinks it's funny . . . and then there's that black dog.'

I felt I could endure no more of this conversation.

'That'll do, Bessie,' I said.

And she went out, leaving me with a terrible fear in my heart.

Nanny Loman had taken Livia to Landower to play with Julian. Ever since that talk with Bessie I had been unable to throw off an ever-increasing uneasiness.

Gossip! I thought. It is foolish to think too much of it. But I could not shut out of my mind the memory of the moors, with those people wandering about, whispering, their attention focused on the mine as though they expected to see black dogs and white hares at any moment.

When Livia returned I would supervise getting her to bed, an undertaking which soothed me considerably. I would watch her absorption in Cinderella and Little Red Riding Hood and occasionally diverge from the text so that she could have the pleasure of putting me right because she knew it off by heart.

I heard them return and went to the nursery.

Nanny Loman looked disturbed.

I said to her: 'Is anything wrong, Nanny?'

She looked at Livia and I nodded. It was something she did not want to say in front of the child.

Cinderella seemed a long time reaching her happy ending that evening, but as soon as I had tucked in Livia I sought out Nanny Loman.

'What is it?' I asked.

'Well, it's very strange, Miss Tressidor. You know Jenny who acted as lady's maid to Mrs Landower . . .'

'Yes, of course.'

'Well, apparently she thought it was rather strange that Mrs Landower had gone off to Yorkshire without telling her and she had not taken some comb or other which she usually wore.'

'Yes,' I said. 'I did hear that.'

'Well, she wrote to Mrs Landower's aunt, because Mr Landower said she had gone to her. The letter she enclosed to Mrs Landower herself has come back with a note from the aunt saying Mrs Landower had never been there and she hadn't heard from her since Christmas.'

'Oh! What can that mean?'

'Well, it means . . . where is Mrs Landower?'

'She must have gone to Yorkshire.'

Nanny Loman shook her head and turned away.

I could not read her thoughts, but I could guess the direction they were taking. I thought that our lives were an open book to them. Sometimes I wondered how much they knew of our secret thoughts. And what they did not know they would guess.

The expression in her eyes when they looked at me . . . were they faintly suspicious? Was she asking: And what part are you playing in all this?

I had the utmost respect for Nanny Loman. She was a good conscientious nurse who took her duties seriously, but because of her virtues it was unlikely that she would ever have been tempted to step out of line. Perhaps this made her specially censorious.

All would know the state of affairs which existed between Paul and Gwennie. What did they know of Paul's feelings for me and mine for him? It was hardly likely that we had been able entirely to disguise them from those ever-watchful eyes.

They would reason: Mrs Landower was in the way. And now Mrs Landower had disappeared.

I had to see Paul.

Suspicion was like a worm that wriggled its way through my mind. It would give me no peace.

I kept seeing his face. 'Something will be done.' What had he said? 'I hated her . . .' and I had replied: 'You talk of her as though she were no longer there.'

Yes, we had said something like that. Why had he talked

of Gwennie in the past tense?

I knew it was probably foolish but I couldn't help it. I walked over to Landower.

It was a pity there were so many servants and I could not see him without its being known.

One of the maids opened the door.

I said: 'Good evening. Mrs Landower isn't back yet, is she?'

'No, Miss Tressidor.'

'No news of when she is coming?'

'No, Miss Tressidor.'

'Then perhaps I could see Mr Landower.'

'I will tell the master you be here, Miss Tressidor.'

Was she smirking? What were they thinking, this army of detectives who recorded our every movement, who lived in our lives, alongside their own?

He came to me quickly.

'Caroline!' He took my hands.

'I shouldn't have come.'

'You could come to me . . . always.'

I said: 'Paul, I've got to talk to you. I've heard the news.'

'You mean about Gwennie.'

'She's not in Yorkshire. Where is she, Paul?'

He shrugged his shoulders. 'She could have gone off . . . anywhere.'

'But why? She's never done it before.'

'I don't know. She has never taken me into her confidence.'

'What happened? How did she leave?'

'Early in the morning. She caught the seven-thirty to London.'

'Why so early?'

'Because she wanted to go straight through to Yorkshire and had to go to London first.'

'Who took her to the station?'

'I did.'

'You? Why?'

'I suppose it was because it was so early . . . and I was

glad to see her go. I took her in the trap.'

'There must have been people on the platform. She must have got a ticket!'

'No. We were rather late. The train was in. She didn't go through the main entrance. She took the short cut through the yard and she planned to get her ticket on the train. It saves time.'

'So nobody saw her get on?'

'I don't know. All I know is that that was how she went . . .'

'But she didn't go to Yorkshire, Paul. Oh, what has happened?'

'She must have changed her mind and gone somewhere else.'

'Where would she go?'

'Why are you asking these questions?'

'Don't you see? They are saying she didn't go to Yorkshire. That girl has the letter from the aunt. She did not go there. She had not written to say she was going. There's all that interest in the mine. You know what the gossip is like here. These people watch us all the time. Don't you see what they're implying? They know how things were between you and your wife. Perhaps they know about us. I don't think much escapes them, and what they don't see they make up. Paul, do you know where she is?'

'What are you suggesting, Caroline, that I . . .?'

'Just tell me the truth. I shall understand . . . I shall understand everything . . . but I must know.'

'Are you thinking that I know where she is?'

'Oh, where *is* she, Paul?'

'I don't know. I saw her on to the train to London. That's all I can say.'

'Paul . . . you would tell me . . . Don't let us have any secrets.'

'More than anything,' he said fervently, 'I want us to be together. I want us to be here . . . where we belong . . . you and I . . . for the rest of our lives. She stops it. But I swear to you, Caroline, as surely as I love you, that I do not know where she is. I saw her on to the train. I know no more than that. Do you believe me?'

'Yes,' I answered. 'I believe you. But I'm frightened, Paul, I'm terribly frightened.'

The main topic of conversation everywhere was the disappearance of Gwennie. Interest in the mine increased and rumour was rampant. Lights had been seen hanging over the mine. A black dog was said to be prowling around but he had appeared only to certain people.

I lived in a state of desperate uncertainty. I believed Paul. I did not think he would lie to me . . . unless he felt he must do so to keep me out of danger.

I could not believe that he would indulge in violence. But there was a breaking-point for everyone, I supposed; and I knew that the tension at Landower had been mounting over the years.

I called in to see Jamie.

He said: 'There's excitement in the air. The bees know it. They can't seem to settle. It's all this talk about the lady up at Landower.'

'People talk to you about it, do they, Jamie?'

'They can talk of nothing else. She's gone off somewhere. Well, she was a fussy woman, too anxious to pry into matters that didn't concern her. She'll be back, I don't doubt.'

'I am sure she will, but I wish she would come soon. I don't like all this gossip. They're talking about the mine and seeing black dogs and white hares.'

'Oh, the mine,' he said. 'There is something about that mine. Lionheart is fascinated by it. No matter how much I warn him, I can see he wants to explore.'

'There are always people there now. They all seem to be expecting something to happen.'

'If you expect something, like as not it will come.'

I wanted to talk of something else and I said: 'How are the maimed and the sick?'

'A little rabbit at the moment. I found him on the road
. . . a broken leg. Something on wheels must have run over
him.'

'Jamie,' I said, 'it's so peaceful here . . . particularly
now. It's a pleasure to be able to call in.'

'Call in whenever you have a fancy to, Miss Tressidor.'

It was true. I felt a little comforted, but when I reached
Tressidor the servants were all whispering together about
the new turn of events.

In view of all the rumours about the mine, the local
police had reported to headquarters in Plymouth, and it
had been decided that there should be an investigation of
the mine.

I shall never forget that hot sultry day.

In the morning the operation started. I heard it whispered that ropes and ladders had been taken on to the moor
and that numerous men were there to arrange a descent
down the mine shaft.

No one said openly that they were expecting to discover
Gwennie's body, but that was what everyone thought.
They had made up their minds that her husband had
murdered her, had given out the story of her having gone to
Yorkshire, and then disposed of her; and it was all because
he was tired of her, had never wanted her, had married her
for the money which was to save Landower for the Landowers, and was now sweet on Miss Tressidor.

It was a dramatic story and one which appealed to their
love of intrigue and showed that those who set themselves
above ordinary folk because of birth and affluence were as
full of human faults as anyone else.

I could not stay in. I could not talk to anyone. I wanted to
be out and alone.

Yet I had to know immediately if anything had been
discovered. I wanted to be with Paul. And I wanted to tell
him that whatever he had done I understood.

I rode out and found him waiting in the lane for me.

He said: 'I had to be with you.'

'Yes,' I answered. 'I'm glad. I wanted to be with you.'

'Let's go away . . . somewhere where we can talk. Let's be quiet . . . away from everyone.'

'Almost everyone will be on the moors today.'

We came to the woods and there we tethered our horses. We walked through the trees. He put his arm round me and held me close.

I said: 'Paul, no matter what . . .'

'What I've done,' he finished.

'You have told me you have not harmed her and I believe you. But what if . . .'

'If they find her in the mine . . .'

'How could she be there?'

'Who knows? . . . Some quirk of fate. What if she were set upon and robbed? You know how she decked herself out in jewellery. What if someone murdered her and threw her body down the mine?'

'But she was in the train.'

'I don't know. Strange things happen. They would accuse me, Caroline.'

'Yes,' I said.

'And you?'

'I would believe in you. I would help you prove your innocence.'

'Oh, Caroline . . .'

'It can't be long now. How long will they take?'

'Not long, I should imagine. We shall soon know.'

'But whatever happens, I love you. I have been so critical of people. Life teaches one so much and when things like this happen one sees so much more clearly. I know how you have been provoked and even if . . .'

'But it is not so, Caroline. I put her on the train. Whatever has happened to her is none of my doing.'

We walked through the woods; the sunlight was dappled on the leaves and the smell of damp earth was in the air; now and then a startled animal moved among the undergrowth and I thought: I want to go on like this. I want to stay here forever.

418

It was strange that in that time of fear and apprehension which was almost too great to be borne, I should know how deeply I loved him and that nothing he had done or ever would do could alter that.

I was not sure how long we were in the wood, but we knew we must part.

I said: 'I am going to ride to the moor.'

'You shouldn't,' he said.

'I must.'

'I shall go back to Landower,' he said.

'Never forget,' I told him. 'Whatever happens, I love you. I will be with you . . . against all the world if need be.'

'If it took this to make you say that I can't regret it,' he said.

He held me in his arms for a long time and then we mounted. He went back to Landower and I rode on to the moor.

There were crowds of people there. I saw the men near the mine. They appeared to have finished their task. I looked about me. One of the grooms was standing nearby.

'Is it over, Jim?' I asked.

'Yes, Miss Tressidor. They found nothing . . . nothing but a few animals . . . bones and such like.'

Great waves of relief swept over me.

'Looks like a waste of time,' said Jim.

Still people stood about. I wanted to ride back to Landower. I had to see Paul.

I turned my horse and went back as fast as I could.

I did not care what the servants thought. Let them do their worst. Gwennie's body was not in the mine. They would have to believe that she had got on that train to London.

I knocked at the door. One of the servants opened it. I stared. Someone was coming down the stairs. It was Gwennie.

'Hello, Caroline. This is a joke. Here I am. I gathered you have been wondering what had become of me?'

'Gwennie!' I cried.

'None other,' she said.

'But . . .'

'I know. I've been hearing all about it from Jenny. They've been searching the mine, looking for my corpse. What fun!'

'It wasn't much fun.'

'No. I gathered they suspected my dearly beloved husband. Well, that'll teach him a lesson. Perhaps he'll treat me better now.'

Paul had come into the hall.

'She's come back,' he said.

'Perhaps we ought to go and tell them at the mine,' said Gwennie.

'They had already finished their work,' I said.

'Oh, were you there? Had you gone to see my grisly remains?'

'Certainly not,' said Paul. 'She knew you were not there. I had already explained that you had gone off on the train.'

'Poor Paul. It must have been awful for you . . . that suspicion. I can't wait to show myself. I'd have loved to arrive at the mine. They might have thought I was the ghost of myself.'

'There was a great deal of consternation when Jenny heard from your aunt that you had not been to Yorkshire.'

'Oh yes . . . I decided against it at the last moment,' said Gwennie lightly. 'I went to see someone I knew in Scotland.'

'What a pity you didn't say. It would have saved a great deal of trouble.'

'I must say it is rather comforting to know that people round here were so concerned for my welfare. I thought they always looked on me as an outsider.'

'They love drama and you gave them the opportunity to create it,' I said. 'They love you for that.'

'I think it's fun. I'm going out now. To ride round and show myself.'

I said: 'Then I'll leave you to enjoy your fun. Goodbye.'
I went home. I was relieved but far from happy.

The neighbourhood was abuzz with the news: Gwennie was back. It had all been a storm in a teacup. I guessed there were some red faces. Those who had seen the black dogs and the white hares were suitably subdued. Why should these omens of evil appear just to announce the deaths of a stray sheep and a few animals? And even they had been down there for quite a long time.

Gwennie continued to be greatly amused. She talked of little else. Jenny was shamefaced. She admitted to some of her fellow servants, who reported it to ours so that it came to my ears, that Mrs Landower did not always wear the comb, and she had mentioned it because she had wanted to know if she had really gone to Yorkshire.

Gwennie came to see me. She said she wanted to talk and could we be alone?

I took her into the winter parlour and sent for some tea as it was afternoon.

She looked different, I thought, sly in a way.

She began talking about all the fuss of her so-called disappearance.

'Why shouldn't I go where I want to? As a matter of fact, I had no intention of going to Yorkshire. I just said so because it was the first thing I thought of . . . having my Aunt Grace up there. I didn't think that fool Jenny would raise all that trouble . . . on account of a comb.'

'I think the comb was just an excuse.'

'But why should she suspect that something had happened to me?' She laughed. 'All the intrigue that's going on, I suppose. Well, Jenny likes to be in the middle of all that. You can't blame her. So all this about my comb.'

She took it out of her hair and looked at it. It was tortoiseshell, Spanish type, not large and with little brilliants set in it.

'It's true I wear it a good deal, but why she should think I would never leave without it, I can't imagine.'

421

She stuck it back in her hair.

'So you had other plans right from the first?' I said.

She nodded. 'I can't bear to be in the dark.'

'I know that well.'

'I like to *know*. It worries me if I don't. I just have to find out.'

'I did realize that.'

'Yes, everything that goes on. My Ma used to call me Meddlesome Matty. She used to say: "Sometimes she'd lift the teapot lid, to see what was within." I forget how the rhyme goes on but I believe something terrible happened to Matty. "Curiosity killed the cat." That was another of my Ma's sayings. Pa used to laugh at me. "It's no good trying to keep anything from Gwennie," he used to say. I knew that it was you and Jago who caused my accident.'

'Oh?'

'Don't look so startled. I saw *you*. I remember your green eyes and your hair was all tied up with a ribbon . . . remember? One day you had it done just like that and I said, "Hello, I've seen that before." It was one of those things that come to you after . . . you know what I mean. Then I found the door in the gallery and the staircase up to the attics. It didn't take me long to work that out. I went up there and found the clothes you'd worn. You might have killed me. That was the first thing I had against you.'

'I realized how foolish we were as soon as we'd done it. It was meant to be a joke.'

'Typical of Jago. To frighten us away, of course. Just get rid of us, never mind the consequences.'

'We didn't think for a moment that you would fall. We didn't know the rail was rotten.'

'Everything in the house was rotten till Pa and I took it over.'

I was silent.

'I couldn't walk for a while. I still feel twinges in my back and when I do I say, Thank you, Caroline. Thank you, Jago. It's all due to you.'

'I am so sorry.'

422

'All right. You were children. You didn't think and I know you're sorry. Jago was always very nice to me. I think it was because of that.'

'Jago was quite fond of you.'

'Landowers are fond of Landower . . . all the glory of the family. I have to admit I like that, too.'

'I think Jago can't be accused of those feelings. He was very willing to abandon it all.'

'He'll be well gilded now. Rosie knows what she's about.'

'I don't think he was all that concerned with the gildings.'

'Everybody likes them. They make the wheels go smoothly round.'

'Do they?'

She looked at me sharply. 'If you let them,' she said. 'I know about Paul, of course.'

'What do you know?'

'That he is after you . . . and I don't think you feel much like saying No to him either. But let me tell you this: I'll never let him go. He married me. Look what he got out of it. He's got to remember that.'

'He doesn't forget that he's married to you.'

'He'd better not. I shall never let him go. You'd better understand that.'

'I do understand it.'

'The best thing you can do is go up to Rosie. She's fond of you. She'll help you find a husband and then you won't have need of someone else's.'

'There is no need for you to talk in this strain. I understand the position perfectly. I am not looking for a husband, and if I went to London to stay with Jago and Rosie for a visit it would not be with such a hunt in mind.'

'I like your way of talking. Dignity, I suppose you call it. I suppose that is what he likes. Lady of the Manor and so on. Well, it's not to be, because I'll never let him go. He's got the house and he has to take me with it. And that's how it's going to stay.'

I said: 'Why don't you try living amicably together?'

'What? With him hating the bargain all the time and trying to wriggle out of it?'

'If you look upon it as a bargain, you'll never live serenely together.'

'Life's what it is, Caroline. You take what you want and you pay for it. It's no use niggling about the price when it's all signed and settled.'

'I don't think that is quite the way to look on marriage.'

'And if you go on like this it seems to me you'll never have an opportunity of looking at it at all.'

'That is very probable,' I said, 'and entirely my own affair.'

'Well,' she said, good-natured suddenly, 'I didn't come here to quarrel with you. I know it's not your fault . . . or anybody's fault. It just is. I came to talk to you about something else. As we said, I like to know what's going on around me. Well, I thought I'd do a little tour of investigation. That's what I've been doing.'

'Where?'

'In Scotland. I went to Edinburgh. I stayed with someone we used to know before we came south. Her father was a friend of my father's. She married and went to live up in Edinburgh. I thought I'd look her up.'

'What made you do that suddenly?'

'It was something Rosie said. Rosie always had her ears open, I imagine. She's like me in a way. That's why we got on. We talked a lot together. I reckon she's had a life of it. She mentioned this after we'd seen him.'

'Seen him?'

'Jamie McGill. I wanted to get some honey for her to take back to London with her and I said to her, "You won't be able to buy anything like you can get from this man. He's a magician with the bees and has conferences with them. He's a little loose in the top storey." '

'I wish you wouldn't talk about him like that. Sometimes I think he's cleverer than any of us. He's learned how to be contented and that's about the wisest thing anyone can do.'

'Well, don't you want to hear?'

'Of course.'

'I took her along. She was interested in the bees and in him and we stopped and talked awhile. When we left she asked what his name was and when I told her she said, "McGill. I'm sure there was a McGill case." Well, as you can imagine, I was all ears. I said to her, "There's always been a bit of a mystery about Jamie McGill. He won't talk and he got a little fussed when I asked him a few simple questions . . . just the ordinary sort of ones you might ask anybody." Rosie said, "Well, I can't be sure, but there was a case and I'm certain the name was McGill. There wasn't a lot about it in the London papers because it happened in Scotland." '

'I think it must have been something to do with his brother,' I said. 'He did mention a brother to me once.'

'Yes . . . that's right. Rosie remembered that this McGill had been involved in a murder case. She wasn't sure what happened, but he got off. Then she remembered that it was because he got off that there was this bit of a stir about it. It was a verdict we don't have here. "Not proven." That was why it was written about and Rosie remembered. Well, I felt ever so interested . . . but Rosie didn't remember anything more.'

'Do you mean to tell me,' I said incredulously, 'that you travelled up to Scotland to discover the secrets of Jamie McGill?'

She nodded, her eyes shining with mischief. 'Though I'd have gone in any case if I'd known what a lovely little drama I was making here.'

'I believe you like stirring up trouble.'

She was thoughtful. 'I'm not sure. I like to know . . . I always did. I like to find out what people are hiding.'

'And did you find out about poor Jamie McGill?'

'Yes. I talked to people who remembered, and you're able to get some of the papers which came out years back. I stayed with my friend in Edinburgh and she took me about the town . . . showing me the ropes. As I said, we found quite a number of people who remembered. It wasn't all that long ago . . . only ten years or so. People remember these things.'

'Well, what did you discover?'

'It was Donald McGill. I thought it might be Jamie.'

'That,' I said coldly, 'was what you hoped to discover.'

'But it was Donald. His brother didn't come into it at all. There was no mention of him. Donald had murdered his wife.'

'I thought you said it was not proven?'

'I mean he was on trial for murder, but they couldn't prove him guilty. She was found at the bottom of a staircase in their home. They had been on bad terms and there she was . . . dead. She had a blow on her head but they couldn't tell whether she had got it in falling or if it had been delivered before she was pushed down. That was why they had to decide and they couldn't, so there was this verdict, Not Proven.'

'Congratulations on your discovery,' I said.

'Well, at least you know about the man you employ.'

'But this was his brother.'

'It's something he doesn't want to come out.'

'I can quite understand why not. If anything like that happens in your family, I dare say you want to get away from it.'

'I had to know.'

'Well, now you are satisfied.'

'Yes, I'm satisfied now.'

'I hope you won't go round talking about this. If Jamie wants to keep his secrets he should be allowed to.'

'I don't suppose I shall say anything, and in any case it is only his brother. Now if he were the murderer . . .'

'You mean the suspected murderer. It was not proven, as I have to keep reminding you.'

'If it had been Jamie, that would have been different.'

'A great disappointment for you!'

'I'm still interested in him. I think there is something very odd about him.'

'I should leave him in peace if I were you.'

426

She looked at me, smiling. 'You're of much greater interest to me, Caroline. When I think of you . . . coming here, getting the estate and everything . . . and then getting your own back on Jeremy Brandon . . . and then falling in love with my husband . . . I must say there is never a dull moment with you, Caroline.'

'I am astonished that my life is so interesting to you. One thing I ask you. Please don't upset Jamie by letting him know you have discovered his secret. Remember it is his.'

'Yes,' she said, still smiling. 'Let's all keep our secrets, eh?'

Disclosures

During the days which followed I did not want to meet people. I knew that the great topic of conversation throughout the neighbourhood would be the search of the mine shaft and the return of Gwennie.

I did hear certain comments, and it amazed me how those who had been so certain that Gwennie's body would be found in the mine shaft now declared they had never suspected foul play for one moment and they had guessed all the time that she had gone off somewhere without saying.

I did not go to Landower. I did not want to see Gwennie and I was afraid of seeing Paul. I just wanted to shut myself away for a little while. All that had happened had been a great shock to me and that was partly because I had suspected that Paul, driven beyond endurance, might have killed her. It was a terrible accusation to make against the man one loved; and it taught me something about myself. Even if he had done so, I would have been ready to shield him.

Because of my immature dreams into which I had set Paul during the time I was growing up, because of my infatuation for Jeremy Brandon, I had sometimes wondered how deep my love for Paul had gone. I was in no doubt now. I loved him for ever and ever.

But our case seemed hopeless and I must come to some decision about my life. I had Livia and I had Tressidor. Livia and I could leave, but could I leave Tressidor? Could I sell it? The ancestral home of the Tressidors. But I was not really one of them. My mother had merely married into the family and my father was not one of them either.

What did I owe Tressidor? I ought to get away. What life could I ever build up here? Moreover, there was this niggling fear in my mind. Suppose what I imagined had happened, actually had? It could so easily, I believed, for would it have been so unusual, so unexpected? Many – including myself – had believed it could happen.

These were more grim thoughts.

Cousin Mary, I said to myself, if you are watching me now, if you know what is happening here, you will understand. I know what this place meant to you. I know that you wanted me to carry on . . . and it was what I wanted. It meant a good deal to me. But I can't stay here, and I feel that what has happened has been a sort of rehearsal, a warning. It has brought home to me so clearly what could be. How can anyone go on enduring this state of affairs? How near to murder can ordinary people come? Perhaps if they are goaded beyond endurance . . . Cousin Mary, would you understand?

I thought: I will go to London. I will talk to Rosie . . . and perhaps Jago. They might help me decide.

Livia wanted to go to Landower to play with Julian. 'The two of them are so good together,' said Nanny Loman. 'Julian is like a big brother to her. I've never seen two play together like those two do.'

So Nanny Loman took Livia over to Landower.

When she came back she found an early opportunity of talking to me.

She said: 'Mrs Landower's gone off again.'

'Gone off?'

'Off on her travels.'

'Oh, where this time?'

'She hasn't said.'

'She seems to like these mystery tours. I hope she has taken her comb with her this time. Did you find out?'

'As a matter of fact, I did. It appears she has taken it.'

'Then all is well,' I said.

Gwennie had been away a week. I had seen Paul and we went together into the woods where we could talk in peace.

'I wonder where she has gone this time,' I said.

'She was so amused at the last upheaval. I suppose she thought she would do it again.'

'Nobody seems excited about it this time.'

'Well, you can't play the same trick twice.'

I said: 'I've been thinking a great deal. I am beginning to wonder whether I ought after all to sell up here and get right away.'

'You can't do that.'

'I could, and sometimes I think it is the only solution.'

'It's defeatism.'

'It is a retreat from something which could become intolerable for us all.'

'That last affair shattered you, didn't it? I think you really believed I had hit her on the head with a blunt instrument and thrown her down the mine shaft.'

I was silent, then I said: 'I'm afraid, Paul. This is getting out of hand. She will never let you go.'

'I could leave.'

'Leave Landower . . . for which you would always crave. It's different with Tressidor. I wasn't brought up in it. I'm not even a Tressidor. I just have the name because my mother happened to be married to one. I don't feel the ties of a home which has always been mine and my family's.'

'You would leave me.'

'Only because I have a feeling that it could be dangerous to stay.'

'People live with these situations.'

'Yes, that's true.'

'Then couldn't we compromise? We can't have what we want but need we lose everything?'

'We have gone over that ground before. I could become your mistress. That's what you mean. But between us there is more than a physical relationship. It would not satisfy either of us completely. We should hanker for the really stable things . . . the things that matter . . . home, family, the honourable life, the honest life. We live in glass houses, as it were. We are watched all the time. And sooner or later . . . the explosion would come. I saw it all so clearly when they were exploring the mine . . . I have to think, Paul. I have to make up my mind.'

He did not try to persuade me this time. There was nothing to be said. We had said it all before.

We walked through the trees, close . . .

And I thought: It is the only way.

I rode out to the moor.

Gwennie had still not returned and there was no news of her. No one seemed to think that strange.

I wondered where she was this time. Had she gone to Scotland to make further enquiries into poor Jamie's past or was she investigating someone else? But it might be that she had gone away out of mischief. She had been so amused by all the speculation.

How desolate it seemed on the moor! How different from the last time I had seen it with the crowd of morbid sightseers gathered there!

I felt an impulse to walk on the springy turf so I tethered my horse and did so. I felt I wanted to go near to the mine and almost involuntarily my footsteps led me towards it.

How lonely it was!

I was near the edge now. Suppose I were to see a black dog or a white hare, what should I do?

The wind moaned a little as it ruffled the grass where it grew tall and I noticed that several clumps of gorse were in bloom.

Suddenly I heard the wheels of a trap and the clip-clop of a horse's hoofs. I looked up and recognized it at once as my own trap. That meant that someone had taken it into Liskeard to get some purchases, I imagined.

The driver had seen me and pulled up.

He called to me: 'Miss Tressidor.'

It was Jamie.

'Hello, Jamie. Have you been into the town?'

He alighted and patting the horse whispered something to it. Then he came towards me, Lionheart at his heels.

'Oh, Miss Tressidor, what are you doing near the mine?'

'I was just having a walk.'

'You shouldn't go so close.'

'I was just wondering whether I should see the black dog . . . and here is Lionheart instead.'

The dog came to me and gave a friendly bark, wagging his tail. I stooped and patted him. He ran close to the mine.

'Have you just been shopping?'

'Just to get one or two things. The trap is handy.'

'It would be impossible without,' I said. 'It's a lovely day.'

'Too sultry. There's thunder in the air.'

'Who told you that? The bees?'

'There's nothing they don't know about weather.'

'Of course. What's the matter with Lionheart?'

The dog was standing on the very edge of the mine, barking.

'Come away,' called Jamie. His voice was sharp. 'Lion, this instant. Come.'

Lionheart came slowly with his tail between his legs. Jamie stooped and patted him.

'Don't you go near the mine, there's a good dog.'

Lionheart looked regretfully back to the mine and for a moment I thought he was going to disobey orders.

'Well,' said Jamie, 'I reckon I'd better be getting back. Up you go, Lion. And Miss Tressidor. I wouldn't linger about on the moors if I were you.'

'Why, Jamie?'

'You were too close to the mine. It seems to have a sort of fascination for you.'

'I suppose it does. It's all the talk about it. Goodbye, Jamie.'

I watched the horse trot away and I walked slowly back to where my horse was tethered, thinking that there was something different about Jamie. He was not quite himself.

I decided that I would call on him. I wondered if something was worrying him. Was something wrong with the bees or perhaps some of the animals?

He was as delighted to see me as ever and set about making tea.

'Jamie,' I said, when he sat down beside me and poured out from the brown earthenware pot, 'is anything wrong?'

'Why do you ask, Miss Tressidor?'

'I just felt there might be something.'

He looked at me steadily for a few moments and then he said: 'Donald has been back.'

'Donald! Your brother. The one who . . .'

He nodded. 'Yes, Miss Tressidor. Donald has been back . . . been here.'

'Oh, Jamie, and you hoped he would never find you.'

'He's been here,' he repeated.

'Has he caused trouble?'

'I'm afraid he will.'

'What does he want?'

'He's just found me out.'

'Where is he now?'

'He's gone.'

'He can't do you any harm.'

'He can, Miss Tressidor. He can finish everything.'

'No, Jamie. We won't let him do that.'

'You don't know Donald.'

'Only what you've told me about him.'

'Donald's wicked. I don't want him here, Miss Tressidor. He'll spoil everything . . . everything I've built up since I've been here.'

'He can't . . . if we won't let him.'

He was silent for a while.

'Donald's a murderer,' he said. 'I always knew he had it in him. When he was a boy . . . I've seen him hurt things. Kill things . . . little animals. It used to come over him. He couldn't help it, I think. He just wanted to kill. Little furry things . . . white mice, rabbits . . . things like that. Pets we

433

had. He'd love them for a bit and then you'd find one of them dead. It was this urge to kill.'

'We won't allow him to upset you, Jamie. You're settled here now. You've got your home in the lodge and everything is satisfactory.'

'I've never told you about it, Miss Tressidor, but if I had told anyone it would have been you . . . or Miss Mary. She was good to me and so have you been.'

'Would you like to tell me about it? Tell me why you are so afraid of him? I promise you he can't harm you.'

'Well, you see, he was married. He married Effie. I loved Effie.'

'You mean you both loved the same girl?'

He was silent. 'Poor Jamie,' I went on, 'and she married Donald.'

He nodded. 'People change. Effie was a bright girl . . . full of fun. She liked going out and about . . . dancing and things like that and when they were married they couldn't do it. Money . . . things like that . . . you understand?'

'Yes,' I said, 'I understand.'

'She went on and on . . . years of it. She was never satisfied . . . she was wishing they never married. Nag . . . nag . . . and one night Donald picked up a poker and hit her on the head and pushed her downstairs. It was murder and Donald did it. But they couldn't prove it. Not proven. That was what they said and Donald went free.'

'How long ago was that, Jamie?'

'Ten years.'

'And all that time Donald hasn't been near you?'

'I got away. I couldn't stand it. I was afraid of Donald. I knew, you see. I remembered that little white mouse we had. I remembered how he couldn't help himself when the mood was on him. And I didn't want to see Donald . . . ever again. I knew there could only be peace for me if Donald were not around.'

'And now he's come here?'

'Yes, he came.'

'When was this?'

434

'Some days ago.'

'And did he go away again?'

'Yes, I told him to go. I said, "Don't come here any more." I said, "You're dead to me. I can't do with you here, Donald, you'll spoil my life." '

'Is it as bad as that? He is your brother.'

'You don't know Donald. He's quiet for a time and you think it's all right and then . . . the wickedness comes out. Donald must never come here . . . not in my home . . . no, no.'

'I understand. But where has he gone now?'

Jamie shook his head.

'And he's discovered where you are? That's what's worrying you?'

Jamie nodded. 'You see, he came back.'

I said: 'You're overwrought, Jamie. You're making too much of this. You're afraid he's going to harm your animals . . . Lionheart, Tiger and your waifs and strays. Look here, if he comes again, send for me. I'll come and see what we can do.'

'You're so good to me,' he said.

I left him then. Poor Jamie, he felt so strongly about his brother. I supposed one would about someone who had committed a murder.

There was still no news of Gwennie. I tried not to think of her but I could not get her out of my mind. That she was mischievous, I knew. She had been very intrigued by all the drama her absence had aroused. But would she go away again? She would know that she could not provoke that sort of speculation again and so soon.

I wanted to go into the town to do some shopping and on these occasions I took the trap. It was early afternoon and I went to the stables to tell them to get it ready for me.

This they did and in a short time I was driving along the country lanes, my thoughts still busy as they had been for some time with the future. I could not make up my mind what it held for me. I would wake in the morning saying I

435

must do one thing and by midday I had decided against it.

I must leave Cornwall, I would say. And then: No, no. I could never leave.

And so it went on.

I chatted awhile in the shops. Everyone knew about the return of Gwennie and the fact that the mine had been explored. They still talked of it.

'A storm in a teacup, that were, Miss Tressidor.'

I agreed it was.

'She's not like the likes of we,' said the postmistress. 'She'm a foreigner, right from up north. They has some funny ways up there.'

I supposed I was also a foreigner; but at least I had the name of Tressidor.

I drove back to the stables and as I was about to get out of the trap something caught my eye. It glittered and was protruding from under the seat. I stooped and picked it up. It was a comb – a comb I had seen before – a small Spanish type with a row of brilliants decorating the top.

Gwennie's comb!

In the Tressidor trap! How had it got there?

There was one thought which persisted in my mind. If Gwennie's comb was in the trap, Gwennie must have been there, too.

I was bewildered. I could not think how it came to be there.

I put it in my pocket and went to find the head groom.

I said: 'Who used the trap last?'

He scratched his head. 'Afore you, Miss Tressidor?' he asked.

'Yes, before me.'

'Well, I don't know as anyone . . . unless it was Jamie McGill.'

'Yes, he did have it. I saw him on the moor.'

'So he would have been the last, I'd reckon.'

'Did Mrs Landower ever travel in it?'

'Mrs Landower? Her have been away . . . and have been this past week or so.'

'Yes, I know. But I wondered if someone gave her a lift.'

'Not as I know of.'

'All right,' I said. I put my hand in my pocket. The prongs of the comb stuck in my fingers. I felt sick.

I went to my bedroom and took out the comb. I could see her taking it from her hair and looking at it.

'I wear it often . . . but not always,' she had said.

How had it come to be in the trap?

I decided to call on Jamie.

I saw him in the garden as I approached. He was among the hives and the bees were buzzing round him.

I called out to him.

'Good day, Miss Tressidor.'

'Are you busy?'

'No. Go into the house. I'll be with you in a moment.'

I went in and sat down and within a few minutes he came in.

'Jamie,' I said, 'when did you last use the trap?'

He looked puzzled and I went on: 'I know you had it the day we met on the moors. But when did you before that, and did you give Mrs Landower a lift?'

'Mrs Landower? I heard she'd gone away.'

'I wondered because I found this in the trap.'

'What is it?'

'It's her comb. It's strange that it should be there. I wondered if you gave her a lift somewhere . . . before she went away.'

'A lift?' he repeated.

He looked strange. He was staring straight ahead of him.

I said: 'Are you all right, Jamie?'

He just went on staring ahead and repeated: 'A lift?'

'Jamie, sit down. What is the matter? Do you know how Mrs Landower's comb could come to be in the trap?'

'You know, don't you, Miss Tressidor?' he said.

'Know what?'

He had a glazed look on his face which gave him an odd expression which I had never seen before. He was like a different person.

'Jamie,' I said, 'you look strange . . . not yourself . . . what is it?'

He leaned across the table and repeated: 'You know.'

'I know what?'

'You know this isn't Jamie.'

'What do you mean?'

But understanding dawned on me and I felt my heart miss a beat and then begin to hammer in my chest.

I said: 'You're . . . Donald.'

A sly look came into his face. I had never seen Jamie look like that.

'Yes,' he said, 'I'm Donald.'

I stood up in alarm. All my senses were warning me to get away . . . quickly. I felt: This man is mad. Jamie was right. He is a danger.

'Where is . . . Jamie?' I stammered.

'Jamie has gone.'

'But where . . . where? I came to see Jamie.'

I moved backwards. From the corner of my eye I measured the distance to the door.

'I'll come back . . . when Jamie's here. I came to see him. Will you tell him I called?'

He just repeated: 'You know, don't you?'

'I know that Donald came.'

'You know she's dead. You know where she is. She's down the mine shaft. That's where she is. I killed her. I hit her on the head.' He started to laugh and took a step towards the fireplace. Hanging beside it were a brass poker and bellows. He took the poker and looked at it. 'I killed her with this,' he said. 'I hit her on the head and then I took the trap and drove with her to the mine. There was no one about so I pushed her down.'

'You can't mean this. You've only just arrived.'

'I've been coming here . . . off and on . . . for some time now.'

He laid down the poker. 'I did it with Effie and I did it with her. Effie drove me mad. She went on and on. She ought not to have married me. She would have been better

438

off if she'd married Jack Sparrow. He got on, he did. It would have been a different life with him. I let her go on and on and then I couldn't stand it any more . . .

'And Mrs Landower . . . She was too nosey . . . She pried. She went to Edinburgh and found out things . . . She was going to talk. Soon it would have been all over the place. It wasn't fair to Jamie. Jamie liked it here . . . He'd worked hard to get it as he wanted. He wanted it to stay as it was . . . and she was going to stop it.'

'Did Jamie tell you all this?'

'Jamie tells me everything. I know Jamie . . . and Jamie knows me. We're different, but we are one . . .'

'I know you are twin brothers, but you haven't seen each other for years. I must go now. I'll come back later and see Jamie.'

'You know now . . . don't you?'

'I know what you have told me.'

'I've told you about her . . . and you've come here with that comb. It was found in the trap. I was careless, wasn't I . . . not to have seen it. It gave it away. No one would ever have known. They would have thought she was playing a game. She'd tried it once before.'

'I must go . . .'

He was before me and he had his back to the door.

'But you know,' he said. 'She had to go because she knew . . . and now you know.'

'I don't believe a word of this. I don't see how you can be aware of all this. You don't live here.'

He took a step towards me and I noticed afresh the strange glitter in his eyes.

'I've got to save all this . . . for Jamie,' he said. 'Jamie is happy here. You're going to make trouble for Jamie.'

'I would never make trouble for Jamie.'

'You came here with that comb. You came to accuse Jamie of killing her. Jamie wouldn't hurt a moth. Jamie loves all living creatures. Jamie wouldn't have touched her, no matter what she'd done. It had to be Donald. And now . . . there's you.'

He was quite close to me. I was in the presence of a madman. I could already feel his hands about my throat.

I tried to speak firmly: 'I'm going now.'

'You'll have to go down the shaft with her . . . with that nosey woman who spoiled everything with her prying ways. You shouldn't have come here accusing Jamie . . .'

I could see his hands. They looked thick and strong. I tried to cry out but my voice was hardly above a whisper and it would be little short of a miracle if anyone was near enough to hear me.

I felt his hands on my throat.

I thought: This can't be happening. Why . . .? What does it all mean?

His face puckered suddenly. 'Miss Tressidor was good to Jamie,' he said. 'Miss Mary and Miss Caroline . . . Nobody was as good to Jamie as Miss Caroline and Miss Mary.'

And then in a blinding flash of clarity, I knew. I saw him clearly as he had been in the gardens with the bees buzzing round him and I cried: 'Jamie. You're Jamie.'

He dropped his hands and stared at me.

'I know you're Jamie,' I said.

'No . . . no. I'm Donald.'

'No, Jamie, the bees have told me.'

He looked startled.

'They've told you?'

'Yes, Jamie, the bees have told me. You're Jamie, aren't you? There is no Donald. There never was a Donald. There is only one of you.'

His face crumpled suddenly. He looked gentle and helpless.

'Jamie, Jamie,' I cried. 'I want to help you. I know I can.'

He looked at me in a dazed fashion. 'So it was the bees . . . they told you.'

He sat down at the table and put his hands over his face. He spoke quietly. 'It's all clear now. There is only one of us. Donald James McGill. But sometimes it seems to me that there are two of us. Jamie that was the real self . . . and Donald . . . he was the other. He did wicked things . . .

and Jamie hated it. There were two of us in a way . . . but in the same body.'

'I think I understand. One part of you killed those little animals whom the other part loved. The impulse came over you suddenly to kill . . . and you felt that was not really you, for you were Jamie, quiet, gentle Jamie, wanting to live in peace with the world.'

'I loved Effie,' he said slowly, 'but she went on and on making me feel that I ought never to have married her, reminding me that I couldn't give her the things that she wanted. And then . . . one night when she was going on and on . . . it was too much. I picked up the poker and hit her. We were standing at the top of the stairs and she fell. I told myself she tripped . . . but I knew I'd done it. Then it seemed it was Donald and they brought in Not Proven . . . and there was a chance to get away.'

'I understand, Jamie. I understand now.'

'And Mrs Landower . . . I always hated her. She wanted to spoil everything . . . not only for me but for everyone else. She was always asking questions and going on and on. She's a natural spoiler. And then she went to Edinburgh and she'd gone on asking questions there and she'd seen it in the papers. Then she came to see me and she said she thought I ought to tell the whole story. She said it wasn't right to have secrets . . . So . . . I took the poker and I hit her . . . just like I'd hit Effie. And then I took her out in the trap and put her down the mine shaft.'

'Oh, Jamie,' I said. I was shivering.

'It's the end, I know,' he said. 'And you know now . . . so the only thing I can do if I want to live in peace is to send you with her.'

'But you couldn't do that, Jamie,' I said. 'Jamie is back now. Jamie would never do it. Donald has gone . . . and now that you've told me, Donald will go forever.'

He covered his face with his hands. 'What will become of me?' he asked.

'I think you'll go away from here. You're sick, I think. It isn't the same . . . if you're sick you're not to blame.'

441

'And Lion and Tiger and the bees . . . what would become of them?'

'There'd be someone to take care of them.'

'I couldn't hurt you, Miss Tressidor. No matter what . . .'

'I know. As soon as I knew that, I knew who you really were. And you were out there with the bees when I came. Only Jamie could have stood among them. They wouldn't have allowed anyone else to go unprotected into their midst.'

'What can I do, Miss Tressidor?'

Again he covered his face with his hands. Lionheart came up to him and leaped on to the table. He began to lick his face, and Tiger came and rubbed himself against his legs.

'Oh, Jamie,' I said. 'My poor, poor Jamie.'

I went to the door. There was no one there. I stood there for ten minutes before I heard someone in the road.

It was one of the grooms from Landower.

I called: 'Will you ask Mr Landower to come to the lodge immediately. Tell him he is wanted . . . desperately.'

When Paul came I clung to him. I was a little incoherent as I tried to tell him what had happened.

He put his arms round me and said: 'Don't be afraid. Don't be afraid any more.'

Then we went into the lodge together.

Diamond Jubilee

I sat in the big bow window of one of the most successful fashion houses in London to watch the procession pass by, and my thoughts must inevitably go back to that other occasion, ten years before, when I had sat at a window near Waterloo Place and watched another Jubilee.

It was so similar, but it was a woman who had taken the place of the innocent girl. It seemed incredible that so much could have happened in ten years.

The sun shone brilliantly – just as it had on that other day. Royal weather, they called it. The little old lady in her carriage did not look much different. There was a feeling of tremendous excitement in the air, just as there had been that other time. On the previous day I had driven through the city and seen some of the triumphal arches, the decorations, and in the evening the gas jets had been lighted and there were even some of the new electric light bulbs which were coming into use.

'Our Hearts Thy Throne,' said one inscription. 'Sixty Glorious Years,' said another; and yet another: 'She Wrought her People Lasting Good.'

And as the procession passed along, it was not so much the magnificent uniforms and all the brilliance of the royal gathering of princes and notables from all over the world that I saw. It was the passing cavalcade of the last ten years during which I had ceased to be an innocent young girl and had become a mature woman. It was not the bands and the martial music that I heard but voices from the past.

I could cast my mind back to the day when I had sat with my mother, Olivia and Captain Carmichael and watched that other Jubilee. It was then that life had taken its dramatic turn and I had a strange feeling that I had lived through the turbulent years to come not only to happiness but to a greater understanding.

I was no longer hasty in my judgements. I saw what happened through different eyes. I was mellow. I did not judge harshly now. I had learned to accept the frailties of human nature and to understand that people are not divided into the good and the evil.

My mother, pleasure-loving butterfly, yet brought happiness to her Alphonse, for the marriage had been a great success. She was content and she made those around her content. I had despised Robert Tressidor as a hypocrite with his outward show of virtue and his secret prurience. But perhaps I had judged him harshly. I was sure he had wished to be a pillar of virtue. He had had to fight his human sensuality and he could not resist the temptation to indulge it; and when he was discovered, he fought desperately to cover it and doubtless the strain had something to do with his early death. And Jeremy, the fortune-hunter? Had he been born rich he might not have been forced into mercenary calculation. He had charm, good looks; if he had not had that urgent need to find a means of living in luxury he might have been quite a worthy young man. And Paul, my Paul, who sat beside me now, what a temptation he had faced when it was incumbent on him to save Landower. I had bitterly criticised him for marrying to save the house for the family, but I now saw how easy it had been for the most honourable of men to succumb to that need.

In my youthful innocence I had endowed those I admired with godlike qualities. But they were not gods. They were men.

I came across some lines of Browning's the other day and I shall always remember them.

> 'Men are not angels; neither are they brutes;
> Something we may see, all we cannot see.'

I wish I had understood that earlier, for to understand the motives of others is surely the greatest gift one can have – and to understand is not to judge and to blame.

I think often of Gwennie . . . Gwennie who wanted to be happy, and did not know how to be. She wanted to bargain all the time; she could not understand that money could buy her a great mansion but it could not buy love. Poor Gwennie, if only she had known that one must give willingly and without thought of recompense, and only then does one reap the rewards of love.

I am sermonizing to myself, but I know I should be grateful for having lived through such experiences which have taught me so much.

I often think of Gwennie whose insatiable curiosity brought her to her death. 'Curiosity killed the cat.' I remembered her saying that. Curiosity killed Gwennie. They found her body in the mine shaft, just as Jamie had said. The story came out at the inquest. She had discovered the truth which he had been trying to hide. The great task of Jamie's life was to keep up the myth that Donald and Jamie were not the same person. There were two sides to his nature. He saw himself as two people in one body. There was Jamie, the gentle lover of animals, the man who wanted to live at peace with his neighbours; but there was Donald who could be swayed by uncontrollable urges to destroy; and the two natures had warred together in Jamie's childhood; and Donald James McGill, unable to live with the murderous instincts which came over him at times, had come to terms with life by dividing himself into two personalities. While he could live as Jamie he was safe. But Donald came back when Gwennie threatened to betray him.

He was judged clearly insane and was 'detained during Her Majesty's pleasure'. I was relieved that he passed into good hands. One of the greatest doctors who specialized in mental disorders was interested in his case, which he called one of split personality. He arranged for Jamie to go to a special institution of which he himself was in charge. I went

...e now and then. He worked in the gardens. He ...ives. I think that he often believed they were his ...nd he was able to forget what had happened and ...agined himself back at the lodge.

Soon after the discovery of the body I came to London to be with Jago and Rosie. I brought Livia and Julian with me — and Nanny Loman, Miss Bell and Julian's nanny, of course. Julian was so fond of Livia and as he was of an age to take note of what was happening around him, we thought it best for him to be away from home.

Rosie was wonderful to be with — so sane, and so was Jago. I was amazed really at the success of their relationship. They were really devoted to each other and theirs was fast becoming known internationally as one of the great fashion houses of the world.

I brought my attention back to the procession. Julian was pointing something out to Livia. The friendship between those two was a great delight to me. I thought: Perhaps one day they will marry. Who could say? Tressidor would go to Livia. I had made up my mind on that. Great houses should remain in families. I was not a Tressidor but Livia was, and Tressidor should go back to Tressidor.

I knew that Paul would make Julian his heir no matter what children we should have. Julian was half Arkwright and it must not be forgotten that it was the Arkwrights who had saved Landower from destruction.

Why was I thinking all this as I sat there looking down on the Queen's Diamond Jubilee from this elaborate bow window of Rosie's and Jago's grand establishment?

Paul was looking at me quizzically. I think he read my thoughts. His hand closed over mine and I knew he shared my view that we should put behind us all the hazards through which we had passed but which had brought us to this happy state — and rejoice and be thankful.

Rhanna
Christine Marion Fraser

A rich, romantic, Scottish saga set
on the Hebridean island of Rhanna

Rhanna

The poignant story of life on the rugged and tranquil island
of Rhanna, and of the close-knit community for whom it
is home.

Rhanna at War

Rhanna's lonely beauty is no protection against the horrors
of war. But Shona Mackenzie, home on leave, discovers
that the fiercest battles are those between lovers.

Children of Rhanna

The four island children, inseparable since childhood, find
that growing up also means growing apart.

Return to Rhanna

Shona and Niall Mackenzie come home to find Rhanna
unspoilt by the onslaught of tourism. But then tragedy
strikes at the heart of their marriage.

Song of Rhanna

Ruth is happily married to Lorn. But the return to Rhanna
of her now famous friend Rachel threatens Ruth's
happiness.

'Full-blooded romance, a strong, authentic setting'
Scotsman

FONTANA PAPERBACKS

New British Writers

Three rich, wonderful novels
by outstanding young British authors

A Splendid Defiance — Stella Riley

Justin Ambrose, a dashing and cynical Cavalier, was bored
with garrison life – until he fell in love with Abby, the sister
of a fanatic Roundhead rebel. With their hearts and
loyalties divided, and caught up in a passionate, forbidden
love affair, Abby and Justin watched the rival armies
prepare for a bloody confrontation.

The Skylark's Song — Audrey Howard

Zoe was born in the poorest street in Liverpool. As the
youngest of five children her life in the Merseyside slum
meant brutality, degradation and appalling poverty. But
Zoe was bright, sensitive and determined to escape.
Freedom would bring her wealth, luxury and love – and
heartache she could never have imagined . . .

A Season of Mists — Sarah Woodhouse

Ann Mathick had a dream. She wanted to make the run-
down Norfolk farm, which she had inherited from a
disreputable uncle, prosperous again. None of the county
believed she could do it. But the only man who could stop
Ann was Sir Harry Gerard, her dashing, reckless
neighbour – a very dangerous man to fall in love
with . . .

FONTANA PAPERBACKS